THE PURSUIT OF COOL

by
ROBB SKIDMORE

ISBN 978-0-9850379-0-1

Book Cover and Interior Layout by Lee Libro

Printed in the U.S.A.

**TMiK
PRESS**

To Ingrid,
The sun in my sky.

I agree with no man's opinions. I have some of my own.

~ Turgenev ~

TABLE OF CONTENTS

I.

II.

III.

IV.

I.

CHAPTER ONE

THE PROM INCIDENT
1986

Lance Rally sat alone at his assigned table. The funk band blasted the room with hysterical sass, yet only static reached his corner. His cuffs peeked out the sleeves of his tuxedo, revealing cufflinks affixed the wrong way. The decorative studs hid inside the cuffs with the swivels sticking out. He was not aware of his mistake. His mind searched for an unknown, as it often did, but one larger and more insidious, a ruin which lurked in a swirl of standardized tests, college applications, and outsized expectations. A feedback explosion pierced his eardrums, snatching his breath.

Where had his prom date gone? His shoulders were rigid, but his eyes darted wildly, as if trying to escape his head. Minutes ago, Tanya had said she didn't like their table and was bored. He didn't know what to do and sank into turmoil. Now he couldn't find her. To him she was impossibly complex. Tanya, the neighborhood pool regular and frequent wearer of a citron zippered neoprene bikini top, the Stephen King reader, the mall enthusiast, the picker of sentimental movies, the habitual chewer of grape bubble gum, had vanished. The funk band stomped their feet and snapped their Jheri curls side to side for a lone couple on the dance floor. The Mason Prep seniors of Alexandria, Virginia had danced themselves into a lather, then lost interest. As fifteen minutes dragged into forty-five, Lance concluded she had left the premises, his evening done.

He stood and flipped his purple napkin toward the table's motorcycle centerpiece. It landed over a candle, igniting, and he yanked it away and stamped it out. The prom theme was "Take

Me With U," from Prince's *Purple Rain* album. "Let's Go Crazy" had been shot down by administrators fearful of stoking youthful destruction. He locked his hands behind himself and tried to stretch his clenched back muscles.

"We're going to a party," Tanya said, suddenly at his side. Her face, glowing with fresh makeup, was a wondrous sight. He gazed as he had when he first spotted her at the change machine in the video arcade. The leonine volume she had achieved with her brown hair was remarkable. In a pink gown with huge shoulder ruffles, she tugged him toward an exit. They shuffled past a tableau with a lavender backdrop where a photographer posed couples. Earlier, Lance and Tanya had posed, she boldly attempting an exotic look, which on proofs resembled a silent film starlet. Lance had looked startled and glued to his date.

The party was in her neighborhood. During a happier moment, they clicked plastic cups of cheap champagne. After many cups he experienced a modest relaxation and a sponginess about his neck. He smiled at her with relief. After five glasses, Tanya's chatter had sped up to indecipherable, and she was giggling and scrunching her face.

He checked his hair in a bathroom mirror. It was not a freestanding creation, not a puffed wave, not an exciting or rebellious color. A sandy brown, it sat flat on his head, doing nothing. His facial features were symmetrical and well-spaced, with a prominent brow on a square-shaped head which seemed disproportionately large for his body. He worried he had a giant gargoyle head. Coming out of the bathroom, he checked his zipper. Tanya threw her arms around his neck and stuck her wet tongue in his ear. This gave him the impression something might happen that night, though Tanya was as predictable as the outcome of a dice roll. The idea cut through the fog and dominated his thoughts, overjoyed him, terrified him, and made him grind his jaw—he hadn't considered this possibility.

They walked across lawns on the way to her house. Lightning bugs flickered. He stole glances at her, amazed she was with him. In a way, he didn't see her at all. He saw ladies from his mother's *Cosmopolitan*, who had so captivated him earlier in his youth, or the underwire-supported and scissor-legged women of J.C. Penney. The models all wore the same facial expression to match their slim torsos and precise hair. This look was in their burning eyes, the sublime crease of their mouths, their shiny lips and the angle of their chins. The look hinted at a terrible boredom, or pleasures they sought to keep from the world, or a closely guarded bit of wisdom, or something he couldn't fathom. It meant everything and nothing.

He felt like he should say something, but could think of nothing. Her pink satin pumps in hand, a mashed corsage swung by a thread from her wrist. She sang softly to herself, *I will be there tonight…*a ballad she'd heard on Hot 102 FM. He wondered intensely: what was she thinking at this moment?

"Oh my God—I think I stepped in doo doo!" she shrieked.

At the Krieger house, she flailed her silk purse against her dress. "Dammit. I lost my keys!" He fumbled in a flower bed, peat chips crunching painfully under his knees until he found the fake rock that hid a key.

"Are you sure they're asleep?" The Krieger ranch house always exuded a mild hostility.

"I'm in trouble if they aren't. They haven't made it past ten o'clock in the last ten years." She pecked at the deadbolt with the key. What Lance hoped but also feared might happen with Tanya would not be the first time. It would be the second; the first memorable the way a car wreck was memorable.

Inside, amid the polished early American furnishings of the Krieger household, fatigue and confusion set in. Lance threw his coat over the couch and unclipped his tie, relieved to be less constrained. A smoky smell permeated the house, a reminder of Mr. Krieger's Firestone franchise. That guy had a punishing handshake.

"Have you had a good time?" she asked, somewhere in the dark.

"Well, sure." The sound of his voice spooked him.

"You don't seem like it."

Then they were kissing on the couch, frantic, as though it were urgent business delayed by the night's formalities. He held her in his arms and she lay across his lap. A classic movie pose. She tapped his lips; he held them too tight again. The muted television was on, flashing commercials. He groaned as he worked his lips, a satisfaction and perfection warming him. There really was something there between them, he wanted to believe. Wasn't there?

He leaned forward and pulled her closer.

"Owww! Are you trying to break me in half?"

"Sorry."

Next she straddled him, her legs settling onto either side of his pants. He pulled his arms out from under mountainous billows of dress and fluff and lace and things he wasn't sure about. More kissing. A *Saturday Night Live* skit unfolded on the television. Two people dressed as pilgrims, part of that anonymous and irritating cast of the post-Eddie Murphy era. Even with sound the skit wouldn't have been funny. It went on too long, beating the initial premise into the ground and leaving only a passing interest as to how the weirdness would cease.

They'd been kissing for what seemed hours and hours, exhausted from it. Each in a dreamy daze. Now see, he told himself, things were fine. Something bumped in the kitchen. She turned her head, then said, "It's just Ranger," meaning, the family dog was nosing around his bowl. She zipped her dress down in the back. This allowed slack in front. Enough to slip his hand inside the silky garment and underneath a breast.

A metallic sound. Then a bright tumble of light from the kitchen door, stinging their eyes. He was slow to recognize the robust figure of Mr. Krieger in the doorway, like it was some vision from the television. Tanya shrieked and pushed away, scratching his neck with a fingernail. She retreated to an unlit corner. Mr. Krieger shook his head, then mumbled something, a dull exhortation without overt meaning, but sounding harsh, like a dog's bark. He slammed the door. In darkness again, Lance stood, unsure if his heart would rupture. The first smashing sounds reverberated inside the kitchen: the hard, terrifying smack of china against floor tile, the explosive scatter of shards. Percussive waves bounced around the house. Chunks sprayed against the kitchen door.

Where was his tie? And Tanya?

"You can't leave now!" Tanya said, pressing her face close, tugging at his sleeve. This failed to interrupt his search for tie and cummerbund. She rushed toward the kitchen in bare feet, her dress swishing. He found his coat behind the couch. Mr. Krieger shouted in gruff tones. Leaving the front door open, he fled down the brick walk. Near the dark street, Tanya called to him from the steps. Mr. Krieger's vibrating form filled the door frame. Tanya flowed toward him, swishing again, holding her dress. Grateful, he anticipated an embrace.

"You need to leave! Get out of here!" she yelled. She put a hand on his lapel and pushed. He stumbled backward a step, stunned, waiting for some whispered communication, a secret apology. "You stupid jerk!" She stepped forward again, this time with both hands. He turned and walked off briskly to escape her. Part of him felt bad for her. The other part hated her.

After a block he slowed to get his breath.

More daunting than his fear of Mr. Krieger coming down the street in a car and more crushing than his date's betrayal was a single confounding thought, about Tanya and all the other Tanyas who populated the world: they could just as easily shove you as stick a tongue in your ear.

He walked home glumly, his shoes scratching on pavement. It was dark, only a trace of moon from a lidded sky. Maybe Tanya had broken up with him and he hadn't realized it yet. He thought of them together and felt depressed. He'd never dated anyone else. This loss would put him at zero. He had always idealized the feminine, his eyes wandering across the playground sandbox to the composed and secretive girls. While he was fidgety and nervous, they seemed freer, happier, possessing some inner magic he could only wonder about. And strange, doom-like circumstances had followed him since. He'd held hands with Karen Dell in Sunday school only to discover a spreading urine stain on his pants. He'd passed a love note to Jenny Whitley in second grade, vomiting on it the next moment.

In a few short months, he would be in college. It was a chance for redemption, to build himself into the person he imagined.

A humiliating moment flooded back—the dance floor. There was such pressure to perform, to be instantly fluid and Travoltaesque. A funky song had inspired him to bust loose and unleash his feet in a daring flourish, but the slick rental shoes betrayed him and his ass hit the floor. He had popped into a martial crouch and scowled at amused onlookers.

He turned into the Linden Chase subdivision at either 3:20 or 2:20 am. The vertical gray lines of his plastic Swatch, lacking numbers, seemed to twist as he studied the black hour hand. He paused at the sight of his family's house, which contained his parents and little sister Vickie. A tall prosperous house on a coveted cul-de-sac lot. The house loomed, serious and self-possessed. He was proud to live there (houses in nearby Willoughby Chase were more expensive, but less new).

The house and thought of his family made him lift his chin. His spine straightened and his chest filled with air. His father, a Harvard Business School graduate, was a senior vice president of a national consortium of aerospace companies. His much older brother, Kevin, was in medical school at Johns Hopkins. One grandfather had been a three-star general. Two uncles were high-powered antitrust lawyers, Yale men. The keen Rally intellect. All the men in his family were brainy, upright people with advanced degrees. A winning formula, it seemed. Lance's own high school showing had been unremarkable, compared to the scholarship bonanzas his father and Kevin had orchestrated, but he had excelled in some areas and showed potential. It frustrated him, his relative mediocrity, the subtle doubts he sensed from teachers.

He closed the front door behind him soundlessly. His parents would be asleep. The excitement of the evening still tickled him, the violence, the wacko conclusion. But could he be arrested for something?

A leathery smell drifted from his father's paneled study. Diplomas and award plaques and antique weapons and a mahogany desk sat in reverent silence, an epicenter of dark power. In the living room (or, more accurately, the television room) he sloughed off his coat and melted into the couch. This room calmed him, with its stacks of *Reader's Digest* and *TV Guide*, and its catatonic wall hangings. The television, that old mischievous friend, sat waiting for him, but it was so late. How many hours had he spent watching his beloved movies? The hard-bitten war flicks, the subtitled foreign oddities, the steady diet of obscure cable fare. His parents, concerned with his obsessive behavior and fearing the contamination of bizarre notions, had restricted his watching when he was a young child. So he snuck downstairs in the wee hours and watched in darkness, the sound low. The movies stood in contrast to the routines of church attendance and Sunday school, the mundane progress of Cub Scout projects, the drab ritual of school assemblies, the exhausting difficulty of grass cutting or leaf raking. Transportation to foreign worlds became possible. The freaky mind-blowing excellence of *Apocalypse Now*, the heroism and steamy undertones of *The Year of Living Dangerously*, the sublime violence and tension of *The Road Warrior*.

The end of the couch was grooved to his slump. A remnant of positive cinematic feelings touched him. That floating, out of body feeling from inhabiting a parallel world. In *East of Eden*, he had witnessed James Dean mumbling and lying about, as cool as the ice blocks he lolled against. This lackadaisical immunity to the opinions of others was amazing, enviable. It drove Julie Harris mad, forced her to fall in love with him. This ability to veg out, to let go and lie around as though near physical collapse was a marvelous invention. If only real humans could manage it. This approach ended with tragic consequences for Dean however, both in the movie and real life. On the big screen things were much easier. In *Easy Rider*, Peter Fonda and Dennis Hopper could toss their watches into the dust and tear across the Western landscape on choppers, finding an awesome freedom. Sunglasses fixed, the wind in their hair! But as the credits rolled, and more so when the music stopped, the feeling faded, as if such freedom was an entertainment trick and unattainable.

Upstairs, he crept down the hall past his sister Vickie's room, thinking of her with consternation. Vick the Stick had turned thirteen and was looking and acting like Vickie the Vixen. With the onset of menstruation and the strange, chaotic forces of womanhood, she had somehow gained psychic advantage. Recently, Lance had walked into the kitchen as she stood in a tight satin nightgown, her pert new chest outlined by the thin fabric. She was sporting blood-red lipstick. "Wear clothes often?" Lance had said. She leaned against the preparation island, eating an instant pudding. Gazing blankly, she ignored what would have been a dagger a few years back. And her friends: Cammy and Tammy and Kaitlin. They'd been hand-holders, whisperers, their greatest joys horseback riding and watercolor painting. They had regarded Lance with respect. Now a wild, she-devil edge infected them. Their main activities were phoning boys and screaming *God, he's so hot!* at *Dynasty* actors. Last week they surrounded and trapped Lance in the kitchen, speaking in a rapid unintelligible code with wet orthodontic mouths, babbling like they had just come out of anesthesia, their richly conditioned hair swinging. And their laughter! The mocking laughter of sadists having achieved final vengeance over an enemy. They invented a spontaneous nickname—Lodo or Loddy or Lano, it kept changing—based on an imperfection in his chin dimple. He escaped this mob, but his face turned crimson.

The truly weird thing was that Vickie now had the ability to read Lance's thoughts. "Why don't you just call her?" Vickie had said impatiently as he brushed his teeth. He had been thinking of Tanya but hadn't noticed it.

He clicked on the overhead light in his bedroom and exhaled, as he could only in his sacred place. He tossed his jacket, kicked off the pants and unbuttoned his shirt, realizing his mistake with the cufflinks. Embarrassment flared with the intensity of a physical ache. He struggled with the shirt. It flapped at the ends of his wrists, sailing through the air, the improper links stubbornly holding tight; he cursed until he was free. Inspecting the pants, he found a triangular rip on the seat, courtesy of the dance floor.

Exhausted, he slumped onto an oversize beanbag chair, mud brown, his hands flopping dead to the carpet. Familiar posters came into focus. He looked about, imploring, as if hoping one might jump off the wall and befriend him. A surreal photograph of a lime Porsche 911 Targa. Max Headroom, the computer-enhanced talking head. Also, a bumper sticker—HE WHO DIES WITH THE MOST TOYS WINS.

Tanya: he recalled the first time he inhaled Jean Naté and grape Bubblicious standing behind her on the mall escalator. Why had she French-kissed him after that argument? Not returning his phone calls for six days? She kidded him constantly about his most sensitive feature—his little toe which lacked a nail. So he kidded, once, about the mole on her shoulder, then felt horrible for causing her tears. She was a sweet-smelling enigma, a Rubik's Cube which had remained scrambled despite months of analysis from his relentless Rally mind. His failure to figure her out, to find her guiding logic—it was infuriating, crushing. He ached for what he thought she had stood for, this notion dying a small, unobserved death. He vowed to figure them all out.

His own behavior baffled him just as much. The swell of discomfort in her presence—brooding, powerful feelings he couldn't identify. They rose into his throat and threatened to strangle. She seemed to trigger an electronic glitch within him. Tanya, composed and emotionally nimble, would watch him squirm.

He studied a taped photograph from *Sports Illustrated*: Cheryl Tiegs in midstride on a beach in a fishnet bathing suit, her nipples prominent and unobstructed by the netting. This vision of Cheryl, so lithe and so sharply erotic, always moved him deeply. The bright dazzling eyes, the kind smile. He pretended a woman with equally fantastic qualities was strolling toward him: a steadier, more powerful version of himself. A woman whose beauty and candor would deliver him into woozy splendor, a sensual nirvana from which he would never return.

His eyes moved to his poster of *Eraserhead*, the early David Lynch film. The shadowed, bulging eyes and illuminated high hair of Henry Spencer struck a note of terror, like a cold steel instrument against his spine. Disturbed, he whistled, covered his eyes and tried not to think about the hellish industrial world Henry blankly inhabited, his wife giving birth to a mutant snake, and that tiny singing woman behind the radiator who provided Henry his only solace. But now he *was* thinking of the movie, which illustrated some cruel truth verified by his evening, that unending torment existed for certain people, possibly himself. He groaned loudly, thumping his head into the bag and carving out a pocket of beans, now thinking about Mutual Assured Destruction and nuclear winter, the planet ravaged, scavenging for food. He did not want to think about these things, but once you started it was hard to stop.

He gnawed on his fingernails, chomping one down to the

quick; this steadied him.

His eyes trailed over to his bookshelf. He scanned the presidential biographies his father had given him, the science fiction titles, the odd gifts. One title was tucked out of sight behind the others. *The Young Person's Guide to Sexuality*, his most embarrassing volume. His mother had given him the book. The *Guide* said sexual intercourse was a very serious gift given to people in love, *married* people, and between unmarried people it was known as fornication, which made God unhappy.

He respected his mother's opinion and decided it would be better to wait, yes. He had experienced a righteous feeling of goodness, of responsibility.

This information had hung over his head like a cautionary cloud, on a special afternoon at Tanya's parents' lake house. In the master bedroom, Tanya with the sneakiest of grins had peeled off her wet bikini. The decision was made for him as his principles crumbled. Added to his nervousness were guilt, and scrutiny from an onlooking, disapproving deity. And then it happened way too quickly, surprising both of them. Tanya was disappointed, a reaction he replayed a million times in a shameful loop. Afterwards, she looked at him differently, her eyes dulled, her respect halved.

He closed his eyes tight, this memory still like rope burn.

His component stereo, his shrine, beckoned him with its scientific blinking lights, its sleek consoles and knobs that begged to be tweaked. A list of bands and albums breezed through his mind. Van Halen. Thomas Dolby hit a special inner point. The Beach Boys' *Pet Sounds* he craved, but rejected. It would have swelled uncomfortable and potentially uncontrollable emotions—he sensed them right at the surface—that bursting sense, which led to crying, which was embarrassing and very unRally. His sadness stayed within, an unexpressed lump.

His ears still rang from the prom band and he lacked energy to get up. He burrowed deeper into the beanbag. Floating within this protective womb, he took stock of himself. He was so uncool. Feeling none of it, zip. This, he realized, was the evening's judgment. It was a complex thing and his mind whirled, considering car commercials, movies, television, comic books, fashion: this steady assault of conditioning and subtle judgments. Cool existed whether you wanted it or not, and was all around. Where to begin? His inability to phone females without using a weird oxygen-starved voice was probably his most uncool quality. He'd read extensively about the lives of American presidents, and tried to emulate their exemplary qualities. He'd signed a Drug Free pledge and had strictly adhered to it. He owned five identical pairs of khaki pants he wore to Mason Prep. Another five pairs of white oxford shirts accompanied them. But the ultimate arbiter of cool, the proving ground, was the dance floor, which hours ago his ass had slid across.

In his defense, he could name chronologically every band Eric Clapton had played in. He'd stolen a watch from a drug store in sixth grade. And watching James Dean marching off his property line in *Giant*, he had felt a joyous tug, a kinship so satisfying surely it was a kindred spirit thing; the thought of it now made him briefly feel he was OK. Except Vickie, who seemed destined to be correct, who possessed natural female cool, no one else in his family understood these factors, or appreciated their implications, or had it. Certainly not Kevin, the violinist. This seemed to work against his chances. Still, the factors were ever-changing.

He made an ungainly exit from the beanbag. Blood rushed, his vision darkened and he swayed. He fell back into the bag and waited for the yellow spots to clear.

A copy of the Mason Prep Spring Report lay on the floor. The school motto: *High Character, High Expectations*. The Report listed colleges each senior had been accepted to, scholarships and accolades granted. Lance had suffered a painful slew of Ivy League rejections, and been waitlisted at

Brown. His final choice had been Langford. He liked that it had four thousand students, was far away and had proximity to a major city, Atlanta. It had a growing reputation of putting students into top tier graduate schools, which was key.

The Report listed no scholarships or accolades by his own name. With a bare toe he nudged it under his bed, next to a grade-school-era bottle of Ritalin. He fought off a yawn and hung his head wearily. It seemed a lifetime of effort just to get to this point. The entrance tests for private schools, the weekend tutoring, the SAT preparation, the constant arms race of scholastic achievement. The stress caused his breath to get tight, made his stomach raw and achy. He also flicked report cards under his bed, like the one blemished by a cataclysmic C in Physics, or that C- in Trigonometry, word of which had triggered raised eyebrows and whispers of alarm through his household. The C- was a poke in the eye, a liver punch, until the hateful report was banished from his presence.

The sight of his Junior Achievement award plaque for Outstanding Project of the Year revived him. His eye often traveled there for sustenance, to the dark mahogany and smooth brass plate with its cursive lettering. He drank in the superlative, *Outstanding!* His project idea had been The Alexandria Game, like Monopoly, but with the city's streets and landmarks around the board. He'd sold hundreds of them to bookstores, civic organizations and friends. At last, a discovered talent. As in his mind, this achievement was echoed by his parents to friends and extended family: he was the *business natural*, a decent scholar but more the *little wheeler-dealer*, the *young gifted economist* of the family.

Standing before the award, a second wind stirred in him; his limbs became weightless and clarity entered his thoughts. In college, where things really mattered, he would correct his wrongs and prove himself.

Energized, he did a side-to-side dance move he invented on the spot. Before his mirror he snapped his fingers, rocked his shoulders. It was conceivable someone in the background of a music video or a cola commercial might do such a dance. He was smart, he assured himself, smart enough; he felt that way inside, the way his brain worked briskly and retained facts, and because he came from good genetic stock, his father being a Harvard Business School grad. Mom had a Vassar communications degree and was summa cum laude. Falling below this baseline was unthinkable. That would mean either he hadn't received the smart genes, or that he was a fuckup.

After his Junior Achievement success came a mention in the newspaper, which he played up big in college essays and which had probably gotten him into Langford (his SAT scores necessitated emphasizing his *special abilities* and where he made a *unique impact*). His college counselor had recommended economics and business school as a *focus plan*. His father concurred. It made sense to Lance. He had to pick something.

You had to think about all this beforehand if you were going to do it right and get anywhere in life. A pain in the ass? Perhaps, but a little foresight paid dividends. And for his trouble, he intended to earn lots of dividends. He sensed across the land a spirit that making it big was good and right and cool, and those who had made it big with hot careers were wearing shocking bright pastel colors and driving sports cars and being celebrated and cheered on by a tax-cutting president. Indeed, his screen idol, Tom Cruise, had illustrated these very principles in *Risky Business*, proving that the right shades, a sharp sport coat and the right attitude could turn your life around, leading to mountains of cash and transformational sex with Rebecca De Mornay. Cruise was ready to grind up the world with those big white teeth.

And the kicker: how could the woman of his dreams turn down such a mighty success? She would not. So he would do what it took to get there.

Armored by the security of his future, his mind turned back to that evening. In a few months he'd be surrounded by college women. Who cared about Tanya? He snorted. He recalled the outfit she had worn to the mall: coral red cotton overalls, striped blue socks, ripped white mesh t-shirt. With two similarly dressed girlfriends, the three of them unconsciously, or maybe by design, skipping along like the Bananarama girls on a sunny London day. And the gobs of makeup she wore! It had first seemed worldly, illicit, like she was an older woman. Not uncommon for clumps of mascara to stick to her eyebrows. She was a constant flirt, always brushing her hair.

He did several irate pushups. This exertion fed a building rage. The thing that angered him—it had frustrated him without surfacing until this very moment—was the feeling he got from her…how to put this?…that he was *doing it wrong*. She wouldn't tell him what it was, she just narrowed her eyes in dissatisfaction. Clenching his teeth, he wanted to scream, to crash cars, to smash someone's face. But carefully, as he had been trained, he calmed himself and stayed rational.

He yanked her picture out of his mirror. Next he started composing a letter to one Tanya Krieger, informing her of her many crimes and outrages and that he was finished with her. He crumpled this page into a ball, however, and pulled himself to his bed in late, late evening, possibly morning. Relaxed for the first time since being lip-locked on the Krieger couch. He could still feel her in his arms, still smell the strawberry shampoo and taste grape bubble gum from that last slow, wet kiss. He savored this memory, holding it tight.

CHAPTER TWO

LANGFORD

He started his new life as a collegian, an adult, by sitting in the back of a car driven by his parents and being dropped off. His father piloted the fragrant black Mercedes, which moved rapidly without seeming to move at all. Each morning he commuted into the nation's capital where powerful senators and House members addressed him on a first-name basis, like he was one of them; and he influenced important decisions at the complex intersection of government and commerce. Lance had driven the car, once, when his father tossed him the keys at the dealership. He had been nervous some spastic failure of his at high speed would destroy the big sedan. But today, Lance stretched his neck, his eyes active on the road as his father, who was an incredibly skilled driver, worked the car. His father drove extremely fast, always making stoplights, choreographing other drivers at stop signs with hand signals, almost without losing speed. But under total control, his mother not saying a word. Cops never noticed him. Never a ticket in his lifetime. Amazing!

"Are we there yet?" his father said, suddenly grinning.

"That's my line," Lance said. "I'll be saying that in about ten minutes." His father in a good mood, Lance relaxed. He eased into the leather cushions.

His father clamped the top of the steering wheel with the crook of his left wrist, his hand hanging over; this relaxation pose was the driving stance Lance had adopted. With his right hand he gesticulated freely. In their car positions, his father's role was storyteller and MC. The subtle modulations of his deep voice, his thick brown hair—he was a natural. He knew every conceivable thing, and was very entertaining in a way Lance wished he could be. "They arrived in Connecticut and migrated westward…" He chatted about their canny Scottish ancestors who fled English tyranny and hacked through the American wilderness. Lance knew the story well, but was still sucked into the instructive tale. They suffered many, many hardships and dangers, but they stayed the course and through miserable hard work they were richly rewarded. Being related to these tough characters had a certain satisfaction. His mother listened worshipfully, touching his father's sleeve. Her face softened, part of her lifelong swoon in his presence.

His father next spoke of his Princeton days, where he was Phi Beta Kappa. He'd had a deep friendship with an esteemed political science professor, his advisor, who went on to be a top confidant to LBJ. The seeming ease with which these things had happened for his father, and continued to happen, was always a remarkable thing.

"*Harold Tagg*," his father said to Lance, looking in the rear view. "Remember, he was hired from Stanford years ago. Harold Tagg is now head of the Economics Department at Langford."

"Oh, yeah. Right," Lance said, faking knowledge of this promotion. How did his father know this? Extra research?

"He was promoted last spring. He's the guy to get to know."

"Definitely. He sounds like advisor material." Lance imagined a similarly intense relationship with Prof. Tagg, a recognition of Lance's intellectual gifts and his great potential, and writing glowing recommendations that brimmed with personal insights. He would get Tagg to be his advisor. His expectations swelled happily and filled out the back seat.

"It's wonderful, the people and things you'll be exposed to. That's a part of college," his mother said, enunciating carefully. She reached back and jabbed his knee to get his full attention. She was an elegant, fine-featured blonde, still quite regal, who had hovered above Lance's childhood like a capricious fairytale queen. "Just be aware that these things can also be distractions from your focus."

"I already know that." Lance frowned.

Like most things his mother said, it was couched with such care he compulsively agreed: she was always logical, usually with insight that surprised him. Then he rethought it. He sensed that she, and his father, considered Lance more *prone* to distraction than Kevin. He leaned forward. "When have I ever not been focused?"

"I'm not saying you haven't been, just that you need to *keep* that focus." She stared forward a moment, then turned her head to glance back at him. Her face was pleasantly nonchalant, but her eyebrows tensed, her eyes suddenly trying to find something. This look he'd often seen from her in fifth grade during those secret-mission car trips to Dr. Henry Shatzer, the prescriber of Ritalin. Lance's grades had mysteriously dipped, and this coincided with Lance running down the street naked, on a dare from Kevin, and offending an elderly neighbor. After an hour of Dr. Shatzer's throat-clearing and gentle questioning about dreams and feelings, and Lance's tight-armed squirming and silences and evasive answers, he climbed back into the car. Again his mother would look at him with veiled concern: half-smiling, but her eyes searching, frantic, trying to find or fearing finding something. She waited for what he was determined not to give. Lance would steel himself with aloofness, as if proving to her, and to himself: *no problems here.*

"Is Economics one of the core requirements at Langford?" His mother shifted suddenly and stared back at Lance with her full face.

"Um. I'm pretty certain that it is."

"It must be," his father said.

"Well..."

His mother's face remained, waiting.

"No. I don't think so. I'm not sure, actually." A heat rose on his neck. He started twisting the plastic end on his shoelace. He clamped his teeth. Back when he was trying to sell them on Langford, trying to justify the premium tuition, he had made an elaborate point about the core requirements. Now this was a blank.

She turned her head back around.

"My guess is that it is not," his father said with great assurance.

Lance started to say something, but stopped. More twisting. He picked at a tear in the plastic sheath, ripping a seam from the shoelace fibers. A sharp plastic edge jammed under his fingernail at a soft point.

Mom turned to his father. "Didn't Kevin exempt out of two core requirements? Because of all those advanced placement credits?"

"That's right. He did."

"It was only one," Lance said. "Math he exempted out of, but that was it."

"I think it was two."

"Wasn't it two?"

"No, it was only *one*." Lance spun the plastic end, rubbing it madly between his fingers, then yanking it off the shoelace. He flicked it onto the floor mat and kicked it under the seat. Kevin, the star medical student, with his monastic-like intensity, his Herculean single-mindedness and eye-popping scores, who had wisely put off "serious dating" until his career was on firm footing. Kevin was impressively book smart, but in certain ways he lacked common sense. A silence fell, the muted hum of the engine the only sound. Lance tensed, trying to remember the core requirements. With his thumbnail, he picked at the rough edge of his other thumbnail and carved a groove.

His mother said something to his father that Lance missed. They exchanged knowing, vexed glances. He tuned in.

"Is it thirteen thousand this year? Langford raised the tuition again?"

"They are going to raise it every year."

His father shook his head, and made several short huffs. News that a new water heater would cost five hundred dollars had once caused him to lean against a wall and grimace at the loss of this hard-won capital.

"Who knows what it will be next year."

"Could this create problems for us?" His mother suddenly looked worried. In a voice soft enough it barely escaped to the back seat, she said, "The miracle of scholarships."

He felt like he might burst. His feet pressed into the floor. He pulled a thread of the seat stitching, jerking it until a seam opened up and separated the leather. Another silence settled in, then stretched out, this one deeper, more enduring. His parents' heads were fixed, staring straight ahead; he sensed grim expressions on their faces, their eyeballs moving ever so slowly.

He reached for his Walkman, clamped headphones to his ears and pressed PLAY. The scene before his eyes blurred as he transported to a distant cloister with walls two feet thick. The Cars, with their power chords and spacey synthesizers on "Just What I Needed," calmed his nerve endings. His mouth inched open and his eyes shut as ecstatic rhythms pulsed in his skull. In this universe, expressionism reigned and convictions were screamed with the full power of a vocalist's lungs. These emotions! What to do with them? At one time he took these emotions as a directive and imagined himself as a rock-'n'-roller; he borrowed money from his father, at huge difficulty, to purchase a pawn shop guitar. But he had zero musical ability, and the sweet sounds of Jimmy Page did not issue from the strings, just unspeakable twanging. Kevin scowled at his attempts, which ended with ripped fingertips and frustration and a loan to be repaid. He sold the guitar back, proof to his father that listening to The Cars was a lot of nonsense. But Lance wasn't giving up his music. He bought headphones and went underground.

At last, they reached the offbeat town of Langford, with its main street, its curious little businesses, his mother cooing and pointing at the darling place. Flags atop the medieval- looking Langford campanile showed the university's colors of yellow and umber. Outside of Szabo dorm, Lance and his father unloaded the car. His father talked to a student with a clipboard. That student waved over two other people, all of them raking through papers. This was his father's genius, his ability to inspire and orchestrate people who performed tasks for him.

A college girl in a clingy tube top walked along the sidewalk—a very complementary tube top. His mother bristled and stared in disapproval. Lance stared also. The clipboard guy directed them to room 310. Szabo reeked of bleach and new carpet. They shuffled up a metal stairwell. And what of his roommate, his comrade, his new hell-raising college chum? Lance reflected that many important friendships began between college roommates. Some lasted a lifetime. Lance found an empty room. Two unmade beds. He picked the one nearest the window. Only Lance's name was on the door. His mother walked in. She brought her hands together before her while taking a little breath, which meant gracious approval. "It's a gorgeous little room," she said. She ruined it by opening her eyes wider, which meant she had grievances. Lance's father swept in behind her. Air puffed out of his mouth to emphasize some irony.

In the hall, Lance asked a guy with a clipboard about his roommate.

"Looks like you don't have one. You lucked out."

"Great." Lance smiled, then wondered if he should smile about that.

"A private room," his father said, tapping him on the arm. "That's quite a luxury. That way nobody can interrupt your concentration."

To Lance's annoyance, his mom worked on his single mattress. She stretched a fitted bed sheet, the blue leaf pattern he liked, then lovingly tucked a cotton blanket. Then she pulled out a nature poster from her bag, a forest primeval brimming with green canopy, ferns and adorable small animals. Lance looked at it, touched, despite its embarrassing qualities.

"Do you like it?" His mother nodded her head genially.

"It's very *green*..." He averted his eyes and disguised his expression, as he usually did, to try to counter his mother's mindreading abilities.

She studied him with her invasive look. "You *do* like it. I knew you would, but you won't admit it."

They made trips to get luggage and Lance's beloved stereo. His father produced his old leather-bound *Roget's Thesaurus*. He flipped through the well-thumbed pages one last time, rubbed the spine, then presented it to Lance. The heavy book sagged in Lance's hands.

"It's yours now," his father said. "I want you to have it."

"Are you sure? This has always been your thesaurus."

As a child, Lance had often borrowed it, always turning the thin pages with the greatest care, studying the handwritten notations for clues to his father's soul, and regarding the archaic words as if they constituted some powerful religion. On the first page, his grandfather had written an inscription to his father, and below that his father had drawn a line, then written the same inscription to Lance: *May you always have the right word.*

His father and mother stared at Lance solemnly. Then their faces softened and their eyes got big with a final rush of love and worry. He realized the sacrifices they had made, the advantages they had given him. His father, not a hugger, surprised him with a vibrating bear hug, the smell of his father's deodorant odd. "You're going to do very well," his father said in an unusually wavering tone. A torrent of warm memories filled Lance: of celebrating a tee-ball trophy, of a balsa wood bridge he and his father had built. He wanted to announce he would do his absolute best, wanted to convince his father this was true, and almost did. His mom hugged him, and told him to call.

Then he felt an excruciating tension, that if his parents did not soon go far, far away he might explode all over them. He waved as they drove off, moisture welling at the corners of his eyes.

His room was quiet and empty. At this dawn of his freedom, he felt lost. It was too much possibility, like he was standing on a high windblown cliff. He remembered his focus plan. He would study like a fiend. The shelves, cubby holes and flat writing surface of the built-in wooden desk were riddled with pen marks, hieroglyphics and graffiti. But as he rubbed his palm across the wood and arranged his father's thesaurus—now his—it welled within him that at this desk his life would begin. He wanted to suck up all the knowledge Langford University had.

He was eager to dig into his Orientation materials, to pick out classes. A good start was crucial. He organized papers in pleasing stacks, imagining he had an academic head start on everyone. He closed his door. His Orientation packet contained a copy of *From Ignobility to Glory*, the autobiography of school founder Theodore Ivan Langford. Langford owned a string of factories and at the turn of the century decided to use his wealth to found a university.

A Career Services memo in Day-Glo orange caught his eye: NETWORKING. This cutting-edge concept involved finding professional mentors and writing each person's name in a Rolodex and plugging oneself into this conspiratorial group to receive information and to procure jobs. This was a brilliant idea! *An assembled network will be instrumental in post-graduation job hunting and ultimate career success.* But Lance had no idea where to meet these professionals. The prospect of job hunting inched his blood pressure higher; it put him on edge.

A sound boomed from an adjoining room: a television blared a warped, vibrating sound common to futuristic cities: *Blade Runner*. What were the rules about such noisemaking? He tapped on the wall with his pen.

He moved on to the TARGETED CAREER OPTION EVALUATION. It had to be dropped at Career Services no later than September 5, the deadline for being assigned a Career Consultant. *The career track must be started as early as possible and matched with compatible course work.* The Evaluation asked: *What are your areas of concentration? Your weakest skills? Where do you see yourself in twenty years?* I just got here, Lance thought.

Movie noises filled the room, making concentration on this life planning difficult. Stray noises came from down the hall, a festive stereo now played. He became curious.

Out in the hall, Lance shut the door behind him. Many doors down, a crowd of freshmen hung out in doorways, listening to music, telling stories, smoking cigarettes, forging alliances. The hallway framed this in a distant square. Tag team duos of roommates worked introductions. Barefoot girls laughed and tossed their hair. These people, vibrating with an ultra-loose vibe, seemed to have known each other forever. He wanted to join this throng. A new social order was being formed. It had gelled without him. He was aware he stood sideways to the crowd. He deciphered the music: Crosby, Stills & Nash, this ridiculous hippie music. But one girl weaved her arms in a psychedelic way, swaying, laughing. She both celebrated the music and pointed out its absurdity. They kept yelling a catch phrase: "We're that type of people!" from that idiotic Chevy Chase movie. They were laughing harder each time, *"We're that type of people!"* but with this mocking, this irony, it became quite brilliant. It was this complexity he was up against. He leaned against the wall, like he'd stepped in glue, studying the crowd out of the corner of his eye.

He looked down at his horrible khakis, wishing to rip them off, to burn them. His white oxford shirt similarly crawled against his skin, the antiseptic white of a medical garment. He looked like a Father's Day advertisement. He crossed his arms, trying to compress himself. He seemed not to have a plan. His desire to walk down the hall was thwarted. Was that a red kimono somebody was wearing? He pondered this thought: When you were one type of person, how did you become another type of person? There was no reason to stand in the middle of the hall, leaning against a wall. He threw up his hands suddenly, like he had just remembered something important, and walked away.

He decided he would do without the social scene. That could be, as his mother had warned, a big distraction. Either he was serious or he wasn't. He imagined a Spartan existence: study, eat, sleep, study more.

Noncompetitive games were scheduled for the next day. He judged this a frivolous waste of time. Instead he scouted out study locations. Scanlon Library he didn't like because the tables and chairs were old and scarred, it had a peculiar smell, and the fluorescent lights had a yellow pall. The stacks of The Ivan, he liked: the serious aura of thousands of shelved books, each carrel offering a slender window, and soothing white noise hissing from air conditioners. As he rattled the locked front door of Lipton, a custodian stared from within, squinting in puzzlement as to why this young man wanted into a library during Orientation.

Parties and excessive drinking took place during the evenings. He was repelled by this lack of seriousness, this cocktail mentality—so high school—and the banal pop music. On rare walks between his room and the hall bathroom, he was quick to bounce on his toes and throw retorts at hall mates and project an intense orbit. He laughed aggressively but was very hurried, as if he might knock someone over to get back to his room within thirty seconds. People stared at the guy who was barricaded in his room, always wearing the same Langford t-shirt and faded yellow tennis shorts, his only clothes not obviously purchased by his mother. Lance ripped off his door a picture of a naked old man and a tabloid headline that said

"Hermit Man"—his hall mates decorating again.

Inside his room he listened to real music, like rare Led Zeppelin vinyl from Japan, and read *From Ignobility to Glory*, impressed with Theodore Ivan Langford's vision and business savvy. But laughter outside made him stare longingly at the door. It was a problem: if he closed the door, he was sealed off like an astronaut; if he opened it, people stuck their heads inside to see *the guy with no roommate*. It was useful to be able to close the door, draw the blinds, hang his head off the bed and stare upside down. Blood pooled in his skull, making him delirious, his scalp tingly with needles. His old tonic to alter consciousness. He had imaginary conversations with girls he'd seen from his window. The TARGETED CAREER OPTION EVALUATION, probably due, lay on his desk. He was too depressed to fill it out. The door opened, casting a bright shard of light. A custodian, maybe that same guy, eyed the overflowing garbage can. He stared at Lance, then started to retreat.

"You can go ahead and get it."

"It's dark in here."

"I know."

He considered calling Kevin for advice about class selection. He picked up the phone, imagined Kevin entangled in serious medical-school things, and put the phone back. *Get to know your professors*, Kevin had advised, using the rare serious tone Lance always appreciated. Then his mouth bunched sardonically and he added, *and whatever you do, don't be a fuckup*.

By the end of Orientation, lethargy had taken hold of Lance. Sleep came grudgingly and was unsatisfying. Lance sensed the stirrings of all the residents of Szabo dorm: flushing, screams, arguments. By morning, his clock radio blared as he slumbered. He missed the Personal Organization and Goal Setting lecture.

At last classes came. Once he dragged on clothes he ran across campus, getting lost, sprinting to make up time in the correct direction. He felt joy as his feet crunched on the needles of Virginia pines. Most paths led to or exited from The Lawn, which anchored the campus. The size of several football fields end to end, each main academic department had a building. Students marched in and out of the Italianate facades. Higher learning! The life of the mind!

In the Economics building he sat in cavernous lecture room 103, on a middle row, among seventy other students. His very first class. Econ 101: Microeconomics, which the heralded Harold Tagg, the Cutler-Swain Professor of Economics, was teaching that semester. He opened his textbook to Chapter One, which he had already read twice and highlighted, and opened his pristine spiral notebook to the first page, ready to note words of wisdom in strict paragraphs. His desire to learn was ravenous.

It was stadium seating, which meant Tagg was many feet below. Lance expected a distinguished fellow, a cross between Paul Volker and John Maynard Keynes, not one of the Fabulous Furry Freak Brothers. Tagg's shaggy head and beard joined in a swirl of flaxen curls around his pudgy face, forming a hair halo. Tagg would shuffle before the class, pin a microphone to his shirt and start talking in a rapid monotone—*What? Slow down!* Lance wanted to yell. An overhead projector lit his face from below and reflected strangely from his glasses. Tagg jerked at the overlays, marking them with black pens and smearing mistakes. The graphs jumped around on the wall, hovering like menacing UFOs. In an amplified mumble he talked about inverse curves and demand curves, which Lance remembered vaguely from the reading, but it seemed in conflict with the reading. In fits and starts, Lance covered his notebook with illegible graffiti that baffled him as he scribbled it. He stewed in confusion.

He usually finished the class irritated and listing Tagg's deficiencies as a teacher: he didn't speak in complete sentences;

his graphs were infantile; he aggrandized himself talking about the national economic council he co-chaired. In one class, Lance made a breakthrough in his understanding of inverse curves and their elasticity. Afterward, he rushed down the stadium stairs to clarify one point. He caught up with Tagg in an outside hall, several students at his elbows as he walked. He had shed all but one student as Lance caught up, like an ambush reporter. "Professor, could you slow down please?"

"I cannot."

"Just a second."

"Another class awaits."

Lance asked his question, zigzagging around oncoming students. Without breaking stride, Tagg said, "The short answer is maybe. If you do the reading again carefully, the long answer will be apparent..." He ducked into another classroom, leaving behind only a scent of musky corduroy. His office hours were booked solid.

It was upsetting, defeating. He hated economics; it was not supposed to be this way. Every day with Tagg ripped away at his careful planning. But perhaps Tagg was using advanced teaching, he reasoned, an inaccessible high theory form of microeconomics that might benefit him in the long run. Lance was stubborn. In first grade he sat in a tree for three hours, waiting out a bully. Giving up was bad.

He strolled out of the Econ building. At the busy intersection of Burk and Langford Way, he paused. People hurried from all sides, streaming around him indifferently, like he was a newsstand. A girl and a guy, lovers, each with a hand snug in the derriere jeans pocket of the other. Wisecracking pockets of friends. Chatting grad students. He looked in every direction, searching for someone he could shout at, who would laugh in solidarity about a quarters game, or some late-night debauchery, or a guest appearance on *Miami Vice*, this spirit reverberating, making it obvious to onlookers that he possessed cool, and was traveling in happening circles. There was no such person. A daily narcolepsy pulled him towards his mattress. He dreaded his room and its isolation. In an essential way he was failing. He was an outsider.

Another student bumped his shoulder, walking on without stopping.

CHAPTER THREE

NAKED CALIFORNIANS

A fluorescent green Frisbee sailed toward Lance, whistling as it spun downward. This was Ultimate Frisbee. All he had to do was grab it for a touchdown, his first catch of the game. Moving easily, he savored this victory, ready for the plastic to slap his hand. He heard heavy footsteps and there was an impact, a cataclysmic smack, like his head was a billiard ball. A pain coalesced behind his lids as his back slid across grass. Acrid phlegm rose in his throat. He opened his eyes. A guy with a Mohawk was on his knees, gritting his teeth, a hand over one eye. His other eye bulged, searching about belligerently. Not a pristine Mohawk; it was unkempt, and dirty blonde hair had grown into stubble around the thick band at the top of his skull. He pulled his hand away, and blood stained an eyebrow.

Lance pushed up using his fists, nervous the punk rocker might throw a punch. The guy was from Los Angeles, maybe even Hollywood, where real punkers existed. Lance recalled his aborted moment of glory, irritation welling up against this guy who had contested the catch like it was the Super Bowl. LaCoss. Ian LaCoss. He wore cutoff fatigue pants and black Puma soccer cleats while everyone else was in sneakers. Earlier, he'd shoved another guy in the back, the guy's face plowing the ground. This was Frisbee, a game invented by hippies. Lance's left ear was ringing; the world had a reddish tint. His teeth felt oddly sensitive. He pushed himself to his feet. LaCoss, the punker, stood also and looked down at his smudged knees. He flicked off some blades of grass. "You've got a hard skull."

"I think I have a concussion. People can die from that." Lance held his head with both hands, as though it might split into halves.

LaCoss held up a closed fist. "How many fingers?"

"You're a funny guy."

It was outrageously funny to LaCoss, who wheezed and convulsed as if suddenly drunk. A tiny silver dagger dangled from his earlobe. The game continued on without them as they walked toward the sideline. Somebody gave LaCoss a tissue and he dabbed at the cut in his eyebrow. He'd written numbers, messages and hieroglyphics across his palms in blue ink.

LaCoss had on a frayed t-shirt minus the sleeves. On the shirt a logo: the letters P.I.L. inside a circle. Lance suddenly craved a t-shirt with an obscure insignia.

"What's P.I.L.?"

"Public Image Limited. Johnny Rotten's new band."

"That guy has been dead for years."

"Sid Vicious is the dead one." LaCoss made a bored, deadpan face, implying this pitiful lack of common knowledge was embarrassing. The cut still bled, though he didn't seem to notice. Lance introduced himself. They shook hands, LaCoss staring at their clasped hands like it was a peculiar ritual. LaCoss laughed. Lance smiled, but was perplexed.

"P.I.L. just put out a new album. It's really good."

"Is it worth a listen? Do you think I'd like it?"

"That depends on how advanced you are."

They walked down University Drive. Lance guessed they were friends, though it was difficult to tell. They were about the same height. LaCoss had a ranginess, a knobby muscularity that made him seem larger than he was. Lance recalled stories about a California wild man who had viciously argued with a tenured professor during a class, a wild man who was dating a beautiful sorority upperclasswoman. A convertible Celica with three girls in it rode by. They whooped and waved breathlessly at LaCoss, screaming *Ian! Ian! Ian!* He pointed and yelled something about

New Orleans—*Whoa, yeah!*—to the girls. Despite the Mohawk, a certain appealing rakishness flared at the sight of the well-wishers. He flashed brilliant white, well-formed teeth and light green eyes. The girls' eyes flitted to Lance; caught off guard, he stood inert like a flash photo and failed to wave back at them.

LaCoss lived in Pichler, a dorm on the opposite side of campus, in what seemed to be the basement, a giant windowless room with bright fluorescent panels.

"I've got my own room too," Lance said, feeling a sudden pride.

"I had a roommate, this *total* idiot character. This cello player. A tennis lover. This nitwit. I couldn't stand a single word coming out of that guy's mouth. So I demanded immediate change. They put me down here." His face lit up with raging self-satisfaction. A bed, a small cut of blue carpet and two folding chairs were bunched into one corner of the room, the remaining two-thirds of the room strangely bare. Next to a sack of oranges was a moist cardboard box filled with peels. Posters of Iggy Pop, Sophia Loren and the Maharishi Mahesh Yogi hung over the bed. Lance raised his fists and revved an imaginary chopper in homage to a Peter Fonda poster, circa *Easy Rider*.

Lance sat on a folding chair and drank some offered Gatorade. LaCoss took a record album out of its sleeve, admiring the black vinyl, and placed it gently on a turntable. It was a cheap stereo—a Krako Multiphonic?—a cassette deck built into a turntable with a dusty removable plastic hood, and shabby brown speakers which might have been used by Nixon for a public address system. Wooden crates on the floor bulged with albums. Lance's eyes grew big as he took an inventory of this musical bounty.

"This is Public Image Limited's latest." LaCoss sat on the other folding chair as the music started. He leaned forward, his body tensing. His pupils widened as he listened, his gaze becoming indistinct, like he was falling into oblivion. His eyes blinked rapidly, his head snapped forward as if a low voltage current surged through him. Lance watched, fascinated. At the end of the song, LaCoss snapped out of it. He looked at Lance, concerned. "You don't get it, do you?"

Lance frowned. "Nope. I don't get it." The music sounded flat, drained, an odd form of experimental disco.

"That's OK. No problem. We'll just back up. Sex Pistols?"

"I've heard of them. I've never actually listened to them."

"Obviously, you've had a deeply deprived upbringing."

LaCoss embarked on a crash course. He plucked twenty albums from the mystery crates, explaining that he was starting from the very beginning, the point of conception, with the Ramones. Static issued from the speakers, then wild hyperactive music roared in Lance's ears, startling him. He knew in a loose passing way that the Ramones had biker jackets that were too small, mop top hair, and an unmentionable frog man on lead vocals. Corporate powers had deemed them unworthy of radio play. The song was crunchy from LaCoss listening to it every morning for the past three years. Lance fixed his gaze on Sophia Loren on the far wall, let his arms hang to the floor and let go. Then their brilliance sunk in: they had stripped rock down to the raw stuff; they were The Crickets, post plane crash, taking up secret drug habits behind the auditorium after a sock hop. The song "I Wanna Be Sedated" blasted, and a feeling of liberation swept through him like realizing some good news he'd been trying to remember for days. A euphoric smile dented the upper reaches of his cheeks. He imagined taping LaCoss's collection, the hours of blissful discovery, a new soundtrack to his life. LaCoss cranked the volume to eight, the loudest setting possible on the Krako. Then he sprung into the air repeatedly like a human pogo stick. He pounded straight arms against his sides and thrashed around unpredictably, twisting with seizure-like intensity; he knocked over his chair and bounced against a wall.

Lance gripped his chair, alarmed. Then he laughed and howled in camaraderie. He jumped into the air also, thrashing, jumping, happily possessed by the music, inhabiting a new body, until he was out of breath and the song ended. With other songs they headbanged to the beat and shook their fists, Lance accentuating a satisfying guitar lick with air licks of his own. How had this musical category been missed? Where had he been?

He *was* deprived, but resolved to make up for it with strict focus.

LaCoss covered the rest of the New York punk scene, playing Television, putting special emphasis on Richard Hell and The Voidoids. These brave souls cross-pollinated with Brits to produce the Sex Pistols, Gang of Four and The Clash (who Lance was perfectly well aware of; I mean, come on). Crunching guitars filled desolate landscapes. Inexperienced fingers rattled and twanged in guitar wires. The voices were scratched, imperfect, though earnest. They told tales of warped joy, of embracing one's torment—an emotion Lance well understood—and taking ownership of it. He ran his fingers over the nubby edges of albums, read liner notes and looked at washed-out backstage photographs: the band in some trashy, poorly lit backstage dungeon. They didn't care about their unsightly t-shirts, about their sneering faces or self-imposed wounds, maybe nothing at all, save their music. The songs were rocky, crude, as if recorded in dank alleyways using abused equipment. He took in these sounds hungrily, astonished, moved by their power and their relentless rage. Lance dropped his eyebrows low, concentrating: it had never occurred to him to rage against society, that there were reasons to spew frustration about the status quo or scream obscenities into a microphone, so the feeling was unfamiliar. But not completely.

LaCoss asked with understatement, "So, what do you think?"

"It's unbelievable. It totally rocks." Envy that LaCoss had mastered the genre softened his response, but Lance was grateful to have learned about it at all. The music was perfection, a surreal joy similar to seeing *A Clockwork Orange* for the first time, or discovering Cheryl Tiegs. The feeling everything could change for the better, or maybe already had. A light shone from the heavens. A spooky rockabilly skeleton on an album cover in a crate caught Lance's eye: The Cramps. He plucked it out, and LaCoss queued it up.

Lance sat upright. "Shit! I've got a class in ten minutes." It was Econ 101, a ten-minute walk. Thus far, his attendance had been flawless. He gathered up his books.

"So what?" A bemused smile from LaCoss, a hint of mockery which Lance disliked.

"You know, classes. Like, the reason we're here."

"Is it?" LaCoss bit into a tangerine. Pulp stuck to his lips. "Would it kill you to miss one? Will this ruin your life?"

"He's supposed to cover demand curves. That's pretty important." Lance rechecked his watch. He'd have to run. He would get there out of breath. Tagg chastised latecomers and stared them down. Lance stood by the door. Not listening to the rest of the album seemed the cruelest of deprivations. But he did have a choice. He imagined flipping off Prof. Harold Tagg in the two-fingered British way, as Johnny Rotten might.

One missed class was no big deal.

It took days to cover the foundations. Lance lost track of time in the windowless room, the bright fluorescent lights and isolation giving his listenings a scientific quality, an importance, an urgency. He saw through a new lens. All his life he'd been listening to dinosaur rock and top 40 nonsense, this generic crap, which screamed of ignorance and conventionality. He wanted to throw his entire record collection into the mouth of a volcano and start over. What else was he mistaken about? What else waited out there, ready to spin his head around? It was rather disturbing, these potential unknowns.

At last they got to the strength of LaCoss's collection: the California punks. Agent Orange, Dead Kennedys, and the masters themselves, Black Flag, each of their shows like having your soul remade. Most of them LaCoss had seen himself, in Hollywood, or at a downtown haunt, or in East L.A. during his infiltration of the punk club scene (Alexandria had no such thing). Incredibly, LaCoss's parents didn't care how often he attended clubs, so long as he came back to their Topanga canyon house regularly, went to school semi-regularly and didn't take on any *serious* drug habits. Lance enjoyed these mad California bands, his chest fluttering with a similar energy as his head pecked to the beat. They also found remarkable consensus on the important matter of movies. LaCoss had discerning tastes as a cineaste and shared similar infatuations with Stanley Kubrick, the films of Malcolm MacDowell and the work of director David Lynch. Lance valued Orson Welles and *Citizen Kane* more than LaCoss did. LaCoss had a fuller grasp of Fellini's oeuvre.

"*Taxi Driver* is superior to *Raging Bull*," Lance asserted.

"I'm sorry, but you're off base. *Raging Bull* is De Niro's best by far."

"That I will grant you, but I'm talking about the film's overall impact."

They played a handball game with a tennis ball against the back wall of the room as punk music blared. The court was marked by masking tape on the floor. They played for hours. Lance missed a Comparative Lit class, skipped another Microeconomics class: supply curves paled in comparison to the excitement of gnashing guitars, of reverb. They ventured into the exotic corners of New Wave, into Soft Cell, Kraftwerk and Devo, which LaCoss held in strangely high regard.

"Listen very closely," LaCoss said, putting his hands together at the tip of his nose, as if in prayer. Lance liked early Devo too, which nobody listened to. But Lance could only take them so seriously. After all, they wore identical yellow rain suits, 3-D glasses, and plastic flower pots on their heads, and they moved like robots. He chuckled thinking of them.

This bugged LaCoss. "Listen. It's very important."

"I am listening. All ears."

"Do you know what Devo means?"

"It probably means nothing."

"It means de-evolution. It's about going backward with evolution. Devolving. The human spirit being twisted by modern forces. There has been this excessive conditioning of young people, this materialism and this increased societal *regimentation*"—pronounced with a hard "g" rather than a "j"—"together they are doing some nasty things to the human psyche…" The whole Devo thing was a core theory, a foundational belief. LaCoss believed aliens existed and that Jim Morrison was a preeminent philosopher. He was making it all up, assembling a value system like a tricycle on Christmas morning.

"What are you going to major in?" LaCoss asked.

"Economics."

LaCoss zipped the needle off a Sex Pistols record. "Econ? Why would you want to major in that? Why would anyone?" His face became riddled with disgust and upset, as if he detected the stench of rotting meat.

"But economics describes how the economy works. There are patterns and rules to commercial activity that are predictable."

"What a god-awful boring subject to learn about!"

"Maybe. But once you get beyond that, it's a versatile degree."

LaCoss groaned, then shook his head in a confounded way: the study of economics was for squares and didn't jive with the anarchistic rage of the Germs or the working-class protest of Gang of Four. And perhaps it didn't. Not the sexiest of majors, it was a supporter of the status quo. For a moment, Lance was embarrassed by his choice and he considered changing it purely on this basis. But it was necessary to have a consistent plan, to make a plan and keep it. This was the way to success. LaCoss kicked the tennis ball hard, like he wanted to pulverize it, and the echo shocked Lance's ears. He was crushed by this criticism from LaCoss, who embodied almost every quality Lance wanted himself. It seemed a serious impasse. Then LaCoss picked up a record. "Oh, man. Wait till you hear this one."

LaCoss had an ease backed by a fierce personal code, his life an intensely cool movie he was acting in and directing. His early life, fleshed out by questions from Lance, seemed a sort of California living experiment. His mom's thing was finding God, or finding herself, depending on the meetings she attended. She had started with the Timothy Leary mind expansion, tripping on the very day she realized she was pregnant with LaCoss. She became convinced she couldn't find God. Mom's solution to this cosmic vacuum was to empower the individual to be their own God. *I am God*, Mom had young Ian repeat before she tucked him in at night. It caught on, attracting followers to her living room. She'd written a book. That such people existed, that such freedom of thought was attainable, it boggled Lance's mind.

"Where do you stand on this personal God idea now?"

"I'm just as likely to be God as anybody else."

LaCoss's family visited nudist camps (Lance tried to imagine his own family naked, but could not). Society repressed emotion and fostered guilt, they believed. The cure was regular recreation with your genitals catching air. His mom enjoyed running in the buff, a jog around the volleyball area to work up a sweat. Little Ian jogged with her. He'd seen her pubic hair and breasts before from taking baths with her. No big deal. The nudie and clothed worlds coexisted. Though one morning he walked to the corner to wait for the school bus wearing only a backpack.

"Clothes are a drag, man. They hide your soul."

LaCoss's father was a set designer. He had constructed Old West towns on several classic Clint Eastwood flicks. Then Dad, who consumed four grams of Vitamin C daily, went into life extension products. Little Ian tramped about the neighborhood with a box of Vitamin B Spectrum bottles of the *LaCoss Life!* brand. He was nine and knew to target the moms, who wanted healthy families, everlasting beauty and weight loss. They would stoop down to hear the little businessman. LaCoss searched their mom faces, sensing what they wanted to hear; he learned how to penetrate the feminine psyche. He flashed the teeth he brushed three times daily and made his eyes glow. Once he detected a certain feeling, that twinkly estrogen-fueled approval, he knew he had them. By age twelve he'd sold over twenty grand of product.

LaCoss swallowed handfuls of pills daily. He convinced Lance to take a giant multivitamin that made him jittery. He said in total seriousness, "Taking these things, you can live to be a hundred and twenty."

Lance saw LaCoss once outside The Fritz playing hacky sack, but he seemed not to be attending classes. He seemed not to have other friends. Lance wondered if LaCoss felt a loneliness too, but guessed he did not.

While they were listening to side two of The Clash's *Combat Rock*, two girls with beaming faces appeared at LaCoss's door. They chewed gum and waved at LaCoss. One with bobbed brown hair, the other with long red hair. Lance waved back, getting their attention before he knocked over a soft drink can with his foot. An album cover slid off his lap into the puddle. LaCoss made his hand into a pistol and closed one eye, sighting these girls with an imaginary gun. Magician-like, his whole demeanor transformed, powerfully lasering his attention. His eyes stirred, becoming intense, his shoulders softening. He stood slowly, the edges of his lips turning up suavely. He approached the girls with open, magnanimous arms and they clung to him like metal shavings to a magnet. He said things that made them weak with amusement. Lance turned down the volume to hear.

LaCoss said in a sweet tone, "Now don't tell me that. That's crap. I don't believe that for a second."

"Oh, yeah. It's true," the redhead insisted.

"Lance, Melissa here says she's sure to flunk a Spanish test tomorrow."

"Use positive thinking. You're going to do really well."

Both girls kissed LaCoss on the cheek and went on their way. More girls came by on other days, more pairs. Always with tweaked, longing expressions, like women in cologne commercials.

"How do you know all these girls?"

"How does anybody know anybody? Human beings interact. These are just girls I've met." Dropped like the dumbest question ever. He was a good-looking guy, no doubt, these girls weren't blind; but unconventional good-looking. His nose was flatter than most, but it added to a rugged, outdoorsy quality. His ears were an unusual shape, slightly cupped but adding distinction.

"Where's your girlfriend?" LaCoss asked Lance.

"Obviously, I don't have one."

"Why not?"

"It's probably a lack of trying."

LaCoss kept mentioning Janeen Gordon, his upper-class girlfriend (infamous around campus because of her jaw-dropping beauty), but Lance didn't believe he was dating her. Impossible. That was fantasy. Then one day, without knocking, she opened the door while they were playing handball and cranking the Germs at a prodigious volume. The tennis ball smacked Lance's nose painfully as he turned to her, the girl of legend. She had almond eyes, brunette hair that kissed the tops of her shoulders, and a pink sweat outfit with sorority letters. A young Ava Gardner. Holding his nose, his eyes watering, he experienced another type of pain seeing her kiss LaCoss on the lips and embrace him with a long, motionless hug. She frowned at the box of orange peels, then gave Lance a hug, which made him quiver with rosy tremors.

They all met that evening for beers at Petro's Pizza, a dive near campus. Lance got there early, sitting at a corner table by a street window. Janeen showed up in a long brown dress that went down to her feet, her hair frizzed out. She sat down without hugging him, which was disappointing. She ordered a pitcher of beer and drank two glasses almost without stopping. She offered Lance a cigarette, which he declined. LaCoss arrived in his punk leather jacket (the words FATAL WOUND painted on the back), a sleeveless t-shirt and black Vietnam jungle boots. He gave Janeen a long-stemmed rose, an origami turtle and a French kiss, then played the pinball machine, winning multiple free games and standing there a long time, the machine clacking and echoing disembodied commands.

"Why are your fingernails like that?" Janeen made an unpleasant face at Lance.

They were particularly chewed and ragged. His cuticles were bad too. "It's a bad habit. I do it when I'm nervous." He put his hands underneath the table and faked a smile.

"Don't ever take Jensen or Klacker for any philosophy classes," she said.

"I heard that Jensen was a monster."

"Jensen is a total egomaniac who hates teaching. I could talk for hours."

"Don't you hate that? Why be a professor if you don't like teaching?"

The more they talked the more he liked her, sensing a playful, intelligent edge. She had a click at the bottom of certain words, a slight lisp which melted his heart. The wooden booth was uncomfortable. Lance straightened his back and winced. "Turn around," she said. She took off his windbreaker and massaged his shoulders. His mouth fell open in ecstasy as she worked. Flooded with the sudden paradise of her touch, his eyes closed, he lapsed into an elaborate fantasy: he was married to Janeen and they were in a hotel on the French Riviera, in a four-poster bed, about to make love. He moaned aloud as her small fingers kneaded. "Are you all right?" Her soft minty breath against his ear. His cheek lolled against her warm hand. When she stopped, he felt enormous gratitude toward her. Hope existed. LaCoss whooped when he won another free game. Hoping he would win several more, Lance huddled next to Janeen like a frozen, chapped-face man in the glow of electric heat.

Lance asked what year she was and she said she was a junior.

"Why are you with LaCoss?"

She bit a pretzel. "I don't know. I guess it boils down to energy. With some people, you just feel that energy, and you want to be with them." Lance cut his eyes away, trying to write this valuable insight onto his brain. But like microeconomic concepts, this seemingly simple principle disguised a complexity—the unfathomable, practical details which almost made the knowledge unusable. He sagged, confused by this mystery energy.

Janeen pointed at LaCoss. "He won't quit that pinball machine. He's got tunnel vision with everything, and that worries me. Have you noticed this about him?"

One afternoon Lance dropped by Pichler. LaCoss stood in his doorway with the redhead girl from days before. He held her face with his hands and they kissed in a lip- rubbing way. Seeing Lance, she turned and walked away, crossing her arms with modesty. LaCoss stood in boxers, his bed sheets tousled behind him. Smelling of dried sweat, he yawned.

"What about Janeen?" Lance asked. He thunked LaCoss on the chest with the back of his hand. At first, Lance was excited by the glow of the tryst, dripped in bad boy energies, but this morphed into outrage that LaCoss had done this to Janeen. He imagined warning Janeen, swooping in like Dr. Zhivago visiting his beloved Lara, hinting at dark possibilities to draw her close.

"What about Janeen," LaCoss said in a thoughtful, though

blank manner, as if seeking reason from another dimension. "We still have our thing. Our relationship. It's still valid."

"So what's-her-name was just nothing, just a throwaway!" Lance said, surprised by his anger. He realized his hands were balled into tight fists.

LaCoss's slow eyelids and tendency to leave his mouth slightly open added an odd sincerity when he said, "You mean Claudia. She's a super sweet girl. I think the *world* of her. Listen, everybody has got their own reasons, OK. Experiences can be on different levels. Oh, man. There's a seminar I was supposed to be at an hour ago." He mashed a hand against his face.

"I don't understand," Lance said, shaking his head. "Janeen is such an incredible person. Why can't you just be happy with her?"

"God, you're so hung up on her. Maybe you should be dating her." LaCoss scratched his chin a moment, thinking. He looked around the hall, then shut his door. He pulled a duffel bag out from under his bed and unlatched it. "You've got to promise me something. You cannot tell anybody once I show you this picture. This is crucial. *Beyond* crucial, since this information has got to do with my heart."

"OK. You have my word."

LaCoss pulled out an envelope and slid out an eight-by-ten photograph. A glossy posed shot of a young woman: a model, surrounded by focused light and wearing skintight jeans. The ends of a flimsy button-up shirt fluttered behind her. Thick, caramel hair blazed around her head. She had full lips and the most perfect, stunning face Lance had ever seen. Her expression was an embodiment of ecstasy from another world. "That's Lucinda Falcon, my real girlfriend," LaCoss said with a controlled voice. "She's about to sign a deal with Guess jeans. Her mom is from Venezuela, dad from Malibu. I met her eight months ago at a car wash near Beverly Hills." LaCoss tapped his heart and closed his eyes.

Lance shoved back the photo, his envy so pronounced he forgot to breathe.

"Me and Lucinda. We're like this spiritually." LaCoss twisted two fingers around each other. "We read each other's thoughts. It's deep, man, totally deep."

Lance was too confused to ask. But he learned something even stranger and more remarkable that day. LaCoss was going to be, of all things, a theater major—an actor. His ultimate goal was stardom. The way LaCoss talked it, it was a predetermined destiny. He said he had already been in a movie, which Lance didn't quite believe. With a videotape of *Repo Man* (number twelve on Lance's all-time list), starring Emilio Estevez and Harry Dean Stanton, they found a VCR in a common room on the second floor. They watched an early scene where Estevez gets fired from a grocery job. Then, quick cut to Estevez whirling around, slam dancing in a parking lot among a sea of tartan- and leather-clad punks.

"Did you see me? Huh?" LaCoss asked.

"Nope."

"Look there!"

"Where?"

They replayed the scene. When the recognition came, Lance put both hands on his head, shocked his friend had actually pierced the screen. He was legit. He flowed across the scene, all shoulders, knees and red plaid, as one of the punks who careened into Estevez. The director shot the scene eight times. The punks went after Estevez more savagely each time he complained to the director about being elbowed too hard. LaCoss chatted briefly with Estevez on the set, then saw him again at the Hard Rock Cafe, having a beer with Rob Lowe and Judd Nelson. Estevez told LaCoss to leave him alone or he would call security.

"I'm on screen exactly 2.3 seconds." LaCoss grinned hugely.

They replayed it again and paused during his lightning

moment at center camera. Jumping above the throng, arms flying, he was actually looking up toward the camera with a smirk, maximizing his face time.

"What a hog. You're a hog in every conceivable way," Lance said, slumping, feeling equal parts of astonishment and envy.

LaCoss was trancelike, a milky glaze over his eyes, recalling a pleasant memory from that day on the set and the love from the big levitating camera. He didn't protest this characterization.

CHAPTER FOUR

THE LEADERS OF MEN

Lance begged LaCoss to go with him to a reception of the Langford chapter of the Young Business Leaders Forum, but LaCoss scoffed that he wanted no part of this "cult of the establishment." So Lance, in navy sport coat and tie, on a Thursday evening, ascended the steps of the Mitford-Geller House alone. He didn't know what to expect, just that the Young Business Leaders Forum was a natural fit for his goals. And graduate schools loved to see quality extracurricular involvement. He touched the spiked ends of his hair, suspended fashionably in the air like porcupine needles, thanks to mousse borrowed from LaCoss. He centered his tie knot. His fingernails were trimmed. Upon opening the front door, an assembled crowd turned their heads and fixed him with aggressive stares, like he had insulted their mothers. An irritated speaker in mid-sentence stood before a mantel. The silence sent blood brightly into his ears and face. He moved quickly behind a love seat. The speaker resumed talking, something about emerging markets in Southeast Asia. Behind him, shuffling sounds as people strained to see around him.

After the talk, he retreated to an hors d'oeuvres table and snagged a beer. He worked on it steadily, seeking to erase his entrance. He wrote his name on a *Hello My Name Is* sticker and shook hands with strangers. Students formed into conversational clumps. Traces of dialogue floated his way, that so and so had snagged a plum summer internship with the Federal Reserve Bank in New York. A girl said, to mild applause, she would be working after graduation with Sotheby's auction house. A guy in a yellow paisley power tie reported that his friend, who had climbed into the godly ranks of Wall Street bond traders, was earning over a hundred fifty grand after just three years. Sweet! The voices were confident, upbeat, at times giddy, reflecting that their prospects were good. The way things were going in America, if their talent proved exemplary or their circumstances lucky, they might do hugely well, as in retire before age thirty-five.

Rubbing shoulders, talking about himself in small bursts, Lance felt an acceptance. He shook another eager hand; a guy pat Lance on the arm as he moved past. Among these scrubbed, responsible-looking students, he imagined rising with them to lofty positions. They would rise, pulling each other along, and then gather in sophisticated settings to talk about their successes in lively tones. He listened to a tall girl with glasses he recognized from the Econ building. She reminded him of people in Junior Achievement circles: smart kids with innate purpose, who, like him, had read many books. Wearing an attentive half-smile, he nodded in hearty agreement with her point. His chest filled with reassurance and energy. He was taking steps to arrive at a bright future. All the crap he'd have to endure getting there would be well worth it.

He slipped into another social cluster which was debating the fairness of a progressive tax code. He met a girl named Stephanie Nalley, who seemed more colorful than everyone else in an electric teal cotton jacket and matching pants.

"Oh God. Please help. Please save me," Stephanie said suddenly. She put a hand on Lance's lapel and stood directly before him, looking over his shoulder.

"What's wrong?" He looked down at her hand.

"That guy. He won't stop calling me. I have tried to explain to him."

"What guy?" Lance whispered. The beer made him lightheaded, made his nostrils flare.

"It's Carson Wombley, Jr., the President of the Forum. Don't move. I will be forever grateful to you." She moved closer to Lance, who froze, acting as a blocker. Close enough to smell L.A. Girl fragrance and notice freckles on her chest between the folds of multiple lapels and shoulder pads, these gauzy layers. He noticed mist blue eye shadow, giant hoop earrings and a white studded belt worthy of some televised championship. Lance turned to see behind him, and she disappeared.

The guy who had been speaking at the mantel was making his way through the crowd, in a three-piece wool suit. Tall, with a long face, he was bobbing down a line of people, getting hosannas from either side. He offered cheery, morale-boosting comments while clutching an open bottle of beer. He extended a hand to Lance, who introduced himself.

"I'm Carson Wombley, Jr. Great to see you here." He laughed, a pleased-with-himself laugh. Wombley had a beak-like nose and jagged pock marks on his jawline, reminders of a once terrible acne problem. "I'm told you're a freshman so I wanted to come over and touch base."

"Sorry about your speech."

"You?"

"That was me." Lance grinned, the beer making it larger than normal.

"No harm, no foul. That's my philosophy. Listen, the group has some great programming you should know about, like our mentoring…" Lance was distracted by Wombley's most remarkable feature, his hair. The blow-dried, feathered masterpiece of an English pop singer on MTV taking the nation by storm. Longish and insanely plentiful, it had a grand, indulgent wave that swept out over his forehead and gravity-defying ridges on either side of his part. Lance didn't want this hair for himself, but couldn't help admiring it. As Wombley talked, he used hand signals and nods to communicate with others in the vicinity. His tone was formal, polished, like the hood of a BMW. He talked about a YBLF fundraiser for a local school for the handicapped, in which Lance expressed interest.

Wombley consulted his leather day planner, noted this, circled a calendar item and checked off two unrelated completed tasks. Lance mentioned his Microeconomics class. Wombley strongly suggested getting Prof. Tagg as an advisor—he knew big shots and his recommendations were "solid gold." Lance said he probably would. They got on the subject of monetary policy, which Lance didn't know much about. Wombley was an expert, easily recalling concepts like "liquidity" and "econometrics." Lance was tempted to feel badly about himself, that he was limping through this discussion. Nodding, he buttoned and unbuttoned his jacket several times.

"I mean, if the Fed wants to tighten the money supply then nobody can do anything about this anyway," Wombley said.

"Sure. They can do whatever they want. That's kind of a frightening power."

"A central bank without power would be useless." Wombley had an annoying lip quiver, as though he was about to snicker. Behind his insouciance was an amusement at points he disagreed with or inaccuracies he would be quick to correct. "Where is that girl you were talking to?"

"Oh, I don't know." Lance took a long gulp of beer. "What were you talking about?"

"I forget specifically. Not that I often forget things. That's rare for me."

They stared at each other, the matter hanging. Wombley put his hand on his hip. Lance fingered his tie knot, enjoying the suspicion he had some connection to Stephanie what's-her-name. He glanced down at his penny loafers, then at Wombley's high-polish shoes. This silence extended into discomfort, into a stark conversational absence. Carson Wombley, Jr.'s eyes grew more intense, like zoom lenses, seeming to make an assessment. He seemed to judge Lance's spiked hair. Seeking to heal the stretching wound between them, a kind of social failure, Lance blurted out the first thing he thought: "Hey, have you heard the new Dead Kennedys' album? It is *amazing*." Rocking onto his tiptoes, he did two strums of air guitar and made a rather loud *bwanna nanna* sound.

Wombley raised one eyebrow in disdain. "Haven't heard that. No. Gotta run. Excellent meeting you." He glad-handed Lance and moved on.

Lance considered that possibly he had lost points with the Dead Kennedys mention. He got another beer. Watching other people talk, he felt suddenly conspicuous. He noticed other strays around the room who were also insular and struggling. He grew bored, a bit restless. He hummed music he'd listened to with LaCoss. Song lyrics came to him from Joy Division's "Leaders of Men." The ones that hinted leaders were created out of disappointment, and were a product of scheming. It seemed subversive, a misplaced sentiment, an eight-track stuck in the cassette collection. He felt a tension between these passionate sounds, which he wanted to hear right then, and the removed intellectual calculation required at the YBLF reception. Briefly torn, he worried this combination was evidence of freakishness, of unsuitability. His collar seemed to constrict around his neck.

He finished beer number three and considered slowing down. But no. Things were getting interesting. He was gathering momentum. Between beers two and three he usually reached a point of departure, of waving his arms and saying things that otherwise would have undergone greater scrutiny. He butted into a conversational clump and blurted some comments, a spit bubble shooting from his mouth. The clump disintegrated around him.

An irritation gnawed at him. A moroseness. It was the D he'd gotten on his first Microeconomics test. He'd studied hard for it, knocking his head against the wall to learn these miserable concepts. The graphs of the hypothetical questions had tiny smudged letters that were impossible to read. Lance's confusion had turned to panic and anger as time was sucked out of the room. He snapped a pencil tip writing the last answer. Then he suffered Tagg's lengthy ridicule of the class: Only two people got question three correct when it was *such easy stuff*! How pathetic! What was wrong with this class? Did they have any brains? Lance imagined hitting Tagg with a baseball bat, and crossed him off his advisor list.

Still smarting from this psychic stab wound, the phone had rung in Lance's dorm room. Holding the test between his fingers, he listened to his father say, *We think about you every day. Have you had any exams yet?* Lance took a deep breath and quietly shoved the test under a pile of papers. He stuttered, struggling to find another subject, the test flashing before his eyes like a demonic test pattern, screaming of dishonor. He wrapped the phone cord tight around his finger, cutting off blood. Yes, my classes are going well, he assured his father, and he was studying on a regular schedule. He pulled the cord tighter. He mentioned his new friend, but didn't explain his friend was a punk rocker with a nudist upbringing who could snap his fingers and get laid.

He stood by the hors d'oeuvres table, alone, his teeth gritted. The Econ test still nettled him. He recognized a spindly guy from his Econ class, in blue seersucker, chatting near the mantel. This guy, upon picking up his test, had thrust a triumphant arm into the air and hooted. Now he told a joke to a willing audience. Lance fixed him with a dead stare, hoping a snarling bassist draped in chains might materialize and shove that guy in the back. He looked away and found Stephanie Nalley looking at him, blinking in a concerned way. Lance smiled bashfully. She had caught him being aggrieved and unsocial. He jiggled his beer and enjoyed this shared moment. An ease mixed with a slight belligerence settled through him. He walked over to her.

"You were thinking so hard," she said, a sheen of condensation on her wineglass.

"That's the only way I know how to think."

"I can tell you do a lot of thinking."

"It's one of my favorite things to do."

She laughed politely. He tried to recall what she had said about herself earlier and couldn't. Her hair had dark and light streaks, variations that made her neither blonde nor brunette. One of those peculiar dye schemes that left a straw texture. She tucked a strand behind her ear and bent to inspect cheeses on the hors d'oeuvres table. "Those are really good." Lance pointed to chocolate-covered nuts he hadn't tried. They looked disgusting. She popped one into her mouth and squared her shoulders at him. A fleck of chocolate stuck between her teeth. Her hair hugged the sides of her face, her wide cheeks and longish nose. Attractive? Sort of, but it depended on the angle.

Lance put down his empty beer. Stephanie handed him a fresh one, which he gladly accepted. "Here's to future success!" Lance said.

They clinked glasses. "Success!"

Lance had hoped to talk more to Wombley and do a better job representing himself, but he was suddenly gone. Perhaps because the Mitford-Geller House was only to be utilized until 10:00 pm. A party broke out. With a greedy thirst, Lance helped to exhaust the beer and wine allotted for the reception. The revelers would have dispersed earlier if a guy named Norton Skinner had not rooted around for and found a case of Coors meant for another function. But Lance, Stephanie and the others, their loud voices bleeding easily into laughter, snorting, and stray noises, did not ask about the mystery suds.

Norton Skinner, who performed an impressively loud imitation of a train whistle and proved he could clap twice in between pushups, was a mystery himself. He had light reddish hair in a neat, armor-proof crew cut and gray eyes that aligned in competing directions. He had a port wine stain under his right ear. He wore a powder blue cotton jacket with the sleeves rolled up to his elbows, a white t-shirt, pleated beige pants and white weave loafers without socks, like a television cocaine dealer.

Earlier, Skinner had had a memorable argument with Carson Wombley, Jr. as to whether Kathleen Turner was more beautiful than Ellen Barkin. Skinner wasn't a YBLF member at all. He'd mistaken the reception for a nearby meeting of the Modern Poetry Society. He did an impression of Wombley—the way he flipped his hair back, wrinkled his nose and pronounced the word *super*—that put two guys on their knees, they laughed so hard.

Lance laughed violently and spilled his beer on the carpet. Stephanie Nalley leaned on Lance, in stitches also. It dawned on him that Stephanie was always beside him, leaning against his shoulder for balance when adjusting a pump, or brushing her hand against his sleeve, or waiting with a charged sense of dazzle as she listened to him. An expression of wonder crossed his face as he made the connection. Stephanie Nalley, a sophomore, for reasons he wasn't certain of and without his intending this to happen, had the *screaming hots* for him. He restrained a smile, his sudden Bond-like magnetism a miraculous thing. Why wouldn't she? He was sporting an expensive maroon and gold rep tie, stolen from Dad's closet. And his hair, spiked—it was dangerous, the hair of a wild man.

Skinner located a strip of cardboard and did break dancing moves on the floor of the parlor. Lance and the others cheered him on. His hands palm down, he spun his knees around, his weight pivoting on his elbows. He carried his weight for several turns, then his legs bucked upward. A knee cracked into a china umbrella holder and busted it into a pile of shards, umbrellas landing on top of him. People turned and immediately fled the room. The front door clicked opened: a rush of footsteps and it whanged shut.

Lance and Stephanie bent down to help Skinner. He clutched his knee and moaned. "You're bleeding!" Stephanie said. The knee of his pants was slit; there was a cut on his knee. Skinner stood up and wiped sweat off his forehead, the broken vessel seemingly forgotten.

"You guys want to go to Prancers?"

"What's Prancers?" Lance asked.

"Dance club. They have over five hundred lights and a fog maker. Two-for-one shooters tonight only."

"I've heard that place is *totally hot*," Stephanie said. "I've been dying to go there."

"We're there!" Lance yelled. The place sounded fantastic. His imagination reeled with the idea of *five hundred* lights.

On the steps of the Mitford-Geller House, Lance noted a pleasant, numb sensation at his temples. He felt washed clean, blithe, his mind a tranquil lake unblemished by ripples. He'd done a fabulous job at the reception, he judged, and was a beloved new member of the organization. Stephanie dug a finger into his belt loop.

"There she is!" Skinner said proudly, pointing down toward the street. A convertible sports car glowed faintly at the curb. Squinting, Lance's eyes adjusting to the dark, he made out the lines of a Triumph TR7, that angular, briefly popular British convertible. It was painted a wild and disturbing array of colors: the hood was aquamarine; streaks of lemon yellow and magenta accented side panels. A black number 5 painted on the passenger door. Expensive radial sport tires and hubcaps with complicated chrome nuts and wire spokes. It was a common sight and sound on campus, emitting plumes of choking gray smoke, gunning through 15 mph zones doing 35 and earning the scrutiny of Langford Police officers. Hearing a screech of tires, you could see mirrored Air Force sunglasses and catch a few notes of heavy metal music as the car sped by.

"I guess I'll have to sit on your lap," Stephanie said to Lance, surveying the little two- seater. The space behind the seats was microscopic.

"I guess so." Lance ran his hand along the cold trunk, uneven from multiple coats of paint. Above a brake light he noticed the painted words *Mary Ann*.

Lance opened the flimsy little door and settled into the

passenger seat. Stephanie got in on top of Lance, her knees pointing toward the gear shift. The little car started, the hum of a sport muffler and the ring of the engine in their ears. Stephanie, with an arm around Lance's neck, shifted heavily into Lance's chest as the car gained speed. Her mottled hair took flight and whipped across his face.

Skinner clicked open the glove compartment and cassette holders rained onto Stephanie's lap: Iron Maiden, Motorhead, Judas Priest—this raucous feast of English metal bands. Also, a black wristband dotted with silver spikes. Skinner snapped it onto a wrist, fed a cassette into the stereo and pumped his fist into the air during a complicated epic song involving a castle siege and the slaying of a sea monster, the lead singer for Iron Maiden belting out lyrics in a high-pitched death wail. Oh, the delicious insanity of this evening! Stephanie was perched on his lap in a quasi-fetal position, his arms wrapped around her hips. Immobile from her weight, he closed his eyes, the gentle lurch of the car soothing him. He nuzzled his head against her shoulder, melting from her satisfying warmth and the rosy smell of her clothes, his body going soft. She tightened her grip on his neck.

At Prancers, Stephanie dragged Lance by the hand toward the dance floor, which pulsed with blinding colors and bewildering sounds. Blinking translucent color squares at his feet gave him vertigo and bright bodies heaved unpredictably around him. Foreboding robot poles of light lowered from the ceiling, spinning and strobing, like they might slice dancers to ribbons. He began to move his limbs, stiffly at first, like his joints were rusty. Stephanie danced before him with closed eyes and a hazy, ecstatic expression. Music boomed from all sides with a godlike omnipotence, each bass note an atomic blast. The music gripped him, possessed him. They danced in a tight space. Stephanie's thing was to turn around and look over her shoulder in a coquettish, mysterious way. She perspired, her hair flattening and sticking to the sides of her face.

The Wang Chung song came on, the horn section pounding his ears. A vocalist urged the dancers to Wang Chung, whatever that meant. A versatile concept, it was also the name of the band. An all-purpose promotional theme and attitude. Lance and Stephanie responded to this guidance, to the Wang Chunging, sensing they were enjoying a trend at its freshest point. He shuffled his feet wildly, waving his arms in a creative rhythmic fashion as if to prevent falling from a high beam, while repeating patterns and keeping the beat. He felt elated by his moves and was overtaken by euphoria. Suddenly, he was hot shit. He was Dance King. An Asian kid with white fingerless gloves and black parachute pants danced in a private pocket. He had all the moves. Lance stole a quick turn move from the guy, but couldn't execute it as smoothly. A recent immigrant Asian kid was always the best dancer: they dove into the pop culture with hellish intensity.

"Look!" Stephanie pointed to where people danced on a huge rectangular speaker. Skinner was up there, doing a complicated line dance with a blonde girl and two energetic guys wearing gold suspenders following his lead. His moves were unreal, his arms fluttering like propellers. It had not been *American Bandstand* Skinner had watched every Saturday morning, but *Soul Train*.

Lance and Stephanie took a break and sat in a dark booth alongside a velour wall. Stephanie was talking on and on, her blurred face approaching and retreating as she spoke. Her incisor teeth seemed unusually large. "…So my girlfriends and I played this game at this dance club. We sat on barstools, and every time a guy asked us to dance, we turned down every guy except for the fourth one. Then, when we danced with him, we only danced with him one time. Isn't that totally hilarious?"

"I guess it was hilarious for you."

"Oh, come on. It's funny."

He made a mental note: *never ask girls on barstools to dance*. Stephanie leaned over Lance to get a napkin. She paused before his face. He nudged his face forward and their lips met. She put her wrists behind his neck. Their tongues oriented themselves, a spearmint and lipstick flavor circulating. This went on through several songs, the waitress coming and going. Lance rubbed his hands along her back. *She wants sex*, he understood suddenly. This prospect amazed and satisfied him, nourishing his ego. Finally! Then it seemed hazy and unreal.

They searched the club but could not find Skinner, so they jumped into a cab. She drew his eyes to hers, then looked away. He rested his hand on her thigh, because he could. His getting out with her was expected, though unspoken. It seemed fantastic in an adult, racy way, like he was watching himself in a drive-in movie. She hurried up the steps in her dorm and hastily flicked keys at her door. That ubiquitous Calvin Klein ad was taped there: the guy in the shiny silver suit who gazed narcissistically at his mirrored image.

He followed her into the dark room, exhaustion pulling at his arms. Carefully made beds stood at opposite sides of the room. The door shut behind him. He expected a lamp to flick on, but one never did. Her hands at the back of his neck, they kissed. She tugged at his shirt, pulling the tails out impatiently, then yanked on his buttons. He undid some of her buttons. There were freckles on her chest. She stared at him with an expression he couldn't interpret, then sat on a bed and leaned back on her arms stiffly.

He was supposed to go over there. He felt her eyes targeting him, tracking him in the semidarkness. His bladder suddenly ached.

"I have to pee. Excuse me a second." He let himself out and squinted in the stunning hall light. He walked down the long hall and made a left where it split into two directions. He found a girls' bathroom, with nobody in there, and urinated. In the bright hall again, he listened to the buzz of the fluorescent lighting, confused as to which direction he had come from. He paused before a door to get his bearings. His head felt under water from alcohol. The door opened and a strange girl in a towel stepped out, shrieking when she saw Lance, startling him. She retreated and slammed the door. He heard a phone being dialed inside. He backed away from the door. The evening came into focus. Was this what he wanted? What did any of this mean, or would it mean something afterward? Whatever happened with Stephanie might create expectations he had no intention of fulfilling. Surely there would be unease the next morning once it was obvious he wasn't so crazy about her. She sat on a bed, looking nothing like Gina Lollobrigida in *Come September*. Each door looked remarkably similar as he walked. Who was this girl? What did she expect? Did she do this every weekend? He was in no shape for complex reasoning. He had no faith he was going in the correct direction, or was still on the right floor.

And what obligations would he have to her? Or, Jesus, what if she was actually insane? She seemed rather desperate. She'd really been the one to pick him. And why was that? But she was more nice than anything else. A niceness that hid a desperation. A niceness looking for torment. She had an edge; she might say something awful, the way Cheryl Tiegs never would, because Cheryl was a kind person.

Around a corner, he heard a radio crackle. Then two armed, beefy Langford Safety and Security officers stood before Lance, scrutinizing him. He tried not to wobble.

"We've gotten complaints," the one with a crew cut said. "You're not supposed to be here."

"I was invited."

The tall, angry-looking one, an exact genetic match of a hated PE coach, made a turnaround motion with his finger and pointed toward an exit. "Visitation hours are over."

"You don't understand. I can't leave. I'm in a situation..." The officers stared patiently, thumbs tucked into their gun belts. "There's this girl..."

"What's her name?"

Lance closed his eyes, but under pressure he blanked. Had he actually been lip-locked minutes earlier with Melanie? Stephanie? Melissa? On passion's doorstep! He shuffled his feet, fuming at this surreal intrusion by lawmen. He lapsed into himself for several moments, opening his eyes only after they asked him if he had been drinking. Crew Cut's hand was now perched on his cuff holder.

"I can smell it," Tall Angry said, now holding a note pad. "Before you leave I'm going to make out a report. What's your full name?"

Retreat was the only option. As Lance walked down the stairs the cops followed, their belts squeaking. Outside, they stood at the exit and watched Lance walk off into the night.

A clanging in his skull awoke him the next morning. He pulled the sheets up to his neck. The severity of his hangover was surprising. Even so, his first moments were bearable. Then he remembered Stephanie, and pulled the sheets over his head, a white canopy sealing him from the world. He imagined her looking out her door, baffled, then crying hot tears of rejection; he closed his eyes tightly, retreating further into blackness. He sensed whispers across campus and a spreading knowledge of his shameful behavior. He suspected he had actually disgraced himself at the YBLF meeting as well: his disruptive entrance, his ill-conceived comments, his excessive drinking. But this was nothing in comparison to his behavior with Stephanie. His most astounding failure yet. The throbbing behind his eyes intensified. Instead of drinking water he suffered the dehydration as punishment.

Hours went by with him motionless under the white sheet. He wanted to never look at himself again. *The Elephant Man* came to mind. Memories of other disgraceful and baffling behavior surfaced from their deep burials, like zombies, to attack him. During horseplay with an antique frontier musket, a valuable Rally heirloom, he'd broken the stock, then panicked and hid it in garbage; a disappearance later blamed on innocent plumbers. A halfhearted car alarm honked outside. A television in another room flicked on to a talk show. Hallway doors opened and closed as people went to classes Lance was missing.

He imagined Stephanie wandering the halls of her dorm the previous evening, heartbroken, then crying herself to sleep. No, anger. She would be infuriated and insulted. He considered making a conciliatory phone call or writing a letter of apology, but quickly dismissed both ideas.

He was supposed to eat dinner with LaCoss that day. He phoned to beg off.

"I heard you had a big night," LaCoss said.

"Who told you that?"

"A guy I know said you were trashed out of your mind and you guys ripped up the Mitford-Geller House."

"I didn't rip up anything."

"What about that girl who was hanging all over you? You guys hook up?"

"Well, sorta."

"Sort of? That sounds like a metaphysical thing."

"Long story."

"I got time."

"I don't."

"You're being very weird."

"I'm on my deathbed. It hurts to hold the phone to my ear."

"How was your meeting? Are you going to join this YBLF outfit?"

"I already have. I met the President and talked to him a long time."

"What else happened? Something must have happened."

"Nothing happened!"

The following evening, Lance received a phone call from Carson Wombley, Jr. "Where the hell were you? The YBLF fundraiser was tonight. We were one person short."

"Oh, I didn't realize it was tonight."

"You let down the kids. We still raised a good amount. Over six hundred bucks. There's also this matter of broken antiques at the Mitford-Geller House." He sighed heavily. "I've gotten reports you played a role in this."

"That wasn't my—"

"The organization has paid for the damage, but frankly, there's a reputation we're trying to uphold. We're young business *leaders*. Unfortunately, you're on probation."

"I didn't break anything!"

"Also, a pantry was apparently looted. Our bylaws are pretty specific about probation in these circumstances."

"Oh, my God!"

"And the campus cops wrote you up about kicking you out of a dorm? Self-control, man. But that's separate. Look, don't sweat it. Our next meeting is Tuesday. We start at seven thirty. Punctuality is good."

Tuesday, he put on fresh jeans and a clean shirt, leaving his room at seven. Outside the Biology building, he realized the obvious: Stephanie would be there, and was probably there right now, spreading poison about him. She would glare at him. He sat on a cement bench, head down, counting the minutes until he would be late. He stood up, sat down, a pantomime of indecision. Then he lay on the hard bench, eyelids heavy, recognizing he would not go to this meeting or any YBLF meeting thereafter. A cloud passed between trees, slowly enough that it seemed to be moving backwards. Lance yanked a weed out of the sidewalk and tried to imagine the night of carnal bliss that could have been.

That night, Lance lay in bed, his arms outside the sheets and pressed along his torso. First with disdain, but later with mild acceptance, he considered he wasn't a one-night-stand kind of guy.

CHAPTER FIVE

THE AUTUMN TRAVAILS

With exams fast approaching, Lance resolved to finally hunker down and study. He turned on his desk lamp, pulled up his chair. Knowing himself to be vulnerable to distraction, he inched his chair tightly to the desk, imprisoning himself. He opened a textbook. Without courtesy of a knock, the door swung open and LaCoss prowled the room. He waved papers before Lance's eyes. "Look at this!"

Lance brushed them aside. "It'll have to wait. I'm studying."

LaCoss flipped the textbook closed and leaned on the desk. "This is more important. The Travails. I've signed us up—"

Lance reopened the textbook. "You never study. I've never actually *seen* you study. What is your GPA going to look like after this semester?"

"As a well-rounded individual, I make time for different activities, like the Autumn Travails." He popped his fingers against the papers.

"I never agreed to that. I want *nothing* to do with that." The Travails was a peculiar Langford thing, part of the Autumn Harvest Festival. A series of physical and mental tests that teams tried to perform, witnessed by a huge crowd.

LaCoss sat on the desk. "This is a longstanding tradition. Come on."

"No way." Conventional wisdom said the fun was in watching, or, as Lance had overheard upperclassmen talk about it in overheated tones, taunting and baiting the participants. Also, Lance had avoided every opportunity for performance, eschewing school plays, musicals and Nativity dramas; claiming he had no talent to stay out of talent competitions.

LaCoss crossed his arms. "I've already told our third team member we're doing it."

"Who?"

"This guy, Charles Boyd. He's a borderline genius. A Langford Scholar. He's a total renegade of the mind. Smoke comes out of his ears. We'll ace the written questions with him. We'll be superstars!" LaCoss was pacing, smacking his hands together, doing quick heel turns and generally vibrating, as if the event had already been fixed in his favor. Lance turned sideways in his chair to watch the pacing, back and forth, unable to stop watching. LaCoss whistled using two fingers and yelled *ha-ha-ha!*

"I'm going to see the guy now. Come with me. Just think about the Travails. You should meet him. You two are alike."

"What is that supposed to mean?"

At the door, LaCoss motioned for Lance to follow him. "You'll see."

Lance drummed his fingers on the textbook. He would get out of the Travails with this minor concession. He told himself he could use a break. One short break. And he was curious about this supposed genius. He was surprised when they walked over to Claxton, a street off-campus. All the Langford Scholars—six in each class, with free four-year tuition, a living stipend and the prestigious title—lived in a plush new wing of Pichler dorm, a perk designed to lure them away from Ivy League schools. The idea was that by living together, their scholastic energies and brilliance would synergize. Charles Boyd had started out there, then left Pichler after vicious arguments with peers and complaints he was belittling and ridiculing other scholars, damaging the atmosphere of intellectual openness.

They knocked on the door of a dingy townhouse. After a long pause, they knocked again. A circumspect fellow in a dirty Jethro Tull t-shirt answered the door. In faded jeans with slit, unraveling knees and dark wool socks that flopped about his toes, he sniffled, staring at them. He seemed unhappy to have been found.

"I'm very busy right now."

"We're set for the Travails, my friend!" LaCoss announced with an exaggerated enthusiasm. "This is my buddy Lance." Angered by LaCoss's assumption, Lance shook his head, then offered a weak wave.

Charles Boyd had a stricken appearance, as if rebounding from a long period of destructive excess. His thoughtful eyes were set in deep sockets and shifted under amorphous black hair. The hair was overgrown, perched over his eyes and grown over the tops of his ears; a moppish, radically unfashionable hairstyle, the result of neglect rather than design. His physique was slack, his shoulders and neck a bit stooped. Showering and hygiene were secondary concerns, or lower.

"I told you," Charles Boyd said quietly, "I don't want to participate." He stared, seeming to hope they would leave. The door wavered, and started to close. It inched forward like an apologetic sinner, until LaCoss stuck his boot inside the doorjamb. The door clunked against it. A second clunk. Lance wanted to laugh. Charles Boyd peered around, then opened it in an invitation to enter. A duo of cats ran for cover as Lance and LaCoss came in, the small beasts knocking against one another. A light odor of corned beef and cigarettes trailed up from the gold carpet.

"Do you live here alone?" LaCoss asked. He looked around as if impressed.

"I have one room upstairs. A married couple owns the place. They do seminars and are elsewhere half the time." A prickly self-absorption underlined his precise manner of speaking. He sat at a kitchenette table and pulled an ashtray and a pack of Camels towards him. He padded his pockets, then seemed to rethink smoking. Lance and LaCoss pulled out chairs and sat slowly, like interrogating police officers. Lance was disappointed. He had expected Charles Boyd to be holding an abacus, or translating Russian poetry, or working calculus problems on the walls.

"Do you guys want any guava juice?" Charles Boyd asked.

"No thanks."

"I'm good. I don't need any guava juice right now."

A cat jumped on the table. Boyd placed it gently onto the floor. He bent down close, scratched the cat's belly and made peculiar gurgling sounds.

"So, what do you say? Ready to participate?" LaCoss asked Boyd.

"*I* don't want to participate," Lance said.

Charles Boyd rubbed his eyes. "I have a problem with contrived competition. Not my thing. Plus, I've heard it's rather embarrassing."

"That's what I've heard also," Lance said. Apparently, injuries happened. A columnist in the *Langford Owl* had deemed the Travails "inhumane" and was agitating to stop them.

"Oh, fine! Let's just immerse ourselves in this negative vibe."

"Tell you what. I'll consider it," Charles Boyd said unconvincingly. He gazed at a cheap clock. "But for now, I've got to take off." He explained he was driving to Athens. He'd heard a rumor REM was playing a gig that night in a hole-in-the-wall joint, using a fake name. He calculated for a moment with a slack face, then added they could join him if they wanted. LaCoss signed on immediately, flashing a hand signal of rotating his outer fingers and making a clicking sound of approval. He looked at Lance. Live music had sudden fantastic appeal.

"Ah, shit. I...there's this review class..." Lance squeezed his temples with his fingers. It was impossible, a no-go. He would miss his Econ review that afternoon. He had forgiven himself for class preparation not done and for general lack of intensity, then had pledged—a rock solid vow of the most solemn kind—that he would start studying, so as to fine-tune the material before the final, and to master this material and retain it, such that he could impress colleagues and get a workplace advantage because he had absorbed this wisdom.

"I just…You see…" Lance's choice was made and it hurt. He grimaced, avoiding his spoken decision as he imagined the alternative rock idols who walked the streets of Athens. UGA was a mega university seething with a spectacular night life that approximated a permanent collegiate Mardi Gras. And the women: curvaceous cornfed beauty contestants, their lustrous hair and shiny teeth blinding people on sidewalks.

Lance slumped, tapping his teeth and falling into himself with irritation.

"Seems like a huge decision you're trying to make," Charles Boyd said, smiling, as if enjoying this torment.

"This is major trauma," LaCoss said. "Major!"

"I think he's about to implode."

"Just let me think for two seconds here," Lance said, closing his eyes.

LaCoss whispered, "Is he going? Will he go?"

"I don't think so. He seems *very guilty* about that review."

"He's a very responsible young man."

To attend the review was the right thing, and Lance recalled his dutiful lifetime record: attending Young Followers meetings at St. Luke's, completing homework assignments *before* watching any television; doing weekly household chores to earn an allowance, his father giving performance reviews of his finished chores…He felt brief revulsion at his record of responsibility. Wasn't taking an occasional detour important? It was healthy. It was possible, yes, to rededicate himself *after* the Athens visit. He lunged on this raw possibility, as if jumping over a crevasse that might be inches too wide. "Let's go." Lance's smile relieved everyone. They pushed back from the table, their chair legs scraping the linoleum.

They roared into the countryside, their arms hanging out

open windows. Lance experienced inestimable joy—oh, to be free of burdens!—while sitting shotgun in Charles Boyd's ancient two-tone Ford LTV. A vehicle with dinged panels like a great garbage can with bumpers. A lime green wave coated the car's interior. Charles Boyd told of his unusual upbringing. His mother was an eccentric academic whose form of day care was to drop him off every day at the local library. Young Charles read and read, working his way down row after row. He slept on the top of a shelf one night when she forgot to pick him up. His father, a geologist with Swiss Jewish roots, had abandoned Charles at age three to move to Africa. At age seven he was writing footnotes for his mother's scholarly articles on Greek literature. He joined Mensa at twelve. His mother crusaded against the evils of television, so they never had one.

"You've *never* seen television before?" Lance was in shock.

"I've seen snippets of it. I've never actually watched a whole program." He smiled in a highly self-satisfied way.

"Aren't you curious? Haven't you ever been tempted to see an episode of *Dallas*?"

"I've figured it out from conversations. All the women are sleeping with J.R. *Bor*-ing. That sort of passive entertainment can be detrimental. It dulls certain receptors. My mother has some interesting data on the national I.Q. versus the percentage of the population with television sets and average hours of watching."

"You're now my hero," LaCoss said with sincerity from the back seat.

To his credit, Charles Boyd did have a quality Blaupunkt stereo. He clicked on his tape player and presented Lance with the cassette cover of REM's *Reckoning*. Music filled the car, a mutant folky rock sound of plinky guitars and gentle percussion.

"I first saw them in 1980 in Raleigh," Charles Boyd explained. "That was way before they had a record deal. I've turned hundreds of people onto them, *hundreds*." He bragged that they had *authenticity*, had an *honesty*, a *humility*, they were regular guys barely out of college. Implying that every other band was inferior and corrupt. Lance sighed, rolled his eyes.

LaCoss also grew annoyed with the dissertation and said, "Yeah, yeah, yeah…"

The REM songs were pretty good, Lance decided, in a jangly folky way. Though they were a bit low power for his taste, Lance understood Charles Boyd's devotion to the band. He had been burdened in high school by all the brainy social handicaps: his voice forever ringing out with the right answer, his busting of grade curves and his trouncing of the SAT with a perfect 1600. But with this identification with a band, made clear by his t-shirt, many would choose not to torment him, or dismiss him as an egghead. He was a fan, connected to and strengthened by a chain of people.

Charles Boyd tapped out a cigarette. He lit up, took a long puff.

"NO!" LaCoss screamed. He snatched it out of Charles Boyd's mouth and flicked it out the window, the tip flaring as it hit rushing air. "Don't you know those things can kill you? Jesus!"

Once they got to Athens they did not see REM lead guitarist Peter Buck on a street corner in his trademark pajamas. They did not see the B-52s or buxom girls in cutoff jeans. They did eat at Walter's Barbecue. Walter, the owner, reported he had not seen the members of REM in a long time. They ate barbecue sandwiches on white bread. A scrawny guy on a stool next to LaCoss was talking up a band named Howitzer Brains. "They're way better than REM. It's just that nobody knows about them yet."

LaCoss laughed, a mocking edge to his voice. "Any band named Howitzer Brains is going nowhere. They'll be gone tomorrow."

"I'm the bass player." The scrawny guy stood up.

"You should get another name. Or join another band."

"Who the hell are you?" He stuck a finger in LaCoss's face.

LaCoss knocked the hand away and inched his face forward. "My name is Ian LaCoss. Remember it. Ian LaCoss. I'm an actor, and I'm going to be in major motion pictures. I've already been in one. Your band is going nowhere. Why? Because you and your band are *losers*."

Four other guys in dirty t-shirts, huge guys, hopped off stools. Likely, the other members of Howitzer Brains. They lined up behind the bass player. Lance stopped chewing.

"Take it back," one of them said.

"Fuck you." LaCoss got off his stool, his entire lean body galvanized and taut, like a knife blade. He was all fearless bloodlust and high voltage current, like he was rehearsing for an action adventure role and channeling *Mad Max*, *Dirty Harry* and several of the *Rocky* pictures. Lance, still sitting, turned around from the counter. By default, the second line of defense. He anticipated a stool broken across the bridge of his nose. He braced himself. At that moment, the Micro review was taking place, without him. He had never been in a real fight and feared violence; fearing the risk of arrest even more. The idea of police, of handcuffs, of the humiliating call to his father from jail. A criminal record was a career ender. A life ender. His hands shook. A punch to the throat—wasn't that supposed to be effective?

For backup he looked to Charles Boyd, who was still hunched over the counter, eating his sandwich. He applied more sauce. One bothered eye noted the scene. This pose was difficult to interpret. Boyd was possibly immobilized by a hardcore pacifist stance ingrained by his wacky mother. Though if provoked, he seemed capable of sneaky and vicious outbursts of fighting. Perhaps he didn't give a shit.

Walter appeared from the grill area and asked what was going on, which led the musicians to back down. Afterward, in the car, Charles Boyd said with dry remove, "That was quite a spectacle." Then he smiled with an open mouth, flashing a childish glee. LaCoss laughed along with him. Lance took guarded breaths, thankful he was unbloodied and not incarcerated; then he joined the celebration. They had put the Howitzer Brains boys in their place.

Phizer Pitts Revolution, the band Charles Boyd had heard was a cover name for REM, actually was a band named Phizer Pitts Revolution. An awful cover band, so painful to hear they forfeited cover charges and beers left on their table to get away. Charles, LaCoss and Lance found a nameless bar packed with perspiring people. LaCoss met a beautiful girl in spandex tights. They danced with athletic abandon. Lance observed this while sitting at a table with Charles Boyd, who snickered and dismissively stated that he did *not* dance. Boyd peeled labels off Heineken bottles with great precision, then stuck them to the table. He glanced often at a hulking black digital watch. He had the oldest, most ragged boat shoes ever, these ancient Docksiders. Duct tape attached the toes to the wafer-thin white soles. He held up his Heineken. "This is pretty weak stuff."

"You mean the beer?"

"I mean alcohol in general, as compared to other intoxicants. You know, hard shit. Pharmaceutical grade." His smile was lizard-like.

Lance leaned closer. "Like what?"

Boyd studied Lance carefully, his expression unchanging. "Oh, never mind."

"What do you want to do with your life?" Lance asked.

"I'm going to be a diplomat. Ultimately, I would like to be U.S. Secretary of State. Or maybe a secretary in the United Nations. There are also a number of foreign policy books I would like to write. I've published two articles so far." He tilted his chin upward, seeming to arrange these goals in a pleasing order. This all involved passing the Foreign Service exam, which, as he described it, almost nobody passed; and surviving a lengthy winnowing process that cut the numbers further. It seemed shaky. They got on the subject of arms control. Charles

Boyd dismissed the Soviet Union as overrated and unimportant. Lance leaned back from the table, amazed at this position. Boyd cited their lack of GNP growth, productivity declines, failures of trade initiatives, etc., his voice humming with numbers and authentic Russian pronunciations. So annoyingly factual it was hard to argue. Lance sat dazed, trying to absorb all this information.

"And you?" Charles Boyd asked.

"I'm going to major in economics." In this context, it sounded dull. But it was practical, doable, and lucrative, whereas the Foreign Service exam sounded much more tentative.

"I see. You're one of *those*."

"What does that mean?"

"Means nothing."

"Then why did you say it?"

"You seem defensive about this economics idea."

"I am not!" Lance said. Boyd's ideas were nakedly grand, but as a Langford Scholar he'd been branded by administrators as *talented* and *brilliant*; he'd been chosen as a high hope for their generation. He was like a lost Rally, a super Rally, the Rally Lance had always wanted to be.

LaCoss collapsed into a chair, tucking a phone number into his wallet. "Here's how I see it," he said, getting his breath. "The Travails is an opportunity. There are choices in life. We can do the usual meek and mild Langford thing, or we can make a major statement."

Lance and Charles Boyd looked at one another. They crossed their arms. LaCoss possessed a certain credibility when it came to making "statements." He was threatening entire bands, easily picking up spandex-wearing beauty contestants, proclaiming his future greatness to strangers, performing from memory entire scenes from *Scarface,* all while wearing a sleeveless t-shirt advertising F.S.L.N., Communist rebels in El Salvador. Charles Boyd's eyebrows went up and down, tacitly acknowledging he could use a statement. He was unbeatable at filling in circles on a standardized test, but every female in the club was steering clear of his disastrous hair and the line of ankle grime above his boat shoes. He didn't know *how* to dance. Lance felt he could read Boyd's thoughts, his secret hunger for recognition, and they matched his own. Boyd was pretentious and something of an asshole, but this ability to read him seemed to indicate friendship. Lance uncrossed his arms and tilted his head.

"We've got a chance to—"

Lance put up his hands. "Yeah, we heard you. Just *shut up* about it."

Boyd said, "Say one more thing and we won't do it."

LaCoss's eyes softened, becoming plaintive. He needed balance from steadier heads. He had fewer friends than you would think.

Nods of agreement came from Boyd and Lance. And so a nervous itch began. Either something wonderful or terrible would result. It was impossible to predict. This, it seemed to Lance, was the essential problem of the universe.

Under a jubilant blue sky, students filled a grandstand. A ninety-by-ninety-foot square of The Lawn had been roped off. The Langford pep squad led cheers in honor of that night's basketball game. The crowd's roar echoed off buildings. The Langford Owl mascot, in brown tights, chicken feet and an enormous square head, pranced and begged them to roar louder.

People were lined up around the rope six and seven deep, girls sitting on tops of shoulders. Lance excused his way through, unnerved every time he brushed past someone. Currents of laughter swirled around him. He wrapped his hands around the rope. A podium and table were set up near the grandstand, a gleaming silver cup on the table. Years ago, Langford's founder had held the first Travails to select a team to go on a Central American archeological dig. The ritual had continued ever since. He ducked under the rope and walked forward, feeling eyes tracking his sneakers and Langford sweats. A heat rose on his neck. A series of smaller rope circles had been laid out. Three students in matching red track suits sat within one, a coed team of two guys and a girl next to them. LaCoss stood within another.

LaCoss shouted toward the edge of the grandstand. Wearing a white kamikaze headband and black sweats, he clapped his hands and whooped, flashing a thumbs up and playing to the crowd. He put his hands around his mouth and yelled *Oh, yeah!* Lance stepped into the circle and did a slow pivot, looking up into the grandstand and at the restless people surrounding the square, who seemed to be considering throwing objects. Some girls at the rope yelled for LaCoss, who flexed a bicep for them.

"This is awesome," LaCoss said, like a giant surprise party had been thrown for him.

"Where's Boyd?" Lance's feet dented the soggy ground as he shifted his weight. An edge of cloud blocked out the sun. The not knowing was at its worst.

"Shouldn't more people be here?"

"Do you think he's backed out? We've only got five minutes." Lance kicked the ground with his toe.

"Five minutes?" LaCoss looked in every direction, becoming frantic. Charles Boyd appeared at a corner of the grandstand and strode toward the circle, his expression irritated and paranoid, his stoop more pronounced. He wore jeans and a matching jacket, the weathered light blue denim of a convict. His one concession to the athletic nature of the competition was an old pair of Jack Purcell sneakers. Chewing a wad of gum, his hands were shoved into his jeans.

"Is this our ring of confinement?" Charles Boyd asked. He frowned and put his hands on his hips.

"You were supposed to wear sweats," Lance said.

LaCoss put his hands firmly on the shoulders of Charles Boyd and Lance, pulling them into a huddle. "Is this great or what?" A wave of noise made it difficult to hear. Lance felt a small surge of camaraderie, which was overwhelmed by a desire for this to be over quickly. Charles Boyd patted his jacket pocket and pulled out a cigarette and lighter. Boyd took a few concentrated puffs, his eyes unfixed, seeming to forget where he was. He offered the cigarette to Lance, who took one hot drag before remembering he wasn't a smoker and was puffing under the scrutiny of hundreds of staring people.

A rotund man in a blue seersucker suit and bowtie made his way to a podium before the grandstand: Simon Worthlin, a professor emeritus of music. He received a warmhearted sprinkling of applause. Worthlin tapped the mike, the *thud thud* of his fingertip quieting the crowd.

"I now call the Autumn Travails to order." The crowd roared, egged on by the Langford Owl crazily flapping its arms. Worthlin cautioned the mascot with a wagging finger. "As always there will be three tests. Four teams are participating this year." Tepid applause, disconnected shouts. The Travail staff, in matching red t-shirts, checked the names of team members from a list, then reported back to Worthlin, who covered the mike with his hand.

"I now call upon my loyal staff to prepare the first test. It will be a height test." A low, rolling sound of speculation rose from the crowd. The staff brought forward what seemed ten- or eleven-foot posts with perpendicular slats at the top. Lance felt trepidation, though some relief too. A popular physical test in the 1960s had been drinking multiple gallon jugs of apple cider, which teams later vomited in gushes while doing algebra equations.

A post with a tripod base was erected within each team's circle. Using a foot ladder, the numbered overhead slats were lined up. Teams had ten minutes to reach the highest slat possible, *without* touching the pole.

"Begin!"

Their first idea was that Charles Boyd would stand on LaCoss's shoulders. Boyd was resistant to being the climber, but he was the lightest. LaCoss went to his knees, but was unable to stand bearing Boyd's weight. Lance suggested he and LaCoss join arms and lift Boyd. Boyd wavered a bit as he stood on their arms; he held their shoulders for stability. The crowd's yelling was harsh, like at the center of a riot. Why did people at events scream like idiots? They struggled to push Boyd's feet into the air, their arms trembling. Boyd reached over his head precariously, before wobbling and falling hard to earth. He landed ungracefully on his side with a squishy sound. He winced, shutting his eyes and clutching his shoulder. He pushed away his teammates and flung his jean jacket to the ground. The track suit team had knocked a bottom slat, the crowd roaring in approval. The all-girl team managed a shaky human pyramid, then the top girl crashed heavily on top of their pole. A red disqualification flag waved.

"One more time!" Charles Boyd yelled. Spunk! Boyd had some spunk.

They set up again. LaCoss suggested they fling Boyd up into the air.

"Yes, fling me! Fling me dammit!" They bent slightly, then pulled up with their full might, propelling him into the air. Extending an arm, he knocked the bottom slat and landed heavily on his feet. This was good teamwork. Suddenly, it felt like a team. The next time, Charles Boyd bent at the knees and leapt, though it was timed poorly in relation to the heave. He collapsed onto his hip. In their last throw, Boyd's jump was well timed and he sprung up with a furious grasping, reaching two more slats. Exhausted, struggling for breath, they waited for the whistle. They had tied the track suit team by reaching the third slat.

Was this fun? No. It was too tense to be fun.

"Well done, participants," Simon Worthlin's gentle voice

rang out over applause. "The second test will be a written test." Notepads and pens were distributed to each team. Lance, LaCoss and Charles Boyd sat cross-legged on the soggy ground, facing one another. They were instructed to list, in fifteen minutes, as many European wars as possible since AD 1000. The History Department would count up points, deducting points for each invalid answer. "Begin!"

Lance wrote the obvious last two world wars, then worked backward into Napoleonic warfare and the Hundred Years' War, losing steam during the Middle Ages. Charles Boyd's pen twitched madly, filling up a page within a few minutes. LaCoss showed Lance his meager list: *WW II, the Revolutionary War* and *Julius Caesar?* Lance tossed it back. He remembered the Franco-Prussian War of 1870. After ten minutes Lance and Charles Boyd compared lists.

"You've got Charlemagne attacking the Huns," Lance said, in a heated whisper. "That wasn't a war. That was barely a skirmish."

"Yes it was. He was consolidating power."

"The Huns were totally unorganized and scattered like chickens. It was an *attack*, not a war."

"That still counts!"

Charles Boyd scrutinized Lance's list. "Hannibal attacking Rome? Hannibal was from Carthage, in Africa. Does that count as a European war?"

"It happened on European soil."

Charles Boyd slapped the notepad against his leg. "The rules are so imprecise!" He winced again, gripping his wounded shoulder. Mud flecks dotted his cheek. Using his as the master list, they struck a few of his entries and appended a list of Lance's answers. Boyd's grasp of naval warfare was impressive, from the Venetians and the Spanish Armada to Sir Francis Drake's many victories.

After a twenty-minute judging interval, Simon Worthlin spoke into the mike, "It appears the LaCoss Rally Boyd team has prevailed in the second test with thirty-one correct answers. Very good. They take the lead." Appreciative applause followed. Faces and arms swayed on the perimeter in wavelike patterns. LaCoss pumped his fists. Charles Boyd raised his arms, suddenly smug, holding back uncharacteristic glee. He bounced on his toes like a child. A similar sense of elation infected Lance; he raised his arms. A surprisingly glorious high, like the performance he had never given, the soccer ball never put in the back of the net. And though he usually sat on his hands for others, he accepted the applause now. Within the cheers were the high pitched *woos* of wildly approving, bouncing young females.

For the final test, staff people brought forth bushels of unshucked corn and jugs of apple cider. Something in the air turned and hostile shouting rose, a gloating, the crowd jabbing their fingers at the contestants. There was something insulting about these agricultural props, and Lance had an uneasy feeling. Boyd stared at him, shaking his head. Now they would have to humiliate themselves. They were captive freaks in a sideshow. This was what happened when you did things for purely superficial reasons. The remaining test was shucking the corn while balancing gallon jugs of cider on their heads. The first team to finish the corn would win. A fallen jug disqualified that team. They sat around a teeming bushel basket and straightened their backs as a staff member placed a jug on their heads. "I don't know how to shuck corn," LaCoss said, his eyes trailing upward to the golden liquid settling in the glass container on his head. "I've never done it."

"We'll show you how," Lance said. He took steady breaths, adjusting to the heavy jug pressing the top of his skull like a foreign hand. Once each team was positioned with jugs, a whistle mixed with piercing feedback rang out. "Begin!"

"We've got a problem," Charles Boyd said in a thin voice. "I've got a pointy head."

Lance rotated his head cautiously. Underneath the dark

mane, Charles Boyd's head did appear to be oblong, tipped. Tiny tremors shook Boyd's jug, the liquid a turbulent sea behind the label. His cheeks were drained, his eyes zombie-like.

"That's OK," Lance said. "LaCoss and I will shuck. You relax. Take deep breaths."

Lance demonstrated and LaCoss got the hang of shucking quickly. The remnant of his Mohawk anchored his jug well. They placed the yellow bare cobs into an empty basket. After several cobs, Lance shucked without looking at his hands. His eyes were fixed forward on the grandstand: a swirl of colors and shadowed faces. He thought he recognized Stephanie Nalley sitting beside Tanya Krieger. But that was impossible. Wasn't it?

A machinelike roar on all sides, a Phil Spectorish Wall of Sound. LaCoss cracked cobs furiously, his jaw set, eyes intense. The noise crowded Lance's eardrums, as if the ropes had been pushed in and people bellowed from mere yards away. The jug seemed to sink into his head, leaden, compressing his spine, his neck muscles smarting from the tension. This discomfort changed into desperation, then into hatred of the screamers. He turned a degree and made eye contact with Charles Boyd, whose red eyes and twisted mouth confirmed what Lance had also discovered—they were suckers. He heard each screamer individually, noting the click of saliva below their tongues. The screams were strained and ugly, like a fight after a JV football game with gawkers calling for heads to be bashed, or a mob heckling a hated senatorial candidate. They yelled not that their team should succeed, but that they wanted them to lose. Who were these people? This was just a stupid college thing. It was for fun. Lay off! Simon Worthlin couldn't resist some cruelty, his effeminate laugh picked up by the mike.

"My neck...is killing me," Charles Boyd said. His face had turned purple. One side of his neck was compressed, buckling, the cider jug listing to the left on his head.

"Hang on!" Lance said. He carefully bent forward to reach

Charles Boyd's arm and steady him. As he reached out, Boyd fell away, his eyes rolling back in his head and upper body tilting slowly backward. The jug shattered when his head hit the ground, his arms dropping dead on either side of him.

An ocean of boos and hisses drilled into their ears. Then came laughter, hard and concussive. A coin, flung with terrible precision, stung Lance just above his ear. A chime rang in his head. He considered throwing it back.

The medical team gave Charles Boyd oxygen. He regained consciousness quickly. His hair was drenched with cider, a bleeding cut on his scalp. He got onto his feet and slunk off into the crowd. Lance looked around for Boyd, then saw LaCoss talking to a reporter for the *Langford Owl*. Lance walked off quickly among the people who had overrun the ropes. A trio of seniors was later declared the winner.

Lance felt an acute sting of defeat; a confused embarrassment, mainly because he'd gotten his hopes up. Walking on campus, he would raise his eyes to find a new notoriety: unwelcome stares from strangers and tragic looks. Everywhere a creepy familiarity. A guy in the post office said *nice try*. Outside the Student Union, some girls with sad faces said *too bad*, but were uninterested in talking further. He longed to give these people the finger, to hurl rocks at them. The word disaster was too soft—it implied there might be recovery.

"Here's one thing," LaCoss said, a blue cafeteria tray before him. "We'll have a leg up on next year."

"Are you crazy?" Lance yelled. "Those people were jeering at us. You want more abuse?"

"They were cheering. Man, it was like a rock concert."

"They booed us. They were laughing. We were *laughed at*." Lance put down his fish sandwich; suddenly he had no appetite.

"They were having a good time. Can you blame them? It was exciting." LaCoss blinked, his face sanguine. His eyes were bright with certainty that he had achieved a sweet victory. His tongue, front teeth and lips were stained sherbet orange. Sticks from four or five frozen desserts, which he claimed to be high in vitamin C, were littered before him. Orange flecks also stained his white t-shirt, with a rough design he had sketched in black permanent marker: a series of concentric ovals, which he claimed represented his soul. Lance wondered: how he had ever listened to this person?

"We disgraced ourselves before hundreds of people. Hundreds! Did you not hear them?"

"That's where you're wrong." A smile blossomed on LaCoss's face. "We had the guts to get in the ring. We earned their admiration. It's all about the good fight, man. What about Peter Fonda and Dennis Hopper in *Easy Rider*?"

"They died in the end. They were shotgunned by rednecks!"

"Maybe so. But they went down with what they believed. They could feel good about their choices. Look at *Treasure of the Sierra Madre*. Or how about *2001: A Space Odyssey*? In one light you could say it ended badly. But did it? I think you need to reconsider this whole win-loss calculation. You've got it all reversed."

Lance worked over *2001*'s ending—that weird giant baby. And what happened to that one astronaut? And that terrifying, soft-talking computer. What became of Hal? Lance threw up his hands, frustrated by this chain of thought. He winced; his neck was still sore. He opened a copy of the *Langford Owl*, to a photo spread, and shoved it at LaCoss. A photo of Lance and Charles Boyd, their teeth gritted, had the caption: "The Agony of Defeat."

LaCoss tapped the newspaper and made a big orange smile. "My quote made it into the article." He dropped the smile and shrugged. "I don't know. I thought it was all kinda cool."

"No! There was nothing cool about it. It was degradation." Lance pushed his tray, jostling the silverware, and got up to leave.

Neither of them heard from Charles Boyd for a week. Was he no longer their friend? Lance felt in need of a sympathetic ear. He went over to the townhouse. Boyd was listening to folk music in his room with a drowsy smile, sitting on the floor at a makeshift shrine to Bob Dylan. Votive candles, burning incense, and album covers lay on a low table. He lovingly stroked a cat in his lap. Lance sat on the floor and the cat wandered over. He paused, unsure if it would scratch, then smoothed its side. Lance spoke to Boyd about seeing people around campus, getting rotten looks.

"What are you talking about?"

"Remember a week ago—the Travails? The *statement* we made." Lance pointed to the scab on Boyd's head, to stitches in a shaved patch of scalp.

Boyd shrugged. "It went the way it did. I've moved on."

"How can you possibly feel that way?"

"That's why Bob Dylan is my hero. He didn't care what people thought. He went electric and half his fans deserted him."

"LaCoss wants to do it again. He thought it was a wonderful experience."

Boyd laughed. "You know about LaCoss, right? His mom tripped on acid when she was pregnant." He whistled and made a circular finger motion by his ear.

Despite his agitation around the peculiar cowboy music, Lance studied the album cover, noting a goofy character with tumbleweed hair not unlike Boyd's. The voice, incredibly, was both whiny and monotone. Dylan seemed to be in the room, sitting with them. The lyrics fluttered through Lance's mind. Lance had been egocentric or reckless enough to do the Travails, and thus was not a person to be trifled with. What was cool anyway? Why U2 and not UB40? Nobody really agreed on these things. It changed constantly. It was this mass projection. It was a strange gift, an omnipotent high, instant admiration, but the whole system depended on people buying into it. It was subjective, which meant his own interpretations were as valid as anyone's.

Dylan lamented his work on Maggie's Farm, using a bulletproof sarcasm. A comprehending light came into Lance's eyes, like a sheet falling to reveal a completed magic trick. The music was something he'd been listening to forever, but suddenly, he finally heard.

II.

CHAPTER SIX

THE POWER OF THE FUZZY SWEATER

Who could have anticipated the exquisite frustration, the subtle pain of spending a summer at home? Home? It was true in a technical sense, a historic sense. He set down his bags, remembering the walls a different shade. The house was familiar enough, though each room was smaller by about ten percent through a mysterious shrinkage.

His mother gave him reports. The younger Harrison, Freddy, with the shorter leg, had won a full scholarship to Chapel Hill. The Marston boy, from down the street, who'd gone to an expensive college in New England, had dropped out and was in Drug rehab (she didn't know what Drugs, just a general poisonous cloud), the poor Marstons going broke. The Fricker girl, Jenny, the tomboyish one, was making over *seventy* thousand a year her first year out of law school, the Frickers relieved since they'd worried about her from the time she cut off her hair. Lance listened, indulging his mother's belief that their family, by comparison, was gifted and lucky, which he also believed. Though secretly, he enjoyed the disaster tales. To his mother's considerable delight, Kevin was now studying to be a brain surgeon under the tutelage of a *world-class* neurosurgeon.

The home scene was distressing. Everywhere he went, his parents seemed to stand in the way. His sister Vickie, when not talking on a pink telephone in her bedroom, regarded him with annoyed detachment. He ate quickly to avoid the claustrophobia of the breakfast table. Escaping the tedium of family television programming, he read Tolkien in his room, sipping vodka and popping breath-masking peppermints. He and his father did spend a long weekend measuring, cutting and framing a new door to the backyard. Admiring their finished work, his father put an arm around his shoulders and gently squeezed, and Lance felt satisfaction.

Then came his freshman grades. He eagerly ripped open the grainy carbon printout, his eyes zigzagging on the page. He found numbers. He looked up, then took a deep audible breath. He shuffled in a semicircle, his mind suddenly blank, and tried again. Yes, it was addressed to him; these were the classes he had taken, true. The numbers, these strange hateful symbols, appeared again: a 2.3 overall GPA on a 4.0 scale, a C-. He wanted a wall to buttress himself. His GPA was mega low, with barely a pulse. His econ grades had yanked him down like bricks in a pond. He couldn't remember a worse report card. His mother called him. He dropped it on the hall table.

To his horror, he later found his father eyeing the document. Looking tall and regal in a black sport shirt and slacks, reading glasses on his nose. He exuded stoic calm, but his eyes worked with a focused fury. He touched his chin with his thumb, the lines about his mouth straining, which meant grave concern. A gesture last seen when the call came that his mother was entering the hospital a final time. He took away the glasses. His eyebrows came together. His eyes shifted critically to his son. The piercing hazel orbits made an appraisal, the pupils tight with pity and worry. It was delicate, this life, requiring careful plotting. A bad turn might set you at a permanent disadvantage. The corneas tensed, straining for recognition, as though adjusting his perception of Lance, who despite a lifetime of encouragement had measured up to less than considered possible.

His father let out a pained sigh. "I see this is yours."

Lance's mouth was dry. "Look, it's not like I didn't try or something."

His father sucked in a deep, uncertain breath. "Well…"

"It's just my first year." A hatred for his father burned, sudden and unfamiliar. Lance looked away, studied the carpet a moment, then felt guilty. Guilt and hatred mixed with embarrassment, and the combination made his face warm.

"First years can be rocky. You'll have to work harder. *Much harder.*"

Lance nodded. A dampness started in his eyes, but he shut it down. A similar past transgression would have earned a detailed lecture and a long pep talk, which he craved now. But he was older, in college, and his father turned away with his lips bunched tightly. Later, he found his mother shaving candles with a knife, fitting them into holders. Her jawline tense, her eyes avoided him even as he stood in her periphery.

That night he couldn't sleep. His breath was labored, as though cinder blocks weighed upon his chest. He imagined future stories shared among the mothers of the neighborhood: the disappointing Rally boy, whose grades had excluded him from the better future he had *seemed* capable of attaining. His father's word stuck, *rocky*, implying that through recklessness he had ended up *on the rocks*. The personal engine that had powered him through Mason Prep, through the SAT and into Langford, had sputtered. His SAT prep teacher's mantra haunted him: *The numbers matter. With so many competing, it is the only way to pick the chosen.* It seemed unfair, but life—as his parents liked to say, and as increasingly seemed true—perhaps was unfair.

He found himself walking about his room in the dark, whispering. He kicked the beanbag. He ripped the *Eraserhead* poster off the wall and shredded it. His engine was a strong and worthy power plant, he assured himself, and it would power him all the way. He resolved to bear down and bring that average way up.

At summer's end he packed up his blue Corolla (his mother's old car, given to Lance). He draped Mardi Gras beads from the mirror and slapped a Clash sticker on the bumper. He waved to his parents, outlined by the big house, their faces round with hope, and somehow, this aggravated him. He vowed this was the last summer spent at home. On an open highway he aired out the car's speakers, the raw salivating fury of the Sex Pistols spilling out the windows to cows and cotton fields. He accelerated, pushing the 4-cylinder harder than it had ever been pushed, white-knuckled from the speeding euphoria—state troopers be damned! Johnny Rotten's blistering vocals and the air rushing through the windows reconfirmed he was young and alive.

The morning after his first night in Oswald dormitory, Lance opened his eyes. Above the bed, on the ceiling, the numbers 3.75 greeted him. Black numbers on white poster board, the numbers thick, imposing and huge, like on the side of a battleship. This was subliminal programming to help him achieve this GPA goal that semester. Another 3.75 was taped above the desk in his tiny private room (a perk of Oswald) and another was behind the door. He yawned. As his eyes adjusted to the numbers, he told himself it was already working. He repeated 3.75 over and over. Like a scholastic robot, he hoped to be pulled inexorably toward this result. This technique was described in *Achieve Every Goal*, a book his father had given him that summer. Goal Strategy #1 was *Visualize your goal*. He and his father, on their knees, had sketched out the big numbers using squeaky markers.

Strangely, a scrap of paper lay on his belly. A torn corner. He pulled it toward his eyes with incomprehension. In a cursive feminine hand, a name written in red ink. Robust loops, sexy end flourishes, but with a consistency and a pleasing uniformity, the nurturing hand of a lunch box reminder.

Lynn Van Oster 377-2297.

His mouth sprung open with a long blissful noise, his head melted into the pillow, and his eyes rolled back. The memory of her blazed. That hair, blonde with shades of champagne and wheat fields. It draped to her shoulders and formed a kind of halo around her face. Cheekbones to melt your insides. This Grace Kelly meets Kathy Ireland type beauty, with an endearing touch of Goldie Hawn in her sidestep. He flung off the covers and paced the room in his lucky game fish boxers. Something momentous had happened. He had waited a lifetime. Lynn Van Oster! She was not merely a paste-up on the wall. She wore jeans with ankle zippers. Though he had been falling down drunk the night before, he felt no hangover, just a lightness in his sinuses, like an idyllic remnant of her.

Still, his memory of the evening was confused. It was clouded, an art student film with quick cuts and fadeouts and poor preproduction decisions. He paced, taking five steps, turning, another five steps back, 3.75 flashing from several angles; yet the mystery of 377-2297 dominated his mind. He ran a hand through stiff, tangled hairs on his head. He had talked to her at the end of the evening. In the common room downstairs. One look had told him she was The One. He recalled a radiating presence. Other girls, defensively checking their hair, were unnerved and guys, gawking, were aware that it was *the* Lynn Van Oster, and were too intimidated to approach.

So why had he? Was he guided by the hand of God?

He started at the evening's beginning. The Trang brothers, Johnny and Nguyen, came to mind. Oswald was coed, an outer satellite of the Langford Dormitory Association, an older unit with an unremarkable brick facade. For some reason, many exchange students lived there. A feeling of celebration had been in the air and the Trang boys had lit a portable gas burner on their floor and heated up a powerful sake-like home brew, sprinkling in mysterious gray herbs. Lance tried some, as Johnny and Nguyen smiled and slapped him on the back. He noticed, from their posters, an unseemly devotion to Michael Jackson. A pain seared his throat. His eyes watered. He experienced a hysterical reckless high, then the sensation his brain was underwater. He drank more.

He recalled barging into Ian LaCoss's third-floor room,

interrupting a group discussion on the true nature of love. Morrissey, of The Smiths, was singing in his tone of endless boredom, and LaCoss insisted to Marcie and Andrea, girls in clingy pastel dresses, that initial attraction could never be controlled, because it was all pheromones and animal ectoplasm, but emotional choices beyond that could be controlled. And giving too much emotionally put oneself into grave danger.

Lance was outraged. "But what if it's so powerful you can't control it? And why would you want to control it? What's the point if you don't give yourself fully over to love?"

"Then you're in real trouble, my friend." Lance swung his arms in the air. "You make it sound so heartless, so clinical." The girls nodded in agreement. "And you're a hypocrite..." Lance was tempted to mention Lucinda Falcon, LaCoss's California girlfriend, who LaCoss was obsessed with, but considered that LaCoss had designs on one or both of these girls. LaCoss and the girls exchanged furtive glances. Marcie and Andrea lunged at Lance. They pushed and held him down, forcing liquor bottles and wine coolers into his mouth as he gagged. An explosion of white light behind his eyes. The room fell into a cinematic turn.

He found himself in a stairwell clogged with people. He wondered about his shirt, a baggy long sleeve shirt with a cheery palette of colors. Did this shirt look ridiculous? It was a bloated clown shirt. He leaned his face against a wall, feeling wobbly-headed, suddenly depressed his life would never change and that nothing good would ever happen. He recalled Goal Strategy #2: *Activity is always preferable to inertia.* Though it had a touch of his father's annoying absolutism, it struck him as brilliant—the raw physics of life! Of roaring comets, of armies clashing on a plain, of Indiana Jones's ability to skirt trouble by scampering away. He slapped his face. He plowed down the stairs making beep-beep sounds, brushing past startled people. According to the logic of a music video, which he now seemed to inhabit, anything was possible: horses might appear from a mist, or ragged post-apocalyptic mutants, or buxom girls on bicycles. He saw two pretentious guys he disliked on sight. He waved his hands in their faces to confuse them. Taunting them, he did a dance he remembered seeing Wile E. Coyote perform. Then he abruptly turned his back, hoping they'd come after him, relishing the thought of tearing them to pieces.

He rolled into a common room. Synthesized music filled the air with a hive-like buzz. His eyes were wild with a dangerous glint when they locked on Lynn. She stood with two girlfriends. She held her drink at arm's length, having just spilled it. Breath held, she did a quick scan to see if anyone had noticed. She stared at Lance, seeming to calculate whether he had. I caught you, his smile said. Moving toward her—there was no question about it, just movement, as if he was on a conveyor belt—a sensation spread under his ribcage, a warm glow. And he was before her, pulling her eyes to his. He introduced himself and held her firm hand before it retreated, her fingers curving and resting on her clavicle. She had a small nose, full lips and vigilant eyes: her features focusing a daunting energy which seemed capable equally of joy or rage. He experienced this weird calm. A grace, a suaveness came over him, as if he was at his favorite point in a movie, but a movie he'd never seen, going on inside him in an unpredictable way. He lost track of what he was saying to her, his mouth on autopilot. She swept a lock of hair behind her small ear. She laughed, a quick staccato laugh. Each detail reverberated within him like a tiny earthquake. What he was saying—something about being an econ major—sounded great, this deep stream of consciousness. Her eyes traveled across his shirt, which now, it seemed to him, draped from his shoulders in a chic and dashing way. She wore a black fuzzy sweater with yellow lightning strikes. It took great restraint to not run his hand across the wispy strands.

Her hand reached out, tapping his arm as she made a point. It seemed obvious she was into him. So he started taking risks.

He got louder, his hands chopped the air. And was he imagining this? He remembered using obscure vocabulary words. These archaic freak words from his *Roget's Thesaurus* that popped out of his mouth. Was this possible? But they seemed fine with her.

Then her friends had to leave. She waved and moved off and he waved with no thought of stopping her, the way you could never control the way a dream ended.

Lance gathered information. Lynn was a sophomore. Jacqueline Tucker had lived in Lynn's freshman dorm. After seeing *9 1/2 Weeks*, Lynn stated she would do everything Kim Basinger had done, except crawl for the dollar bills. That was demeaning and wrong. She danced with a modern dance troupe called Dyna Dance. A recent playbill showed Lynn, mixed with other performers, wearing a white unitard, a garment so sensuous it left Lance stricken. Dana Washington, another dancer, described Lynn as having great creativity and balance, unusual flexibility. She was respected by other dancers, but always ended up with most of the flowers tossed up on stage. In a weird coincidence, Charles Boyd's mail slot was four slots across from Lynn's at the Student Union. Not that Charles Boyd had ever spoken to her. Lynn read all her mail standing before her slot, oblivious to others reaching around her. He'd seen her tear up twice reading letters. She never tossed junk mail onto the floor, putting it into trash receptacles each time.

"So, you've got the hots for Lynn?"

"She has the hots for me. I'm going to go out with Lynn." Lance smiled.

Charles Boyd sat Lance down on a bench, staring at him in a worried way. "Let's be realistic. She is so far out of your league." He patted Lance on the back. "Dreams are fine, but some dreams can become painful. Some notions will only lead to pain." Charles Boyd shook his head vigorously, his dark hair swishing around his eyes. His own dating record was poor, in fact nonexistent, and Lance suspected jealousy.

"It's going to happen. I have her phone number." Lance held up the scrap.

"The campus directory also has her number." Charles Boyd smirked, then got up and walked off. Lance rubbed his hands on his jeans, sweat leaving a trail of moisture on his thighs. The specter of failure loomed. This opportunity carried significant risk. Like having the soccer ball in front of an open goal. Suddenly, the ball bounced deceptively and your foot seemed only capable of jamming into the ground.

First, he had to dial her number. The phone was treacherous. Lance had not made friends with the medium yet, with its immediacy and the problem of accomplishing things by listening to a faint voice, then speaking into a plastic dial, which might as well have been a hole in a wall. His father was good. He was direct, commanding on the phone, though he also soothed people in small ways. He filled up phone space skillfully and could be funny. He got what he wanted. Phoning was trickier when you were dealing with girls. Verbal communication was their forte. According to scientists, that part of their brains was more refined. When he talked on the phone with girls, Lance always sensed a charged silence, a hyper attention to his voice. He sensed a judging, a sifting of his worthiness. He felt they could see him from overhead and he was being scored. Goal Strategy #3: *Proper preparation is crucial.* So Lance wrote out an imaginary phone conversation, underlining key points. He positioned his chair in the middle of the room and straightened his back. He shook out his hands, dialed her number, then hung up. He balled up the paper and kicked it. Being too scripted was bad. How pathetic and anal-retentive was that? But now he had material. He was prepared. He sensed he was entering mind game territory, so he punched in her number again. He listened to static, then a soft, trilling sound as Lynn's phone rang.

"Hello?" Was it her? It didn't sound like her. "Yes, hello?"

He was behind already, his hesitation earning a prompt.

"Oh, hi. Lynn?" He sounded like a television actor playing himself.

"Yes."

He waited, then realized it was his turn again. "Hi. This is Lance Rally. You were at my dorm last weekend…" A sound like crackers crunched under a shoe. "…Do you remember me?" He reached for the balled-up paper, just in case, and pulled the phone off the table. It crashed against the floor, making a sound on the line like an explosion at a cymbal factory.

"Oh, my God. What was that?"

Lance stood, waving his free hand like he was imploring a superior court judge for leniency. "Nothing. Listen. Dinner with me. Say, this Saturday. Dinner. Saturday. With me."

Another silence, like she'd been distracted by something. "I think I remember you. You were wearing that shirt, the real colorful one." Appreciation or mild mockery? He couldn't tell.

"Yeah, that shirt. You can't go wrong with colors." He laughed and waited, but she did not laugh.

"Oh, so sorry. I can't do Saturday. I've got plans."

"Friday? We could do Friday."

She made a clicking sound. "No. My roommate's parents are here Friday."

Was it the delicate brush-off? The parent thing sounded bogus. He threw his pen against a wall. He considered hanging up.

"What about next Saturday?"

During the pause, he imagined her tabulating a score sheet. "I can do next Saturday. That's open."

Her affirmation was like a cool salve all over his body. Over the next week and a half he rode waves of triumph and raging euphoria. He walked past her dorm, hoping to catch glimpses of her. He crawled into a stand of tall bushes across the street, waited an hour and was rewarded by seeing her come back from a class. He told several remote friends he had a new girlfriend.

Saturday his euphoria crashed when he confronted himself in the mirror, post-shower, wearing a towel. He scrutinized his features: his skull which had always seemed bigger than the rest of him, his eyes which suddenly seemed too wide, his ears a bit cupped. But his chin was good. Solid, with a hint of dimple. A Rally chin. He sat on his bed and considered he might be out of his league. What did he have to offer? What did he add up to? His blood pumped heavily in his limbs. He considered getting drunk to duplicate his performance the other night. A vision came to him, something he had imagined in various ways as a child: his grandfather Zachary Rally, who before he chaired the Physics Department at West Point had run a gauntlet of Nazi gunfire, carrying a crate of ammo to a forward position. He must have been terrified, without a gun, just holding this crate, bullets zinging everywhere, but he ran seventy yards during a crucial point of a battle. He just did it.

Lance listened to Joy Division's "Love Will Tear Us Apart" three times at a bracing volume while doing pushups, playing the speedy drum parts and singing the chorus in a wistful voice. He realized pulling off the date would require something deeper and more improvisational than his usual knapsack of tricks. He worked huge gobs of mousse into his wet hair, combed it back; pulled on freshly washed Levi's, an expensive Genera collection shirt and a tweed sport jacket.

It was late September, and the air was balmy. At his blue Corolla, he stared at his window reflection. He marveled at his hair; he had achieved perfection. The entire feathered helmet was airborne. A perfect spread, like an early-career Don Johnson or midcareer Sting. He turned his head cautiously, like his hair was a bird that might fly off. He sat in the hot car. The car smelled stale. He ripped open a package of lemon-scented liquid air freshener. He dabbed at the tiny vial and rubbed his finger onto the carpet in a few spots, noting a clean pleasant smell. The oil spread down the side of the vial, which slipped from his fingers and fell under the seat. In horror, he watched the vial slowly empty. He plunged his hand under the seat, scraping it against metal, unable to reach it. A dewy cloud filled the car, like an attack of poisonous lemon gas. He pinched his nostrils. He rolled down both windows. He drove with the fan blasting on high. He waved his arms. He found Fricker, the side street to Juniper Dormitory.

Outside 4B, he inhaled deeply. He knocked.

"Come on in," a voice said.

He opened the door. From the middle of the room, Lynn looked at him and regarded him with stark caution and honesty. A piercing, truth-seeker look, a cannon blast, and it struck him in mid-step. The date was very serious; there was much at stake since she was an attractive young woman skilled at repelling unwanted males. The look set off a slow panic. His stomach knotted. He could not match his performance from the other evening. What had he even said? It was as though he was using false pretenses. I was really drunk, he wanted to admit. God, just so drunk!

"You look terrific," he said, extending his open palms toward her.

"Thank you." Lynn tilted her head slightly, her expression going soft.

He stepped into the room. A smooth, moist glow surrounded her. She had achieved a perfection of hair and makeup, assembled with such delicacy and artistry he was hesitant to go near her. He could have stared indefinitely. In a black velvet half-jacket with shoulder pads, a frilly white blouse, black miniskirt, dark hose and pumps, she appeared vaguely Spanish, like a female toreador.

"I'm having trouble with this clasp." She held a plastic bracelet, an irritation in her exhale. This schedule delay she clearly did not like.

"Can I help you?"

"I'll try another one." She bent to a vanity littered with

makeup and jewelry.

Lance stood on a shaggy white rug. The sweet, light scent of the room mellowed him. Mint toothpaste and roses mixed with fresh laundry. Pillows, comforters, and stuffed animals surrounded him. He could have fallen in any direction without injury, cushioned by brilliant hues. He picked up a monkey from a nest of silk pillows on what he guessed was her bed. The monkey held tiny cymbals. He switched it on and the monkey jerked and screeched and clashed the cymbals together. It delighted Lance. He held it toward her and mimicked the screeching sound.

"That's Chachi the monkey. I've had him ever since third grade." She smiled, but her eyebrows rose in mild concern.

"That's a long time. I usually destroyed my toys pretty quickly."

"I have always been able to count on Chachi."

He clicked it off and carefully placed it on the bed. The monkey shifted, rolling off. He caught it by an arm, and yanked that arm out of its socket. With Lynn's attention directed to the vanity, he quickly jammed the arm back in, hoping it attached correctly. He wedged Chachi between pillows, burying him. A big smile shot across his face.

Outside, he opened her car door. The vision of Lynn getting into his car, her hair shifting in the late afternoon light, was surreal. Inside the car, Lynn wriggled her nose several times. She distorted her lips and her face became distressed. "Oh my God! What on earth is that?" She opened her door and put a leg outside.

"Don't leave!" Lance tapped his forehead twice on the steering wheel. "I can explain. I bought this concentrated air freshener, and I kinda dropped it."

"You did that for me?"

"I'm sorry. My car reeks of lemons—"

"You just bought it?"

"Yeah, yesterday. Normally my car stinks. But differently."

"That's so sweet of you!" She threw her head back against the seat, pulled her shoulders together and her face was beautiful again. Amazed, Lance noted this reaction, filing it away in a mental dossier. He drove her around campus. At the four-way stop on Brickland, several pedestrians glanced into the car. Lance could hear the future gossip: It was Lance Rally driving Lynn Van Oster...Rally, who was a likable fellow, but with a history of erratic behavior, on a date with Van Oster, the ice queen!

At the Kon-Tiki restaurant, with its ornate pagoda roof and fish tanks, the hostess sat them at a booth with palm fronds and bamboo supports like a little hut. They opened menus.

"So, what are you studying?" Lance asked.

"Psychology. With an emphasis on applied rather than behavioral. Also, I'm leaning more toward cognitive than psychobiology. Though what really interests me is childhood psychology." So many psych major girls at Langford. The place was clogged with girls carrying clipboards, handing out questionnaires or asking for volunteers to punch keys in a lab experiment. He loved the idea of these scientific, highly stable, preprofessional women with insights into the human psyche. But maybe his psyche was vulnerable. Were his neuroses obvious? "And psychology is also cool to figure people out." She batted her eyes, then focused them on him in a way uncomfortably similar to the molten stare of Dr. Henry Shatzer.

Lance held up his menu, staring into it. "Are you going to be a psychologist?"

"Absolutely. It's a wonderful field, with business applications too. There are so many linkages with other disciplines, it's becoming a breakout field." He wasn't sure what that meant, but it sounded good. She popped a fried wonton into her mouth. "What's your major?" The most dreadful of Langford clichés. She laughed in a self-deprecating way.

He was determined to make his career info sound as good as hers.

She leaned forward. "Of course, I already know all your plans. You told me about them the other night."

"That's right. I did." Under the table, he weaved his fingers together tightly. A knuckle popped.

"It really impressed me you've thought so much about these things. And you were so willing to express them. I mean, starting your own company takes a lot of courage. And you have some great business ideas. Like your idea about delivering groceries to homes." He forced himself to smile and nod, shocked he had told her these things, plans that had only briefly nibbled at the edge of his consciousness, that were barely plans. They had passed through his mind years ago like feverish hallucinations and it was unsettling to hear them now. Her feelings were intense: her nostrils flared slightly, and the veins alongside her neck grew taut. "It drives me crazy the way some people are so directionless. They have this idea they can lie around and things will happen for them. Get a life. If you don't try to be the best, then why try at all?" She described taking ballet at six a.m. before school for four years, and how she had won an audition for *The Nutcracker*, even though she was the youngest at the tryout and had a broken toe, and how she worked three extra hours a day on the balance beam to make a junior gymnastics team. "Which business school do you want to go to?"

"I haven't decided yet. My dad went to business school at Harvard."

"Wow. That's so cool!" Her blue eyes became bluer. She smiled richly, tilting her head with approval, which made his heart swell and affirmed it was a wise and worthwhile path. She knew! She knew of the hardship of having a plan, an adult plan, and she recognized this and cheered him on with that smile. He applied duck sauce to a wonton with the single-mindedness of a young man with ambition, a future top earner with a vision. A man with a plan. He felt himself growing into the role before her eyes. She said, "I've gotten flak from people for caring about my grades. But that's really important."

"Absolutely. I just implemented a goal-oriented study strategy that is working really well. I'm using some subconscious techniques."

He piled Kung Pao chicken onto his plate. Lynn scooped a spoonful of shrimp in lobster sauce. She sat perfectly upright, her free hand in her lap. He was so grateful to her, for every detail, like that tiny birthmark on her neck. He rejoiced when she leaned her face forward and flashed an expectant gaze. He could have sat there for an eternity, silently grooving. In this case, the not knowing was exquisite, allowing a sensuous future to be imagined between them. She had lived all over, she explained. Her dad was a senior engineer and they had lived the last five years in Huntsville, Alabama.

"I heard that you know Ian LaCoss," she said.

"He's one of my best friends." He sensed this was a poor direction.

Lynn frowned, bristling a bit. "He had a...fling with a friend of mine. Heidi. That guy is a total male slut. I can't respect that."

"He is kind of a male slut. But he's still a good guy. He has qualities not everybody knows about." Lance noticed a white hot speck inside his cheek from his last chewed mouthful. The spot burned, until hot spittle rose in his throat and his eyes watered. A chili pepper had lodged between his cheek and gum. Lynn looked at him, alarmed. He fumbled for his glass. He swallowed water, but the offending pepper lodged in his throat, sending toxic fumes into his nasal cavity. He gagged. He placed his napkin before his mouth in time for an involuntary cough, a retch, the pepper shooting into the napkin like a baseball into a catcher's mitt. He put down the napkin and took some hesitant breaths.

"Are you all right?"

"Oh, fine." He wiped tears from his eyes. He sensed the pepper's juices burning a hole in his stomach lining, cooking him from within.

Lance smiled, nodding his head—choking on chili peppers, that was funny stuff, no? She lapsed into a series of private thoughts, and stared at her plate. He wanted to slit his throat. She put down her fork and placed both hands in her lap. She stared at him coldly. "You seem different from the other night. You were more talkative. How much did you have to drink then?"

"Oh, I guess a beer. Well, more like two beers." His knee bumped the table.

"There was this one time you were talking and you said the word 'display,' but it came out like 'dispay' "

"I lose that L sometimes."

Across the table, she was further away from him than the other night. He tried to pour soy sauce onto his rice. The spout was clogged, and he tilted the bottle back and forth, back and forth. He shook it.

"I hope this isn't too forward of me." She licked her lips and her eyes narrowed. "Are you one of those people who are usually a little nervous?"

"No. No. I get nervous at certain times, sure. Everybody does. But on whole, no, no, I would not say that." His heart started banging wildly. He kicked his ankle with the heel of his shoe. He stared into his plate. A numb silence descended upon their booth. Asian ladies soundlessly took things from their table. He scraped food into various shifting piles and inhaled to a count of six, exhaled to a count of six: this technique had saved him during his second taking of the SAT. Goal Strategy #4: *Adjust to adversity.*

He put the bill on his credit card and suggested they go to a movie, *Dangerous Liaisons*. She dabbed her lips with a napkin, her face unfathomable. With a nod, she agreed to go. She was composed, full of courtesy, which he feared might be a facade.

An all-purpose, social cheeriness to mask disgust. Mothers seemed to ingrain these qualities. His own mother was always sniping at Vickie, reminding her of things in a strange code, sometimes without talking. Possibly, he was mistaken about this theory.

"Listen to this," she said in the car. "The campus police are looking for this guy, who has been loitering around my dormitory. Somebody saw him hiding in the bushes."

"No way."

"It's some kind of freak." She shuddered.

In the parking lot of a multiplex, he found a spot for the car. With the engine idling, the radio became audible. He reached to turn off the car. She touched his arm. "Don't…" A lonely, ringing guitar came over the radio. The intro of U2's "Bad" from the spacey second side of *The Unforgettable Fire*. She turned it up. She looked off, blank, as though she were blind. The circular guitar riff filled the car and she titled her head back dreamily. Bono's voice touched their ears, the singer accentuating each syllable. Her eyes slid shut and her face slackened as if an intravenous tranquilizer had kicked in.

In awe, Lance observed this direct hit on Lynn's warm, milky core, this capitulation at the hands of musical notes. Had she stopped breathing? Was she going to weep? He craved a way in there. He hovered near her, holding his breath. He wanted to touch her face, which reflected a pure, unadulterated pleasure he had never felt, a contentment he had never experienced. Oh, to inhabit her beautiful Disney world, to lay side by side in her serene fairytale. It would end his every problem. She snapped out of it and opened her eyes. He turned off the car.

"Sorry. I'm ready now. His voice just does things to me." She stared straight ahead. He realized she wasn't going to move until he opened her door. They walked toward the theater. A breeze blew and she crossed her arms. Her pumps clicked on the pavement. "I hope we're not late because of me," she said vacantly. "His voice just touches me."

Lance forced himself to say, "His voice is great."

The interval in the car seemed like abandonment. His general failure at entertaining her was now obvious. He had almost choked—a pitiful spectacle. Now the movie, then he'd take her home, and that would be it. Then, the long wait until death. He wanted to pound his skull on the pavement and moan between bashings, to set himself on fire, to be executed by firing squad. Lynn walked with perfect posture, grace, her face lovely and unreadable. He slowed to find the right walking rhythm with her, his eyes on the ground. At the curb, something touched his right hand, slender and soft and strange, delicate fingers working in between his fingers. He tightened his own to confirm it was her hand, embracing his like a tiny inseparable lover. A miracle. As he studied movie times, she sidled closer and rubbed his forearm. Her chin brushed his shoulder.

"Looks like they still have tickets," he said, smiling at her. She smiled back. An exuberance pumped through his body. The glass of his happy meter shattered from an all-time high. They held hands again in the lobby. He led her to center seats. Trying to amuse her, he put his feet on the sticky floor and pulled them up, making crinkly sounds. He spoke softly, "This is always my favorite part." She stared at him, seeming quite absorbed. "It's hushed and dark when you first sit down. Everybody is real quiet. You can totally relax here. Kind of like sitting in church." He nodded, surprised by the strength of his feelings.

"It is nice."

"Wouldn't it be great if you could just sit in theaters for hours? Movies wouldn't have to be shown. People would just sit and think, or maybe whisper."

"I'd pay for that." She stifled a laugh, like it was too weird.

Dangerous Liaisons was more intense than he had anticipated: the manipulations and gender warfare between Glenn Close and John Malkovich. Glenn Close dryly told Michelle Pfeiffer that men got happiness when they received it and women found happiness when they gave it. When Close explained that a woman relying on love for happiness would only find misery, Lynn nodded slowly. Maybe not the best subtext for a date movie. They wandered out of the cinema with loosened, post-movie expressions, that dreamy swelling of their features, the back of their hair tousled from their seats. This, combined with her warm hand finding his again, led him to feel he could do no wrong. In the car he put his hand on top of her seat, suddenly the Cary Grant of backing out of parking spaces, his nicked, paint-challenged Corolla now a grand vehicle. With a manly generosity, he waved at pedestrians to cross. He found his favorite Cars song on the radio, thrusting his arm in the air like he had summoned it with his touch.

They nursed beers at a campus watering hole. While this relaxed Lance, the alcohol seemed to harden an edge of her personality. "Heart of Glass" came on the jukebox and Lynn sang a few verses, doing a passable tough girl Deborah Harry. A disconcerting number of guys trailed past them and said hello to Lynn. She answered every greeting cheerfully, but he noted grievances in the curtness of her replies, the speed with which her politeness was turned off.

"Have you dated any of these guys?"

"God no. I went out with this upperclassman last year. He just wanted to screw me. Didn't succeed. Guys are all the same. Though in your favor, you haven't tried to feel me up yet." Her jaw tensed. She recrossed her legs swiftly, convincing Lance those toned dancer legs had slammed powerfully into the shins of those who transgressed her value system. He had used great care when near her, scrupulously avoiding any hint of such overreaching.

"That guy was a cad," Lance said.

"A what?"

"A playboy, a philanderer, a rapscallion." This

pronouncement, in the style of Alfred Hitchcock, embarrassed him as soon as it slid out.

"You have a great vocabulary. You used some amazing words the other night."

The music changed on the stereo, leaving a quiet space.

"It's a shame you've had to deal with jerks," Lance said, taking a chance. "Cause you're so beautiful." A faint sigh came out of her. She refused to look at him, as if she badly wanted to believe it, but did not.

"Actually, there was only one guy who was really cruel to me. Well…" Others obviously came to mind; she worked hard to banish them. "It was this uneven power situation. I was so stupid. But that will never happen again. Never." She drew both hands into her lap and steeled herself, as if she regretted talking. He wanted to crush skulls, to drive to distant cities and seek vengeance. Something fell away from her expression, a stiffness, a resistance, and her eyes reddened. Lance sensed her need, this discovery awe-inspiring, like the wailing zenith of a guitar solo. A need not unlike his own. For the first time he was certain he'd read a girl's emotions correctly. A need and an opportunity. He placed a compassionate hand on her back, just below her bra strap, with all the gentleness he could. His diagnosis was proved correct when she tilted towards him. "The question is whether I can trust you."

"A fair question. You've only seen me twice."

"I saw you before in the Autumn Travails. You were trying so hard. I respect that. You seemed like a good teammate."

He would later report to his father he had implemented all the Strategies in *Achieve Every Goal*, and expected real progress that semester. Strategy #5 was: *Keep advancing in positive directions.* Awash with the righteousness of a good teammate, he leaned in for a mouth kiss, his lips exposed, hanging for several torturous moments. Then he moved forward and pressed his lips, where they were accepted by hers.

CHAPTER SEVEN

THE WONDERFUL WORLD OF LYNN

They studied together. For Lance, this consisted of reading a few lines of a textbook about Trotsky's vision of the New Socialist Man, or the role of derivative assets in the economy, then glancing furtively at Lynn, who highlighted with precision and focus. He would shift his eyes around, as if considering an esoteric point, or making some multidisciplinary connection, while stealing glances at the downy, faint hairs between Lynn's cheek and ear, or the point where her neck met her gentle clavicle. If he lingered she might catch him. She wore black reading glasses, managing to make them sexy. "What?" she'd say.

"Oh, nothing. I was just thinking." He ruffled random pages.

Lynn liked to study in Tuttle Library, a hushed, creepy repository off The Lawn, where books smelled like roach bait. She fanatically made outlines of her notes, on topics such as the influence of heredity on antisocial behavior. She used a ruler to construct perfect columns. Every fifteen minutes she held her left wrist upright and twisted, clicking a mass of bracelets, rubber loops and bait clamps together. Lance managed only sporadic concentration. The problem was distraction, but also sedation. Lynn's presence was a soothing balm rubbed over his psyche, her composure and subtle rhythms making him woozy. Her eyes traced smooth trails across the page. Her lips moved silently as she devoted two inches of flash cards to memory. His mind wandered as he considered Trotsky's death at the hands of Mexico City assassins. His intention to master the determinants of aggregate consumption before an Econ quiz was dulled. She pulled her hair back into a bun, her shirt tight against her chest. A nipple pressed the fabric. The prospect of her unhaltered breasts tightened his stomach, made him momentarily crazed. Her library stamina was amazing, extending into three- and four-hour sessions, exhausting Lance. "Are you bored?" she asked, using a forceful tone to indicate distractions were unwelcome. "You can't be finished."

"I was just taking a break." He slowly sat up straight, assembling himself like a puzzle, and lowered his eyes to a paragraph for the hundredth time.

They ate lunch every day, went to seminars on Far Eastern mysticism and the oppression of Central American dictators. They laughed at student improvisational comedy. He sent roses to her room, the first she had ever received, which reduced her to tears. They met before classes, after classes; he even stopped by an auditorium to watch her sitting in a class. His professors talked too slowly, on subjects so annoyingly obscure as to insult him. He counted minutes, wondering what Lynn was wearing that day. Maybe those jeans, the stonewashed ones. When their discussions of mysticism had been exhausted, and after his impressions to relive the comedy, and times like when all the food had been eaten, moments would occur when they looked at each other and nothing was said, and a seriousness burned the air. A sensation dropped deep into his intestines, like he was about to jump off a building, and it made him look away.

"What?" she asked, intercepting his anxiety every time.

"Nothing."

On the sidelines of intramural softball, he was lulled by the slow game and her sweet scent of lilac shampoo, and a thought slid out as a strange discovery, something he had never consciously admitted: "I once was afraid of being hit by a softball. I thought it might kill me if it hit me in the head." She turned to him, her face moving closer with a look of deep fascination. She slid closer to him on the metal stands, seeming to scrutinize the inside of his ear.

"When was this?"

"When I was a kid."

"How old?"

"I don't know."

"Did one ever hit you in the head?" Her eyes widened.

"No." He began to fidget.

She blinked, consumed by a strange joy. "But you were afraid of the ball. That is so cute. Did you cry during a game?" She shook his arm in a pleading way, like a birthday kid a few feet away from the pizza parlor. "What else did you fear as a kid? Do you still fear dying in strange ways? Fear of death is quite common. Many times, childhood fears have to do with separation anxiety." He nodded and looked away, unsure how to respond. Her stare was unwavering. A pressure built behind his ears. He refocused on the game, pointing out activity in left field to her. Walking back to her dorm, she did a pirouette in front of him. "Look out! A softball, coming toward your head! Duck!" Her balled-up fist zoomed toward him. "Here it comes! It might kill you!"

She laughed and he laughed, but he cursed himself. In her eyes, he was wracked with weird childhood fears. Surely no woman wanted this. It was only a softball, something tossed among churchgoers, not like a hard baseball. He had exposed himself. He wanted to be far away from her, to take his freaky, disturbed self and regain composure and make sure it never happened again. She jumped on his back, wrapping her legs tightly around his waist. He liked having her arms around his neck, though she was strangely heavy. He plodded along, determined to carry her a long time. Her mouth came close to his ear. "Now you have to tell me your other fears."

"I don't have any."

"Everybody has their fears."

"I've got none."

"You're lying. Your face gets funny when you don't like talking about something. Your face is like that now."

"No it isn't." His legs burned with each step. He pushed on.
"Yes it is."

He stopped to let her down.

"I'm not getting off until you tell me." She tightened her legs.

"Lynn, please. I'm in pain."

His legs buckled and she dropped onto her feet.

Her favorite TV show was *thirtysomething*, about these hopeless, navel-gazing boomers. He found them insufferable. But watching it gave him an opportunity to pull her toward him and plant his ecstatic lips on her cheek, then her lips. Lynn was excellent. She observed a proper give and take; she was limber enough to absorb an advance, then press the advantage when he let up. Mouth set to a proper opening, her breath minty tongue came into play only with delicacy. A groan vibrated in his chest, his hunger growing. He found a gap under her shirt and touched warm, bare skin. She pulled back.

"I'm not just a one-night stand." Her neck veins stood at attention.

"Of course you aren't. We've know each other two weeks. Not that I'm saying that's enough time…"

"Are you and Ian LaCoss having some kind of contest?" Her eyes became hard and accusing.

"We're friends, but that doesn't mean I'm like him."

Her eyes fixed on him in an expectant way. She studied his face like a map. A long murderous pause followed. He felt a squirm brewing deep inside, like his spine was about to jump out of his mouth. It had been two weeks, two days already. She had tightened her policy. It might be months, he thought. It was Victorian, or some Third World practice. Over any two-week period, modern couples, who were what some would call morally bankrupt, might exhaust every known sexual position, transmit diseases and then forget one another. Strangely, he didn't mind this lazy schedule. Every day a rosy space within him grew rosier, and the chance of a misunderstanding or a misstep destroying their relationship decreased. And his hunger for her was matched by uncertainty as to what would happen when that magic bell finally chimed.

"What are you thinking about?" she asked. "You're always thinking."

"Oh...this class today."

"You're sublimating. Acute sublimation." Her psych major at work again.

"I'm what?"

She jabbed at his belly with her hands. He squirmed, laughing uncomfortably. "Oh, no! No tickle! No!" Her hands worked at his sides like mischievous terriers; he pulled in his arms tightly to fend her off. She gained leverage and they vibrated with laughter and moans of anguish.

What had happened to him? Suddenly, his limbs were more fluid, his movements smoother, as if magical oil filled his joints. He softly crooned lyrics to The Plimsouls or XTC or Echo & the Bunnymen in a rolling improvisation. Every piece of clothing—the Levi's with the gently worn knees, the soft-washed pastel oxfords with the flapping tails, the band t-shirts—seemed draped onto his body by some fashion genius. A column of sunshine followed him, shining on a boundless smile. Then he came upon Lynn strolling with two girlfriends. She glowed with an Ivory girl health, and he looked great too, and they mauled each other with hugs. He winked at Marie and Linda. The girls beamed as he squeezed Lynn: he was the famous and wonderful Lance! Look at that face. Look at them together. Other students rubbernecked while detouring around them. He backpedaled, on his way again waving, yelling *Catch you later!* and *Let's get together for sure!* and *Be good!* while making unpredictable hand gestures. How cool was he? He was hesitant to admit it, but her presence justified it, necessitated it. He was Harrison Ford with Carrie Fisher, Tom Cruise with

Kelly McGillis (he'd purchased a green nylon flight jacket six months *before* the release of *Top Gun*). He felt brand new and other students seemed to freshly consider him, as if they had overlooked him, or just discovered the intense and hip qualities of Lance Rally, who was dating—did you hear?—the comely and illusive Lynn Van Oster.

Lynn drained a White Russian and jumped off her barstool to dance. It was like her personal music video. Other dancers backed off. She was dazzling, dynamic, doing outrageous turns with choreographed perfection, balance from a lifetime of dance classes. She did funky body rolls, crazy hip gyrations; she was a master of retro stylings. She motioned for him to join her. Lance considered staying glued to his barstool. No way to compete with her. None. But her abilities spurred him to the most incredible dancing of his life. He abandoned previous moves and got carried away with frenzied arm-swinging and spirited feet-shuffling. He turned off his mind and his body produced what seemed a pure expression. They waggled their tongues and carved an impossibly hot space.

That evening in his room, they tottered toward the couch, lip-locked. The cushions cut out his legs from under him. She straddled him, her knees bouncing on either side of his legs. Still infected by dance energy, she pressed her face to his and made a delicious pleading sound. He pawed at the buttons of her blouse. She did a magic trick to free her bra, then flung it away. He ran his hands under her breasts, awed, humbled, like a prostrate peasant before a throned and all-powerful empress. She pulled off his shirt. He fumbled with her hiked-up skirt to locate a zipper, a button, a clasp, a Velcro strip, anything. An erection pressed against the zipper of his jeans into a space agonizingly small, further cramped by her shifting weight. Their breathing had reached a frenetic plateau when she placed her hands on his shoulders, put her nose an inch before his and stated with a graveness, a seriousness that startled him: "I've been praying about this!"

He took several labored breaths. "Just now?"

"No. I mean in general. If we should do this. If we're ready."

"And?"

She shut her eyes as though overcome by terrible pain. She groaned, then said in a desperate voice: "Sex without love is just fucking. And I do not fuck."

He applied brakes to consider this information. His heart raced as if he'd just stepped off a roller coaster. The obscene word lingered, raw and unfamiliar from her lips. He kissed her neck. Had she called for a time out? Was this a problem? Or did she merely want this on the record before they proceeded? He kissed her lips, seeking to dispel the obscenity with tenderness, to disprove the harsh word. She pushed away from him, her eyes fixed on his. He rubbed her ribcage. She grabbed his wrists.

"Well?" She lasered him with a truth-serum look.

He rubbed his teeth together. Her weight pressed him, his legs falling asleep. These monster concepts, these loaded universal ideas whirled in his mind. He wanted a week to digest them, then get back with answers. Sex he was in favor of. He wanted to know the carnal pleasures that hissed from every billboard and movie preview. Fucking, as an activity, sounded violent, impersonal and possibly injurious. Middle-aged people on the verge of divorce did that while drunk. He was after something else. And Love, well, it seemed obvious he was madly in love with her. That powerful, jittery feeling when her eyes found his, and the helium head he walked around with. But it frightened him; did these things add up to love? He had long considered the word absolutely serious and had vowed not to say it until he was ready to commit it all.

He opened his mouth with uncertainty, as if staring down into a canyon. "I…"

"Lance, you never talk to me about your feelings." Her

head tilted to the side, her voice was an unpleasant whimper. "You won't even tell me about your grades."

"Oh, come on. I told you, they are OK, but I want to bring them up."

"That's saying nothing."

"And the goal-setting system I've put in place. You know about that."

"You've mentioned that fifty times. Just because you read a book from your dad doesn't mean your grades are suddenly perfect."

"That's saying a lot."

"No." She shook her head. He'd told her about his high school scores in detail, hoping she would assume his college grades were similar. After every exam and term paper grade she recalibrated her own GPA (3.67) on a calculator.

The mood was now ruined, completely deflated. He felt trapped, too close; her breath was too warm. Her eyes observed him with a clinical probing. "Why are you suppressing? Is this an aversion response? Is there something wrong with you?" Her fingers tugged on his earlobes.

He sighed, propped his head against the wall and closed his eyes. The pattern was clear: her desire to intrude into his skull, to wrench out every fact and feeling, like he was an experiment and she wanted a certain result. He expected to hate her, to have their first argument, but on looking at her again he noticed a mournful edge of gray to her blue eyes, her eyebrows wilting: an expression of longing. He understood she might be hurt by him, perhaps more so than he might be by her. She just wanted to get to know him. She poured out all her emotions, no matter how trivial, crying one instant, leaping in joy or sulking the next. What was wrong with him? He'd never reached this point of explanation before. Lance took a deep breath, determined to hold nothing back, yet uncertain, like he was about to speak Japanese for the first time. "Lynn, I think that you are, you are so amazing..." What did that mean? The Eiffel Tower was amazing, photosynthesis was amazing. He wanted to kick himself.

She blinked, anticipating an important sentiment about to be expressed. The crease of her mouth was horizontal.

He cleared his throat, searching within, into a hazy and unexplored place, a treacherous jungle, a place with no defined path. A place full of scary possibilities and repressed feelings. The possibility of ruination loomed, roaring in Lance's ears. He would say the wrong thing and she would storm off, or turn against him in some crafty way. He came from a family of stoics. Masters of the long silence. So many dinners where his father had radiated anger or tension or great stress or something, a mood—Lance guessed the complexities of adulthood were involved—this mood nameless and unexpressed but powerful, heard in the echoed scrape of utensils on china; his mother reactive but controlled with a similarly intense mood, also nameless; and Kevin filled space with talk of his classes and grades, and Vickie hummed a private tune, and Lance stared into his plate.

"It seems to me..." He spread out his fingers, trying to grasp the right thing to say. He licked his lips and swallowed. Impossible; the jungle was impenetrable. He tilted his head forward in defeat and leaned it against her sternum. She put her hands to either side of his head and shook gently, as though a rattle or slosh might help her guess its contents. Her warm hand slid over his thumping heart. Her fingers tapped, like she was trying to coax a cat out from under a bed.

Talk more about self, he vowed. Talk more about self.

The next day he waited outside her class. She hustled past him, barely looking at him, saying she had to get to the library to do research. That night he called her room and got no answer. Something was wrong. He knocked on her door. It took her a long time to answer. Her hair was tied in an unraveling ponytail. She wore no makeup, gray sweats and round glasses he'd never seen. She smiled weakly.

"May I come in?"

She motioned for him to enter. Dark bags were under her eyes. Did she have a test coming up soon? Then he heard James Taylor, one of the folk singer's many introspective songs, which he always found horribly melancholy. The room's air was heavy, a swamp air. He wished she hadn't let him in. He also noticed albums by Cat Stevens and Jim Croce. A depression-fest. She settled onto the carpet, pulling a blanket around her legs. He stepped over discarded clothing and sat on her unmade bed.

"What's going on?"

She picked at blanket nits and pretended not to hear.

He wondered if he should repeat the question. It was as though combustible gases surrounded her. Maybe the relationship thing was too intense, too painful, maybe not for everybody, and maybe he should run away.

"Are you OK?" he said robotically. "You can talk to me," which seemed the scripted thing to say.

She inspected a toe, chipping off polish with her fingernail. She kicked off the blanket, stood and slapped her hands against her hips. "I don't know if you do want to hear!" Her voice sounded strangely gruff. Then she began stalking the room, tugging her hair and kicking clothing. His eyes grew big: he had not considered her capable of such agitation. Did he know her at all? "I've learned," she said in a raised voice, on the verge of cracking, "I've put things in my life into context. With my psychology I've put things into perspective, like my first boyfriend in tenth grade who I slept with after two weeks and who then immediately broke up with me. I am not going to internalize that rejection." And her next boyfriend had made up a rumor she had screwed three guys after a football game, causing girls around her to whisper the word slut. This was adolescent peer cruelty. She picked up a pillow, worried its fringe, then slammed it to the floor, saying she deserved happiness and respect, and now and forever would expect it from those around her. On her bed, Lance pressed against the wall. He tried not to breathe. Was that rumor true? Suddenly, Lynn held up Chachi the monkey and his detached arm. "You broke Chachi and said nothing! I know you're the one!"

Lance affected great shock, trying to show horror to deflect this charge. Before he could speak, another unbearably sad James Taylor song started. He thought turning off the music might further provoke her. There was a knock on the door and Alice, Lynn's dowdy, freckled roommate appeared. Lynn stamped her foot and shouted, "No! No! This is my time now!" sending Alice away quickly. And, Lynn continued, her freshmen-year boyfriend had cheated on her with several girls, one a known disease-carrier. Lynn stared at Lance, her eyes enraged points. He nodded slowly in the most understanding way he could.

He saw an opening to try and cheer her up. "You just need to think about happier times"—he remembered the photo on her wall—"like when your family took that vacation to Florida!"

"Nobody cared about me then either!" Her voice boomed, her hands became frantic. A pillow crashed into the wall next to him. "Don't you remember me telling you about that? Do you listen to anything I say to you?"

His forehead fell into his hand; he groaned. He'd screwed up because her family visiting the Magic Kingdom in 1974 had started out like a happy story. Lynn had watched *The Wonderful World of Disney* every Sunday night at eight with her sisters Margo and Tina. They begged and begged until Daddy announced a vacation there. That whole summer they dreamt of the castle and seeing beautiful Cinderella. Lynn knew during the parade Cinderella would look directly at her from her carriage, acknowledging Lynn's kindred princess spirit. The spires of the Magic Kingdom she could see from the Contemporary hotel window—there they are! Once through the gates, the family ended up on dull Main Street. Mama and Margo, the shoppers, dragged them all through store after store. Lynn did find a cute

Mickey Mouse pen that was within the family budget; the watch she craved was not. If I buy one, I buy three, Daddy said. Then Daddy insisted on the boring Hall of Presidents: Can you see Lincoln? He freed the slaves. That's Truman, a fine president too. He dropped the bomb. Lynn begged for Adventureland, but there was no splitting up. Next they stood in line for mouse ears, as a man stitched the names Margo, Tina and Lynne on three hats. My name is wrong! Daddy seemed not to hear. Anticipation for the Jungle Cruise died after an hour and a half in line, Lynn at eye level with the rope maze, sweat and fart smells everywhere. On the Ten Thousand Leagues submarine, she looked away from her portal and the chlorinated underwater tableau and took her new pen out of her pocket. It was a pen she would use and enjoy for years and years. She could see Mickey's gloved hands as she rotated it. Leaving the submarine, she felt her pocket. She ran back to her seat and found the pen under a man's foot, slowly turning a pool of water blue. The horrible unhappiness she felt defied everything. It poured from the Florida sky at every turn. This is not happening in the Magic Kingdom, she told herself. No. Not happening. But it continued. During their second hour in line to ride Space Mountain, rumors of mechanical trouble spread down the stagnant line as the family huddled in a dark corridor of the metal mountain. Employees turned everyone around to march out the way they had come. Outside, the family staggered in sunshine as Daddy fumbled with a map. That was when Lynn started to cry and complain and threw her misspelled ears to the ground. Her father collapsed the map into one hand, and with the other hand, a large hand, he smacked her on the rear end, hard. In disbelief, she crumpled to the ground. Her father had been the first man to break her heart.

   She stood before Lance, hands on her hips. She yelled, "All of a sudden you won't talk to me! The first night we met you were so open about yourself. How do I know you're any different from the others?"

Her actions now made sense and he felt stupid. He tried again, "But all of that is over. I'm with you now. I'm not going to cheat on you or say rotten things about you."

"These are just words. Don't patronize me."

"I mean it more than I have ever meant anything."

"Are you just saying this?"

"I'll never do rotten things to you. I promise." He smiled, but inside he braced, awaiting her response. She sat on the bed, leaning against the wall with crossed arms. She wouldn't look at him, but after a while she shifted until her shoulder touched his shoulder. He made a silent vow: it would be his mission to make her happy, to be loyal and to heal her childhood wounds. He had an idea. He would express in writing what his mouth seemed unable to.

CHAPTER EIGHT

THE DEIFICATION OF HAILE SELASSIE

Y ou never knew with Charles Boyd. He might not speak to you for hours after losing a heated game of Donkey Kong, or he might give all his cash to a homeless person, or he might suddenly lecture on Hindu asceticism, sending you straight to the library with a hunger for more knowledge; or if you knocked on his door hoping for refuge from seemingly intractable problems with your girlfriend, hoping the hermetic dead zone of his book-stuffed room might steady your nerves, he might crack his door and stare at you without recognition.

"Let me in," Lance said.

"Why?" A bloodshot eye, presumably Boyd's, stared back.

"It's me. Just open the door."

"Did someone put you up to this?"

"Oh, hell."

Lance kicked the bottom of the door. Charles Boyd sighed, then let him in. He was wearing corduroy pants, shit brown and worn through at the knees, and his faded Jethro Tull t-shirt. A stew of smells crowded Lance's nostrils: armpit odor, dirty socks and a subtle rubbery smell. Boyd squinted and studied Lance, as if planning an amusing prank. "Something's wrong. Something's missing." He pointed to Lance's hip, using his sharp ability to detect weakness. "Where's that girl who's been attached there?"

Lance shrugged, doing his best to feign nonchalance. "Lynn's fine. She's studying. At least I've got a girlfriend. She exists."

A faint smile on Boyd's face. "Then why aren't you with

her? I'll drop it." He sat on a suede ottoman, curling his legs underneath him. A week ago Lance had introduced Lynn to Boyd and he made a fool of himself, bragging about his teaching-assistant responsibilities in a crude, pathetic attempt to impress Lynn. It was obvious: despite Boyd's numerous late-night assurances that he couldn't care less about females, he suffered at the slights and snubs he faced regularly from them. In spite of this, he trudged across campus in stinky, unfashionable clothing, sneering at all things "popular" and paying a social price for having chosen the opposite; then he returned to his room's isolation, cracked open a book and lifted his head, satisfied that everything was under his masterful control. This intrigued Lance: Boyd possessed dangerous knowledge that sprung from his books but went beyond them.

"Have you seen Lucinda Falcon yet?" Boyd asked. The L.A.-based model and actress had flown into town that afternoon to visit LaCoss, who had been hyper for days.

"Not yet. You?"

"Nope. Do you know the plan for tonight? Our welcome for Lucinda?" A mad glint came into Boyd's eye. He reached underneath the cushion of an armchair and pulled out a plump green plastic bag. He cracked a crease in the air lock and inhaled in a sexual way. "Oh, yeah. That's real good. Didn't LaCoss tell you the plan? We're all going to get baked."

"We are?" Lance did a double take, giving away his neophyte status.

Charles Boyd said with a guarded voice, his eyes as dark and wary as a Doberman's, "Is that OK with you, Rally?"

"Er..." Lance scratched behind his ear. His facial muscles tensed. He restrained a nervous laugh. Lynn was the social chair of the Langford Drug Free Coalition. Somebody once passed him a roach at a Tears for Fears concert. He'd passed it on, fearing it was packed with angel dust or that undercover narcs were monitoring him.

All those Mason Prep assemblies came to mind, the

testimonials from invited speakers. We're going to hear something about Drugs today, Dr. Archer would say somberly, which meant horrible things had befallen the guest speaker or their loved one, and they were telling the world. Do you know about Drugs? Do you young people think you know about Drugs? the speakers would say, like they were talking about a radioactive element, or a fatal disease. Those shocking assemblies! Girls left the auditorium crying after seeing slides of the black, diseased lungs of someone long under the nicotine grip of cigarettes; teachers shook their bowed heads in remorse after hearing about a daughter hooked by inhalants. Think you're smart? How smart are you? asked the cousin of a vegetative patient, his psychosis induced by monster quantities of LSD. Lance had felt queasy looking at the bruised veins of heroin addicts. Are you dumb? It's no laughing matter—not after what Drugs did to my son. He started with the alcohol, smoked his lungs out with weed and on to pills and cocaine. He was hooked. Now my son is gone. The speakers never used the podium, they paced, jabbing the air with pointed fingers. Drugs tricked young people, kidnapping and reprogramming their brains, doing a Jekyll and Hyde number on cheerleaders and steering them into white slavery, wiping out the life savings of families. Cars were smashed, educations disrupted. First Lady Nancy Reagan, in designer vermilion, had told them to Just Say No. How many of you are going to avoid Drugs? Stand up! a graying Marine corporal had shouted. Everybody stood, except one wiseass, and hundreds of spring-loaded seats fluttered. Many students just crouched over their seats, waiting for the all clear to sit. The Marine then handed out Drug Free Pledges, which Lance took home to his mother and signed, and she taped the Pledge onto the refrigerator and kissed the cheek of her wise and responsible boy.

So Lance considered it might be best to leave the room. His heart beat insistently. But Madonna had toked in that silly movie. And Captain America and Billy, according to rumor, smoked the real stuff throughout *Easy Rider*. Giving authorities the middle finger suddenly pleased Lance and stirred his youthful juices. He mourned that motherly kiss, recognizing this offer was a demarcation leading to points unknown.

"That's the plan," Boyd said, trying to prompt Lance.

A nervous smile broke across Lance's face. "It's good to have a plan."

"You're more of a remedial case than I thought," Boyd said with perverse glee. "You've got a long way to go." He reached behind him and grabbed a red plastic tube, which Lance somehow knew was a bong. Boyd sat on the edge of a chair, holding the pipe low near his knees and working a lighter delicately with his free hand. This scene was framed by a black and white poster over Boyd's head: the haunting face and hat brim of Robert J. Oppenheimer, the brilliant, troubled nuclear physicist. Another Charles Boyd hero. The poster's caption was Oppenheimer's quote, taken from the Bhagavad-Gita, after the explosion of the first atomic bomb: I Am Become Death, the Destroyer of Worlds.

Lance followed suit, with Charles Boyd working the Bic lighter and giving him the signal to inhale. Voluminous skunky smoke streamed from his mouth, as if venting a fire in his abdomen. Lance reclined in his armchair, a clunker with shredded suede upholstery at the armrests. A melting sensation pulled at his forehead. He became acutely aware of his ears, of a silent roar expanding between them. Everything was on the verge: of an important thing being said, of the moment repeating itself, of possible hysteria.

Boyd tapped his finger on a huge, leather-bound book. "What did Jesus and Buddha and Lao Tsu and all the great god figures say?"

A long pause. "I don't know. That life sucks."

"I'll tell you what they said: Know thyself."

"How does this happen? Am I supposed to hypnotize myself? Does this knowledge come down on a flaming pie?"

"Zen monks can meditate and achieve it in an instant."

Lance endured anxious seconds as he concentrated and tried to accomplish this. He rubbed the armrests of his chair like twin golden retrievers. By smoking, he had taken a path. Vines overhung the path. It was a paved path, but irregular and cracked in spots. Rotting fruit, plums maybe, littered the ground. A heat rose in his cheeks. A profound terror took hold, exactly seven times worse than his first SAT. He feared his life plan was all wrong. Was it flawed in some fundamental way? Oh, God. His mind searched wildly, prodding for unhappy outcomes. The not knowing enveloped him like a suffocating cloak. In a *Twilight Zone* scenario, which seemed highly credible, his futility might only be revealed when it was too late. He imagined himself in a gray business suit, the seams unraveling and splitting every time he moved, a sleeve falling to the floor. His life, so huge, so important, seemed a responsibility he was ill-equipped to handle. It cried out for someone more qualified.

"You've got the fear! You've got it real bad!" Charles Boyd yelled, a relish in his voice, like a hard-ass sea captain. He pulled a rubber ogre mask over his head, stood on a milk crate and began laughing and waving his arms. Lance was distracted from this disturbing spectacle by a Grateful Dead poster. He'd never given hippies enough credit. Now he understood why they liked to dance naked. Oh, those nutty hippies! They were free. They had all skinny-dipped in that pond at Woodstock, and this wild abandon gripped Lance.

And wouldn't you know it, the antimotivational syndrome had already set in. He knew he wouldn't be outlining his Econ notes until exam week, if then, and until then, only a strong wind would disturb the wire-bound pages.

"Bingo!" Charles Boyd held up a record album. He grinned, shaking it triumphantly. He lowered the vinyl record onto a turntable. Pops of static filled the air, followed by rhythmic breathing and Laurie Anderson's soft intonations of "O Superman" which was exactly the soothing touch that Lance needed. Boyd rubbed his glasses with a silk cloth, consumed by insane deliberateness, like a fastidious old man. Lance felt a great fondness for Boyd, a kinship. They were both angel-headed hipsters, outlaw brothers!

Boyd was developing a fascinating theory: "...the point of the music's repetition is that it mimics the human heart, it being ironic that Superman, possessed with super powers, still has a vulnerability, that being kryptonite, and ultimately this humanizes him, so Laurie Anderson is playing around with iconography and mythology..."

The door flung open and Ian LaCoss and Lucinda Falcon breezed in. She was not just a glossy fabrication from magazines or the imagination of Ian LaCoss. Long brown hair fluttered behind her alarmingly beautiful teen face. She had on a black silk dress which flaunted her curvaceous body, and thong sandals. Her legs were tan and slender. A heat surfaced on Lance's neck. Lucinda was proof LaCoss existed on a higher plain, his acting career attainable. LaCoss wore a sky-blue Hawaiian shirt, his hair wetted and combed back. They stood arm in arm, this glamor couple, like conquering young stars at a premiere. They each seemed a bit flushed, as if fresh from a tryst.

"Hey, dudes. Smells like a party," LaCoss said.

"Let's get groovy," Lucinda said, shaking her hips.

Charles Boyd sat on the edge of his seat, frozen, stricken by the vision of Lucinda Falcon. His smile changed into a hard grimace, as though his heart was a window, its panes shattering from rocks of envy and lust and disbelief. "This is my buddy Charles Boyd," LaCoss said to Lucinda, patting Boyd on the face to try to rouse him. Boyd stood and she gave him a European double kiss, which seemed to reawaken him. Likewise, she kissed Lance and scent traces of hyacinth and rose petals from her smooth face sent him into a frenzy. He couldn't take his eyes off her. She and LaCoss sat on the couch, smoked and caught up.

"Look at you," Lucinda said to Lance. "You look so sad. You're the saddest guy in the world."

"Oh, my God! Do you think that could be true?" It was the worst conceivable thing she could have said to him.

"He's having some problems with his woman right now," LaCoss said. "He's rather uptight. Actually, he's always uptight."

Lucinda put her hand on Lance's arm and closed her eyes. "Oh, I feel it. You've got a serious psychic blockage."

"She's got para-cognitive abilities that are pretty advanced," LaCoss said.

"Oh my God."

"Don't freak out. It can be changed." She extended a lithe hand to him. He held her long, delicate fingers. "Close your eyes. Lose the fear. Just let it go." Their arms swayed and kept swaying like they were all alone in a meadow. She had a wonderful touch, a strong, positive energy he felt moving up his arm, and he thought her touch was something like love, and in this small way he loved her back, and he was convinced she had para-cognitive abilities or possibly was an alien, and realized LaCoss was smitten, totally in love with her, dangerously so, and after what seemed several minutes he opened his eyes and felt much better. She winked and he winked back. LaCoss, who had introduced her to his talent agent, bragged she had just acted in her first movie, a Scarface of the L.A. barrios. Offhandedly, she described stunt guys crashing a car into a house.

Lucinda, who regarded Charles Boyd as being loveably odd, said to him, "I don't know if I can take that anymore." She nodded toward the Laurie Anderson on the turntable.

Charles Boyd located a Bob Marley album. Lance had never been crazy about reggae. It had always seemed repetitive and awkward. But this record sounded fantastic, making their heads sway and nod like waves on the ocean. Lucinda burst into laughter. She tossed her head back, trembling and laughing in a hearty way. She pointed to the top of Charles Boyd's head.

Boyd looked about, panicked.

"He's got one big strand that's sticking up. Kind of like Ed Grimley."

Lance and LaCoss stood to inspect Charles Boyd's head. One clump toward the back did point skyward, much like the Martin Short *SNL* character. They wheezed with laughter, convulsing violently, stoking Lucinda's laughing. This epidemic infected Charles Boyd, until they all bounced and quaked like cartoon characters. Lance's stomach became painfully knotted. LaCoss began to cry, and hung on to Lucinda to steady himself. They took deep breaths.

"*Saturday Night Live* totally sucks right now," LaCoss said.

"It's so bad I can barely watch it," Lance said.

"Why can't they write better stuff?" LaCoss went into a lengthy description of his idea, The Pharmacy Sketch. LaCoss planned to star in the sketch on the night of his guest debut on *SNL*, shortly after starring in his first hit film. In the sketch, the cashiers and pharmacists at a pharmacy have obviously been sneaking drugs. One person snockered on Valium who can barely stay awake; one person on speed who yells at customers; one person hallucinating on Dilaudid. A state auditor who suspects pilfering shows up and the pharmacy people struggle to keep it together; the guest star is the "new guy" who is puzzled by the odd behavior. Lance found the idea brilliant and entertaining. Lucinda urged LaCoss to mail it in to the writers.

"Nope. I'm saving it. I'll tell the writers once I'm on."

"They'll never do the skit," Charles Boyd said. "It's funny, but the censors won't allow it. They'll see it as glorification."

"I think he could be right," Lucinda said. "The feds are constantly trying to shut my parents down. They run a head shop near Venice Beach. My mom is a licensed sex therapist." Lance marveled at this combination.

"It's not just your parents." LaCoss cut his eyes to make sure he had everyone's attention. "A master computer in the basement of the Pentagon knows everything about everyone.

They can read a license plate from outer space. Once, for two weeks this mysterious yellow car followed me around. Freaked me out."

"When will the madness end?" Lance said, being sarcastic.

"It won't stop as long as Reagan is around," Charles Boyd said, close to rage at this mention. A picture of the commander in chief popped into Lance's mind. Not the happy-go-lucky Reagan, but the one who talked in clipped, determined tones. The avenging granddad who bombed other nations. The Gipper stared down into the room with disgust, ready to fling them into a federal penitentiary. Lance sneered back defiantly at the old man and his old ideas.

The opening strains of "No Woman, No Cry" played, the group quieted by Bob Marley's lilting, mournful voice.

"Reggae is religious music to the Rastafarians," Charles Boyd said. "It's like gospel music to them." He slipped into a stirring monologue. Lance, LaCoss and Lucinda listened, rapt, their mouths ajar as they fixed on his tales of the disaffection of black slaves on Jamaican sugar plantations, the spawning of Afrocentric religions, and the prophecy that a messiah would lead them back to Africa. Then, in 1930, a new king of Ethiopia was crowned as Ras Tafari—the Emperor Haile Selassie I. In Jamaica, they latched onto him as the black Christ, and created a religion with its own sacraments. Charles Boyd spoke grandly, waving his hands, easily recalling details from his fluid and impressive mind. His audience was awed by him and hung on every sentence like he was a cult leader with the keys to heaven. They were ready to follow him, throw roses at his feet, obey his commands.

"What happened?" LaCoss asked, shaking with anticipation. "Did the Rastafarians go to the promised land to find their messiah?"

"Selassie was overthrown in Ethiopia. Bob Marley and others went and found an ignored, broken man. It was quite traumatic."

Everyone sat wide-eyed, holding their breath, considering that catastrophically bad things might happen in their lives—ruin, disease, crushing disappointment—and this dark vibe was a bummer. It passed, and they all laughed for no reason.

The group spilled out of the quiet dorm. On the steps, LaCoss and Lucinda snuck a kiss. Charles Boyd yawned and scratched his sprawling bohemian hair. Staring into the void of night, Lance reflected on himself with a sparkling fascination. Things had become fantastic. He had these cool amazing friends. And he had Lynn, who embodied a continuing miracle.

He had written a customized poem for her, mailing it the day before. He'd wanted to impress her by composing an expression of how he felt, the written word less threatening than face to face. A love note, though without using the momentous L-word. Instead of a sappy letter or clichéd verse, he wanted to pioneer a radical new form. He brainstormed during an Econ class, his heart leaping to the ceiling with elation, his mind unusually focused and lively with this creative task while his dour classmates were bent over their desks. Its creation consumed an entire evening.

> Lynn
> with the luxurious skin
> skin like the Milky Way   like blown galaxies so far away
> Her ocean eyes
> her lovely thighs   cheekbones high to the eminent sky
> to kiss her oh so rosy lips
> to touch her golden hair   her gossamer stare
> my heart
> would ache and probably break
> should she never see me again.

Now, his eyelids heavy, he still felt very tweaked, but he burst with pride as he reflected on the brilliance that lurked within his creation. Lynn would flip out. Out of the darkness came the sound of rushing feet. A dim figure padded across the lawn. A ghost? Then Lynn's tearful face and radiant hair came into the light. She ran up the stairs, holding the note Lance had mailed to her. Then she was embracing Lance, saying she had never gotten anything like it before. He tightened his arms around her in a satisfying embrace.

"So…you liked it?"

"I love it! It made me cry. I had to find you. Is that stupid? Hello everyone."

LaCoss said, "Way to go Robert Frost," and tapped a chummy fist against Lance's shoulder. Lance realized LaCoss's silence while reading the poem days before had not been confusion or embarrassment but sincere appreciation. Boyd smiled with unusual warmth at Lance and Lynn before melting into irritation at being a fifth wheel. Lynn and Lucinda regarded each other intently, then seemed relieved to be going separate ways. LaCoss, Lucinda and Boyd descended the stairs. Lance watched them go, moving across the lawn, sentimental about his evening with his friends. He wanted to yell something clever and memorable, but what? He could think of nothing.

"I didn't know you could write," Lynn said.

"I'm not sure I can."

Lynn's joyous face was pressed up into his, filling his field of vision. A deep and thorough terror shook him. Here was Lynn, in all her wholesomeness, with her vulnerable and impressionable heart and here he was…a drug-user, under the influence and unstable, his mind a hardboiled pair of lobes. His heart lunged with irregular beats, like a madman twisting synthesizer knobs. It was exactly the way the guest speakers had predicted: communication difficulties, wedges driven between loved ones, calamity and disaster from even a single usage. They hadn't even had sex yet. "Let's go for a walk." He thought he might escape negative energies this way. She gripped his hand tightly and they turned right on Duncan, heading away from campus. Her presence at his side gradually calmed him, though the tilt of her eyebrows seemed to indicate her antennae were picking something up.

"How long did it take to write my poem?" she asked, gushing, "The vocabulary is so amazing."

"Oh, several hours. I wrote like six different versions."

"Have you written poems for anyone else?"

"Of course not. Only you." His answer caused her to make several small jumps.

At a neighborhood park they ran onto the playground, pulling each other along. He sat on a plastic frog with a steel spring and rocked it with childlike abandon. She ran to the whirligig and jumped on. He got it spinning, then scrambled up to the raised middle part. Lynn climbed up to the pointed metal center also. She weaved her legs around him and pressed her face close. "You seem different tonight," Lynn said, locking her eyes with his.

He studied her shadowed face as the world spun around them. It was hopeless. Like them all, she was a mind reader. This was so oppressive.

"I have to admit something."

"Yes?" She pulled on his arm, alarmed.

"I smoked pot tonight."

She breathed in quickly, "Oh my God! I didn't think you were into that."

"I don't know that I am. My friends were doing it, so I tried it. Is that OK?"

She stared at him, looking concerned. "I know this girl, and she got really messed up using drugs."

"I don't even know I'll do it again. Probably not."

"Tell me you won't. Promise."

"I promise I won't do it again."

The playground was a protected pocket of dark. The

seesaws and monkey bars cut mysterious shadows. A small airplane droned overhead. "What are you thinking about?" she asked softly, peering up at him. "Please tell me. Please."

Several things immediately dominated his mind. Things he had never discussed with anyone, that he preferred not to think about himself. In a cruel turn, he experienced a mind lock and realized he would either talk about these things or have nothing to say. The idea of letting them out pained him. They were behind a watertight submarine hatch, maybe for good reason. These things might offend or frighten her. Perhaps he would expose something dark and hideous, like a mutant creature that would extend its deformed claws and flash blind eyes when exposed to the light of her attention. She might be horrified, or flee.

"I…"

"Yes?" She smiled, rubbing her chin on his arm.

Being close to another human being, this intimacy thing—it was much harder than merely staring at Cheryl Tiegs on the wall.

"Ahhh. Umm."

"Tell me." She set her teeth together, as if all her patience were about to end.

He squirmed.

He sensed Lynn would not ridicule him or judge him. Her interest was quite moving. Her soft, warm lips pressed against his cheek. A pathway within him opened. He was suddenly flooded, overwhelmed, as if he sat beside himself and had X-ray vision into his own soul. "You   remember   the   Junior Achievement project I told you about, the one I won that award for, that everybody said was such an original idea?"

She nodded, her eyes filled with wonder, as if she expected a delightful present.

"A guy at a California chapter did the same thing. That's where I got the idea. So I kinda borrowed the idea. OK, stole it. I just couldn't tell people. Every time I see that award on the wall, I think what a fake I am, and that maybe I should have told." He hung his head and regret burned.

"It doesn't matter where the idea came from. That doesn't negate all the work you did. You should feel proud."

"You think so? It's true I did all the work." He sat up straighter, his head lighter. The sound of his voice pleased him and he wanted to hear it again. She smiled. In fact, she was enthralled, clutching his arm tighter. Her big eyes and quiet observance lent this admission an importance. Suddenly, he felt invincible. A realization came, a leap. Here was the big one. He considered holding it back. If anything would send her away or horrify her that he was a vacillating wussy boy, it was this: "Sometimes I think I am completely screwing up in every way. That I'm not doing it right. And despite everything, I'll end up as this huge disappointment. There's so much...pressure. For as long as I can remember I've felt it. I just hate it." His hands were tight fists, pressing into his thighs.

"I know. I feel it too."

"But beyond that, sometimes I think, am I going in the right direction?" His head tilted to the side, toppled by exhaustion. Had he betrayed himself? Was such talk ruining his chances?

"Yes, you are! You are definitely going places, Lance. I think your career idea about business school is wonderful. That has great versatility. You'll be very successful." She tightened the grip of her arms around his arm, pulling it tight to her side. "It's really important to have a plan. And to stick with that plan. If you don't have a plan then you're just sailing to nowhere. So many people don't and that's sad. That's just a waste."

"I just wonder about being happy. I worry about this."

She brushed back hair from her face. "It's not easy to be happy. It doesn't just happen. You have to work for it, and make sacrifices to get it."

He had to agree. It had been his experience too, though he disliked the idea.

Lynn was enthralled, tracing her finger along the seam of his jeans, the jeans of her fascinating and mysterious man. He felt unburdened, elevated by an immense helium cloud. He had once thought of emotions as weakness, girlish things, but he realized honesty about them, feeling at one—it was power. She rubbed his full thigh now. He leaned back to facilitate more soul-searching. Lynn said in a soft voice, "Tell me more."

His mind jumped to Dr. Henry Shatzer. Don't mention that, he thought. No. It was evidence of insanity. Skip it. But he couldn't resist. "In fifth grade my parents sent me to this psychiatrist for several months. It was for no good reason." He glanced at Lynn, pausing, trying to gauge her reaction. She looked concerned, but like she was working hard to be neutral, clinical. "Anyway, he asked me these creepy questions and I spent a long time thinking before I answered them. Some I ignored, because I was convinced if I answered them wrong he would think I was insane and I'd be yanked out of school and sent to the nut house. You know in *One Flew Over the Cuckoo's Nest*, when they stick that metal pole up Jack Nicholson's nose to lobotomize him? I figured that might be me so I lied, I lied to all of his questions."

Her face remained kind, but her eyes were enlarged. "So what? You were scared. You were just a boy then." The Dr. Shatzer thing, he sensed, was a little too weird for her. It was late. Lynn had her arms around her knees.

"Cold?"

"Yes. Let's go back to my room." She took his hand.

Under a streetlight Lynn kissed him, forcing her tongue into his mouth. Apparently, words were a powerful aphrodisiac. Lynn's roommate was out of town.

At her dorm room he had a long satisfying pee. He slurped at handfuls of faucet water. He opened the door to find Lynn standing completely naked, her light orange complexion consistent all over. She put her hands gingerly behind his head, with an ultra-serious, almost stunned expression. He found her naked self touching, though it was an intimidating sight, since the time was now, right now. It was go time, whether he was ready or not. At that moment, decidedly not. He was tempted to be anxious and to have ruinous thoughts. But Lynn was calming and very appealing.

"Do you have anything?" she asked.

Of course, he didn't. Lynn walked over and dug inside one of Alice's drawers. She walked back in a delicate way and handed him a condom, which—after thinking a long moment—he tossed onto the bed.

She stood before him again, blinking.

He lost his pants and boxers. Then they were on the bed, rubbing, kissing and blowing little breaths of air on the other, the naked expanse of the other wondrous and overpowering. Teenagers, doing what maybe they shouldn't be doing and loving it. Things moved fast; each seemed to need the other badly. He concentrated furiously, wired, drunk on stimulus. She was a naked bus that had struck him. There was nothing not to savor or celebrate, oh boy, and they were linked, with nothing else to expose or explore. He possessed more nerve endings than seemed possible. God, or universal intelligence, or some powerful force like it, existed, and this force, if it was a person, would be a wonderful friend. She seemed more of a natural than him, and he struggled to match her rhythm. She gasped, her breath warm on his face. That glorious tension reached critical mass and he gasped, his vision blurring, and for several seconds he had no idea where he had come from, no idea where he was going or even who he was, and a strange white horizon stretched and flickered before his eyes.

They slept. He woke before her and rolled out of bed on a cold morning. He peered out her frosted window. Feeling tingly and tranquil, he watched her sleeping swaddled in the covers. He felt this incredible head buzz, like lucky breaks kept falling his way. Also a vigor, a strength worthy of a superhero, like he could suck more air into his chest than a mere mortal. A goofiness too, as if he were about to sing la la la from a pop song. He leaned close to her soft face, framed in a golden glow by a random though ideal arrangement of hair. When she woke she would welcome him under the sheets, their hearts pressing against each other, keeping time. She was the perfect girl he had always dreamed about. There she was! Right there! A huge portion of his personal prophecy had come true. At that moment—a majestic double gate swinging open, welcoming him—he believed, for the first time with sincerity, that life would be generous and kind, and all the success he wanted would be his. He really loved her. That was how he thought—curious he hadn't voiced this. Why not? So he shook her awake.

"I love you, Lynn."

In a sleepy voice, she said she loved him too. Then she wanted to hear it from him again. And again.

CHAPTER NINE

A SUCCESSFUL FUTURE

Kevin called to chat, but also in an older-brother mind-control way to ask if Lance was aware how grade-conscious grad schools were. Without the grades, forget it. And was he aware how much their parents were paying to send him to Langford? It was "a huge hit on their savings." Kevin, the brain surgeon in training, inquired as to how things were going that semester—better than last year, right? Certainly Lance was improving the situation? Lance smelled the stench of family conspiracy and slammed the phone when he hung up.

He found a 3.75! GPA poster under his bed. This subconscious device had ceased programming his brain when it tore loose from the wall during a passionate night with Lynn. He wondered about exams. When were those pesky things? Another month or so. He found his calendar under a stack of mail. November 15. Three days until his first exam. A shock tensed Lance's limbs and soured his stomach, like he'd been told he had three days to live. He considered downgrading his GPA goal, but to correct last year's damage he'd need to get a 3.75 this semester to get into a top tier business school. No problem, he thought, ashamed by his false confidence. He inventoried the work to be done; made calendar notes of reading, outlining, notes to be borrowed, an Econ paper to be written. The tasks, stacked chockablock, occupied every day, beginning from that moment until his last final.

Step one would be to locate Carson Wombley, Jr. and borrow notes from an Econ class they both were in.

On the first floor, Wombley was parked on a couch in the common room. His slicked- back hair glistened with a foul-smelling gel he combed in every morning, like he was a bond trader or a mafioso. He wore a yellow Polo shirt and seventy-dollar stonewashed jeans with horizontal razor slits down the length of each leg. He was watching *Lifestyles of the Rich and Famous*. Robin Leach followed around Donald Trump on Trump's new gleaming yacht, inspecting the gold faucets. When asked about his Bahamas casino swap with Mike Douglas, Leach hinting that Douglas had been had, Trump said with a smug glint that Douglas had received a quality casino.

Lance had seen this one. The pitch of Robin Leach's voice climbed higher, hysterical from the intoxication of moneyed privilege. The show was fairly pretentious, but it snuck up on you. The black sand beaches of Tahiti. A lush Monte Carlo estate. Who didn't dream? The possibility existed, if Lance worked hard and played his cards right—this possibility dancing before him, luring him like an exotic beach—that fantastic things might happen, that he might be super successful. A career that was not just a standard climb, like his dad, like Kevin, but a wildly lucrative career, one that provided primo vacation homes and early retirement. This happened with some people, so Lance didn't rule it out for himself. Not yet.

"That's one crazy bastard," Wombley said of Trump, with a brooding jealousy. It was a high compliment. Only a sick bastard, like T. Boone Pickens or Adnan Khashoggi, or a serious hard-ass bastard, like Michael Milken, dwelled above the crazy bastard category.

"Could I borrow your notes? I missed all that stuff on monetary policy."

"Macro hasn't exactly been a priority for you, has it?" Wombley leaned back, sinking into the couch. He inspected Lance with mild disappointment. Then his eyes narrowed, seeming to consider him more unfavorably. Lance might be an outright loser.

"I went to most classes. I missed four, maybe five. I've been busy."

Wombley took a swig of his ubiquitous diet soda, blinking. "Lynn is in that modern dance troupe, isn't she? You are one lucky guy."

Days before, Wombley had intruded as Lance and Lynn were eating lunch and made a big show of trying to remember Lynn's name, holding her hand too long. Wearing a t-shirt that said I CAN S.E.E. CLEARLY NOW, Wombley went into a lengthy description of the organization he had founded, Student Entrepreneurial Encounter. Lance rolled his eyes while Lynn gave her cheerful, clear-eyed attention. He had gotten a $2,000 grant from the Langford Senate to set up student internships with small companies. Encount erships, he called them. There was an article in the *Langford Owl* with his picture. And it was just voted Best New Organization! Lynn opened her mouth in socially appropriate awe. But Lance knew no encounterships had been set up so far.

Then Wombley passed out his fresh two-page resume to Lance and Lynn. Two Rotary scholarships and a Cantrell Scholarship. GPA: 3.59. He had been stockpiling organizations and titles since his first day on campus: senior warden, Zeta Alpha Millennial Society;   president, Young CEO Forum; president, Young CFO Forum; co-captain, Accounting and Actuarial Team; co-chair, Mentors For Middle Schoolers; cofounder, Excellence in Action. He hadn't slowed down during summers. An internship with Robinson Humphrey;   an internship with the Council of Economic Relations. He'd gotten his real estate license and sold three houses the previous summer. Wombley's resume was an action verb masterpiece. He was an organizing, volunteering, achieving juggernaut. A dim hatred welled within Lance for Wombley and every wonder kid who had started a multimillion dollar business at age seventeen. Who could keep up with these people? What was wrong with them? Every precocious noser who turned in their algebra first, who ran to the front of the lunch line, who gleefully busted grade curves. They always had to be first. They left everyone exhausted. Everyone had to stand around them and applaud, awed by their perverse effort and the glow of achievement that clung to their determined faces.

Wombley said to Lynn, "I'm a little worried that with everything I've done it's too long."

"One and a half pages is acceptable," Lynn said with authority. "Two full pages is pushing it."

This was several days after Lance had pieced together his first resume. Lynn had convinced him it was necessary. He gladly would have procrastinated further had she not pulled out her resume guide and a pad of paper and started writing. It had been painful to fill just half a page with his meager college accomplishments. Lynn had patted Lance's hand and said they needed to talk about some quality extracurriculars to go along with his rising GPA from this semester.

"I just need your notes for an hour to copy them."

"Dancers, oh man. They got that flexibility." Wombley leered, his acne scars prominent. "They can twist those limbs in every direction."

Lance grimaced, trying to hide how offended he was. "OK. About your notes."

"What can we do about my notes?"

"You can let me borrow them." Lance didn't know anyone else in the class.

"Could I?"

"I just want to copy those days. Not a big deal."

"Let's see what we can do." Wombley gave no sign of leaving the couch.

Lance's annoyance level rose dramatically. This was a negotiation. Wombley was calculating what he wanted. He had a cassette series called Power Negotiating. Stuart W. Higginboth, the creator of this "system," stood on the tape covers in a double-breasted suit, leaning against a Rolls Royce. All of life was a negotiation, Higginboth said in his high-pitched cajoling voice, a give and take with winners and losers.

Wombley used negotiating skills, usually with a loud voice, to argue away library fines and get free meals in restaurants.

"Dammit. I forgot to call my dad this morning," Wombley said.

Lance rubbed his eyes in frustration.

The Wombleys were a recognized Atlanta family. They got their money from huge real estate development deals in Florida and elsewhere, which had set them up and made them Wombleys and allowed their lifestyle of skiing in Colorado and meeting at Arizona spa resorts for Thanksgiving. His father, who Lance had seen driving Carson around campus in a convertible Jaguar, was a thick-necked man with a conspicuous tan and a knack for land speculation. He now indulged himself in stocking his 3,000-bottle wine cellar and his photography collection. Having put the system in a headlock and given it a few noogies, he now did whatever the hell he wanted. That was very appealing.

This all contributed to Lance feeling he was on a lower social rung in Carson Wombley, Jr.'s presence. Though Lance's father did well, and many properly considered Lance a child of privilege, being a Rally involved fretting, bargain shopping and trying to appear middle-class. Like the Rallys had made an uncertain beachhead into their tax bracket and had dug in, brows furrowed, lest they be rolled back by wasting any precious treasure. It was up to Lance's generation to storm the cliffs.

"About the macro notes."

"There's a practice test on file at the Student Union," Wombley said. "Maybe you could get a copy for me?"

"Just give me your notes without a bunch of negotiating bullshit."

"The practice test would help both of us."

"All right, whatever."

They went to Wombley's room to get his notes. His answering machine blinked urgently. In the taped message, Wombley's older brother Dirk blurted out sentences in a loud voice.

Carson Wombley, Jr.'s face lit up with admiration for his lovable, wild-ass brother. He told a story about Dirk starting out as a stockbroker at Shearson Lehman. "Dirk was making thirty phone calls a day and the quota is a hundred. The other junior people are dialing their asses off. But Dirk takes two-hour lunches, then reads *Road & Track* for an hour. Everyone is like, earth to Dirk, the end is near. The senior broker calls him in and says he is most displeased. Dirk laughs in his face and walks out. He says 'They can't fire me.'

"And they don't, because Dirk has his own clients already. At lunch he was meeting rich people at this restaurant bar. He signs them up one after another. He drinks Manhattans and tells them how he blew out his arm in the college World Series, how he's getting married in six months. It's all bullshit. So Dirk goes to management and says, 'I need my salary tripled and two people under me to handle my client portfolios.' They give it to him. Their attitude is, whatever you want, Dirk."

Lance's eyes bulged enviously. "How do guys like that do it? For some people grades mean nothing."

"Dirk pulled a 3.8 at UNC. He never took notes, but Dirk could snap his fingers and ace the class. He was even a borderline alcohol rehab candidate. He was banned from three bars."

"Amazing," Lance said. A small piece of him folded in on itself, knowing he was incapable of such feats. Though Dirk was a liar, a cheat. Rallys were honest to the point of detriment. Also, he lacked the nerve to lie convincingly and the guilt made it not worthwhile. It was rather sad, to grow up thinking the world worked a certain way, then find people like Dirk and Carson Wombley getting anything they wanted. The triumph of assholes was always upsetting.

Wombley handed the notes toward Lance, then pulled them back. "Maybe you could get a Sociology practice test while you're at it. Or maybe—"

"No!"

"Maybe—"

Lance wrestled away the notebook and walked out.

His Econ exam went poorly. He wandered away from the Econ building with an aching head, a sour stomach: the feeling of a journeyman boxer leaving the arena after a pounding from a contender with hands like mallets. The next day, Lance met LaCoss to review before their Philosophy exam. In a room on the fifth floor of the main library, LaCoss sat on a conference table, cross-legged like some anarchist yogi, in a black Charlatans UK t-shirt and pentagram necklace, his hair pulled back and fixed by a rubber band. He blinked his eyes rapidly at his spiral notebook. Weirdly perfectionistic about spelling, LaCoss used erasable pens. Their greasy blue ink stained his fingers and wrists. "Hey, man. This one Immanuel Kant idea really screwed with my head. It affected me for days."

"What's that?" Lance sat at the end of the table, taking the CEO spot.

"This idea that there is a difference between perceiving and thinking, right? One of those distinctions within a priori judgments. That your senses and your brain are working on different levels."

Lance felt panic. LaCoss actually knew more than he did. But then LaCoss had taken the class very seriously. He did each assignment without fail, his finger tracing sentences as he read. He would whisper *I like that part* during lectures, seeking additions to his grab bag of beliefs. Lance had found LaCoss inside his room one night, the lights off, a bandanna wrapped around his eyes, trying to enter the Aristotelian realm of pure reason. After an hour he got there, he claimed, but only for two minutes, during which he channeled the spirit of Jimi Hendrix. Lance had no idea about LaCoss's GPA or if he was even keeping score.

"Didn't Descartes make the same distinction?" Lance asked.

"I don't believe so."

"Or was it Bentham?" Lance yawned. "I'm getting confused. I could use about twenty hours of sleep." He had intended to read the Bentham chapter two weeks ago, but instead he smoked a bowl with Charles Boyd and spent two hours contemplating why Moe of the Three Stooges was such a cruel and power-hungry hard-ass.

LaCoss slid off the table top. "Sterile knowledge is forgettable knowledge. To remember stuff you've got to fuse emotion with knowledge. You've got to feel the material." LaCoss demonstrated this technique by, as he described it, doing Nietzsche. LaCoss took in a deep breath and gritted his teeth. His body quivered, his fingers bending into claws, an expression of tortured elation passing through him. Then he looked up to the ceiling and jumped on top of the table. "I will not be bowed! I will not be restrained! HA-HA-HA! I will not conform to the repression of bourgeois society!" He pounded his fists on his chest, warping his shouting. A couple passing the room stared in with alarm. "I am the happy warrior! My will to power will be satisfied! I will become a higher being!"

Lance applauded mildly, reflecting on LaCoss's rabid endorsement of Nietzsche. LaCoss was a Nietzschean sort of person.

"You'll never forget Nietzsche now, will you?" LaCoss said.

"I will not."

"Now you give it a shot."

Lance was unsure if he was capable of blending scholasticism with Method acting. He tried Plato's *Crito*. Sentenced to death, an Athenian business man offered to buy Socrates out of prison but Socrates refused, choosing to serve his sentence instead. Lance stood and held his index finger in the air, a possible gesture of classicism. In a reasoned voice, "I will accept the laws of my beloved state. I have enjoyed its benefits and protections. Now I place my own obligation to the law above my own desires."

LaCoss flipped his pencil onto the table, frowning. "I give you a C for presentation, but you get an F for interpretation. He was condemned to death because people didn't like him. His trial was a joke. Why should he obey?"

"The principle is good. Every citizen must obey the law, right?" Lance nodded. "There would be chaos without that."

LaCoss winced. "That 'my country, right or wrong' stuff is horseshit!"

And so LaCoss divided philosophers between the lackeys to the powers that be and those who sounded the call to arms. He performed his philosophic repertoire. For Aristotle's natural masters theory (only a few had the rational ability for self-rule) he clutched his arms as though straightjacketed and struggled valiantly, like a determined Tom Cruise. Kant's Categorical Imperative (the moral value of an action could only be judged by the motives for acting) sent LaCoss to his knees, clutching at the air as if beaten down by heavy-handed do-gooders, like Brando circa *On the Waterfront*. He embraced Mill's utilitarian directive (that the greatest good be done for the greatest number) with the hippie purity of an extra from *Hair* by opening his hands around his face like the petals of a sunflower.

Lance drank some of LaCoss's coffee. He wasn't normally a coffee drinker, but he needed to stay up well into the night to cover the material. It made him feel warm and jittery. He poured more.

"Slow down on that stuff, java monkey. It's late," LaCoss said.

"I've got hours to go. I need to rack up a big number on this exam."

"It's all grades with you. Grades, grades, grades. Your payoff is in your liberal arts education, not the numbers. Wasn't that Theodore Ivan Langford's whole point?"

Riding a caffeine power surge, Lance felt argumentative. "There's this whole system that's been devised. Called a grade point average. You are accepted or denied admission into graduate schools because of it. Jobs are given on this basis. It's a society-wide kinda thing."

"You don't have to give in to it."

"I didn't create the system. I don't like it either. But it exists, so I am dealing with it. I am dealing with my present circumstances."

LaCoss pulled off the rubber band and shook out his hair. "Fuck the systems. What I'm about is freedom. That's why I'm an actor. Remember in *Easy Rider*, when Captain America and Billy rode across America on their choppers? That's what I want my life to be."

Lance pointed a finger. "How did they get their freedom? What did they do to buy those bikes? They turned a cocaine deal. They got a huge wad of money and then set off."

"They didn't need the money."

"Oh, now you're telling me money doesn't matter."

"Hah! You haven't covered Thorstein Veblen yet, have you?"

Lance had not. LaCoss accused Lance of falling into Veblen's trap. "With the Industrial Revolution, the new leisure class became the most admired class. The rich, sedentary capitalists were seen as skillful, and labor of the working class seen as undesirable. The commoners tried to mimic the leisure class to feel worthy, this shame fueling a competitive envy that motivated them."

"That's all very interesting," Lance said, slapping his notebook on the table. "All I know is I'm going to be a member of that leisure class and I'm going to laugh at people like you."

LaCoss laughed—a cruel, haunting laugh. "Congratulations, Lance. You have now officially become your father." He packed up his books.

"Shut up!" Lance tried to refocus on his notes.

Alone in the conference room, Lance felt the evening slide past. The Lynn cravings began. While studying, he'd secluded himself from her for four days. A sweet conjugal certainty had consumed his semester, and with each day of separation the longing became more intense. She would be crawling under her comforter at this moment, wearing only panties and a baby-blue t-shirt graced with a cartoon kitty cat. Maybe just the t-shirt and nothing else. The shirt swishing against her upper thighs, that soft and healthy swell of muscle. No! he told himself. Stop it! Focus! Too late. This flashback led to another, then another, to an evening of the symphony and a chichi restaurant and then Lynn's black dress slinked down to her ankles—remarkably like that scene in every Raquel Welch movie—and she whispered in a direct and possessed voice, Do whatever you want to me. The most provocative thing ever uttered, it froze him, like their other times were merely a warm-up. She wanted the super fantastic. She wanted Michelangelo and he was still dawdling with crayons. He hadn't thought much about creativity; it was all he could do to stay under control and execute the basics. He had ripped off one of his shoes and flung it across the room, hoping raw enthusiasm might bring improvisation.

The library closed at 2 a.m. Back in his room in Oswald, Lance spread notes around his desk with jittery hands, still drinking coffee. Around 4 a.m., a sludgy, burning sensation gnawed at his stomach and his thoughts slid together. He read sentences over and over. He lay down. His eyes dropped shut like dehydrated marathon runners hitting the pavement, but his rapid heart pounded to prevent sleep.

He was roused at 7:30 a.m. by shouting. The exam was an hour away. Tracing the noise, he walked down the hall to LaCoss's room. LaCoss stood, holding a book. "Listen to this from Westermarck. This totally rips!" He read a convoluted passage about ethical relativity Lance couldn't follow. Lance sat in a chair and rubbed his eyes. He sensed a dropping sensation in his abdomen, like a terrible diarrhea brewing.

"Showtime, my friend." LaCoss clapped his hands next to Lance's ear. "Fight or flight, man. Get psyched. I'm loving it!" He poked stereo buttons. A staccato roar of drums blared from speakers: a Husker Du song with a sheer, powerful sound. LaCoss performed a savage air guitar, a surreal morning sight. He threw a cardboard box to the floor and jumped on top of it, crushing it, doing a stylized dance of kicks and spinning fists. Feeling fragile, Lance put fingers in his ears. He wondered if the exam thing was new to LaCoss, if he had attended a gradeless nude hippie school in California. If you believed Kierkegaard, that reality was the internal subjective consciousness of each person, then Lance's reality was confusion and growing unease. He sensed a panic attack coming. He clicked off the stereo. "We've got an exam in forty-five minutes. Not a rugby game."

"Same difference."

They walked quickly in the brisk outside air, their coat collars pointed skyward and hands dug deep in pockets. Warm rushes of vapor shot from their mouths. Lance was suddenly alone, so he looked back. Ten paces behind, LaCoss stood motionless. His mouth slowly fell open and his eyes became dazzled, as if a stunning hallucination had halted his progress.

"What is it? What's wrong?"

"I was just thinking about that Nietzsche quote: 'The doer alone learneth.' Also, what Kierkegaard said, 'Life has its own hidden forces which you can only discover by living.' What I'm getting at…is flying to Europe, right now. There's our education. We'll dye our hair jet black and sell hash to tourists. We'll be street poets! Or we'll get BMW motorcycles and ride to the southern tip of Spain! We'll unleash the floodgates of our lives. Just imagine that, we never show up for our Philosophy exam. Instead, we get on a plane. How cool would that be? That would be the ultimate." LaCoss let out a loud, crazy cackle, balling his hands into tight fists. "We've got to do it! You know we have to do it!"

Lance thought LaCoss to be quite insane; he was irked by

this delay.

"Well? What do you say?"

The sleep deprivation had left him vulnerable. Slowly, the vision took hold in Lance's mind and it tugged at him. It was remarkably complete, so powerfully appealing that a strange heat overtook him. He unzipped his jacket. He'd always liked airports—their wide spaces, that happy transitional feeling. A montage of European faces, of ancient cities flashed before him. It was so rich. His ability to make this choice became terrifying; that a mere idea—somebody else's idea!—could overtake him, consume him, and that he might do such a thing. Possession of such choice was frightening. He opened his mouth to speak but nothing came out.

LaCoss laughed and continued walking. Then he stopped and looked back. "I was only kidding."

Lance had an embarrassed smile. "I thought you were serious."

"You wanted to do it. Admit it."

"I did. You bastard."

They checked watches and hurried to avoid being late.

Lance chose a seat in back of the classroom. Students filed in, glancing at papers, game faces all around. Nobody talked. They were battle ready, ready to excel. Lance felt calm, only because he was still selling hash, which he'd never used or seen, out of the saddlebag of his BMW superbike on a Madrid sidewalk, Castilian accents in his ears. Looking at the first essay question (John Stuart Mill and Schopenhauer meet at the donut shop...) his mind blanked. Nothing, a bare upstairs cupboard. He reminded himself of the importance of this grade, which only extended his thought famine. The room's silence disturbed him, then he became hyper-attuned to the faint scratching of pen tips in blue books. He flashed back to more sounds, to the zippering and rustling of Lynn taking off her jeans. The slither of elastic underwear down her legs, a moist click and catch of lips, then the whisper of hands sliding across sheets. He had grown highly sensitive to her sounds: the quick inhale, the smallest and most delicate of sighs, or a hum from her nostrils that only an ear next to it could detect. Each sound was startling and precious, more meaningful than any dry wisdom from books. An hour ran past before he could disengage from Lynn. He reread the essay question and again, nothing.

LaCoss saved him. Two rows ahead, LaCoss opened his hands around his face like petals; he was doing Mill, whose theory of utilitarianism stated that the greatest good should be done for the greatest number...

Lance started writing.

Charles Boyd favored studying in the big auditorium rooms of The Ivan. On a lit stage before two hundred empty seats, a billow of smoke rose from his ashtray. At the top of a dim aisle, Lance took a breath. He felt shaky, wrung out from stress and too little sleep. Ordinarily, he avoided studying with Boyd, but with his focus waning before his next final, he hoped to borrow some of Boyd's famous concentration. Wearing round Lennonesque glasses, Boyd took a drag on the cigarette, watching Lance's progress to the side of the stage. Lance dropped his backpack on the table and sat in a molded laminate chair. Charles Boyd's hair was greasy and flat, though his eyes seemed tranquil, rested. Volume One of Gibbon's *The History of the Decline and Fall of the Roman Empire* lay on the table. Lance opened it.

"Of course," Lance said, "Gibbons has been greatly discredited. Recent scholars have found considerable bias in his work and some obvious errors."

"What?" Charles Boyd's face wrinkled with disbelief and anxiety.

"HA-HA. I gotcha!" Lance drummed his hands on the table.

Boyd rolled his eyes, beyond the matter in an instant.

The fragrant glue of the binding smelled like history. The name Bernice Madden-Boyd was written inside the cover. Charles Boyd's mom, the classics scholar and professor who had penned three textbooks on Greek mythology, the sole parent who had raised him. Lance opened his own textbook and took the cap off his pen. The dark space of the auditorium seemed calming. He felt some energy; he might rebound and possibly do well on his last two finals. He rolled his sleeves up to his elbows.

"What exams have you had already?" Charles Boyd asked.

"Philosophy and Macro econ."

"I thought you hated econ. You always complain about it. Where does that lead?"

"It leads to getting an MBA."

"Is this something you actually believe in, or is the business thing just your standard answer to people's questions?" Boyd raised his eyebrows, suddenly tentative, as if worrying he'd crossed some line of their friendship.

Lance scoured his backpack with consternation, unable to find his highlighter. "I guess it's some of both."

"What area do you want to concentrate in?"

"I don't know yet." Business occupied a wide landscape, and surely there was a niche, an area which might be tolerable. An area to exploit.

Charles Boyd stared without blinking, the incompleteness of the answer hanging. "Are we talking finance, marketing, management, international?"

Lance flopped a notebook on the table. "I don't know. Any one of them. Look, I need to cover some serious material. I need to study."

"Seems like a lot of unanswered questions—"

"Not every person has got their entire life mapped out. OK?"

He remembered his hesitancy about studying with Charles Boyd, for whom it was all too easy. He maintained an effortless

4.0 GPA. He'd earned extra credit that wasn't reflected, which would have made it even larger. His Physics term paper had been published. A Langford alumni publication had trumpeted him in a feature article as a "shooting academic star." Because of his excellence, any number of institutes, universities, brain trusts and corporations were eager to recruit him and assign tasks to him. Lance found these facts both unreal and all too painfully real.

Boyd's look of unsatisfied scrutiny remained.

Lance bent over the table, trying to concentrate. Charles Boyd picked up a newspaper from the floor: *USA Today.* HART—BACK IN PRESIDENTIAL RACE? The Colorado senator, after being caught with Donna Rice on a yacht named Monkey Business, was considering reentering the nomination race. The headline grabbed Lance's attention. "Seems like your man might get in the race again."

Boyd's voice sounded bored, "It's hopeless for the guy. He won't."

"People might forgive him."

"People are stupid. They don't want the truth. They want schlock. They want some phony moron to smile and wave. They want crap." He examined the front page with a disdainful frown. "What have we here? An important story about Bruce Springsteen. Here's some hard news about real-life party dog Spuds MacKenzie. Looks like the coup in the Philippines is only good enough for page 6. It's the goddamn Easy Reader." He flicked the paper aside. "Such crap."

Crap. His mother's word. Charles Boyd was very much his mother's creation, Lance realized. Boyd mentioned her frequently, but beyond this, he had adopted her world view. She had breastfed him until age three, Charles Boyd had explained late one drunken night, uncharacteristically sentimental as he spoke. Weaning him by teaching him to read Homer's *The Iliad.* She drove a '64 Volkswagen Beetle, still drove that car. Young Charles's geologist father had taken off and they were broke.

Too broke to afford kindergarten. She was earning her doctorate at Princeton. Someone gave her the car. It had mismatched doors but ran strong. At six, young Charles could barely see over the dash. His mom would play Bob Dylan on an eight-track player, encouraging him to sing along. The eight-track had replaced the radio, which played too many commercials and filled your head with annoying jingles and materialistic craving.

Driving in the Beetle they sang Bob Dylan songs, passing up the fast food places with their greasy, processed fare. They served fattening crap and young Charles would not be poisoned that way. They drove past movie theaters. The theaters played oversexed movies, movies with generally worthless, antisocial and misogynistic themes. Movies with pointless car crashes, blood, gunfire, glorified rapes. The movies were crap, so they didn't stop. They drove on, singing "Mr. Tambourine Man." Past the 7-Eleven with its sugar-water refreshments and revolving cancerous hot dogs and pornography behind the counter, past an environmentally devastated tract of dirt a strip mall would soon occupy. They lived simply. They had a garden. Didn't own a television. There was so much crap on TV, so much mind-numbing garbage it was out of the question, with its violent cartoons, its advertising propaganda for cigarettes and luxury cars. The only show she allowed Charles to see, at his grandparents', was *H.R. Pufnstuf*, since Sid & Marty Krofft seemed to have a nature-centered progressive consciousness. They drove past the pizza parlor, Charles never attending any birthday parties there. Pizza as nutrition, as food, was crap, the violent *Sinbad* movies they projected even worse crap. So they drove on, they drove past it, singing "Subterranean Homesick Blues," young Charles looking at the strange, flashy world on either side of the road, the world of so much crap.

Charles Boyd frowned, still glancing at the newspaper. He slumped, putting his elbow on his knee. He'd just finished reading Allan Bloom's *The Closing of the American Mind*, Lance knew. "It's such an impersonal grind out there. It's impossible for individuals to make a difference at all. People are so interchangeable and expendable these days. Suicide rates are way up."

Lance squirmed. "I'm trying to concentrate. Some of us actually need to study."

"And idealism. Where has the idealism of young people gone?" Boyd shook his head.

Lance remembered students in front of the Student Center, at a table for some philanthropic organization. A guy and two plainly dressed girls, with well-meaning, selfless smiles. They were collecting money for victims of an earthquake in East Asia and Lance had breezed by, not even looking at the pictures of devastation. But as a result of their efforts, their young-person energies, an East Asian person would rebuild their meager house. Or get some food. Or medicine for a sick child. They were making a difference. Lance hadn't cared about the crying people, hadn't even stopped to think about them. So maybe he was a selfish creep. Maybe those students were right to not care about being cool. Maybe he watched too much TV and was lazy. He was guilty, and it made him feel like shit.

And what of Lance's ideals? What stirred his soul? The lodestar of his enthusiasm could be described in three words: Lynn Van Oster. He had probably hustled past the pictures of stricken people without helping them, without caring, on the way to her dorm room, the thought of sex moving him faster. How rottenly self-centered was that?

"Do you..." Charles Boyd rubbed his chin, looking weary beyond his twenty years. "Do you sometimes wonder about the point of everything? About what your work—wherever you work—will mean. Will it mean anything?"

Lance groaned, slamming his pen on the table. "If things are really so rotten, then why do you want to be a diplomat?"

"The beauty of it is that I'll be living in other countries. I'll be assigned to green places with indigenous cultures and authentic people. Places with thousand-year histories and people who are aware of them." Charles Boyd would rent some hilltop mansion in South America or Asia and have cheap servants. Probably marry a village beauty queen with Old World values.

Lance stared up into the dark ceiling. He took a slow breath. Maybe Charles Boyd's mom was right. Maybe everything was ruined and pointless in the prefabricated, preprocessed world of crap. What was the point? And from that moment until his next final, he didn't feel like studying for exams, or striving to achieve. He felt like getting very drunk, or taking a long car ride. A ride so long he'd step out with no idea where he was.

In a subterranean library room, Lance struggled to keep his eyelids up as he crammed for his last exam. The hours slid into a deep, hushed night. Focus: as a child, his father told him that every invention, progress in civilization and personal success came as a result of proper focus. This had inspired Lance to stare at quarters until Washington's bust burned into his brain, and study clouds as they shape-shifted, imagining his focus sharpening like a weightlifter's pumping biceps. Yet somehow, his focus on exams never came until well after midnight, and only immediately before each final, and only when he needed every remaining hour to conceivably absorb the info and get a decent result. Then this enlivened focus was as likely to target other things, like a pink Day-Glo flyer under the table:

THE LANGFORD AMAZON SOCIETY SAYS:
THINK ABOUT IT

The television shows *I Dream of Jeannie* and *Bewitched* must be strongly condemned as anti-woman. Both shows are centered around women, Samantha and Jeannie, who with either a nod or nose wrinkle have the ability to invoke "magical" powers: the ability to fly, change identities, stop time, etc. These creative powers are vital to their individuality. The male figures in their lives, Darrin, a husband, and Major Nelson, a male without formal connection other than having found Jeannie's bottle and claimed her as chattel, are obsessed with preventing use of these powers. They are agitated at any display of the women's gifts, convinced there will be punishment from ruling male authority figures if these creative powers are discovered.

The men are humorless and nondescript, Major Nelson always wearing an Air Force uniform, Darrin wearing a dark suit. Both men are obsessed with conformity and pleasing authority, i.e. Col. Murray and Mr. Tate. Col. Murray suspects Major Nelson of insanity and suggests psychoanalysis when he shows any sign of individuality. Darrin's only motivation is to prevent loss of his precious advertising accounts and to please his boss, Mr. Tate. Indeed, Darrin is so hollow and interchangeable that another actor, Dick Sargent, plays him when the original actor, Dick York, leaves the series. Neither character has an identity outside his work. The women accept this restraint of their powers by the males (Jeannie even referring to Major Nelson as "master") and live in constant anxiety.

These shows have destructive implications to young women: that men should properly oppress them; and to young men: that men must assert dominance over women in order to please male authority figures.

GET A CLUE, AMERICA

He had to agree with them. The Langford Amazons, that secret feminist clique, had struck again. He loved the idea of these mysterious, intellectual women. Their last propaganda was about the need to develop a female urinal. Many times on campus he would pass a girl on the sidewalk, a pasty-faced, serious girl who seemed to be thinking revolutionary thoughts, and wonder: is she one of them? Lynn considered it a sham, found their ideas absurd, and had heard a women's studies professor was behind all of it. LaCoss claimed the Amazons were actually a coven. He checked his watch; he'd lost a half-hour of focus.

It was a shame he hadn't spent any time on Modern Art, his one fanciful class selection, because now it was making sense. He had attended some slideshows and vaguely liked the weird, colorful and surprising arrangements, yet he had been put off: everything made complex for the sake of complexity, in that endless college way. Bearded, self-important guys pontificating about the pontification of other bearded guys.

He yawned hugely, a spit drop falling onto a Renoir reproduction. Eyes closed, he remembered the speckled horse pill in his pants pocket. Carson Wombley, Jr. had been handing out "brain pills," claiming that they were primarily B vitamins which focused your mind like a laser beam, and that he took them every day. Lance had imagined some grad student mixing them in a dirty bathtub and pocketed it with distrust. But he felt himself lagging, his mind wandering. It would be a long night. He swallowed the pill and chased it with 7UP. On a bathroom break, he heard retching inside the men's room. In a stall, he recognized Norton Skinner sitting on the tiles, panting, leaning against the stall divider. His face was sallow, an odd glint in his eye. He wore a frayed chamois shirt and fraying jeans, like he had suffered through a natural disaster.

"Hey, man. Are you sick?"

Skinner wiped sweat off his brow. His hands shook. "It's those brain pills Wombley is passing out. I've been up two days. No sleep." His voice became amused, childlike. "Can't seem to drink enough water."

"What, did you take ten of them?"

"Only takes one. Those things are basically speed."

Lance swallowed hard, his heart striking several deep beats. This was bad.

"But Wombley? He takes them and he's fine." Lance nodded, trying to establish this as fact.

"He won't touch them. All I know is they're kicking my ass." He wiped his nose with toilet tissue.

Lance pulled close to his study table, as if locking into a roller coaster seat, and resolved to ride it out. Maybe the pill would help. He admired the Impressionists, wandering around London or Paris with a canvas under their arms, established artists saying they were doing it wrong. The door creaked and Skinner wandered into the room and sat at the opposite end of the table. His face was ashen, drawn. He cleared his throat several times on some recalcitrant phlegm and spread out a ratty mess of notes. "Are you studying right now?" he asked moronically.

"No talking!" Lance considered moving to another room.

Skinner drummed his fingers, vibrating the table, humming a tune with a strangely high registry. He looked up at the ceiling, his eyes unfocused.

In a half-hour, Lance felt the first energizing jolts, while admiring the passive, elongated limbs of Picasso's Blue Period figures. After some reading, he finally understood cubism, the psychological fragmentation and distortion. Trouble started with the Dadaists. He drank water, unable to cure a dryness frosting over his tongue. He studied Marcel Duchamp's *Bicycle Wheel*. Where was the artistic value of a bike wheel attached to a kitchen stool? It lacked traditional creativity. But this was the point, wasn't it? His heart rate elevated to a more deliberate plateau, but not a threatening one. He focused on a Max Ernst collage: a sphinx gazing into a train compartment, a chicken head on top of a passenger. He noted the scale distortion and lack of logic. He felt dumbstruck, confused. His confidence faltered. I know nothing of art. A ringing picked up in his ears. A tension strained his neck and shoulders.

He was thankful for the Color Field paintings of Mark Rothko. Warm happy shades, one on top of the other. The emotional self-evidence was a great essay filler. A moisture seemed to be building on his scalp. Skinner was mumbling things, as if talking to ghosts. He was near personal collapse—oddly, it was reassuring to Lance. He was nowhere near that bad off. He sensed what the painters of the New York School were up to. Just ripping away and airing out their souls without inhibition. That was art. He felt the jagged power of their work surging on the page.

Looking at *Convergence*, Jackson Pollock's brilliance punched Lance in the gut. Earlier, he had been dismissive of the drippings and splatterings. What kind of mess was that? But in an instant, the meandering lines and crazy patterns made total sense. They embraced him like a hug. He pressed his fists into the table and wanted to scream, to cry over the beauty of Pollock's work. He made connections between academic disciplines, between Freudian theory and Aristotelian thought and the urbanism of the fractured twentieth century (a row of bearded professors rising in ovation). At the height of his career, *Time* magazine called Pollock's work drivel; then he wrapped his convertible around a tree. All these artists: toiling in obscurity, penniless, fighting fits of neurosis, searching for what was true, seeking recognition from a society so ready to call them frauds. They were so courageous! They were incredible.

For one full shining moment Lance wanted a radical path, a truth, a passionate cause. To pursue something that mattered intensely and uniquely to him. A canvas to throw his soul onto. Was that too much to ask in your life? What could it be? He concentrated to find it, to latch onto it that second, but experienced only his mind searching. A search which could not be concluded easily, such that his cause seemed not to exist. This moment flared, a torch light in a deep cave, then died as soon, lost in the weariness of exam week.

Lance startled and dropped his pen. Skinner was standing behind his left shoulder.

"What is that?" Skinner pointed to the page.

"That's Jackson Pollock."

"He can't draw worth a damn."

"That's not the point! He was an incredible artist."

Lance stared at Skinner until he moved away. Skinner walked around the room in irregular patterns, like a lost ant, mumbling things. He stood on the far side of the room, picking at his earlobe until it bled.

The next few hours Lance slipped in and out of jittery self-satisfaction. He had reached the end of the material! He congratulated himself by lingering over Pop art, some Roy Lichtenstein comic book stuff. Sleep seemed unessential, a tyranny only foolish people gave into. At the end of the table, Skinner spoke to himself in a low voice, answering questions he posed in a higher voice.

Lance decided on a bottom-to-top review. A big mistake. With one long look at Edvard Munch's *Self Portrait: Between the Clock and the Bed*, the full weight of Northern Expressionism fell on him, knocking the wind out of him and pouring ice along his spine. The collective delusions, deaths of siblings, nagging illnesses and sanatorium visits of every artist of that period descended on him full force, suffocating him. He snapped the book shut. "Oh, God…"

"What is wrong with you?" Skinner sat cross-legged on top of the table, staring down at Lance. A sheet of paper balanced on his head. "Are you…are you freaking out on me now?"

"I'm not the one talking to myself."

"That's a study technique. Haven't you heard?"

Lance had felt a degree of responsibility toward Skinner, like he was an erratic but lovable elderly person. Now he was too far gone. And Lance's own problems had turned serious. He fled the room with one eye over his shoulder, hopeful Skinner would not follow.

It was 6:30 a.m. The exam was at 9:00 a.m. Lying on his bed in Oswald, Lance decided to scrap the review and go into the exam with a pat hand. First he had to pull himself together.

He was tempted to close his eyes, but sensed he would fall into an irreversible coma. Fear kept him awake. Also, his legs and the muscles along his spine were tight, twitching, agitating for some action Lance couldn't interpret. The pill's power was fading.

It was time to hunt down more from the man. Lance wanted two pills. After the first was safely in his possession, he intended to shove the second up Wombley's nose. Lance knocked on Wombley's door. Nobody home. Walking around the second floor, his legs working robotically, Lance ran into Charles Boyd.

"Have you seen Wombley?"

Boyd was wearing a white Ramada bathrobe, his hair mussed. "Good morning."

"Where the hell is he?" Lance grabbed Boyd's arm tightly, and bared his teeth.

"What's wrong with you?" Boyd opened Lance's eyes with his thumb and forefinger, like an experienced emergency responder, and examined a dilated pupil. Lance brushed him away.

"Have you been taking those pills Carson Wombley, Jr.'s been handing out?"

"I'll give you twenty bucks if you have any."

"You don't need any more of those."

"Oh, I do. I've got an exam in two, no one...hour..." Lance's face tightened, the difficult math of time calculation escaping him.

"First, you need a shower." Charles Boyd walked toward the second-floor bathroom. Lance followed, feeling reassurance someone was intervening in his time of need. Boyd was being unusually kind and Lance felt grateful.

"Semi-cold will do you the most good." Boyd adjusted a stream in one of the stalls. "We'll get your mind in shape afterward." Boyd walked out. Lance got under the water, which at first felt catastrophic on his skin; then he relaxed. The water seemed to drub something negative out of him. He put his clothes back on. Charles Boyd sat on the floor of his room with his legs in the lotus position. He pointed to an open spot next to him. "A clear mind is your greatest asset on an exam." Lance sat and wrestled with his stiff legs. He settled on one foot propped on a thigh.

"Close enough. Now some deep breaths."

Lance felt dizzy after giant breaths. Charles Boyd pulled a record out of an album sleeve and placed it on his turntable: *Inner Space Voyage*. Computer-generated spiral art leapt across a black background dotted with wispy stars. "When the music comes on, don't think. Just concentrate on the music. Free your mind."

"I have to think about something."

"Don't think, just listen."

Charles Boyd assumed his position again, closing his eyes. Lance straightened his back. Breath filled his chest. The music began with soft rhythmic drumming, sounds from a distant village. Then bamboo sticks and chanting voices. An electronic pulse surfaced, hollowing out a spacey groove. Lance's brain stretched—like so much celestial taffy, like a highway, a flat blacktop to nowhere, a scalding desert highway, with Dennis Hopper and Kevin, Lance's brother, racing choppers past a mesa, their saddlebags filled with hash, cheered on by naked dancing hippies, cheered by Charles Boyd's mom and her crappy Beetle, and by Donald Trump, with his arm around the waist of Lynn, wearing her blue nightshirt with the cartoon kitty—and then it emptied.

Charles Boyd snapped his fingers. Lance opened his eyes.

He walked to class with a strange calm—a focus! A mindset that would have allowed him to do well if he had studied properly, and if he'd had some of sleep, and if...At the Humanities building he labored up a long set of steps. A weight pulled his shoulders downward. He ached to lie on the top step, to rest his cheek on the cool stone. But had he laid there, he never could have gotten up. He wished for an end to his struggle. But it was just beginning. A certainty graced him: his GPA would not improve much. It would be a drop added to a puddle. His goals would slide further from reach. He sniffled with a sense of dark surrender, of feeling lost. A result was a result, he realized, and you went on.

Outside the classroom, he stretched his arms over his head. He swung them around his body to prompt a final surge of adrenaline. At that moment his art professor, in a trench coat, walked up. "Are you prepared today?"

Lance held up his blue book, saying sarcastically, "I'm going to create a masterpiece!"

CHAPTER TEN

THE PROFESSIONALS

In America you could always hope. A new album, a new song on the radio, a movie to turn your head around: they came out of nowhere and any of them might pull you through. But you never knew when or where. Similarly, from an unexpected place, you could hear a woman's voice on the phone: smooth, officious in a sexy way, calling to conduct real world business. A woman from Patterson French International—say one more time?—called to say Lance had been selected to interview for a summer internship. "Your interview will be with Mr. Grafton. On the 4th. 2:30 p.m."

"That's…er, terrific."

Lance struggled to sound competent, and to mute his excitement. Patterson French International. They were high-powered consultants, movers with tentacles everywhere. Funny, he couldn't recall sending them a resume. It was stunning; just like that he'd gotten into a very hot category. He leapt and touched the ceiling. It was manna from heaven! If he got a job with them, the hell of getting into grad school would be unnecessary.

Jesus, but what if they picked someone else? It was unthinkable. He would crush the competition with interviewing fundamentals, research of the organization, and an injection of winning attitude. He slipped a floppy disk into his Mac Plus and pulled up his resume, remembering he'd given the disk to Carson Wombley, Jr., who'd offered to take it to the resume drop at Career Services (before the brain pill). He moved his face close to the computer screen. Frantic, he phoned Wombley. "What the hell is a Winglet-Pearson scholarship and why is it on my resume?"

Wombley smacked gum. "Made that up. I found your resume to be, frankly, on the thin side." Lance's GPA was now a robust 3.8. He was also fluent in Spanish.

"Spanish? I don't know any!"

"Companies love bilingual. The international side is getting very hot."

"What if they try to talk to me in Spanish?"

"Oh, congrats. See, it paid off. You gotta be aggressive. Who with?"

"Patterson French International."

"No way! They were the hottest company on the list. I would give anything to intern there. You rock. You are so cool!"

"Don't you think you should have asked me before—"

"Gotta go." Click.

He closed his eyes. It was no good. He would have to point out these inaccuracies. It would be highly embarrassing. No interview, no internship, he explained to Lynn, expecting a warm echo of his character and integrity. "But what if they picked you because of your other legit experiences?" Lynn reasoned in her soft voice. "Or what if they pulled your resume off the top of the stack?"

"I don't know that. Are you telling me to lie?"

"Of course not. I'm just saying 'be real.' " She stepped closer, searching him with confounded amusement. The blue of her eyes deepened. Her eyebrows hardened unfavorably: rather than witness this expression, he preferred banging his finger with a hammer. "You're not going to throw this opportunity away. You deserve the interview."

"It's not right." He stared at his feet, his resolve weakening.

"It is right. You need this internship." She pressed her teeth together and poked a finger repeatedly into his chest. "Take it." He pressed his teeth together, imitating her. They both laughed, and she embraced him happily, like they'd achieved something wonderful together. She pushed her lips into his and suddenly, all his cells vibrated with a god-like Beach Boys harmony, Brian Wilson at his most tender and introspective. He'd never really intended to abandon the interview, he realized; her endorsement made him feel vindicated, more mature. A man with airtight morals, the old-time variety tinged with masochism—say Jimmy Stewart or Jimmy Carter—would have called it off. But why punish yourself because of the malfeasance of others? Looking out for Number 1 was necessary. It was an ugly truth.

Lance opened his closet to liberate his Maxwell's suit. A charcoal gray, custom tailored two-button slayer. In a rite of passage common to Alexandria's young men when graduating from high school, his father had taken Lance to Maxwell's, the brick storefront. After much tugging and measuring from old guys with hairs in their noses, his first suit was pronounced to fit properly. A suit is your armor, his father said. Wear it well. It tells the world you are serious and must be dealt with. On a pedestal, mirrors surrounding him, Lance had wanted badly to feel armored and credible. But the dark suit was foreign, daunting, like his head was popping out of another body, or a leap of seriousness was required to occupy the fabric. The suit had hung, unused, in his closet at Langford, a grim cousin, a stiff cryogenic stranger.

On interview day he assembled the parts, first pulling on the pants. Then he buttoned on a white dress shirt, heavily starched. And a yellow power tie swimming with baroque sperm-like paisley. His arms through the jacket, the tortoiseshell buttons flashed at his wrists, the shoulders firm and elemental. He pulled the ends of the jacket, snapping the lapels—his father's habit. The solid shoulders seemed to complement the symmetry of his head. He relaxed, as if behind a diversionary curtain, and tried out some expressions: stern, competent, free and easy, conversational…At last, he felt at one with the suit. He admired himself.

Patterson French International occupied a glass and steel monster that loomed over the northern edge of Atlanta's perimeter highway. Driving, he reviewed his strengths and weaknesses. Not his actual ones, but the ones he thought sounded best. His strengths were a great work ethic, creativity, eye for detail and a natural ability to be a team member or lead, whichever was needed. Patience too. Well, no, patience was too passive. Go-getters like him didn't sit around on their asses waiting. His sole weakness was perfectionism to a fault, working too hard and too long, way beyond the call of duty, demoralizing less perfect souls. It was a terrible thing.

He parked his car in the Parkway North deck. He gripped a leather folder under his arm. The east tower loomed, the sky reflected in its myriad panels. The reflection pained his eyes. He rubbed his hand against his slacks, losing a coat of moisture. How many other Langfordites would interview for the same position? Probably every backstabbing, calculator-toting, pre-business creep, with their day planners, Cross pens, and stacks of recommendation letters. No matter: he was going to mind-lock with Grafton, communicate with nonverbal cues. They'd yuk it up like old friends.

Alone in the mirrored elevator, an obscene Dead Kennedys lyric occurred to him. He strummed several nasty chords of air guitar and bounced on his toes. An unnatural quiet haunted the carpeted corridor outside Suite 1620. A white cornice, like a mini Greek temple, stood over the massive walnut doors. Inside, a woman with fantastically arrayed hair sat behind a configuration of desks. In a confessional tone, he said, "I'm Lance Rally." The woman put aside the phone and said, "Gerald Grafton will be with you shortly." The waiting area was like an art nook in some eccentric wealthy person's house. He sat on a long gray leather couch. A smooth alabaster vessel lay on a glass table before him. Copper ingot-looking things, backlit, hovered on pedestals on either side. The people working there were making ungodly super salaries. He peered into the alabaster vessel, guided by a notion candy might be inside. He leaned back, embarrassed by this reflex.

Lance forced a breath through his mouth and felt his tie knot. If only he could get into this place. It would be an end run around B school and the hell of postgrad job hunting. One of those lifetime moments, that handful, when delivering would leave everything smoother afterwards. A time when the pros came through and the wannabes walked away still wanting. The specter of losing out tightened his stomach. His fingers fluttered against the leather.

Se habla Espanol, Senor Rally? Comprende?

Another nail of worry: maybe he was so full of techniques and answers and bullshit there would be a lack of human connection. On the other hand, an outfit like this was sure to sniff out the non-interview savvy, those not aware of the contemporary protocol.

A smallish man in a navy suit, handsome in a delicate, refined way, moved toward the waiting area with an open hand. When he reached the carpet, Lance stood and shook hands, remembering to introduce himself. In a conference room, a sheer glass wall looked out on a downtown skyline. Grafton sat at the head of the table, spreading Lance's resume and another paper before him. He had graying hair, a thin mustache and a kind face. A loose dam of flesh bulged at his white shirt collar. Lance sat at his immediate left side (a power seat of equal esteem to Grafton's was unattainable) and pulled his torso fully upright. Grafton squinted at the resume, tensing his forehead.

"I'm wondering why I never have my glasses when I need them," he said.

Lance could think of nothing to say to this. He nodded cordially.

"My niece is thinking about going to Langford. It really has a wonderful campus, quite green. I went to Columbia. It's pure concrete jungle. Either blazing hot or dead cold. That's no good." Grafton's mouth wriggled, punctuating what might have been humor. His brown eyes fixed on Lance, studying him in greater detail.

Grafton had left things in limbo. Lance considered commenting about Manhattan, or concrete jungles, but opted to say something about Langford. As he opened his mouth, Grafton cut in: "Yes. The summer position at our Atlanta office. We have offices in New York, Boston, Los Angeles and Dallas. I spent eight years in the Dallas office, working primarily with ailing oil companies. We are consultants, not magicians. We had a Langford student three years ago. She's now working in our Los Angeles office..."

Lance actively took in these comments, like a Labrador on point. Grafton had a pleasant, confident voice, a newscaster voice devoid of accent. Several mustache hairs flirted with the edge of his mouth. Odd scents blew toward Lance, a sour breath mixture of coffee, a Lifesaver consumed earlier, an ashy smell. "...Human resources to our clients. Our clients are business professionals, Fortune 500 companies, many of them. So we pride ourselves as being professionals to the professionals. You can imagine the job of evaluating and turning around a struggling acquisition. We specialize in process-driven solutions, fully integrated with the needs of our clients. Again, we are professionals to the professionals..." A keen look, a fulfillment in Grafton's eyes. These people were business sages, so smart that other smart people listened to them; they pulled powerful levers. Lance's eyes wandered to the giant window opposite the table. Down near the floor, small dashes zipped by on the thin interstate, the vertiginous space beyond the window looming suddenly, palpable to Lance.

Lance opened his mouth for his debut into the conversation. The first exhalation came out, a low stirring of A's and H's, as Grafton asked, "Have you read any of these business bestsellers? Read *In Search of Excellence?*"

Uncanny. Lance about to drop the same reference. A mind meld!

"Yes. I read it last summer. My father gave it to me. He's trying to implement some of the very same things at his consortium—the decentralization of decisions, small units operating better than a hierarchy—"

"Great, good for you. I find reading causes one to evaluate things. Important. And if nothing else because the clients all read that stuff…" Grafton talked with the steady, impenetrable momentum of a Clash song. He would not shut up. The question was a softball toss, but Lance hadn't gotten past the three-sentence mark. Grafton had soft little hands. Had they been pitted in combat in an alternate universe, Lance imagined he could have stomped him. His head reverberated with quick nods, in recognition of points from Grafton.

Grafton said he wanted to introduce Lance around, then he stood. Lance stood also. Grafton tapped on the resume. "Looks like you have a Winglet-Pearson scholarship. I think I've heard of that. Prestigious, isn't it?"

Lance buttoned his suit quickly, the fabric wrapping him protectively like a force field. His chin dropped against his tie. "That's what they tell me." It sounded cocky, but as his lips curled into a smile, it felt like a fitting response for a Winglet-Pearson recipient.

Grafton paused, seeming to expect more. "Is it merit-based or need-based?"

"It's based on…well, merit, and some need. I mean, a general excellence."

"And what kind of excellence are we talking about?" Grafton's mouth curved upward in what seemed like mild mockery.

"Well…it's all there on my resume."

Grafton looked harder at the resume, pulling it closer. "Let's look at what you've written." He pulled glasses out of his pocket, propping them quickly on his nose. Lance feared they were about to sit down again. "I had a Rotary scholarship," Grafton said vacantly. "3.8 GPA, good man. Ability to follow through is crucial." Then he stared hard at Lance, in the searching way of police officers and principals. "How many

Winglet-Pearsons do they award every year?"

Lance inhaled fully, shoving his hands into his smooth pockets. "Last year...Let's see, the committee..." He cursed himself for creating a committee, imagining stuffy people with New England accents. "You know, the trustees, they—I believe it's twelve per year."

Grafton smiled and motioned to the door. "That's not many at all."

He followed Grafton down a plush hallway with framed pastel abstracts. Each office was beautiful, with polished furniture. Grafton explained the work of associates: so-and-so restructuring a textile plant, so-and-so computerizing a brewery. Grafton would say Hey Roger, this is Lance from over at Langford, or Say Evelyn, meet Lance. They extended their hands over crowded desks and it was an edgy dinner party. Mindless talk all around. In each office, during one terrible moment, conversation ran out and Grafton and the associate glared at Lance, whose eyes ping-ponged between them. Then he ran a hand down the front of his suit and smiled, as if suddenly pleased by his smooth jacket. Grafton signaled to leave and whispered in the hall that Roger's wife just had twins and he was a little tweaked, or Evelyn was a terrific tennis player who could whip your butt.

"This is where we put the intern last year." Grafton pointed into an unoccupied office, lights off, with a mahogany desk and high-backed swivel chair. A window wall magically reached floor to ceiling behind the desk. As Grafton turned away, Lance touched the doorframe and wanted to linger there, wanted to walk into the empty office, to run his hand along the desk, to sit in the regal chair and stare a few quiet moments into that glorious open sky where traffic copters buzzed by. The thought that he might not get the job wrenched him, destroyed him, having seen his place, his would-be office at Patterson French International.

They'd made a full circle and were back at the receptionist.

Grafton surreptitiously checked his watch and hummed. Lance slowed his walk: the interview was going too fast. Was he getting the rub off, the quick hook? Had the smell of impropriety ruined his chances? He gathered himself for the final sell, the strong ending. This was it. He took a full breath, lowered his chin and pointed his hands at Grafton. "I think I would really be an asset because—"

"Would June 2nd be an agreeable start date?"

"Sure, listen, I really think—"

"Then we'll see you then."

His mouth dropped. "So I've got the internship?"

"Didn't Joelynn tell you over the phone you'd been selected? This was a get-acquainted meeting today. You thought it was a regular interview?"

They both laughed, genuine laughter. It was pretty funny, this whole mix-up.

"Joelynn," Grafton chided her, "why didn't you tell Lance he had been selected?"

"Because you didn't tell me that."

"Whoops." More laughter. "Sometimes it's best to laugh at a mistake. Hopefully the client will too." They shook hands, Lance pressing his vigorously, feeling the promise of an eager newcomer with an experienced mentor. In the elevator, he felt so fantastic he seemed to levitate. If the job had been in question, he still would have gotten it. He had killed today, had slayed. He struck a martial arts pose and did karate chops. Ya-ya-ya! Doing a high kick, he lost balance. At the car he remembered his folder. He'd left it somewhere.

That evening he took Lynn out to dinner to celebrate his internship. It paid four hundred dollars a week. As he drove, she stroked the back of his neck, seeming to find him sexier. Falling in love, getting in with Patterson French—the world was lying down before him. He was recruited, valued. He was tugging on the fattest, baddest bass line ever. He had busted out of a carapace and left behind a deformed former self.

On his first day, at 8:30 a.m., Lance walked through the gilded doors of Patterson French International wearing the blue Brooks Brothers suit his parents had purchased in honor of his summer position. Well done, Lance! his father had written on a card. We're so proud of you, his mother added. This parental praise put an extra bounce in his step. He was ready to be useful, resourceful, to prove his mettle. Grafton wasn't there yet, so Lance gabbed with Joelynn, the receptionist. Associates trickled in, their heads down, issuing good mornings out of the corners of their mouths. Lance said good morning to Roger, who stared back blankly. The late ones asked Joelynn secretively: Here yet? asking about Grafton. She would pivot her head like a huge manicured shrub, and stretch her face to pronounce a silent no.

At 9:45 Joelynn said, "When Mr. Grafton is this late he's somewhat bitchy."

Lance found the office Grafton had promised. The room glowed from brilliant morning sunshine. He unbuttoned his jacket and sat at the desk, bare except for a phone. An empire could be launched from the pristine glossy surface, acquisitions and fortunes arranged on it like game pieces. The cushy high-backed swivel welcomed and massaged his back. The air was perfectly conditioned, clean-smelling. Somehow, he had done it. He was on the fast track. He spun to look out the massive window over the city's even carpet of trees to the downtown skyline. The full power and prestige of Patterson French International surged in his veins, nourishing him. How cool was this? Ian LaCoss was washing cars that summer.

A familiar figure flashed past his office. Lance stood and gave chase. He caught up with Grafton as he conferred with his secretary at the door to his corner office suite. "Good morning," Lance said, pulling his shirt cuffs smartly out of his jacket.

Grafton looked at a letter in his hands, then at Lance and

then his secretary, rotating among the three. A briefcase at his feet. A flash of partial recognition.

"I'm Lance Rally, the intern. This is my first day."

"Yes. Precisely. This is the week you start." Grafton took a long sip of coffee, his eyes glazing a bit. "Right. Have a seat in my office and we'll get things going."

"You're late to a 10:30 in the conference room," the secretary said.

"I'll have to get back to you. After lunch."

"You got it," Lance smiled and made a slight bow.

Lance admired the perfect gloss finish on his desk. No scratches. He considered getting a *Forbes* or a *BusinessWeek* from the waiting area, but reading magazines might set a bad first impression. He moved the phone to his right elbow and put a legal pad on the upper left corner of his desk. Things wouldn't seem quite as nude that way looking from the hall. People were doing double takes because a young man in an immaculate blue suit was sitting in the usually dark office. The place buzzed with muted phone conversations, the tight clack of typewriters. He picked up his own phone, got a dial tone, hung up. He wandered down an unfamiliar hall and found the break room. Evelyn, the one who whipped asses in tennis, sat at a round table, a newspaper spread before her. She held a donut.

"Hi there," Evelyn said. She wore glasses and had a long, distinguished face. Like everyone else there, she exuded a brusque intelligence, as if a stopwatch tracked each sentence. Everyone had an MBA, plus some two or three other degrees.

"Hi. How are you?" Lance filled a cup with tap water, unsure if she remembered him.

"Are you the intern now?"

"It's true. I am the new intern." Lance felt inadequate suddenly, that maybe he'd ruin the tasks he would be given, or that he didn't know enough to make a contribution (did he know anything?), or that they would fire him once they gave him the big Spanish translation project.

"Don't sweat it. Nobody else here does. Well, that's not true. In fact, watch your back." Her expression was unreadable, then she half-smiled. "I'm kidding you."

Lance laughed lightly, though he found her perplexing.

Around 4:30, Grafton, in profile, stopped in front of Lance's office. He turned his head and wagged his finger. "The intern. I will talk to you first thing tomorrow, good sir." He saluted, grinning in a jolly way.

Grafton was out of town the next three days. Lance waited to have the summer program laid out. He found a World's Fair pin in his bottom left drawer. Ignoring the altitude, he made estimations of traffic volume by counting the cars on I-285 that zipped past a window seam in thirty-second intervals, difficult when all five lanes moved in unison. He tried to figure out what was going on at Patterson French International, what the phone calls and conference table huddles were about. How were they making money? He brought *Tropic of Capricorn* (Charles Boyd's recommendation) to work, to supplement his magazine reading. Taking in Henry Miller's exploits as a manager at the Cosmodemonic Telegraph Company of North America felt like a double heresy. With memos and trade publications scattered on the desk, Lance held *Tropic* in his lap, secretly turning pages. Miller couldn't give a shit about his telegraph job. He was openly insubordinate, spreading subversion to the very messengers he managed. Hot for every harlot, hussy and available woman he could force himself on, he was a borderline sex offender.

Lance ran into Grafton getting his coffee on a Thursday morning. He sat in Grafton's office while Grafton answered three phone calls and used the phrase "efficiently multiply" during two. "How are things going?" Grafton asked, as though Lance had been there for months. Henry Miller's tryst with an Egyptian woman on a couch flashed in Lance's mind.

"Fine. Very well. I'm ready to go."

Grafton, as if hearing a silent signal, launched into a

monologue about Patterson French starting out as a boutique consultant firm, then expanding purely because of overwhelming client demand, how they were the professionals to the professionals...He borrowed heavily from the interview spiel.

"Is there a main project you have in mind for me?" Lance asked, his face brightening.

"Not precisely, no. You will be working on a freelance basis. I've made a pun there, ha- ha—a troubleshooting rotational assignment. Marla!"

A startled woman outside his suite stuck her head in the door.

"What do you have for Lance?" Grafton asked.

A big-boned woman with frizzy red hair, she shuffled into the suite and squinted at Lance, looked at Grafton in a puzzled way, then said she would figure something out. Grafton said "Great!" with a finality that compelled Lance to leave as he answered a phone call.

At two that afternoon Marla buzzed. Lance jumped as his phone blared the interoffice signal: accelerating intervals of bwap bwap bwap like a nuclear panic code. He pressed the wrong button, then waited until she buzzed again. Marla wanted Lance to send a letter to an actual client, which excited him. It was real work. The letter had to get out today. She handed over a letter from the client, a southeastern printer of periodicals, which asked numerous questions regarding payroll automation software recommended by Marla, as well as a booklet describing the software. Lance isolated and separated the questions, giving each a separate legal pad sheet, then dove into the materials. He quickly became enraged at the obscurity and complication of the explanatory text. How many bytes of memory did you need to run the stupid Payroll Plus 1.4? Wasn't it logical to state this? And why hadn't Marla figured it out? No worries. Using professional language, Lance would answer their questions and smooth things over. The client letter bore a resentful edge:...*after significant delay, we need these matters addressed.*

Lance buzzed Marla. "What's the deal with system backup?"

She was miffed. "You've got the materials. It's four o'clock already."

He composed his letter with furious intensity. These printers were going to hang on his every word. He imagined them having fits after a botched installation, throwing darts at his letter and cursing his name. He wrote a draft in pen, double-checking each sentence for clarity, using the words "methodology" and "transmogrify," his Langford education hard at work. He found an open computer terminal in an alcove. A crusty IBM PC with a primitive monitor, the searing ghost-green letters jittery on the screen like something off a decommissioned Russian submarine. The letters were followed by a blinking square at a bottom corner. There was no point and click, no overhead menu bar as on his beloved Macintosh Plus. It wanted a command. Lance spun around as he heard footsteps.

"John, what command do you have to give this thing?"

"Type in RT, then option."

The thing buzzed and groaned, as though it recognized unfamiliar fingertips and was considering noncompliance. He typed out the letter. Trying to indent triggered a series of disasters. He was switched into a parallel universe, then into some backwater of nonsense code. It taunted him with CODE ERROR messages. He was doubtful his file still existed. Through persistent and daring use of the option 5 key, he found his letter. Then the computer had a brain fart and locked up as he attempted to set a margin. He turned around hoping for help from a passerby, but people were keeping their distance from the stench of computing failure. Walking around with his handwritten draft, his tie disheveled, he arrived at Joelynn's desk.

"I'll do it on my computer," she offered. "It'll take me two minutes."

Lance composed himself, then came out to the lobby to find his letter printed on letterhead. Joelynn slung a purse over her shoulder and waved goodbye at 5:15. He plopped into the chair across from Marla's desk as she read. Of course, she would be impressed.

She tensed her face, as if considering the complexity of an Eddie Van Halen guitar solo. "What is 'transmogrify'? I can't sign this. Do the whole thing over."

What had been joy upon entering the building each morning settled into boredom. Grafton was rarely around. He was in Dallas or Chicago or out sick. There was no discernible second in command. The rare times he was there, Grafton seemed to assume Lance was working madly. Lance, his sleeves rolled up, coming down the hall with a steaming morning coffee and a thumbs up, couldn't bring himself to dissuade Grafton from this and didn't care to hear Grafton's long-winded spiel again either. At first he was bothered by nervous guilt, as though be bore responsibility for the administrative void he'd fallen into. But the first rule of business was to act like you knew what you were doing. If he begged for assignments, the flood of questions and disorientation triggered by the rare project would have put Lance in a position where he obviously did not want to be.

So he found ways to stretch days out.

He read the newspaper in the break room, lingering over the baseball box scores. He read Charles Bukowski's poetry, another Charles Boyd recommendation, reveling in the poet's misanthropy and drunken antics—insulting his own fans! He window-gazed, hypnotized by the pleasant ennui of the flow of digits on the superhighway below. He listened to New Order and Black Flag with earphones, hiding the wires by threading them behind his neck. He made a phone call to get the sad story of software problems the neglected printer client was having. Other projects he sloughed off. He was just too busy, he explained. At 10:30 each day, the sun cast a warm bath across his chair and back. He put up his feet and loosened his tie, listening to the chirping of phones. He wasn't the only window-gazer who hedged about his workload and fended things off. In fact, with this approach, he seemed to rise in stature.

On Friday afternoons the office would gather at a bar, the celebrants arriving in high- powered German sedans and handing over credit cards to start tabs. On an open air deck yards away from traffic, they sat around white plastic tables speared with umbrellas. After rolling up their sleeves and putting on Ray-Bans or Vuarnets, they wedged lime slices into the necks of Coronas and tore into the skin of chicken wings, complaining the sauce was way too hot.

Lance found a table with Patterson people. They were cackling and licking bits of lime pulp off their lips and complaining about the clients, the damn clients with noodles for brains, who were running their companies into the ground, who would fall over cliffs without the expert guidance of the consultants of Patterson French. The deck talk surprised him. Unlike neutral office chatter, deck chatter was all ambition and self-promotion. This was the real deal.

Lance reached for his wallet when his Corona arrived.

"Put that away," the expansive J.M. said. "You're drinking on my tab, friend." J.M. winked at the waitress.

"What year are you at Langford?" Roger asked, a Harvard man: proof of either the caliber of Patterson French or that Roger was the runt of the Harvard litter.

"I'll be a junior next year."

"You're halfway home, or halfway to being evicted from paradise, more like it."

"Jesus Christ," J.M. said. "I graduated from Duke in three years. What was I thinking? What was the rush? In hindsight I wish I'd stretched it out to five. Maybe even six."

"Things seem to have worked out for you," Lance said.

Hewing and hawing from the table.

"Sure. Correct. Don't listen to them, Lance. I've been with

Patterson for…six years now. I cannot say they have treated me badly. They are not chintzy with your bottom line if you contribute to the bottom line—"

"It's the clients. You're blessed by God with the clients you've had," Marla said.

"-- on the other hand, you never know about shakeout. There's always some shakeout," Roger said. Lance's eyes jumped around, absorbing these gems of real world wisdom.

J.M. waved his hands. "Hear me out. If you had read the company's quarterly circular, as I do religiously, you would know that one Jack Dalrymple, aka Mad Jack, has been promoted to Vice President of Operations. Mr. Dalrymple is currently confined to the New York office, but I have heard whispers."

"So what? The VPs have to be aggressive," Roger said. This was Roger's thing. Nothing professional surprised or upset him. It was all within his careful purview. Lance craved such masterful certainty.

"Dalrymple is a croc in the water. Mark my words."

Lance forced a lime through the neck of a fresh Corona. The abstract idea of Patterson French International was its best feature. The work was doable, when they gave it. But the work was secondary; this much he had learned. He was handling Patterson French well. That was what mattered.

He walked into the office late one morning. A strange hush had fallen over the place. Except for one barking, insistent voice from the largest conference room. He poked his head into a staff meeting. The entire office, fifty people, was wedged inside, around a huge table and in scattered chairs. From the doorway Lance gazed around, then sat in a chair just inside the door. All jackets were on, ties straight, scarves affixed, dots of hairline moisture, all eyes solid on the loud figure at the head of the room.

His large limbs bulged under the constraints of his suit. He had a thick head and neck, the wave of his slick graphite hair held frozen by some gel/spray combination. His voice was a controlled growl, doing violence to the air before his mouth, as though only his collar prevented him from unleashing complete rage. A Midwestern accent, harsh on the consonants. He took off his double-breasted pinstripe jacket and hung it meticulously over a chair, the gold of his rings and watch flashing, revealing a swollen chest accented by braided leather suspenders. He smacked his hands together. It could only have been Mad Jack Dalrymple, the rogue Vice President, come to the Atlanta office to clean house. Grafton sat in a chair behind Dalrymple, looking small, dispassionate.

"…Let me give some details. Number one. Eight people arrived in an inappropriately tardy fashion to this morning's meeting. You know who you are. It makes me wonder how many times we are late to meetings with our clients. Number two. This one is so idiotic I hesitate to spend time. If you must come in late, do not linger at the door and distract the proceedings…"

Lance swallowed hard and looked down, fearing a glare from Dalrymple might trigger sudden vomiting. Had he lingered? Was he guilty of distraction?

Dalrymple rolled up his sleeves, yelling numbers—the ten percent reduction in billing, market share of system integration installment down five percent for the year, expenses for the Atlanta office up six point three percent. In shocked disbelief, Dalrymple noted the ten percent increase in sick time taken. He ripped a sheet of paper off an easel. His hand slashed across the fresh sheet, the marker squeaking, banging his knuckles against the pad for emphasis. He drew pie charts, wrote action phrases and retraced them to make them bold: IMPLEMENTATION, MULTIPLE   TASKING,   LEADERSHIP,   SERVICE INTEGRATION! He told a story about working with National Semiconductor, the top brass so thankful for his input and leadership and professionalism that they'd given him, Jack Dalrymple, free use of their corporate jet for three months.

"Changes will come to the Atlanta office. I promise this," Dalrymple said. He made an analogy about pruning dead branches to save the tree. Lance's heart raced, pounding in his ears. "...to maintain our integrity as professionals to the professionals, we must justify our existence. Everyone here, top to bottom, must be pulling their weight or they must go."

For the first time Lance feared termination. He loathed the raw authority of his jargon-wielding superior and wished for mercy. His insides plunged. He would be fired for general incompetence and an inability to justify himself. It wasn't his fault he'd been reading pornographic literature and making long-distance calls to Lynn Van Oster. Had a college student ever been fired from a summer internship? Oh God, the humiliation. It would be the darkest of black marks.

Everyone sprinted out of the meeting. Lance lingered around Grafton's secretary's desk, hoping for a word with him. A stream of people were hauled into Grafton's suite for closed-door meetings, where Dalrymple and Grafton sat in chairs before Grafton's desk. Ruth told Lance he would have better luck talking to Dalrymple himself, since Grafton was transferring to the New York office and Dalrymple would run things in the interim. She put a finger on an interview signup sheet. Lance lingered over the sheet as she watched, then he signed the name Marvin Gottshalk. She squinted to read it. He pointed to a snapshot on her desk of a girl on horseback and said, "Oh, who is that?" to divert her.

Marla held back tears in her office and refused to talk to Lance. He found J.M. in the bathroom down the hall, in a stall reading *Sports Illustrated*. J.M. said, "The bastard can't fire me if he can't find me." Lance closed his office door and paced behind his chair. He placed his forehead against the window, making a damp seal, and tapped his fingernails on the glass. He considered going to Dalrymple directly, offering a full confession of the unfocused nature of the summer internship program. But this was the wrong approach. It would be the end of his huge weekly salary.

During that tense siege day, Dalrymple appeared in the hall outside Lance's office, staring in. A sixth sense alerted Lance. He looked up to find heavy eyebrows focused on him, Dalrymple's meaty fingers hanging at either hip, twitching. By a stroke of luck Lance was reading a trade publication; an impressive ruffle of papers occupied the remaining desk space.

"Are you Marvin Gottshalk?"

Lance modulated his breathing, like he'd been pulled over by a state trooper. "No. I am Lance Rally. I haven't seen Marvin around today."

Their eyes locked. Lance detested Dalrymple's naked power. The idea of the bossman, who held your fate in his fingers, wasn't something Lance had anticipated. He had imagined everyone at Patterson pursuing excellence in an undisturbed, collegial way. But there was a hierarchy which, all at once, seemed intolerable. It was oppression, a fancy slavery. Had his Scottish ancestors fled English tyranny and hacked through the American wilderness for this? He was busting his ass for this? The stare-down deepened, like they were Cro-Magnons at the watering hole. Though he was smaller and younger, he calculated he might use guile to bash Dalrymple over the head with a rock, and thus win out. A traffic helicopter flew past the building, roaring and zooming by Lance's window, shaking the glass. Dalrymple tensed, his eyes flashing in a fight or flight response to the din of the blade chops. Distracted, he unwrapped a breath mint, popped it into his mouth and walked on.

Lance felt doomed. So he surrendered to fate and waited. By the end of the week he'd heard nothing and thought he might slide under the radar.

Meeting coworkers for lunch, Lance slid into a closing elevator. Dalrymple, occupying half the elevator, stood in a dark pinstripe worthy of the closet of a military dictator. Up close he had a swarthiness, a heavy jaw. Luckily, Lance had his Maxwell's suit on, his shields up. A woman stood between Dalrymple and Lance, holding a mug. She took a sip of coffee and the elevator jolted to a stop. The splat of hot liquid meeting Dalrymple's expensive shoe. He cut a pained, mocking look at the woman and pulled up his trouser hem, noting the contamination. The fouled shoes were Italian, black calfskin and giant. She chanted apologies, then bent down to dab the drops with a balled tissue.

"That won't do any good. You'll ruin the leather," Dalrymple said.

The woman swabbed his shoe, clots of tissue sticking in the laces. His foot bucked her away. The doors gaped open at an empty seventh floor, this halt for no purpose. Amused at Dalrymple's misfortune, Lance half-suppressed a grin. At the lobby, Dalrymple watched the woman hustle off, his eyes trailing her like he wanted to report her for punishment. He sighed deeply and rubbed the length of his newly moist face. Lance imagined him often tormented by such accidents, or by a crush of so many bigger problems it was intolerable. He faced Dalrymple suddenly and said, "Put a coat of mink oil on them. They'll be good as new." One hand was jammed in his pocket, the other motioned casually.

Dalrymple's face softened, reflecting a seriousness about this shoe care advice. "I might have to try that."

"Mink oil." Lance smiled, rocking on his heels. He knew nothing about shoe care. Quite possibly, this would ruin the shoes, and the absurdity of this exchange was delicious. Dalrymple squinted, like maybe he recognized Lance, or didn't recognize him but thought he might be a wiseass. Lance extended a conciliatory hand, which Dalrymple shook; then he strolled out of the elevator at a contemplative pace. He felt a daredevil satisfaction that could not have been spoiled had he been fired on the spot.

Dalrymple left the Atlanta office after two weeks, ending a time of frayed nerves. Only an older guy and a woman no one liked were fired. "He was trying to scare people to get more work out of us," Marla summarized.

With the departures of Grafton and Dalrymple, the office manager position was unfilled the rest of the summer. It became a stretch for Lance to occupy himself an entire day. Then a package arrived from Ian LaCoss. The letter said he was appearing in an avant-garde production in L.A. Every night, he played teenage and geriatric versions of the same character. The audience no bigger than a handful. He and Lucinda Falcon gravitated between being madly in love and savagely fighting. He was planning a change to a one-word name, in the tradition of Cher, Sting and Limahl. He was considering Dal, Waddo, and Plex.

The bulk of the package was a 270-page screenplay titled *The Man Who Would Be the King*. LaCoss wanted Lance's feedback. Lance was amazed LaCoss had had the perseverance to plink away at a typewriter that long.

SCENE # 1
(1962. Davenport, Iowa. The Burris household. A mother and father sit in a living room watching television. Their infant son, Wyatt, toddles about on the floor. Footage of an early Elvis Presley concert comes on the screen. Presley holds the microphone and gyrates. The toddler, barely able to walk, also gyrates.)

FATHER: Say, look at that little fella go.
(The MOTHER gets out of her chair and puts her hands to her mouth.)
FATHER: Take it easy, Sweetums, he's only imitating the TV. No harm there. Is that dinner ready?
MOTHER: He can barely walk. What if he maims himself somehow?

FATHER: Look at that little pipsqueak go!

MOTHER: Do you think this is natural?

FATHER: It doesn't seem unnatural.

MOTHER: The potatoes! I completely forgot about them in the oven.

FATHER: Why, the little fella is trying to sing. Can you hear him Sweetums?

From what Lance could gather after skimming several scenes, the movie was the story of Wyatt Burris, an Elvis impersonator seeking fame and fortune. Wyatt believed himself to be the reincarnation of Elvis Presley's stillborn twin brother.

SCENE #4

(Wyatt and his girlfriend Wendy sit on a grassy slope outside their high school.)

WYATT: What a lot of people don't understand is that the man had size 12 shoes. He was only six feet tall but he had these giant feet and big, rangy hands.

WENDY: I bet that wasn't all that was big.

(They share a laugh.)

WYATT: Most people don't know the facts. They have a perception of him based on someone else's skewed perception. Pretty soon nobody has the truth.

WENDY: Why do you have to talk about Elvis so much?

WYATT: He was such a great man.

WENDY: He's all you talk about. You never talk about whether you want to go to college or what your plans for the future are. Someday you're going to have to think about these things. You can't daydream about Elvis for all your life.

WYATT: I already know what my future is.

It was LaCoss's *Rocky*. Obviously, he imagined himself in the title role. It showed promise, but was ragged. Lance spread it across his desk at Patterson French. Unlike the intern projects he'd undertaken that made him feel incompetent, he felt qualified to critique the screenplay. He'd been entertained and failed to be entertained his whole life. He went about striking lines and writing in the margins, then realized whole sections needed rewriting. An intense joy consumed him, similar to what he had experienced writing Lynn's love poem.

He went to work.

Lance drove to Huntsville, the high tech enclave, on a Friday. That evening he would have his capable and professional arms around Lynn Van Oster. He sang boisterously to Depeche Mode's *Music for the Masses*. The melodrama of electronic dance songs filled the car, the sonic womps and pows, the mournful vocals, and he pounded invisible drums to the beat. He crossed the hinterlands of Alabama, which seemed dubious and primitive, a place incongruous with effeminate British popsters. He pushed his Corolla to high speeds, not caring that in a crash it would fold up like an aluminum can.

The setting sun cast a hue over Lynn's upscale neighborhood, its well-manicured lawns, vault-shaped brick mailboxes and accent sculptures. He turned up the drive toward Lynn's house, a two-story stucco with huge French windows. Mr. Van Oster, the senior engineer, was doing well. He pulled his car to the side of the drive. A light, warm breeze touched his jeans and short sleeve polo. He pressed the lighted door button and looked for movement in the beveled side windows. A sturdy, bespectacled man with a ruddy, serious face, an inch or two taller than Lance and heavier, opened the door.

"I'm George Van Oster," he said, shaking hands firmly and focusing eyes that seemed consumed with a complex analysis of Lance. His eyes trailed over Lance's shoulder. He winced, pointed a solitary finger, and said, "You've got a tire on my lawn. Two tires."

"I didn't want to block the driveway. Sorry. I could move it."

Van Oster chewed on his lip and said softly, as if to himself, "Has Lynn ridden in that?" Lance turned, seeing not his proud, fuel-efficient ride, but a shoddy vehicle: its tires nearly bald, its panels bolted together in a second-rate manner, an ugly scrape on the bumper. "Come on in. Everybody is around the pool right now."

Lance stepped into a high-ceiling foyer with quality finishing. Van Oster wore khakis, loafers and a blue and black striped golf shirt. He yelled for Lynn. He held a plate of hamburger patties with one hand, his thumb wedged among the ground meat. As much as Lance had rehearsed meeting Lynn's dad and making a good first impression, he felt dumbstruck staring at him now. He fought the urge to say something stupid like you've got a swell house or those burgers sure look good.

"We're doing some grilling today. I have a steak I can cook for you if you like."

"That would taste terrific."

"Some young people don't like meat. They get on these exotic diets."

Lynn appeared from another room in white shorts, a clingy white top and sandals. Lance's heart leapt into his throat as she put her arms around his neck and kissed him. He became a hundred pounds lighter. He lifted her in the air, feeling aroused. Lance opened his eyes to see Mr. Van Oster pressing his teeth together, looking off into a corner of the room.

"Isn't Lance a wonderful guy?" Lynn sided up to Daddy, rubbing his shoulder. She scrunched up her face.

"He's quite a guy all right." Lynn and Mr. Van Oster laughed, a weirdly similar high-pitched laugh. Then Lynn pulled Lance into the kitchen to meet Mom, a puffier, older version of Lynn. Mom put out her arms and waggled her hands and gave

Lance a clumsy, loving hug, pressing his head against her neck. A hug that left Lance wanting more and feeling a little embarrassed. Then Lynn dragged Lance through the living room, commenting that his shirt was wrinkled and was one of his worst shirts. Lance looked down but couldn't find anything wrong. She pointed to a stain on his collar, then flicked her finger under his nose and laughed.

She pulled him through a door onto a cement patio that glowed with Mediterranean optimism in the diminishing light. A turquoise pool had globular shadows flashing along the bottom. Lynn's sisters sat on rubber strap chairs near the shallow end. Lynn made introductions. Tina, two years younger than Lynn, was thinner and prissier. Tina's friend Nell and guy friend Kyle sat with smudged bare feet on the cement. Kyle, stringy-haired and morose, couldn't stir himself from his slouch to acknowledge Lance. Margo, the oldest sister, with the dark hair and the tall genes, shook hands formally. Lance sensed she was looking inside his mouth while he spoke.

Lynn and Tina presented a succession of cats, grabbing them and pushing them toward Lance. Lynn explained that Hokey Jones, an orange tabby with a sagging belly and crusty stuff under its tail, was her favorite. Misty Moo Moo, a demented, Egyptian-looking hairless gray thing, was known to bite occasionally, to draw blood, Tina warned, and was easily startled. Lynn introduced Lady Chum Chum, putting the white puffball on her shoulder. The cat shifted and slid down her back, its feet hitting the cement with a thud. "Oh my God, Lady Chum Chum, I apologize so much!" Everyone shrieked and laughed loudly, including Lance, who felt a degree of inclusion.

Lynn sat in a chair next to a circular transparent table and shook out her hair. "Have a seat," she said, not looking at Lance. He sat beside her and put a hand on her arm, but she seemed to be in another time zone. He was bursting with a million things to say to her, privately. Mr. Van Oster walked out with his meat tray and a scotch and water and headed to the grill. Mom placed a giant bowl of salad on the table. Lance was cornered, surrounded on all sides by Van Osters. They all had a habit of staring too long. Lynn offered him a beer and he immediately drank half of it.

"Lance, I guess you've met the cats," Van Oster said, in a deep theatric voice. He pulled out a chair from the table, all attention shifting to him.

"I know them all very well."

"I could tell you liked Hokey Jones the best," Lynn said, trying to gently embarrass him.

"What's not to like about Hokey?"

Everyone got a plate with salad. Van Oster crunched loudly, mumbling it was marvelous. With a dogged insularity, he put down his plate and ambled over to the grill. Lynn put her feet up on Tina's chair. Her legs were wonderfully tan, the smooth mass of muscles looking firm and sleek. An erotic flashback jumped into his mind: the time Lynn had gotten on top, grinding away on him while balancing on her knees. Mom looked at him suddenly. "I hear you have a wonderful job this summer. We've heard you're an ambitious young man."

He had been looking forward to this topic. "It's a great internship. It's with Patterson French International. They're a big consulting group." Lance discovered that his beer was empty. Lynn grabbed another beer from the ice, then studied Lance, hesitating before giving it to him.

"I've heard of them," Van Oster said from the grill, raising his drink. "That is very impressive. How did you get that position?"

Lynn said, "He got the job after being picked from a huge pool of students."

"I had to interview. It was pretty nerve-wracking." Lance smiled big.

"And what are you working on there?" Mom asked.

Lance put down his plate and beer to gesture freely. "It's on a project basis, troubleshooting mostly, hot projects like the

Delray Corp software installation. They're something like the biggest printers in the southeast. I had to straighten out a situation there on short notice. Though my exposure has been multifaceted, to all the industries they're involved in, which is practically everything." Some hyperbole perhaps, but he had a right to be proud. He'd survived there. Kyle, the sloucher, blew spit bubbles. He and Tina were whispering things.

"That sounds wonderful. That will look so good on your resume." Mom pointed at Lynn. "You need to do less dancing and more interviewing for internships."

Lynn extended her arms in a defiant arabesque, as if onstage. "Thank you, Mother. What do you think I'm doing at the mental health clinic every day? That's an internship too." She'd been reading Jane Austen and Carl Jung that summer, wearing a white coat and referring to the clinic people as "my patients."

"We're very pleased with Langford," Van Oster said, adjusting his voice to a public speaking mode. "Lynn is getting a quality education. The psychology program there is just what she needs to move into a top graduate program. Lance, I went to Stanford on a full scholarship. I won a national science contest with a project on the reverse polarity of magnets. Two of my findings ended up in symposiums that year."

Mom said, "The rest of the story is he has two patents based on those findings."

Van Oster, licking his lips amiably, gestured for Lance to come over to the grill. Lance nodded and pushed back his chair. Lynn brushed her hand along his hip. He touched the back of her hand, stroking it and letting it trail behind him. On his feet, he felt electrified, witty, loosened by the beer. This call to the grill endorsed the gravity of his relationship with Lynn, and of him as a young man. He sensed Mr. Van Oster was seeking a connection. He swaggered over to the grill, a multilevel Swiss stainless steel grill with teak preparation counters. Van Oster lifted the hood, proudly revealing hamburgers, chicken and steaks that sizzled underneath. He and Lance leaned over, inhaling, as smoke warmed their faces. Lance pulled back his shoulders and swirled his beer, feeling the bonhomie of men who stood around grills. Then a feeling of absurdity about this enthusiasm, like an overhead TV camera knew better. Van Oster studied Lance, stirring a dish of fragrant buttery sauce. "I make my own garlic butter, add some spices, and it tastes unbelievable." He dabbed a brush along two skewers of shrimp that were shaded pink. "That's great career exposure you're getting. I can tell your parents did a good job. It's not automatic."

Lance stared at the crackling meats. "I'm not sure I follow."

"I've seen it many times. Guys I grew up with. Their parents got things wrong and they fall away. Guys who seem like they have everything in the world going for them. They get nowhere." He blinked as smoke wafted into his face. He lowered his voice and moved closer until his sleeve brushed Lance's. "I hate to say it, but Kyle is headed in that direction."

Kyle was flicking stringy hair off his forehead. His t-shirt had jagged lettering, the name of a band that couldn't be interpreted. He leaned toward Tina, his thin shoulders caving in his chest. Suddenly, there was a sour taste in Lance's mouth. "He's basically OK," Lance said. "I've got a good feeling about him."

"There are rumors about bad apples he's running with."

"Can you believe rumors?"

Van Oster seemed surprised. "Not everybody is like you and me. In a matter of time, that kid's got a record. I'm not thrilled with Tina."

"I think he'll be fine. He's just a kid." Lance's blood pressure rose.

Van Oster pointed a grill implement with sharp prongs. "If I hear you correctly, you seem to think I'm being unfair." Said to make it easy to back out. And indeed, it seemed up to that point their relationship might be strong, a mutual fondness might spring up, but now it required some backing off. Lance's summer frustrations returned. He was back at Patterson French, facing off in a boardroom, armored, searching carefully for words.

Lance stared at Van Oster. His voice was harder, more aggressive than he'd intended: "I just think you should give him a shot." Lance faced the pool and drank his beer.

Van Oster poked at a steak, squinting, studying the marbled fat. He grunted, as if he might suddenly become enraged; then he lowered the hood and the mood seemed to pass. Lynn was correcting her mother on the pronunciation of the word protégé. She'd lightened her hair. Lance waved feebly and mouthed I miss you, but wasn't sure Lynn had seen him. He thought he might cry. Van Oster gazed over the pool, up into the tree line and took a deep, contemplative breath. He talked nonchalantly of how he'd lettered in two sports in high school, was offered scholarships by MIT and Yale, worked with Bell Laboratories his sophomore year. He then stepped forward and addressed the whole group, making these things clear for posterity. Lance's jaw tightened. His voice reverberated off the patio as he recounted his Tale of Success. He'd gotten hands-on experience working with the Department of Defense. Maybe he should have accepted offers from General Dynamics or McDonnell Douglas, he wondered aloud. Then he would have participated in designing the Space Shuttle or the Stealth fighter most certainly. Shut up, shut up, Lance thought. But, now he knew as much as anyone about laser optic technology. Silicon Valley firms were ringing his phone off the hook.

Mom said, "Many of the people that went into defense haven't done nearly as well." Lines around her eyes reflected grave concern for these people.

Van Oster continued talking, with ample crumbs of inspiration for the younger folks. Lance finished off the dregs of a beer. He grabbed another from the ice chest, shredding his palm as he wrestled the twist-off cap. He sat on the lid and lost track of what Van Oster was saying, something annoying about his retrofitting work with NASA. Lance imagined working savagely hard the next twenty years and blazing a ridiculous trail of achievement, just to show up this bastard. All right, the guy was impressive. He was loaded. He had this giant beautiful house and this healthy brood and he was definitely smarter than Lance in math and science. He'd come up during the great Fat and Happy Era, the American salad days, when radio crooners were easy on the ears, and every schmo with a brain got into the college and grad school of their choice, and the white males all gathered round to compare class rings and divide up the pie.

"Lance, do you have any scholarships?" Van Oster asked.

"Stop interrogating the poor boy," Lynn said.

"I was just innocently wondering."

"Actually, I do have one scholarship. It's a Winglet-Pearson scholarship. Only ten people in the nation get one every year. It's like seven hundred applicants or something ridiculous." Lance avoided looking at Lynn. When he did, she looked like she was holding her breath.

"I've never heard of that one. Is it merit-based or need-based?"

"It's a continuum of factors. The trustees pick them." Lance tilted his beer up to his lips and pretended to notice something floating in the pool.

They ate the hamburgers and steaks with potato salad and chips. Lights under the house eaves came on. Lance chatted absentmindedly with Mom. The white fluffy cat kept jumping into his lap. A telephone rang inside the house. Margo got up to get it. She returned and whispered to Lynn, "For you Lynn..." then something else Lance couldn't make out, two syllables she mouthed quickly: your friend? it's him? it's not? it's Scott? Who the hell was this Scott? Had the secret Van Oster sister code been used in his presence? Used as a means to deceive him? Lance's face flushed, rage warming his neck.

Lynn was gone at least ten minutes. Margo glanced at him

several times. Lynn sat back down, mouthed sorry and stared at the pool. Mom explained to Lance that the bottom floor guest room was ready for him. Mom and Mr. Van Oster said goodnight and faded off into the house for sleep. Tina, Nell and Kyle went off to a neighborhood party. Margo sipped straight bourbon before her friend picked her up. Lynn went inside the house to help Margo get ready.

A stabbing, searing pain hit Lance's full bladder. He glimpsed inside the dark house; no idea where a light switch, much less a bathroom, would be. He feared breaking valuable heirlooms stumbling around. So he went over to a fence in the shadows, to a tuft of grass behind the grill. He enjoyed a wildly satisfying piss. It rained against the stainless steel. A brushing of whiskers at his leg. It was that vicious hairless cat—the biter! Lance directed threatening brain waves at the thing and it slinked off. He sat back in his chair. Lynn stepped onto the dark patio and did a slow groovy walk, pointing out her elbows in a Latin dance way. After her neglect of him and the mystery phone call, now this crap. He considered ignoring her. But her outline was so irresistible.

"Do you remember me at all?" Lance said, opening his arms wide in exasperation.

"Aw, poor baby. No attention for baby." She pulled a chair, and then sat directly before him. She wagged a finger at him. "You were very bad. You and your scholarship."

"It's on my resume. And plus your dad was laying it on pretty thick."

She put a hushing finger to her lips and looked toward the house, then said quietly, "My father has every right to be proud. He's worked incredibly hard."

Lance put up his hand and she weaved her fingers into his and he pulled her forward until he kissed her. He opened his mouth wider, trying to consume her, like a desperate patient in need of a transfusion.

"Oh, my God. No. Stop that. Stop it now."

"Why?"

"This is my parents' house," she said, her voice stern. She flicked hair over her shoulder and pulled away from him. The house loomed with seriousness, as if it embodied the distinguished and lucrative career of George Van Oster.

"Who was the phone call from?"

"What phone call?" She crossed her arms in a restful way.

"Don't play dumb."

"Oh, that call. That was just a friend."

"Why did she call?"

Lynn licked her lips. "Actually, it was a he. Michael. He's from the clinic."

His blood rushed. He gripped the metal frame of her chair, studying her face in shadow. Her eyes were small, distant, her face slack. Her wrists hung off the armrests.

"He's just a friend, Lance. Lose the acute paranoia. I have male friends. Jesus." Her eyes glimmered with outrage. Something rushed inside him, like he was about to shout at her or kick the chair. He couldn't demand she not have friends. He gave up trying to figure it out. He wanted to believe she was faithful, required it, and so he did. The alternative was too awful. He lowered his head onto her soft knee and let his body go slack. An hour spent on her knee would have been a great hour. He loved her hopelessly. She rubbed the top of his head.

He remembered the contents of his right jeans pocket—his surprise gift. He leaned back and made a big show of digging into his pocket and pulling out the thin black velvet case. She rubbed the velvet, looking at him wonderingly. She skittered over to a light under the eaves and opened it: a five-gemstone bracelet of white 14-carat gold! An impulse purchase while walking through a mall. $420. A huge, insane quantity of money, this insanity thrilling him.

"Oh, my God...it's beautiful!" She dangled the bracelet before her eyes like a starved person about to eat. He explained the five gemstones, the topaz, garnet, peridot, amethyst...he forgot the fifth one. He fixed it on her wrist. She hugged him around the neck, so tightly it interrupted his breathing.

A direct hit on her feminine core. So brilliant! An intense elation buzzed inside him, in a way never experienced by pleasing just himself, like that crescendo in "Under the Milky Way" when the bagpipes kick in and it feels like your head might blow apart because nothing in real life could ever match that perfection; but Lynn hanging on him, heavily, was quite real. Overtaken by delirium, he told her about his summer: about Patterson, about Jack Dalrymple staring at him, and the hatred he had experienced for this man. And the screenplay LaCoss had sent! With a little work Lance could see it being made into a motion picture. He described all the changes he was making. He rambled on with excitement. "Working at Patterson French wasn't what I expected at all. The people there are so stressed out. I can't say I like it. I guess I'm rethinking my plan, like going to graduate school and everything…"

He expected her to say something. He leaned closer, detecting in the shadows of her face a building horror. She seemed about to choke.

"Are you crazy? Have you lost your mind? You've worked so hard to get to this point! Don't you realize how many people would kill to be in your position? You can't give up now! What if I gave up on my goals now? It's senseless." She clutched his hand tightly. Her body shook with alarm, with an outrage he sensed might cause her to fling the bracelet into the pool and never speak to him again.

"But it's not a matter of giving up—"

"You're so close! Don't get mixed up with LaCoss. He's insane. He's going exactly nowhere in life! I can't imagine his screenplay would make any sense."

"It's not that bad."

"You are a person who is going places. You have a great future."

A sliver of stray light reached her bare shoulder, a

quivering, delicate shoulder. He seemed to have trampled upon her deepest beliefs. She seemed on the verge of panic, that her every comfort and assurance and means of happiness was about to be stripped away forever. He wanted with all his being to reassure her, to prevent this.

He valued her opinion. Maybe she was right. Maybe insanity had crept into him. Or a notion spun from the sex-crazed mind of Henry Miller, or the twisted, drunken poet heroes of Charles Boyd, or from Boyd's demented mind itself. There at the poolside of that expensive house, secured from years of diligent effort, Lance considered the way the world really worked. This was Lynn's point. He'd experienced some of the world that summer, some of it to his liking, much of it not. The world didn't care. But he did have a claw hold, a notch to pull himself up. It had been a struggle just to reach that. And with it he might summit. The Jack Dalrymples and George Van Osters of the world were unavoidable. They had to be dealt with. He imagined introducing Lynn to his parents, who would love her and be impressed by her. His parents and Lynn, Kevin and Vickie would surround him, a warm huddle, showering him with praise and love, telling him that he, Lance, was so terrific.

"A gymnastics coach gave me this amazing advice," Lynn said, using her excited voice, her eyes big, which immediately made him want to follow this advice. "I'd been dogging it, I was ready to quit in the sixth grade, and he told me, 'If you don't push yourself, you'll never know what your gifts really are.' And I went on to be number one on my team the next year."

He imagined the fury of jumping, vaulting and flipping this advice had inspired.

"Promise me...you're going to pursue your full potential," she said, her lips pursed in a pre-smile, showing her love of promises as sacred things and her certainty of his answer. She also swayed slightly, indicating that not promising would be unwise.

"I promise."

They went swimming. Lance put on a pair of her father's overgrown swim trunks in a little cabana house. She changed into a white bikini. He jumped in feet first, the cold water disorienting and shocking. He swam underwater and grabbed her leg. She kicked and swam away. He floated on his back, staring up at stars, the water thick and plasma-like beneath him, insulating him, freeing him.

III.

CHAPTER ELEVEN

HONEYMOON IN 6B
Fall 1988

Streams of blinking, weary people came off the flight from Los Angeles. Lance tried to manufacture some happiness for Ian LaCoss's arrival, but it wasn't there. His sweet intern paychecks had ended, his office abandoned. He wasn't ready to sit in classes, to grind. The hell of cranking out business school applications would soon be upon him. At least Lynn was back in town. LaCoss would be pumped up, sky high over his latest idea. He was always good for that. A gym bag swinging over a shoulder, LaCoss bounced through the opening. His hair was long and greasy, down to his shoulders—the rocker cum hippie look, a retro psychedelia common to bass players and used record salesmen. He smacked hands with Lance, a braided rope on his wrist, and grinned. Lance hoped this compulsive optimism, baked in by California sun, would be contagious. After some initial elevated small talk, Lance was weirdly serious, and his depression returned.

"You look like shit. What is wrong with you?" LaCoss asked.

"It's half over and counting. We've got this year as juniors, then we're seniors. Nobody has fun as a senior. Hell, this year is over in a blink. It's almost over now." Lance frowned. The time-acceleration factor was one of those hard truths it was best to ignore when possible.

"You're missing an essential perspective," LaCoss said.

Before Lance started his car in the economy deck, LaCoss put his hands up and opened his eyes wide, as if gripped by a grand idea, or a terrifying memory.

"What?"

"This moment. Right here. Us sitting in this car. Fall semester. The airport."

"Yeah. And?"

"That's the key to all existence. Bango! This moment is totally perfect. No other moment is better or worse. Nothing else exists." LaCoss shook his head in quick spasms, which Lance once mistook as sarcasm, but he'd learned indicated sincerity. "Are you with me on this?"

"Somehow, I know exactly what you are talking about." Lance beamed. A roaring sound built up, the deck shaking from an overhead passenger jet. They both suspended their hands in midair, shaking their palms and moaning like possessed shamans as the rumbling crescendoed to deafening proportions and faded.

"Bango! You've mastered it," LaCoss said.

"I read *The Man Who Would Be the King*," Lance said.

"It's a piece of crap, huh?"

"In its present form, yes," Lance said. "I've taken it upon myself to rewrite parts of it."

"We'll split the writing credits and the advance fifty-fifty. Bueno?"

Lance shook his head. "It's your invention. The glory should be yours alone." The thing would never see the light of day anyway. It was a piece of crap. LaCoss insisted on splitting the writing credits, so Lance said fine.

"Have I got a drug for you, my friend," LaCoss said with a sly grin.

"What drug would that be?" Lance both feared and hoped his friend would produce something from his pocket, some wildly intoxicating and regrettable and tempting substance.

LaCoss had discovered a new favorite band in the clubs of L.A.: Jane's Addiction. A concert experience that summer had formed the foundation of his latest theory, the moment-oriented Bango! philosophy. On a steamy Thursday night, the Santa Ana winds lashed the city. LaCoss and his model girlfriend Lucinda Falcon pushed their way inside a club named the Dead Rock, on a forgotten block of Sunset Boulevard. Young bloods, avant-garde underground scenesters and punk freaks inside. These people would never be seen at standard venues. People with attire and attitudes so radical, so unclassifiable, so edgy they were either cutting-edge cool or hopelessly obscure and off the charts. Only time would tell. (How was it Lance never knew about these places?) Lucinda, the knockout brunette, wore knee-high zip boots, a velour cape and a bustier: she fit in anywhere she damn well pleased. She held LaCoss's hand tightly as he parted the human waters, his steel-tipped boots shuffling until they could touch the stage. The opening band came and went after noisy pointless banging.

Are you ready for an adventure, love? Lucinda asked. She reached inside her ample left brazier cup, pulling out a single hit of Ecstasy. She'd mentioned it earlier and LaCoss hadn't quite believed her. She broke it deftly in half with her turquoise nails, popping half into his mouth as the band took the stage. Jane's Addiction was a foursome (all the great bands had four). A blue collar bassist with chopped blonde hair, stripped to the waist. A razor sharp lead guitarist, a master of metal and acoustic chops. An inventive, though steady drummer. A raging freak vocalist, a poet subversive who was willing to confound. LaCoss was close enough to absorb their sweat, to feel the percussion of the singer's leaps. A roiling mass of slam dancers stewed and collided behind him. LaCoss corralled Lucinda between himself and the stage to protect her.

He couldn't say the name of the song he heard when he felt his soul flutter. It was a hard-driven song, driven through crashing operatic heights into a slow lyrical part, an eddy of beauty and sweetness, when they both opened. One arm around her shoulders and one tightly round her waist, they sank into each other, melding, the purest love vibe sealing them. He was ashamed to report it, but he cried, the tears rolling into her hair.

It might have been their love, or the letup in horrendous decibels from a PA stack that vibrated their lungs, or just the magic of a perfect concert and a perfect song, or it might have been the drugs. But it happened! There was a tightening and a relaxing and something filled a space within LaCoss that had been empty. Then a stray elbow from behind him—Bango!—cracked the base of his skull. He slumped onto Lucinda, seeing orange spots, then fell to the floor.

"I can't believe it. Your moment was ruined!" When would Lance's transcendent moment come? Why had it not come already?

"It was all part of it," LaCoss insisted. Lucinda and a stranger pulled him off the floor. They dragged him out an exit to a metal stairway. His hands went numb. Lucinda rubbed his face, but he couldn't speak. He stared upward: an angelic halo bathed her face in soft light. After a half-hour he said the words love and death. In another hour he remembered saying nothing.

Lance made a mental note never to do this particular drug.

"What does this mean?" Lance asked.

"I don't know what it means. But listen to this. The first sentence I spoke after love and death was this: 'Let me have what I want.' " LaCoss's green eyes glowed with brilliance. The creeping smile of a maniac spread over his face.

"Oh, yes!" Lance's hands trembled with enthusiasm. The statement crystalized something, a yearning, a spirit he'd sensed growing in his last doldrum days at Patterson French. A vision came to him of the first three words, LET ME HAVE written over the last three, WHAT I WANT.

They vowed to make t-shirts and sell them for cash.

Lynn moved into an off-campus apartment. She was now on the Pill. Lance carried her television up the winding metal stairs; imagining their steamy adventures in her bedroom, the TV almost slid out of his hands. He was confident this delicious proximity and the perfection of their intimacy would allow him to discover Lynn's magic key, that double helix which tied together her actions and motivations. Wouldn't this naturally follow? Wasn't it inevitable for people so physically close? He sensed the Lynn Van Oster code (and the secrets of all womankind) would soon be revealed. Ali McGraw and Ryan O'Neal's college nest in *Love Story*, living atop one another, came to mind. He imagined wearing white robes and gazing into each other's eyes by candlelight, fingertips touching, understanding each other without talking, intuiting the other's psyche like beings with higher intelligence.

The Pill! That modern champion of contraception opened them up to a new universe of sensation. It released him from the tyranny of prophylactics. With the miracle pill no barriers remained, no fears, and at last, they truly became one. Nothing but full-on passion the way nature intended, just her sweet scent and smooth fit. A final door within him gave way; a last stingy holdout, clinging to the failed moralism of his adolescence, was kicked in, blown off its hinges—and he let the floodgates go. His nerve endings howled with astonishing greed. He wanted a life lived entirely in these moments. Bango! Pleasure so intense it seemed foreign, so uncomplicated, so pure it banished all his fears, anxieties and responsibilities. Pleasure so raw it was a wonderful sin. They lost themselves, this frenzy at times lasting a modest duration. He rested his cheek on her ribcage, full of wonder, willing to do anything for her, wanting to give something valuable and eternal. Bango! They spent solid days and nights together in her bedroom, Lance grooving on Lynn's bright, soft-spoken spirit.

His new textbooks sat in a pile in the corner, unopened. Business school applications gathered dust atop them. This heap she occasionally pointed at, blinking her eyes to gently admonish him. He felt fuzzy with her, guileless, joyously stupefied, like one of her stuffed animals. His happiness seemed to mirror hers. In her bed he slept like never before: ten, twelve, fourteen hours a day of dreams and splendor, no stimulation beyond the subtle shift of her weight, the rub of her well-lotioned skin. The rest was exquisite, as if he'd spent ten years running ten thousand miles and could finally, post-race, collapse on the trainer's table for some much-needed attention.

With her encouragement they moved essential stuff from his dorm room into her bedroom: his stereo, his wing chair and most of his clothes. Though she objected to his black and white picture of a Siberian gulag gracing her wall. "Too holocaust and scary," she said, smiling innocently to soften the blow, but still creeped out. Lance saw it did clash with her Ansel Adams posters. Her nose was triggered with a raging sensitivity. Even after a complete washing, some of his clothes—his Levi's jean jacket—retained a scent she found unpleasant; it was banished to a corner. He was stopped several times from entering the bed on a personal hygiene warning, her eyebrows conveying entry to be an infraction. So he showered, and her pleased smile more than repaid him. Her refusal to touch his used socks he found absurd—toxic waste as soon as they came off his feet. But he felt forgiving of almost anything, and would have gladly burned clothing for her.

Lynn's roommates, Gwen and Gennifer, similarly sized, pasty-faced girls with brown hair and dark eyes, either regarded Lance with polite tolerance or glared at him as an invader. Gwen had a Bible on her nightstand, a serious boyfriend and a quarter-carat diamond pendant which embodied a pre-engagement contract. Gennifer had a goal to be a veterinarian and an iguana named Petey.

"I'm surrounded by married people here," Gennifer said to Lance.

"You can't be talking about me. Hah. No way." The idea intrigued him, then frightened him. Marriage, that dull artifact of his parents' lives—the opposite of what he was experiencing with Lynn. It was something grander, more stirring, like the end of *An Officer and a Gentleman*, or the middle of *9 1/2 Weeks*, or the end of *Sixteen Candles*.

"Smell the coffee, Lance."

He sniffed the air. "I think I smell Petey. Did he just drop a turd?"

The intensity of physical intimacy did not necessarily lead, however, to a more comprehensive understanding of Lynn. He worked a few answers on a crossword puzzle she had gotten stuck on—working the puzzle together, mixing their brainpower, conquering the world together. She shrieked in frustration, her face reddening: "Now…it's no longer a test of my own abilities."

"I thought you'd appreciate help. Just erase my answers."

"That's totally pointless because I know the answers now." She trashed the puzzle, and guilt washed over him.

One morning, leaving the bed, he kissed her toes, for no reason beyond a fleeting desire to honor those shy digits. She sprung upright. Her mouth opened hugely and a disbelieving exaltation came from her mouth, then a series of adoring sighs. It was like he had honored her greatest wish. He was very wise and knew how to make her happy. A toe kiss: pure genius. The next morning he kissed her kneecap, puckering up and hamming the gesture. She smiled again, but it quickly passed. He had probably overdone it, he thought. Too much production. And toes were more intimate, more delicate; knees weren't that sensual. On another morning, he cupped her foot with his hand. Her ankle caught his eye, specifically, the eraser-sized birthmark above the bone, a brown spot he chose to honor with a kiss. She yanked away the foot, pulling the comforter up under her chin. "Why did you do that?" Her eyes scolded him. He scolded himself. The spot always triggered horror, self-loathing and threats to have it surgically removed. It accentuated an upsetting nonexistent flaw in her ankle bone and so sickened her she sometimes covered it with a Band-Aid. "But I really think it's beautiful!" he said, and this upset her further. He backed off all foot and leg kissing for a week, then recreated the original foot kiss, same emphasis, same sentiment. She watched him sleepily, as if he were invisible, then sunk deep into her pillow and closed her eyes.

He walked into the bathroom one night. The little drawer where she kept her contraceptive pills was open and she looked up at him, vaguely embarrassed.

"Is everything OK?" he asked, smiling.

"Fine." She seemed outraged by a miniature, though devastating hurt.

He brushed his teeth; she checked her face in the mirror, reaching for the pink dispenser only as he left. The whole system hinged on her remembering. Did she think it was a bad reflection on her? Was he imagining this? He sensed questions would be met with a how-dumb-can-you-be-so-get-a-clue look.

A streetlamp cast a half-light into her bedroom. Her head lay on his chest, her bare leg scissored over his. He always sensed when she was examining his face. Her eyes pried, patiently waiting. "How do you really feel about me?" she asked. Her voice trailed off in deliberate understatement, which meant watch out.

"You're the best. I love you." He kissed the top of her head, inhaling its sweet scent. He liked using the L word. It underscored that what they were doing was momentous, unprecedented. She liked hearing it, craved hearing it constantly, as though it were a guarantee.

"And what else?"

"What else? OK…Does there have to be an else?"

"Oh, yes. What else?"

"Must everything always be explained? Is this necessary—"

"Yes. It must." She stared at him, as though about to conduct an audit inside his brain. Now serious, almost professional, like Sigourney Weaver in *The Year of Living Dangerously*.

He adjusted his pillow, stalling, then asked, "And how do you feel about me?"

She kicked the comforter off with her powerful toned legs, now restless. "I feel wonderful about you. I mean, there are different levels of emotion and I think we've gotten to a deeper one. Some things we don't talk about, but some things…We're doing well."

"It sounds like we're working on a science experiment," Lance said, weary from this analysis. He sensed an intensified glare, gears whizzing in her head.

Just as tangents of her personality came to light, so she discovered new aspects of his personality. "Who you chatting with in there?" she asked, bright-eyed, as he came out of the bathroom. He looked at her with incomprehension and she said in her even, informative, psych major tone, "Are you aware you talk to yourself in the bathroom?"

He laughed nervously. "What are you talking about?"

"Sigourney? You were chatting about her. What's your thing with her anyway? Every night with us lately—a Sigourney Weaver movie." She paused, as if considering an unfavorable leap of Jungian connection between defecation and a personality disorder. Indeed, he had been thinking about the actress, unaware of his talking. The shock of embarrassment passed through him; he'd probably been doing this odd thing a long time. He quickly ran through possibly incriminating things he'd just thought/talked about. "Nothing wrong there, c'mon…" he said, smiling unconvincingly. "Lots of people do that."

"Sure, like maybe if you're schizophrenic."

"Why are you listening to me in the bathroom? Are you spying?"

"Relax." She smiled, placing a gentle hand on his chest. "I'm not condemning you, baby. But it is very weird." She shook her head slowly, her eyes enlarging, as if about to make him feel bad; then she laughed. And he laughed too in relief and hugged her. That evening he felt no restriction. Indeed he felt liberated. He played New Order's "Ceremony" five times in a row, reaching a point of perfect, transcendent mimicry of the lead guitar, as if he were the Manchester hipster from whose hands the melody had sprung, or an artist capable of a multitude of other brilliant expressions. He missed Lynn entering the bedroom, her bottom jaw jutting forward, looking beyond his pile of dusty Russian books she begrudgingly tolerated, to the sight of potato chip crumbs and an open Sprite can on the floor alongside his discarded white tube socks, a ratty pair with a particularly egregious odor. He turned his stereo up to a throbbing volume, singing along with eyes closed—capable of vocals now!—in a voice he found tuneful and suave. Lynn pressed her teeth together, wincing. Then she held before her outraged eyes her white and silver unitard, now marred by a Sprite stain. She was to wear it for the Fall Interpretive as lead dancer in movement #3: Exodus. Her hands flew to her head. She shouted, "I can't take it!" and stormed out. He sensed something amiss.

That day she had three classes, a professor meeting to protest a term paper grade, a Power Aerobics class to teach and a lengthy DynaDance rehearsal. She returned to find the bedroom cleaned and free of Sprite cans, dirty socks and potato chip crumbs; the entire room and bathroom vacuumed and straightened the way she liked it. Lance motioned her in grandly, like a master of ceremonies. She rubbed her head lovingly against his chest, then stepped back to gaze at him, at her boy with his beautiful sincerity, who enthusiastically read strange things about the inner workings of the KGB and who talked at length about the implications of replicant life in *Blade Runner*, who was sensitive and ready to please unlike any male she'd met, with a quick mind and a soft kiss, and from a good family, the type of family that kept perpetuating itself in its lifestyle and achievements.

"Welcome to your suite, madam," Lance said.

"And look, you even vacuumed..." She smiled warmly, then opened her mouth wider, her eyebrows troubled, as if she suddenly wanted to ask him something but could not.

"Yes, it's totally clean!" He gestured again, further milking his efforts.

She combed the room until her eyes settled on his backpack. It had not moved since that morning, had not gone to any classes on this day, none of the books inside it opened. Her tongue met a groove between her molars, a cue Lance understood to rarely have good implications. He pointed to his neatly folded clothes. Later, she'd learn his Russian reading wasn't for a Soviet Studies class, or any class, and meanwhile class excerpts sat unread in the campus bookstore. What he had done that afternoon was clean for an hour, then finish Solzhenitsyn's *One Day in the Life of Ivan Denisovich*, then strum a giant rubber band next to his ear to find a certain pitch, then browse Lynn's latest *Cosmopolitan*, offended by the scheming and insincere articles: how to tell his real emotions when he hides them; how to send out signals to guys without them knowing it; when to back off to make him wild with interest. Then he flipped through *Architectural Digest*, Lynn's other subscription, wondering why she enjoyed looking at ornate, adult houses, spending hours evaluating each home. Lance found these houses with their rare artifacts and precise spaces to be beautiful but foreign, dull and too controlled, places for middle-aged people.

The room-cleaning seemed to trigger a funk in Lynn. He found her listening not to James Taylor and Rickie Lee Jones, but Simon & Garfunkel's "The Boxer," over and over. Lying on her bed, she wore a ratty blue robe, staring deep holes into the wall. That she was not crying, which she usually did quite freely, was the most unsettling thing. Lance sat on the bed softly, as if she might flee from him like a squirrel. Using Richard Gere's disarming and soothing tone from *Officer*, he asked her, "Hey, what's going on?"

"Basically, dysphoria." Her voice disembodied, she pulled her knees to her chest. "Classic short-term depression. I feel like I should be happier."

"You've got so much...I mean, I really love you. How many people have that?"

"What if things go wrong? What if I get hurt?"

"But you won't." What did he have to do to convince her? "There is no reason to be unhappy. We're together—that's happy. Nothing that seems really bad is ever that bad. OK, sometimes things seem messed up, but if you look at things another way, then, it seems totally different..." His shotgun approach was producing great stuff.

"It's not helping!" she whimpered, her eyes now fixed points of rage. This was an essential failure of his. Put away the white robes, douse the candles. He feared he knew nothing about her, zip, had made no progress at all, and this nothingness now pained him. He watched music videos on MTV, seeking escape, but was unconvinced by the petty melodramas of girls gaping at rock stars from an audience, of school girls rushing into the arms of bad boys, of couples in sunglasses driving in convertibles. The lack of dialogue sustained all this happiness, and would have been destroyed had these people actually talked. He watched numbly, finding this old reliable pleasure slipping away.

Her funk settled into an aggrieved boredom. Several afternoons he couldn't find her. She revealed she liked to drive to a construction site. Parked across the street, the process fascinated her, how the hardhat men used raw boards, sawing and nailing them together. A house slowly appeared. They kept attaching boards and windows without the whole thing falling down. It was her secret desire to join them—to be a woman carpenter. Why? he asked. She liked the certainty. It was guaranteed the house would appear after they put together the boards.

Her explanation puzzled him. He mulled it like a Zen koan, hoping to find enlightenment.

CHAPTER TWELVE

SEEMED LIKE THE THING TO DO AT THE TIME

Lance finished his fifth beer, then slapped himself in the face because his whole life he had been a sap. He had been wound up, stressed out, foregoing pleasure for reasons which now made little sense. He'd been consumed by the slow, responsible march toward supposed adult happiness, which seemed less and less likely. A conspiracy was at work to suck the youth out of his veins. It had begun innocently enough, a Charlie Brown lunchbox, a pat on the rear and off to kindergarten where the learning was fun, fun, fun; then the intensity ratcheted up each year until he was vomiting before final exams and wishing death on professors. All this leading to suit-wearing thugs yelling in boardrooms. He'd been a fool, running on a gerbil wheel. Killing himself. He had missed out on good times. So now he was making a direct grab.

Their habit of carousing through Langford's night haunts started on a memorable Tuesday while celebrating Lance's twentieth birthday: "I feel so old now!" He, LaCoss and Charles Boyd had hit the town, reaching a point of howling intoxication, of release and insanity and sublime pleasure—Lance taking this theme from Lynn's mattress and championing it. They went back for more on Wednesday. Why not on a Thursday? Fridays and Saturdays were command performances. Lynn didn't mind; it was good for both of them to get some space. Sure, it cut into Lance's academic output: the classes slept through, the punishing fog of recovery, the undone assignments. When academic guilt surfaced, he clung to the notion he could get a job at Patterson French International (he told himself unconvincingly).

They started at Tooties, social central of the Langford goodtime scene. LaCoss poured, filling glasses precisely when they emptied, keeping track of who'd had how much. He cut off Lance or Charles Boyd if they were ahead or made them drink more if they were behind.

"Can't I drink however much I want?" Charles Boyd complained.

"It's very important to maintain a level playing field."

"Oh, yeah…that's life or death," Lance said, pointing at his empty glass.

LaCoss could be superstitious, insisting they order one or two more pitchers before moving on, or insisting any more would be a huge mistake. His reasoning involved full moons, or working through negative dynamics or a prevalence of uptight ions or a need to push the cosmic envelope. Lance and Charles Boyd indulged their shaman friend. In his odd metaphysical way, maybe he was right.

"Man, I feel like Experimental Expo Theatre is opening up so many horizons for me." LaCoss leaned back in his chair, smiling. His eyes blinked wonderingly. "It's just a totally natural fit. It's taking my work to a new level."

"Still doing that Primal Scream stuff?" Boyd asked, as skeptical as Lance about this claim.

"I mastered my screaming. We've moved on to Body Positioning. I mean, wow, it's incredible, I feel like this whole new awareness…" He lifted his elbows, bobbing his arms as if underwater. It was hard to tell if he was lying, or had convinced himself he didn't really want to be in Langford Theatre's stage production of *The Wild One* after all. LaCoss had gone all out for the lead role: motorcycles, Marlon Brando, terrorizing a small town…forget it, man! On the day of casting he'd buzzed the street on a moped, waiting for the director to show. He dented a car in a parking space, and hopped off in jeans and t-shirt, a cigarette pack tucked into his sleeve. The casting panel scratched their heads as LaCoss used a James Cagney accent and the mannerisms of a Chicago crime boss when reading the main part of Johnny Strabler. They crossed out his name after he jumped on their table during an improvisational scene they tried to dissuade him from doing. That evening he was seen French-kissing assistant director Sara Dalton, and was later offered a minor part he rejected.

LaCoss laughed incredulously, then said, "Those idiots at Langford Theatre couldn't get their heads around a reinterpretation of Johnny Strabler. Come on, it's college theatre."

"It's a fifties movie," Lance said, unmoved. "Cagney is a thirties actor."

"It's lunacy to try to do Brando. That's *so stale*." LaCoss's head tremored, signaling a state of advanced drunkenness. With drink his ideas became weirder, and he more convinced about the correctness of these notions.

Charles Boyd, on the other hand, became looser and chummier while at the same time meaner and more defensive. His eyes darted around Tooties, excited by his proximity to girls, yet also tentative; more rejection was close at hand. A guy patted Boyd on the shoulder and said, "How's Charlotte doing?" with a shit-eating grin, then moved on. Boyd held his breath, his face reddening. His freshman year, Boyd had talked up his hometown girlfriend to ridiculous lengths, giving her the improbable name Charlotte Westminster, even showing an Olan Mills wallet photo of a stunning redhead, until a girl from his high school came forward to say Charlotte didn't exist and the girl in the photo was ten years older. Boyd's acerbic ways had earned him many scholastic enemies who capitalized on this fraud.

"Really," LaCoss said, leaning in thoughtfully. "How is Charlotte these days? I heard she's married now, several kids."

Charles Boyd placed beer to mouth unsteadily and emptied his glass, with nothing to do but let the matter pass. Lance couldn't let the matter pass until adding, "Didn't she marry into

Spanish royalty?" Then he and LaCoss slapped Boyd on the back and apologized halfheartedly. Boyd faked a smile, a vengeful Jack Nicholson grin. He continued to endure a horrific female drought. He was a nonuser of deodorant and couldn't be convinced he reeked. A thready mustache and goatee remained from his summer beard. Girls smiled at it, he thinking they dug the look, the girls thinking it was hideous. LaCoss took it upon himself to help Boyd. He opened his mouth in a siren-like yell when Boyd was about to ridicule the course load of a prospective female, or reached over to prevent him from pointing in an unintentionally threatening way, or tapped his watch to keep a lecture to a swim team girl on the dangerous reactionary nature of Republicans to a minimum. But LaCoss could only do so much.

Some nights they knew everyone at Tooties. They were quasi-famous. No evening was more glorious than the night they brought a box of LET ME HAVE WHAT I WANT t-shirts. They had been selling them on Saturdays in front of the Student Union, the proceeds financing the barhopping. At Tooties they sold out a box of forty in two hours. Imagine almost every patron and several waitresses, chanting the slogan at deafening volumes...LET ME HAVE...sporting identical cream t-shirts, pounding their beer glasses on tables, waving fists...WHAT I WANT! They had started an uprising! A revolution! Lance stood on a table, waving the last shirt as Charles Boyd and LaCoss orchestrated more noise.

And then—snap!—the scene at Tooties deflated. On Hiflin Street, little gusts of wind nipped and invigorated them. In twilight they bumped shoulders, rolling down the sidewalk. On the verge of laughter, alcoholic contentment swimming in their heads. What a perfect formula for happiness! Lance took smooth strides, sniffing the fall air noisily, feeling loopy and languid. Intoxication demanded surrender of control. His tyranny of analysis was disabled, allowing a random process which seemed like freedom. He recognized a lack of control in the randomness, a danger, but he enjoyed this. The sky's multi-hued glow held out before darkness. This moment! He fixated on the pink-orange mélange, giving no thought to the tabulation of GPA numbers in computers, or the blinking answering machine in his dorm room with unreturned calls from his father. What could ever be worth worrying about? he conveyed with his effortless gait. He was young, strong and untamed. The conspiracy would not succeed—the old men who wanted to snatch his youth, to break him, to put him in a hole and kill him.

O'Grady's Cantina was in an obscure brick building next to a dry cleaner. Standing inside on moist carpet, their eyes adjusted to the velvety dark: nothing Irish or Latino about the place. Something about the decor put LaCoss in the mood to discuss *The Man Who Would Be the King*. His mind flared with nonsensical story ideas. "Wow, mind quake. Check this out, Lance." He talked while scribbling illegible notes on a bar napkin. Drunkenness caused him to switch the first and last letters of words—a dyslexic tic that had caused him torment and relentless teasing as a kid, and had been exacerbated by a motocross concussion. "OK, once Wyatt Burris finally gets to Las Vegas and he falls in love with the show girl, it turns out the show girl is a psychic and she predicts this catastrophe, which is this massive earthquake in California."

More often than not, Lance had to shoot him down. "But what does an earthquake have to do with Wyatt's story? Unless he was there during the earthquake. But why do that?"

"All right, I follow." LaCoss tapped his forehead knowingly.

"Maybe the psychic could predict his eventual triumph as an Elvis impersonator."

"Maybe instead of a showgirl, it's a prostitute…"

Lance shook his head sadly. The screenplay wasn't working. They had tinkered with *The Man Who Would Be the King*, Lance rewriting scenes, both of them reading sections of dialogue aloud. They had tried to make Wyatt a heroin addict, then a lifelong insomniac, then a kleptomaniac, then a junkie kleptomaniac. But his quest to be the greatest Elvis impersonator remained incomplete. It wasn't clicking, in part because they worked on it after a night of drinking, or in some debilitated state of mind. Lance was getting bored with the project. He coughed down a shot of Bushmills, then asked LaCoss, "What is your play about? The Nuclear what…?"

LaCoss had done a shot of vodka schnapps and chugged down a boilermaker. This combo worked on him as if he had been beaten, then injected with truth serum. His eyes dropped to the floor and his chest went concave. "*The Complete Nuclear Family*. It completely sucks in every way. It's embarrassing. Wallace Dennis wrote this German Expressionist, avant-garde piece of shit." He shook his head, clearly experiencing the stage moment Johnny Strabler, leader of the Black Rebel Motorcycle Club, roared into Weaverville on a chopper. Experimental Expo Theatre was the lesser cousin of Langford Theatre, with a third of the budget, and no hope it would grace the cover of a university or alumni publication.

"Sounds Cold War-related. What's the plot?" Charles Boyd asked.

LaCoss rubbed his fists into his eyes, his voice muddled and weary. "Jesus, I wish I knew. I've got theories, and frankly these theories are driving me insane. You've got your postmodern alienation of the soul, then you mix in adolescent confusion and…oh, man, lately I'm thinking it's like God versus the Devil, and God is losing." He pressed his forehead into the table and sighed.

The door creaked and an Asian girl in a red spandex skirt and denim jacket walked in, followed by two girls. Long black hair trailed the girl. "Oh my God, I'm so in love right now," Charles Boyd said, the palm of his hand bunching up his cheek. Asian girls were his greatest weakness.

"That's awfully fast," Lance said.

Boyd gazed dreamily at the table where the girls sat. He slid to the end of the booth, then stopped, as though rethinking approaching them.

"Where you going?" LaCoss asked.

"Nowhere." Boyd became glum; he stopped looking in their direction. Lance felt bad for Charles Boyd. He was getting to an age where shyness and youthful fumbling were no longer excuses. He was either going to get a girlfriend soon or be one of those lonely, troubled guys whose missteps, rough edges and resentments became more and more severe, each rejection cutting him until he had a hide like an armadillo that would repel every woman on sight. He was in danger of never getting beyond Charlotte Westminster.

"Have you ever been in love?" Lance asked Charles Boyd.

Boyd paused, uncomfortable with the topic, his eyes tentative. "Well…sure. I was so in love in high school I couldn't eat."

"Did she love you as much?" Lance asked.

He paused again, longer. "She didn't know I existed."

"Then that doesn't count."

LaCoss agreed—it didn't qualify.

Boyd's mouth fell open. "So, I've had zero love. Great. That's comforting, guys. Shouldn't I get some love?" The corners of Boyd's mouth twitched: a signal, Lance had learned, that Boyd had made an important admission and though he would try hard to mask it, a nerve had been struck. His eyes trailed down to the table. Then they hardened, as if remembering a lifetime of hurt.

"It's all a matter of instant chemical reaction," LaCoss said, framing his hands scientifically. "Endorphins. It's animal. It's programmed, like nature. It's got nothing to do with wanting."

"Love can develop over time. That disproves your theory," Charles Boyd said coldly.

"It doesn't exist."

"If you think about it," Lance said, "love is the central concept of human experience. It's the reason people marry. The basis of parent-child relationships. Everyone wants it desperately. But it can't be quantified. Can't be explained. It's like defining what art is."

Boyd fixated on LaCoss, stoking his indignation. "Doesn't exist? How unbelievably hypocritical. Then what is all that hippie crap about your magical relationship with Lucinda Falcon?"

"The vibe is overwhelming. It's really special. I write her every week. Wow, I am really missing her."

Boyd became loud: "That's just plain wrong! That's a violation. You're screwing all these other women. What's so special about that? And you deny the very existence of love!"

"Those are emotionally platonic relationships. That's allowed. They can have a sexual component and remain valid."

"Bullshit!"

The bartender looked suspiciously in their direction.

LaCoss said in a quieter, hurt tone, "What's between me and Lucinda is a rare thing."

"I'm super confused," Lance said. "Who can deny love?"

"Love is a bunch of shit," LaCoss said. He smacked his palm on the table and paused, getting everyone's full attention. His nostrils flared. "It's dangerous. My mother has been married four times, my father three. You know how many weddings I've attended, all the bullshit I've heard? Love sparkles like a jewel in the ocean. Our love is the brightest star. Love is the most sacred thing…And what happens next?" He swallowed; his voice began cracking. "Cars peeling out of driveways at 3:00 a.m., drunk people screaming about money—that's the best. I think of screaming as the language of love. Then your new stepdad threatens you with a baseball bat…As soon as you say love then bad mojo is coming your way."

A chill trailed up Lance's spine, as if, suddenly alone in a forest, he were being stalked by a huge predatory beast. How many times had he used the word? Could it possibly be true with Lynn? Charles Boyd stared apologetically, then looked down at his hands. LaCoss crossed his arms and unfocused his eyes, collapsing within. Misery descended on them, this emotional turn leaving them incapable of responding. It was a grenade blast, and they lacked the coping skills to crawl to the other. The silence lasted four minutes, like they occupied separate suspended animation capsules aboard a spaceship, until a song came on the dormant jukebox. A lost song, fallen off the AM dial. A singer with a warbling voice. The tune had a plucky Motown flavor and a melancholy subtext: "The Israelites" by Desmond Dekker & The Aces. Everybody in the bar stopped and gazed off. As though the music was a collective projection of a heartbreaking memory—a failed romance, a regret. Are these people really that different from me? Lance thought, looking at the regular stool-sitters and hard cases. He felt an odd kinship.

Buddy Holly crooning about Peggy Sue broke the spell. They threw money on the table, eager to leave troubles behind. They crunched the metal arm on the front door and moved on. It was brilliant, Lance reflected, to be spending your time this way, so wildly free, and to be outsmarting the whole world.

"LET'S RACE!" LaCoss screamed, bolting ahead with a head start. Lance jostled for position, hooking Boyd with an elbow. He had superior foot speed and was ahead of Boyd by the edge of the parking lot. His feet smacked the ground as he pumped his arms, feeling totally alive, strong and sure on his feet, his lungs expanding to full capacity. No one could catch him—not the conspiracy that sought to confine and enslave him and stress him out, not Jack Dalrymple or George Van Oster, because they were old, fat and slow. How dare they try! It felt too good to stop, so he darted in front of a speeding car, honk honk, as he sprinted right across Vigden Boulevard.

They arrived at Jumping Johnnies! in tatters, wet hair plastered to their foreheads. Welcome girls in halter tops yelled whoooo! and plucked beers from an arctic tableau and thrust the dripping cans at them. The wha-wha-wha beat of the dance floor could not be escaped: the power ballads and hot rock hits and dance faves vibrated under their feet and pounded their ears. A time warp occurred, during which LaCoss went missing and Charles Boyd danced, in his herky-jerky reluctant way, with a girl—a hopeful and rare thing—then was cruelly ignored by that girl, sending him into crisis. He stood before Lance, his *Clockwork Orange* t-shirt drenched in sweat, screaming, but his voice barely audible as a speaker the size of a steamer trunk hung from chains overhead, blasting a Steve Miller greatest hit. How ridiculous is this, Lance thought, over one dance? Yet Boyd was suddenly vulnerable and desperate. He'd cracked; his mouth stretched in a fierce attempt to communicate. Tears welled in his eyes, behind his round wire rim glasses, but did not flow. He and Lance glanced around, aware of surrounding people, aware of the girl, who resembled Charlotte Westminster, engaged in a mocking celebration with girlfriends. Both Boyd and Lance were horrified at the possibility of open weeping. Boyd used all his energy and willpower to not cry, focusing this energy into shouting. Lance realized this monologue was intensely personal. Something Boyd had never dared speak before, not to his migraine-ridden, manic-depressive mother who spent days locked inside her room, not to any listening, caring female of any age, not to anyone. It was monumental and it came out as a torrent, his eyes burning. Lance wished he could think after his last Jagermeister shot. Or the song would change so he might hear Boyd, and give a word of advice and be a decent friend, but his attempts to yell back were obliterated by the pounding music. It was all he could manage to lock eyes, firmly grasp Boyd's shoulder, and give several meaningful shudders. Boyd's head slumped and he turned away. The last time he would be seen outside his dorm room for a long time.

In mid-evening, the enraged ex-girlfriends of LaCoss began swarming. LaCoss's hands went up defensively as a dark-haired girl darted toward him, her face tense with hurt. It was Celie Banks, a petite angel-faced girl, who LaCoss had broken up with twice. Her head twitched as she yelled epithets. A gaggle of Celie's friends gave LaCoss mean looks. Why were girls still willing to sleep with him? How had he found time for all of them? LaCoss talked with Celie firmly, though not unhappily. His attitude toward these girls was always charitable, understanding, like they were still on good terms. His raging optimism guided him. A past lover screaming curses? No problem, the shared good feelings were sure to return. An arm punch from a recent fling partner? He cast forgiving eyes, finding an attractive fire he wanted to rekindle. Celie Banks shouted over him, then took off into a crowd seam.

Lance caught up to her near the front door, putting a hand on her shoulder. She spun, whipping her face around. Oh, that wounded face, that tiny defiant nose! And the upheaval, the heartbreak, the emotional storm consuming her. It was so beautifully irresistible and reminiscent of Lynn's Disney outburst.

"I'm Lance. A friend of Ian LaCoss."

She scowled. "Tell him I hate him!" She narrowed her eyes, rage coiling her body until it was perfectly still. They always suspected it was some sort of trick.

"Hey, I just saw what was going on. And I was concerned." All true, the sincerity coming across. Celie studied Lance closer. Heartache gathered around her moist eyes again. Lance knew he had her then. "Let's talk outside." Lance moved toward the exit, putting his hand around her in a courteous way, but without touching her. They walked out to the parking lot. Celie had her slender arms crossed, multiple Swatch watches on one wrist.

Her voice touched a distressed high registry. "How could I have been so stupid? Ian LaCoss is the most selfish person alive. And a complete liar. My friends told me—don't get involved."

"I realize he doesn't have the best reputation, but the guy has a decent soul. These are matters of the heart. These things get…confused. And…also…" She was wearing this tight little top. His head felt like an inflated lawn bag. He grasped at what his point had been.

"Are you drunk?"

"No. Well…just buzzed. No more than you."

"I haven't had anything. I have a test tomorrow."

Dealing with these enraged girls was beyond challenging. He fell back on instinct and what he considered a budding talent. He loved his role as the healer, the white knight, the charitable emissary. The depth of their despair astonished him; it came from simple misplaced trust, or from an incorrect perception. He was strangely drawn to it. And that this deliberate male trickery had happened to them (why me? how could he do this to me?) struck them as horribly unfair. It was unbearable. These things weren't supposed to happen to them. It was gravity reversed, water flowing upstream. The shattering hurt, the intensity of these feelings! If translated into physical pain, it was worthy of an emergency room visit. Was it weird Lance wished he'd been the one to break up with them? Surely something here would give insight into Lynn.

"All that crap about him starring in movies. That's never going to happen. Ian LaCoss is just a total loser." Her voice whiny at the edges.

He held up his hands softly, like she might explode. "You can't just stomp on somebody's dreams like that."

"I don't know why I'm talking to you. I don't even know you." Celie tightened her crossed arms.

"But now you do."

Lance leaned in to Celie, awestruck by a thought. "Think about this. Whether this moment was preordained or not, it doesn't matter, because the moment is here nonetheless. And right now it's you and me. And we have an essential freedom. Look at this beautiful sky. Your eye can just zoom right up there. But, maybe in its own way this moment was preordained. Like this thing with you and LaCoss. Painful perhaps, but it's over. You're moving on." Celie seemed to relax, to consider his thoughts. Balancing on one leg, she uncrossed her arms and put her hands to either side on the car trunk behind her. Lance kept talking, convinced he was onto something very profound. He leaned against the car, putting his arm in the crook between her hip and her arm. She chatted about LaCoss and he nodded with sympathy.

"My friends are leaving," she said. Celie stepped away from the car, then turned back.

"You'll be OK," Lance held out his hand, business-handshake style.

She gave him a polite goodbye hug. A strand of hair trailed over his nose a second, citrus-scented, and she was off. He imagined seeing Celie strolling across campus. She would wave. There was a little bond there. Jen Salter, whose blabbering he'd listened to for an hour and a half, thanked him days later. Mandy Turnbull, an early case Lance had botched, who had tried to slam a car door on his hand, even wrote him an apology.

The most challenging enraged girl case of all: Veronica Boyer. She was a good friend of Laurie Stark, who had quasi-stalked LaCoss after a breakup, a *Fatal Attraction* thing. Then Laurie threatened to quit college, ending up in the care of a university psychologist for a tense weekend. In a revenge attack, Veronica Boyer tossed a drink into LaCoss's face, kicked his shin and told the stunned girl he had been dancing with that he was a "womanizer" and a "ritual abuser of women." LaCoss staggered from the stinging liquid, pawing his blood-red eyes and cursing. Lance followed her out to the parking lot, shocked as much as anything. She was a brunette, tiny, in a clingy black vintage dress and pink stockings. Beautifully pale skin, this flawless porcelain. She seemed out of place among Langfordites.

"Do you know how painful vodka can be in someone's eyes?" Lance asked as she moved away fast into the night. The kind of enraged woman you gave a wide berth to.

She turned around, but without looking at him. "I've done worse."

"Who are you to get involved?"

"I could ask you the same question." She spun around, sucking in her cheeks. She had a startling, curvaceous little figure. These full, amazing lips.

"I'm Lance."

"I'm Veronica."

His instinct was to console, but this was not applicable. It was a whole other situation. He struggled to adjust.

"Am I distracting you from the singles action? Is this a parking lot pickup attempt?" She tucked a lock of dark hair behind an ear. A beauty that radiated intelligence.

"Actually, I came here to punch your lights out for doing that to my friend."

She put up her dukes. Lance put his fists up too and made a few jabs in her direction. She turned and started walking again, her heeled boots clopping an up-tempo beat on the pavement. At a yellow Karmann-Ghia, she pulled a noisy mass of keys out of a black purse, rubber insects and bullets dangling.

"You go around assaulting people without explanation?" Lance asked.

"Lance, Lance, Lance. Someday I'll give you the full explanation." She shut her door and her car sputtered off into the night.

Proving Jung, and Sting, correct in their theories of synchronicity, Lance spotted Veronica Boyer sitting on a marble pediment alongside the stairs of the Humanities building a week later. She was eating a tuna fish sandwich, her fingers poking out of black lace gloves. With sprouting, Bangles-type hair and a black denim jacket. He walked the length of the pediment and plopped down next to her, swinging his legs over the end.

"You're actually enrolled here," he said.

"Naw. I just like to hang out and pretend."

He reached into her bag of Fritos, pulling out a freakish off-color cluster that was glued together. She raised her eyebrows, not exhibiting aggression so much as full concentration. She pressed her lips together, but couldn't hide her amusement.

"So, where's your girlfriend at?" she asked, her voice trailing off. He crunched loudly, a wayward chunk tumbling out of his mouth. "The one you were groping at the President's Day concert. The blonde. Are we having memory troubles?"

"Shoot. The time has gotten away from me." Lance glanced at his watch. "We must do lunch another day."

He jumped from his perch. He took about twenty steps on the walkway before getting a glimpse of her in his periphery. Veronica, now in sunglasses, gazed into a thick book.

In late hours the dance floor of Jumping Johnnies! thinned. They waved off waitresses, fighting to keep from spinning into incoherence or complete malfunction. Then a euphoria softened Lance's face, like he was suddenly in a movie dream sequence with pixilated edges and shimmering light: he was going home to Lynn!

It was twenty minutes in a steady jog, but it seemed like no time at all. No traffic on the side streets, just dull orbs of street lights. He ran down streets, cars be damned, footfalls wisping underneath him the only sound. He took easy strides, consumed by a floating sensation. He ran across the tip of a yard, jumping from a retaining wall and gaining acceleration on the sidewalk below. He could have run for hours, could have taken the gold medal away from Bruce Jenner. He turned off his mind, save for an idealized vision of a bare-shouldered Lynn. He could see being with Lynn for a long time, for the duration—marriage, the ring, all of it—and that would be so good. Yes, a ring!

He charged on, crazy-legged and illusive, protected from detection by an invisible coating. At her apartment, at the top of the metal staircase, fourteen feet up, he hung over the metal railing to see if he could balance with his feet in the air. The ground undulated below, swirling clockwise. He teetered and tottered—wheee! Enjoying the sensation, he mumbled lyrics he couldn't place. He made sure it was the right door, 6B. He'd knocked loudly on 3B the week before, at 2:30 a.m., running away before anyone answered. He raised his hand, then remembered the key they had given him. He shut the door behind him in the dark interior. He stood still, not wishing a repeat of last week's destruction of Gwen's side table: the one her grandmother, just deceased, had passed on to her. He had been so blitzed he body-slammed it, snapping a table leg and splitting the top. Lights flashed on, girls rushed out of bedrooms. His leg was bleeding, further defiling the shattered heirloom. Gwen fell to her knees, wailing. The other two stood over him and frowned. Lance had it fixed, though it remained rickety.

Moving gingerly through the living room, he found the hallway. A light shone under Lynn's bedroom door. His hunger for her was peaking—so near, it was overwhelming. He ducked his head into her room, squinting. In sweatpants and reading glasses, she was curled up on the bed, surrounded by a nest of papers, the same as when he'd left that afternoon. Her hair was tied back, making her face strict, revealing a rare zit on her forehead. He swayed, his loopy smile directed her way. He inhaled the girl smells of her bedroom, the talcum, the conditioner fragrances, the scented lotions, and said, "It is soooo fantastic to see you," while he stumbled toward her bed. She hastily swiped papers and a calculator away from his landing zone.

"How much did you drink tonight?" She used a judgmental tone and sniffed his hair unfavorably. "Confess. Tell the truth."

"No more than usual." The comforter muffled his voice. He squirmed until his cheek found her soft thigh and his muscles relaxed. She pulled a hand through his hair and he looked up at her, feeling like a beached and satisfied sea lion.

She picked up his ink-stained hand. "Is this a phone number?"

"This weird song played in O'Grady's. I had to write down

the name." Lance noticed all the papers. More papers were on the floor. "What's all this stuff?"

"It's called studying. Remember that? You need to do some of that." She tugged his ear painfully. Psychology and Statistics was probably the most work-intensive course at Langford. She devoted several hours a day to it.

Lance grunted, consumed with the bliss of her thigh. It was so reassuring and safe. He closed his eyes. His voice sounded foreign to him: "OK, here was a lively discussion that took place tonight. About love…"

She cocked her head to the side, focusing her full attention.

"About what a weird, indefinable concept it is. It's all you hear. It's like the ultimate goal of everything, right? Love. Love. Love. But what is the objective measure of it? Is it more a personal rationalization than anything else? How does anybody know anybody else's view of love is the same? It's a feeling, but feelings are notoriously subjective." Had he opened his eyes, he would have seen her reaching for a Kleenex, then dabbing a tear from one eye, then the other. "…It's probably the shakiest concept to base anything on, much less commitments between people. I mean…" It was impossible to keep his thoughts organized. "I don't know what I'm saying…" Sleep overtook him like an oncoming bullet train.

She slid from under him, then stared at Lance. A steady flow of tears coursed over her cheeks. She went into the living room and found the phone. She would have called her mother, but it was too late.

His body pressed into the bed, squashing a red rose in his jeans pocket. He had purchased it that evening for Lynn, but would only remember days later, when the brown shriveled remains fouled the inside of a dryer, and he discovered, inside the pocket, the rose never given and its clump of a white tag, which had said: I Love You and Only You!

CHAPTER THIRTEEN

NINETY-NINE PERCENT

E very moviegoer and would-be screenwriter knew about the devastating reversal. But deep inside the story, you forgot it was coming. Every *Rocky* comeback, every WWII mission led by Lee Marvin, and every *Godfather* movie—just when things looked fine, personal conflicts turned poisonous, a rain of blood and chaos from opportunistic enemies. Musicians fared no better. When your favorite band reached a brilliant pinnacle, the horrible concept album wasn't far away, an insult to make you deny ever having liked them and send their concert tees to the bottom of a drawer. When Lance phoned Lynn the day after his crash landing, he was determined to broach the subject of their future plans, of a life lived together, but before he could he was puzzled by a pensiveness on her end.

Lance took a deep breath, then said, "There's something I want to talk about—it's big. I'll drop in tonight."

A rustling sound, then a pause. "I kinda wish you wouldn't."

"Huh…what was that?"

"There have been complaints. You have destroyed furniture. I mean, just think about your behavior lately. It's been pretty bad."

"I fixed that stupid table."

"Lance, what is your GPA going to be after this semester?"

She was gathering steam; it worried him. "Of course, I'll study for my exams."

"You're just on that borderline," Lynn said, using the sensitive, helpful voice he found impossible to defy. "If you worked harder it would make a huge difference with grad schools. That is really important." Lance placed fingers against his cheeks and pressed upward until his face was distorted and his teeth showed. He had taken such determined, punishing lengths to not think about these things. Now he was forced to think about them.

"Meanwhile, I'm working my ass off this year. Sometimes I wonder about your commitment to your future."

Irritation crept into his voice. "I am committed to my future." What did this even mean? It sounded like being committed to breathing, or to gravity.

"Have you even thought about your business school applications?"

He guffawed. "How long does it take to type an application?"

"Doing things last-minute, this is not your strength."

That night in her room, Lynn stared unhappily into her lap. His hand nudged her leg; her hand did not embrace his as it customarily did. She said, "I just don't know about things. You announced your whole theory of love the other night."

This was a relief. He could clear up the confusion. Lance lay back on the bed and smiled. "I was babbling. I don't know what the hell I was saying. It was theoretical stuff. Nothing to do with us." He shook his head.

"The way you think about love has everything to do with us and whether or not you love me the way you say you do."

He straightened up and put a reassuring hand on her knee. "I totally love you. How many times have I said this? In fact—"

A weird high-pitched edge entered her voice. "But you said the whole idea about love was the least understood concept ever. You said it was all but meaningless!"

"I didn't say that."

"Yes, you did!" Blood had risen into her face.

"You're attacking me over nothing."

"I think you finally revealed the way you really feel." She

glared at him.

Lance found it difficult to breath. He restrained a surging anger. This wasn't happening. He'd done nothing to deserve this. He had just been honest. Wasn't that an honorable quality, even desirable?

LaCoss was incredulous. "Why didn't you just tell her she's butt-ugly or you secretly hate her guts? It would have had the same effect."

"I was only talking theoretically. It was this completely esoteric conversation."

"Nothing is theoretical with them, or esoteric. Everything pertains directly to them. To them and them alone."

LaCoss was so right. Lance wanted to pound his head against a wall. He resolved to win her back, and remove any doubt planted by his raving. He went on his best behavior. He even fixed the toilet in Lynn's apartment when management stalled sending someone out. Using the toolbox he kept in his car, he replaced a leaking flapper. Lynn sat on the edge of the shower, complaining about smells. The tank filled up and Lance smiled with satisfaction. Lynn seemed not to notice this successful result. Her tongue rubbed her front teeth and she squinted. "Someone told me they knew you the other day."

"Who's that?"

"Celie Banks. She's in my Statistics lab."

His chest constricted. Lance pulled his grimy hands out of the tank. "Celie. Yeah, she used to date LaCoss."

Lynn's voice quieted in a sly way. "You think. You talked to her for over an hour in the parking lot of Johnnies." Lance sensed one of those deeply searching looks boring a hole into the back of his head.

"I talked to her awhile. So what? She screamed at LaCoss that night."

Lynn was looking out into the hall, slack-faced. "I don't understand why girls put up with him. Maybe you've figured it out from hanging around him so much."

"Look, Ian is my friend."

"Fine. I just keep getting reports about girls you're talking to."

It was unbearable. This interrogation, while he slaved over their stupid toilet. And how many guys did Lynn regularly chat with between classes, or while standing around in her aerobics outfit and dabbing her head with a towel? Lynn insisted on sleeping alone for the time being. Over a several-day period, Lance failed to get Lynn on the phone, his old nemesis. He dialed and dialed. Gwen and Gennifer were cheerful in their ignorance of Lynn's whereabouts. He got no return calls. He was whipsawed between fury and raw panic.

"It's taken a dangerous turn, my friend," LaCoss said. "She's using your screw-up as leverage. You can't let her get away with this." LaCoss had rules for dealing with girl turmoil. First, resistance or avoidance on her part should not be answered with more pursuit. Second, if he were to apologize for any crimes or excesses on his part, she should be made to do so also. Third, weeping or emotional outbursts on his part were strictly verboten. This was pure female manipulation, a trap often used as a test of devotion. She would hold it against him. Knowledge of this dangerous phase further stressed out Lance. LaCoss urged caution. If Lance made concessions during this period or if her outrages were ignored or prematurely forgiven, then their relationship would continue in a weakened and impossible state, like a surfboard without fins. Groveling and lowering himself to pathetic depths would only result in hating himself later. All her girlfriends would give him amused, piteous looks the rest of his college career. Or worse, Lance might win her back but be emotionally enslaved.

"You've got to hold her feet to the fire," LaCoss said. He held a dollar bill close to his eyes. He had heard if you studied Washington's curled hair long enough, a likeness of Karl Marx could be seen. "If she doesn't want to talk, then she doesn't get the pleasure of your company."

"Right. I see that now. I'll wait for her to call me."

"Good man."

Lance got up from their booth in O'Grady's and went to the bathroom. Why was he listening to LaCoss? His tactics were driving girls to screaming and drink-tossing. He found a quarter in his pocket and dialed Lynn's number on the pay phone, despising himself. Gwen answered and he hung up. He let out a long groan, thinking of the way Lynn hugged him around the ribs, her face even with his clavicles, the sweet flowery smell of the top of her head. A wetness strained his eyes. He held it back, recalling a shouting tirade his tee-ball coach, Coach Bronson, had directed at Jerry Ravy, who struck out and cried, and at the whole team, that only sissies cried, that criers let down the team and lost ball games and were losers at life. This echoed the modeling of Scout leaders, coaches and assorted dads, that manly behavior was a kind of lock-jawed determination and wariness, a hardness, and emotional displays led to undisciplined behavior, and eventually to being queer.

Lance held the tears back, feeling horrible shame at his need to cry.

Lance gave up expecting Lynn's voice with every ring of his phone. Then she called. She was sweet, though insistent; she wanted to talk about some things. They agreed to lunch at the South Campus Cafeteria. He ducked in from a glass side door. The ancient hall had the depressing eggshell ambiance of a V.A. hospital, with gray carpeting between the Olympian tables. Twin portraits of Theodore Ivan Langford and Fritz Szabo Langford hung under dusty banners at a far end, sheets of Plexiglas protecting them from stray ketchup.

Lynn was already seated alone at a long table, a blue tray before her. His heart bucked inside his chest. He tapped his fingers on the backs of chairs as he walked. She wore a loose unbuttoned blue oxford shirt over a white t-shirt and jeans. He put his hand on her arm and stooped to kiss her cheek. She held her face up, accepting the kiss, not smiling, but not being unfriendly either. It gave him hope. Lance pointed toward the steam lines. The place smelled of broccoli, detergent and mop water. He gathered fish filets and hush puppies, a corn dog which looked appetizing, a soft-serve ice cream cone and some orange juice in a sealed cup.

Lynn wiped her mouth with a napkin, her eyes lingering over him as he sat down and positioned his tray across from her.

"I'm hungry," Lance said, like it was any usual lunch.

"It looks like it." She stared at his tray with a numb face.

He popped a hush puppy in his mouth, chewing with a smile. He was infused with a spirit he could fix things and was going to. They were going to have a good laugh at their rift, pointing at it like a rude monkey in a zoo cage, then walking away happily. She placed a morsel of cottage cheese into her mouth, then morosely picked at salad remnants on her plate. She turned her head to glance at food workers gathered by a cashier.

"Who are you going to vote for in the presidential election?" he asked.

"Mmmm. I don't know. Doesn't matter in my case. I'm not registered." She leaned back with a bored composure, her hands in her lap.

Lance laughed to himself, then leaned over the table. "You wouldn't believe Charles Boyd. He's gone nuts or something. He's obsessed with the election. He won't leave his room. He's been in there for days, hunkered down like Brian Wilson." Lance nodded his head vigorously, seeking validation that this was amusing.

She raised her eyebrows, opening her mouth in a disturbed way. She found Charles Boyd disturbing, though she was always friendly to him. Boyd was icky; just how she could never explain. Lance plumbed deep inside himself for something entertaining to say, something to draw out her sparkle. She was frowning. He was bloated from the fish filets, the sweet juice making him feel sick. A couple ambled down the aisle, his arm around her neck, her hand shoved in his back pocket. People with trays were hovering, then choosing other tables, steering clear of the stink of bad relationship mojo.

Disappointment sunk in. He had imagined her suffering for days leading up to her phone call, immersing herself in crying jags and looking at his picture with longing. He had further imagined what he'd say, I understand how you might confuse what I said with how I feel, which would pave a return to their cheery past, her blue eyes loving him, her face radiating joy. Later, he'd rub his lips against her breasts.

Instead, she planted her elbows on the table. She pointed her face at his and brought out the stare. A test and a method to wear him down. He met her stare, trying to match its intensity; when he didn't do so, she always interpreted this as unseriousness about their relationship and a lack of devotion to her. But he could never sit still because he feared failing the test and revealing, falsely, that he valued things less. Also, it reminded him of *Blade Runner*, when Harrison Ford tests Sean Young to find out if she is a replicant. Lynn's dead-eyed glare was very replicant-like and unpredictable and creepy. Also, he worried she'd use her mindreading to discover he was actually a replicant, or somehow defective, rather than the sweet guy she wanted. So he tried to relax, thinking purely devotional thoughts, yet he soon broke and glanced down at his orange juice.

She took a deep breath. Then, in a professional tone: "I wanted to meet to talk in person. My period is late. It was supposed to come two weeks ago."

He was working on a corn dog stick, chewing off the last breaded crumbs. He almost asked when it was going to come, since it was late, like it was a delay in mail order delivery or a flight in need of rescheduling. He put down the stick. The air in his lungs grew heavier. He stared at her. "OK. So it's late."

Red rose in her cheeks. "This never happens to me. Every month it's like clockwork. I don't know it means anything."

People at other tables seemed to be glancing over. Lance lowered his voice. "So you think you might…"

"I don't know." The corners of her mouth turned down with irritation.

She was pulling him into a chasm, a paranoid bunker. She only knew enough to scare herself and felt the need to frighten him as well. He racked his mind to recall details from a Health class, what he'd learned between the snickering—the arcana of ovulation, of insemination, the Fallopian tubes, the shedding of the uterine lining…

But she was on the Pill! It was impossible!

"Have you been taking your—"

"Of course I have."

"Isn't it ninety-nine percent effective?" He was nodding, trying to convince her.

"It isn't perfect. Some women get pregnant on the Pill. Not that…" She took a deep, uneasy breath, then snapped her head angrily.

A milky river trickled down his soft cone, puddling on his tray. Armpit sweat ran down his ribs. He leaned back, staring into a corner of the room.

"I thought you should know. I'm assuming you're interested, but I probably shouldn't assume." She threw her knife onto her plate, bouncing it, then looked away. The sharp ping of the bouncing knife disabled his vocal cords, and soured him against trying to say anything else. He looked down at his melting soft cone, which he never ate. They stood at the same time, without looking at each other. He left the South Campus cafeteria via the University Drive exit, not paying attention to where he was going. In the stairwell, graffiti had been written with a fresh black marker:

THE LANGFORD AMAZON SOCIETY SAYS:
In the near future,
men will become unnecessary.

He walked past with an eye fixed on the mysterious words, as if they might jump and bite him. Was it a threat? A prediction? It seemed a projection from the darkest corner of Lynn's mind. On the sidewalk, a crowd was gathered. The Langford Owl mascot and two cheerleaders were handing out balloons in anticipation of a basketball game. Lance skulked past, wondering if he had said the right things. The Langford Owl, holding a black balloon, broke through a semicircle of onlookers and raced toward Lance. He tried to avoid the silent giant-headed mascot. The Owl's knees, covered by yellow tights, pumped as it worked for Lance's attention. Ducking his head, weirded out, Lance kept walking. The Owl tied the balloon around Lance's neck to laughter and applause.

The balloon bobbed behind his head like a pursuing malignant cloud.

An October cold front frosted his dorm window, obscuring the world beyond. The heat wasn't working in Oswald, so Lance donned a double layer of sweaters. He sat on the floor, consumed with the terrifying possibility a tiny human being could be developing in Lynn's uterus. The idea taunted him, like a shadowy dream villain. Pregnancy. The word which sounded like a disease. Fatherhood was so alien he couldn't go there. It was still only a possibility. Wasn't ninety-nine-percent effectiveness good enough? Had those scientists lied about the Pill to every high schooler in America? He had been lulled into a false paradise, into the belief that you could do it like Adam and Eve, like Mickey Rourke and Kim Basinger, like Jack and Diane, over and over, free of any consequences. He wasn't sure how Lynn felt about abortion. He knew she wanted babies once she was married. Maybe she wouldn't turn one away now. After all, it was their biological role. And insemination wasn't necessarily a precise thing.

He answered his phone in an automatic motion. Both parents chattered in his ear like hungry birds. They wanted to visit him that very weekend! They had the weekend open, and could meet that girlfriend of his. It was catastrophic, this threatened visit. Lance put his hand on some unopened textbooks to stand up. They shifted and he hit the floor. He sensed what they really wanted was to investigate, to get past his shifty pseudo answers and get real answers. And Lance knew that if he were with them long enough, he might give them some, about his grades, about the girl he had lived with, who he had impregnated and who now wouldn't speak to him. What Lance most dreaded was a new feeling toward his parents he didn't want to feel and would not express, but would richly experience in their presence: a terrible negative feeling, a dark spear of resentment, perhaps hatred. This feeling would be awful and confirm he was a rotten person. So he rattled off excuses, so flimsy and implausible he forgot them as soon as they warbled in his mouth. The next weekend was bad too, sorry. Bye. When the phone rang five minutes later, he put fingers in his ears. That evening the dorm resident advisor put a note on Lance's door: *Please call your parents*.

Two days later, Lance answered a ringing phone, sensing and hoping for Lynn, yet found himself speaking to his brother Kevin. "What's your problem?" Kevin wanted to know, using his condescending voice. Lance stonewalled, wondering about the answer himself. "Thought you might want to know they've made calls and figured out your grade situation. They're going to yank you out of Langford if you don't get your act together." The phone dropped away from Lance's ear. He rested his hand in his lap and took some deep breaths. He couldn't dispel a gnawing pain. He'd been considered in the same thought with being yanked out of college—the hallmark of the modern fuckup. Another low. It was as disturbing as premature fatherhood, but somehow seemed less real.

"Guaranteed she is not, I repeat, is not pregnant," LaCoss said.

"But she never misses. This is very unusual."

"First off, this is what she has told you. The invented crisis is not beyond them in terms of tactics. But menstruation is not like trains running in Germany. Delays happen. Physiological changes or stress can throw them off schedule." LaCoss was the most convincing guy you could imagine sometimes. If you scrutinized it, his thought process was often shaky, but it seemed to work for him.

"Ask Lucinda. We went through the very thing last summer. It was nothing. She just skipped a month. But that whole maybe, maybe not stuff has been pulled on me before. I said no you don't, and that was the last of it."

"Lynn wouldn't do that. She has integrity." Lance almost said: unlike the girls you hook up with. In contrast to the carousel of meaningless sex LaCoss enjoyed with his goodtime chicks, Lance's love with Lynn was unprecedented and entirely spiritual. So rare and precious that losing Lynn was like the Taj Mahal burning to the ground.

"Don't underestimate her fear of losing you. I find it curious the preggers thing pops up after you guys haven't talked for a while."

Lance didn't want to imagine Lynn was capable of that, and resented the suggestion. But the last several weeks had caused him to reassess who she really was.

He tired of LaCoss's stressful guidance, so he went downstairs to Charles Boyd for a fresh opinion. The bunker-like insularity of Boyd's room appealed to him, as well as the possibility of taking some therapeutic hits off Boyd's giant bong. Lance knocked. There were muffled sounds, bumps against the door. Charles Boyd stuck his face in the crack of the door, just his mouth and watery eyes. Gray recesses under his eyes. "What is it?" His thready mustache was longer.

"I gotta talk to you." Smoky, fetid air blew into the hall. Lance's plan, if it was a plan, immediately seemed flawed.

Charles Boyd's eyes darted around the hall behind Lance in a paranoid way. "I'm really quite extremely busy."

"Too busy for a friend?"

Boyd sighed, shutting his eyes. He backed away from the door. Lance pushed it open, and stood among boxes and packaging peanuts. The room reeked with an unsavory stew: of soiled socks, armpit odor, and burnt incense sticks. Discarded plastic bags of microwaveable cuisine sat atop a full trash can. Adlai Stevenson darted out from a hiding place, startling Lance, and rubbed against his ankles. The cat's litter box was in a closet below hanging clothes; strangely, the only smell absent. Lance shivered. The room was freezing. He read address labels on boxes. Boyd had been ordering things off the television. A peculiar weakness. When channel flipping he had been sucked in by the ingenuity of the Pocket Fisherman, sold on the nostalgia of owning a double record compilation of Folk Classics. Boyd sat on a swivel chair, focusing on an old typewriter, and mumbled to himself, repeating "balance of power" over and over. There was an odd delicacy and fluidity to his gestures. He wore a U.S. Marines t-shirt, boxers with yellow smiling faces and hunting socks with snap pockets for batteries. The desk and table were arranged to form a console, a control bridge he sat behind. Everything was in a circumference around the typewriter: boxes of cereal, his mini fridge, a blue neon telephone, his stereo, a translucent yellow acrylic water pipe, disassembled watch parts and a jeweler's eyepiece, a red lava lamp, a GAF View-Master, a sketch pad with an elaborate aquatic monster drawn on the top sheet, a black and white TV showing C-SPAN coverage of the House of Representatives, and a color TV with a talking head news anchor.

"How much longer is this going to last?" Lance asked. "You've been holed up in here for two weeks." Books of every color and type were stacked four to six feet high, covering each wall. They seemed higher than ever, about to tumble and crush them both.

Boyd snorted and shook his head. "How much longer will our democracy last?"

Lance was concerned that Boyd had possibly broken from reality. Or maybe Boyd was using harder drugs. Maybe as a responsible party Lance should take some action to save Boyd before he became a corpse, waiting to be found. You did nothing, Mr. Rally? The idea Boyd was cracking made Lance feel better about himself.

Charles Boyd fixed his gaze on Lance, studying him, like he was performing an elaborate analysis. He nodded in an unnerving, conclusional way.

"People are beginning to talk about you," Lance said.

"People are stupid. Nobody gives a shit about me anyway. Half the population, the female gender, prefers I never speak to them again."

Boyd turned up the volume on the color TV...the presidential campaign shifting into high gear with this Ohio visit...the all-important electoral college...He turned it back down, shaking his head. He wrote notes on a pad, tapping his skull to recall a specific word. Lance picked a typed page off a chair from a stack of pages. A letter addressed to the Editor of *The Washington Post*:

> *Dear Editor,*
> *Have we read the 1st amendment lately? Where are your constitutional balls? The dog and pony show some refer to as a presidential election could be different if the free press dared to go beyond merely serving as a deaf and dumb mouthpiece, as a public address system for the vulgarities of the Bush and Dukakis debate squads.*
> *How does it feel to be used like a cheap date?*
> *Charles Grindler Boyd*
> *Junior, Langford University*

The neon phone buzzed softly. Boyd picked up the handset, setting it in the crook of his neck. "Hello. This is he...Terrific.

It's going to run in this Saturday's edition? Yes, I wrote it…That's fine with me." He hung up and said, "*San Francisco Examiner*. They're running my latest op-ed piece. Fourth piece I've published this week."

"Are you serious? Congratulations."

"My stuff is better than most editorial content out there." Charles Boyd patiently painted his thumbnail with Liquid Paper, doing a surprisingly neat job. A Tom Waits record was playing. Boyd sang along to "Innocent When You Dream," and matched Waits's raspy vocals. Adlai Stevenson jumped onto the typing table and nudged Boyd. He head-butted the cat in likewise spirit.

Suddenly, it was all too weird and Lance rubbed his eyes and moaned.

"You think I've lost it! Don't you?" Charles Boyd said. "I'm the sanest man in America. You know why? Because I give a damn. Representative democracy is important and what is happening in this election is a disgrace."

"Have you been eating?"

"It's because I care. Nobody is asking these candidates any hard questions!"

"It's no longer sanitary in here." Lance held his nose.

Boyd flung a shoe at Lance, missing his head by an inch, startling him and the cat. "I'm passionate about this. I want the world to be a better place. That is the focus of my career and my life. What do you know about passion, Lance? Do you have any passion? Or are you planning to just go through the motions in your stupid career? Huh? Answer me!"

Lance was speechless. Passion? Real passion had a significant downside. Maybe this was why Rallys tended to be cautious, dry and methodical. As a result of passion Charles Boyd was a shut-in, flirting with a psychotic break. Had Lance let passion rule with Celie Banks or any of the other girls, he would have ruined his relationship with Lynn Van Oster. And his passion for Lynn was being slowly turned around on him, aimed at his heart like a knife point that dimpled skin, about to plunge. That was what passion got you.

"Look at you." Boyd affixed the jeweler's eyepiece over his right eye. "Obviously, things are falling apart with Lynn. And more than that." He laughed like a vengeful god in a Greek myth, viewing the pitiful efforts of mortals. "The rats are jumping ship. The aid workers are being pulled out of the country. You're the amazing dart man, or should I say, the amazing non-dart man. Everybody is throwing and nobody can hit you. The question is, how long can you keep it up? The question is, what kind of man are you?"

"I didn't come here to be harassed. I am having problems with Lynn. Not that I'm getting any sympathy."

"He's avoiding the issue," Boyd said quietly to Adlai Stevenson. "Is it any wonder, considering...the league she's in?" Boyd half-smiled at Lance.

"I'm in the same league." Lance pointed a threatening finger.

"Of course you are."

Lance felt suddenly weak, desperate. Now it was his turn to hold back tears in front of Boyd. He'd momentarily forgotten the pregnancy thing and didn't want to bring it up. "Things are really messed up with Lynn. She won't talk to me. It's unbelievable, it's beyond awful...I feel like...like I'm dying..." Lance faked a cough to prevent weeping, realizing how destabilized he had become.

A concerned look came to Boyd's face. Then discomfort and puzzlement, as if he'd been called on by a professor and for the first time, he had no answer. He put his hands together under his nose and concentrated, channeling the wisdom of every book in the room. "Yeah, it's usually that way. Isn't it? At least, in every romantic comedy I've seen. They fight, they fall in love, they fight. That's the extent of my expertise." He shrugged.

Stuff Lance already knew. He felt no better.

"Don't you have a midterm exam coming up?" Lance

asked. "Next week or something?" Even the thought of someone else taking exams made Lance nervous.

"I have two. Tomorrow."

"Oh, man! What are you doing? Aren't you supposed to be studying?"

"I've done the reading. I'll do fine." Boyd scissored his legs, hiding his feet. The tiny chair was obscured, as though he were levitating. He smiled grandly.

Lance thought: He's going to ace his midterms and he already knows it. Was this fair? Even in lunatic mode, Charles Boyd was publishing editorials in major news outlets, provoking whirlwinds of national agitation. He would ace the Foreign Service exam and rocket through the ranks of the State Department. He would negotiate peace in troubled nations and be mentioned in fat headlines. Lance resisted this truth, just as he resisted he was losing Lynn. A survival-jamming radar was broadcasting within him, a high megahertz signal which blocked an honest appraisal of his academic situation and his rapidly approaching future. The signal weakened and in a clear moment Lance understood from where he stood, flicks of dirt and rock were being dislodged into the fuckup pit, that bottomless, steep-sided hole. No escape once you fell in. A crevice Charles Boyd could dangle over and dance around without ever taking a plunge.

"Mail these, please." Boyd handed over a stack of letters. He strapped gravity boots to his shins, grabbed a metal bar hooked inside his closet and hung upside down. On the floor, two lit jasmine incense sticks bled smoke that wrapped around his torso.

As Lance closed the door behind him, the future ambassador of the free world windmilled his arms, inhaling deeply.

What else could Lance do but start listening to Bauhaus? He'd gotten into them through LaCoss's friend Sy Terlinger, the anarchist actor who lived in the most decrepit rental in the West Downs. Terlinger was intense, maybe the coolest guy on campus, earning the reverence of people like LaCoss. His bio fascinated Lance. Terlinger had been attending Langford as an undergrad and postgrad for eight years. He was a teaching assistant in Organic Chemistry. He had welded a twelve-foot muffler sculpture in his yard, in the shape of a Celtic cross. He had exhibited his nude art photographs of middle-aged women in a local gallery. There were rumors he manufactured drugs in his basement. He was a Yokohama Karate black belt instructor. He carried a .25 caliber semi-auto pistol in his motorcycle boot. He'd rigged four IBM PCs together to form a supercomputer that calculated the distance between stars. He was a pen pal of Doors keyboardist Ray Manzarek. Terlinger listened to Bauhaus first thing every morning, likely ingesting the day's first drugs while doing so.

And the guy knew good music.

It was dark, intense stuff from the late seventies and early eighties. In those years, in his boring mainstream existence, Lance had been unaware of Bauhaus. There were always things going on you didn't know about until they were over. All the current music—the sugar rock barf from MTV-created hair bands—turned his stomach, so he dove into the old stuff for nourishment. Terlinger made a tape for Lance using a ninety-minute high bias cassette, recording two albums, some amazing live songs and a bootleg EP.

"Are you ready for this?" Terlinger had said before handing over the tape. He tapped the plastic holder against his black leather vest. He'd filled the blank cover with blue India ink sketches of the band, four emaciated deadpan Englishmen.

"You bet." Lance smiled, unsure of what Terlinger was intimating.

It was musical heroin. The screeching, icicles-on-your-spine guitar work of Daniel Ash and the charismatic, wounded-vampire vocals of Peter Murphy. That commanding voice, it started narrating Lance's dreams. The songs sprung from a strange poisoned well of punk, but with a hypnotic insistence that put them in their own category. They pounded out an eerie furious landscape, riveting his attention as a manifestation of his inner turmoil. Dark forces had surrounded him, creating the fetal confusion, whispering doubts into Lynn's ear.

No! It was her fault, he realized. She was causing all this. The great Love controversy was a cheap argument, an excuse for her cruelty. The unfairness of it enraged him. He had done nothing but love her, without ever cheating on her, and treat her well. He respected her career motivations, allowing her due as a modern woman. He'd vacuumed her apartment! She'd chosen to shit on his best intentions. To mock him. The Bauhaus shed new light on Lynn's mysteries. What had seemed innocent, endearing, now became monstrous. He had miscalculated, wrongly assuming she had positive intentions.

He was listening to his Bauhaus tape so much, he heard guitar chords while in line at the Bursar's Office. The lyrics of "Stigmata Martyr" ran through his brain during sleep.

He fell into the Walkman habit for additional Bauhaus fixes. He became a campus walker who piloted in a contained world, cords dangling from his ears, the ephemeral buzz of miniature noise trailing him. The guitar twitches, ricocheting explosions and sonic slithering added new meaning to everyday campus sights. He'd never noticed the grim architecture of the journalism school. The upper floors of The Ivan were hideously streaked with purple pigeon shit. And the typical Langford student—with their sad backpacks and shoulder bags, like so many lost travelers—they had no idea of their ridiculous selves. Packs of sorority girls roved, smug and clueless. Weight room dudes trudged about in chopped shirts, the morons. They knew nothing of their mistakes, their life miscalculations, blissfully dumb about the folly of their efforts. They were like those plastic football players who randomly collided according to electric vibrations. He wished them all misery. Beside the Economics building's fountain he consumed an apple as the endless dire melody of "Béla Lugosi's Dead" unwound in his ears.

Lynn was mocking him. Well, screw her!

Lance liked that the headphones suspended the pretense of connection with other pedestrians. He was oblivious to his haunted expressions, the moving lips and dazed eyes, the times he blurted lyrics aloud. He'd see people he knew, acknowledging them briefly with wary eyes. His belligerent body language and quick pace made it seem he suspected others of violence, or was planning a violent outburst himself. He sensed the confusion of innocent people. He anticipated their reports, but didn't care: Rally was marching down Hawthorne with this demonic expression and he didn't even say hello.

He preferred walking to sitting in his room. He went on long forays off-campus. One day walking around the West Downs he dropped by Sy Terlinger's house to thank him for the music. Terlinger was in the backyard, site of the altar-like muffler sculpture. Industrial music played from roof speakers. Terlinger threw paint bombs against large canvases. This was to be the set of *The Complete Nuclear Family*, the production Terlinger and LaCoss were acting in. Terlinger was also designing the set.

"The Bauhaus is awesome," Lance said, taking his headphones off.

"I can tell by the look on your face. Too bad it's splitsville for the band. It's a royal shame." Terlinger's dark hair was in a massive braid that hung to his belt. He let Lance toss a few paint bombs. Lance missed with a green one that splattered against a garage.

"Oh, sorry. My bad."

"Good one, man." Terlinger nodded in appreciation. He tossed a yellow bomb at the garage to add contrast. He singed parts of a canvas by igniting lighter fluid. He dipped arrows in paint and shot them. Lance shot a few, then suggested mixing more colors and Terlinger agreed. They exploded firecrackers gobbed with wet paint. They were creating art! It looked fantastic. Jackson Pollock would have been proud. It was pretty cool to hang with a guy like Terlinger.

"Did you want anything else?" Terlinger asked. His peculiar gray eyes twinkled. "I can set you up." He meant drugs, and Lance was flattered. Terlinger considered him cool enough, worthy of this secretive confidence.

"I'm good for now, man. I've been trying to sort out my head. I was just doing some walking in the neighborhood."

"There's no better way to enjoy the day. That's the mark of true freedom." He held out a fist, and Lance bumped it with his own. A joy poured suddenly from the sky—Lance's first in weeks. Standing in Terlinger's backyard was a fine moment. In his rebellious way, Terlinger was a genius. He smiled. His top lip pulled back, revealing gray, problem teeth. On the other hand, it was hard to tell if Terlinger was actually going nowhere, or had given up on going anywhere.

Walking out of the neighborhood, Lance passed a yard sale. A coat hung on a rod. It was slate blue, with sublime strands of gray and black, an ultra-thin lapel and tortoise buttons. Fashionably wrinkled. Its retro slim fit was so perfect he took it as an omen and paid three dollars. He imagined an American secret agent in the early '60s—played by James Coburn or Steve McQueen—wearing the suit in a South American airport, smoking Gitanes and looking for a contact. When Lance wore the coat with an old pair of jeans, frayed at the knees, listening to Bauhaus, he felt armored from the world. A newer, tougher, more resourceful Lance. The coat triggered a fantasy about living in a West Downs rental, joining an experimental musical combo and dating artsy tough girls. He took measured strides, his fingers tucked under the shoulder straps of his knapsack. His anger was firmly clamped onto a defiant pleasure.

He crossed a leaf-covered patch of The Lawn. Out of the

corner of his eye, he recognized a familiar gait. Radiant blonde hair like Lynn's. Probably wasn't her. These scares happened all the time. But the threat caused his breath to catch. He kept his gaze fixed forward. The girl walked directly across his field of vision, thirty feet ahead. It was Lynn. "God in an Alcove" was playing, during the verse he could never understand. Lynn held her books to her chest, looking peaceful—a surreal sight, a vision of her earlier self. She turned toward Lance. He hoped this wasn't happening. He had no plan. Their meeting was unavoidable, disturbing him greatly. She moved toward him in a slow-motion sequence, looking wholesome in a jean jacket and caramel suede skirt. Her soft face loomed closer. Weirder still, she was holding back a smile.

He yanked the earphones off, plunging him into the hollow world of fall, into the dull crunch of leaves and distant voices.

"My period came," she said happily.

"It did?"

She nodded, biting her bottom lip. She moved to within a foot of him, cheer in his eyes. "I'm sorry if I put you through anything. It's over."

He couldn't stir himself from a flat feeling. He tried to remember all his grievances against her. He wanted to scowl, but only managed a frown. She rocked up on the balls of her feet and drew closer, rubbing her hands together. "That's such a cute jacket."

Tougher, more resourceful, he told himself, monitoring the distance between them.

She flattened down the lapels and felt the fabric on his sleeve, her eyes flitting between the jacket and his face in an animated, giddy way. The sensation of her hands made him tingly. He told her about buying the jacket. Before he got to the secret agent thing she threw her arms around his neck. Having no choice but to catch her, he embraced her. Inhaling the sweet honeycomb of her hair was like waking from an operation.

"It's all been so ridiculous. I've missed you so much," she said.

"I've really missed you too." This statement, and its utter truth, shocked him. He squeezed her, pulling her off the ground a few inches. He moaned in relief.

They spent the afternoon lying on her bed, fully clothed, lethargic, an inertial weight gluing each to the mattress. They talked in careful, confessional tones. He occasionally lifted his eyes from the pillow fringe he picked at to glance at her, resisting the urge to cling to her like a piece of lint. She rubbed the synthetic tufts of hair on Chachi the clapping monkey's head, then looking sheepishly at Lance with big eyes. She put her hand on his chest, slowly moving her fingertips. "It was really hard for me not to be able to talk to you. I mean, with a lot of couples there are problems. It's hard when you can't talk about things."

He tensed his eyebrows. "You weren't returning my telephone calls."

Lynn didn't look at him, pretending she didn't have to respond. An aggravation stirred within Lance. It was best to drop it, to grant an amnesty for this transgression.

"I definitely suffered from not talking to you." He ached for her, every inch of her, dying at the thought of her with another guy.

"It helped me to read this." She picked up a book from her bedside table: Kahlil Gibran's *The Prophet*. Lynn read from a passage on Love. Something about love having wings and a sword. Lance imagined an absurd flying elven creature from the Tolkien trilogy. Love also thrashed you. Love was a giving, taking, floating entity. Lynn teared up, accelerating into full sobbing by the end of the passage, which made Lance feel bad he'd wanted to ridicule the book. "I guess I just needed reassurance," she said. "Trust is everything to me."

He kissed her head. He did love her, or at least he had and probably still did. They kissed, suckling, as if supplying oxygen to each other. He pulled her shirt out of her jeans, rubbing his hands around the smooth toasty region of her lower back, anticipating that lovely piece of physical transcendence soon to occur between them. Something lunged inside him; he wanted to consume her.

She put her hands against his chest. "I don't know about the timing." Her voice was smooth but her eyes were frantic, darting between his eyes like he was a stranger. Lance decided it was code. The saving menstrual flow was flowing still. Intercourse was off-limits, which was fine. It would have to be.

Experimental Expo Theatre's production of *The Complete Nuclear Family* opened. The play's debut. Just the kind of neutral entertainment Lance needed for his first post-difficulties evening out with Lynn. They walked to the Student Center. A cold bite of early winter had swept in, turning the sky to steel gray. He wore his canvas duck jacket. Her hair settled across the puffed collar of her blue cotton-fill jacket, a perfect backdrop to her face. She had on exactly the right amount of makeup, worthy of a Cover Girl. They ran across Sedge Avenue, his arm around her jacket. She in the wool skirt that made her legs look so dynamite. On the far sidewalk a gust hit them; he whinnied, trundling his feet and braying like a horse. She let loose a full laugh, bending at the waist—an accomplishment that always exhilarated him. She latched onto his arm with glee. She was coming back to him.

He was being careful. He didn't want to break the spell.

They held hands, the beige Student Center in the distance. She kept her red-cheeked face fixed on him. She kissed his cheek spontaneously. He felt so good, so connected with her, so pumped. He could have ascended to a pulpit and converted millions of followers, could have convinced them all to cut off their own thumbs. He almost said to her: to hell with the play, let's go back to my place. She would have said yes. But LaCoss had a leading role in the play and was already upset Charles Boyd wouldn't leave his room to attend.

In the theater lobby a crowd in dark wool coats and long scarves milled around. The hearty, cliquish Langford art crowd, in all shapes and sizes, wine from plastic cups dribbling down their pale chins. Lance was surprised how many people he knew. Lynn chatted with a girl. He purchased cups of Chablis using his last ten dollars. Ominously, the quarterly spending money from his parents was weeks late. Gingerly holding full cups, he looked around. He immediately recognized the back of a raven-haired head. He spotted Veronica Boyer at the crowd's fringe, by a potted palm. In a black coat with fur collar, antique but very elegant, she turned and faced Lance, like she had sensed him telepathically. A black flapper dress sparkled and shifted between her coat folds. A cosmetically pale complexion and the reddest lipstick he'd ever seen. She stared at him directly, a bold daredevil look, a taunt to say something to her. Sipping wine, he stared back. Then he pivoted, sensing danger from Veronica's presence. He located Lynn, who was motioning Lance over to introduce him to somebody.

Inside the theater, they sat in the middle section, toward the front. They glanced at their programs for *The Complete Nuclear Family*. The program used the phrase "a dissection of the postmodern family unit." Four actors. LaCoss's character was Baby Johnny. Sy Terlinger played Fury.

"Do you think he's nervous right now?" Lynn asked.

"I'm nervous for him," Lance said. LaCoss used a strict Stanislavski Method approach to acting. At that moment backstage, a towel over his head, he was reliving his most traumatic memories: age nine, when he suffered a double fibula break in a BMX race; age twelve, when his stepfather shoved him into a wall; age fourteen, when he saw his best friend drown in a rain-swollen culvert. Then LaCoss would listen to The Doors, making one prayer to the Lizard King for stage presence, then another to the spirit of Humphrey Bogart that he not forget any lines.

The lights dimmed and the curtain opened. In darkness, a

buzzing sound droned, which changed into a space liftoff as the lights grew brighter. Terlinger's scorched paint bomb canvases lined the ominous backstage. Three dark squares were center stage, arranged in Olympic-medal podium style, the center one highest. LaCoss stood on it as Baby Johnny. Wearing black monochrome, his arms embraced himself as though straightjacketed, his eye sockets darkened, his hair slicked back and pulled into a tight ponytail. Lyle Rudner, as the Father, stood stone-faced to LaCoss's left. Liz Williams, as the Mother, looked aloof on the right.

Liz was a black girl with a Boston accent who maybe had had a tryst with LaCoss, maybe it was gossip, but neither was talking out of consideration for the production. Lyle Rudner was rumored to have a current thing going with Wallace Dennis, the writer and director, though they were hush-hush as well. To further complicate things, Lyle had made it known to the crew he had a thing for LaCoss, which had creeped out LaCoss briefly, but he was over it. This was showbiz.

LaCoss, holding himself, wriggling, twitching, let out a bone-shattering scream. "Why, why, WHY?" Baby Johnny wanted to know, looking up in agony to a post-apocalyptic sky.

Mother and Father stared into the audience without reaction. Baby Johnny reached toward his parents with unsteady hands. They gazed at him admiringly. "We are lucky parents indeed," they chanted. The Father, looking over the audience, recounted Baby Johnny's birth in stark terms. This was how the production went, the characters unaware of each other much of the time, blurting things and throwing tantrums. Lyle was doing a great job, discarding his usual nonchalance and morphing into the elemental, solid Father, coming off like a steady Hugh Beaumont. Liz Williams had marvelous presence, sweetness and calm surrounding her every movement.

Lance wasn't sure about LaCoss, whose physical gestures all seemed weirdly prolonged. Rapid emotional changes flashed across his face, like a cartoon character on speed. LaCoss stepped on Liz's line, then paused, unsure whether to speak. Lance fidgeted, fearing his friend was bombing—oh no, oh God!—and that he had no acting talent. LaCoss, it was painful to admit, was delusional about stardom. But the unevenness of his performance was partly due to the way his character was written. Baby Johnny was full grown, yet he might revert to a colicky state. At other times he plotted with a Tom Cruise-like intensity, breathing through his teeth, his chin tucked. He did a good job in the breakfast scene, using the exploration of a cereal box to great effect. When Lyle Rudner backhanded him, LaCoss spun away, recoiling yet still balanced. It was vaguely Martin Sheen. In Baby Johnny's tenacity, Lance also caught glimpses of Wyatt Burris, the Elvis-obsessed protagonist of their stalled screenplay. Was LaCoss successfully portraying the complex soul of his character, or just exposing poor acting technique? Maybe Brando had once been this bad.

During the set change Lance put his arm around Lynn, asking how she was doing. She nodded, then bunched up her nose. "It's so much shouting." Though a performer herself, she could be highly critical.

Act Two contained LaCoss's big scene. A pyramidal, ziggurat-type structure was wheeled out, Baby Johnny crouching on top of it. Twin slide projectors cast pictures onto a screen behind him. LaCoss's monologue, backed by a tribal drumbeat, veered from a calm recitation of his life story to hysterical complaints. Slides of industrial wastelands and birthday snapshots of toddlers. LaCoss's face lit up with a frantic hope, a longing. His voice fell into a groove as black and white Native American portraits flashed over his shoulders. "What I did was to sleep with these thoughts held tightly, so tight I shall never give them up, because I know when and if I do then it shall be the end of me…" The play had hit a mark. Something of LaCoss's essence had surfaced as well, a hint of a modicum of talent. Cheering silently, Lance rubbed Lynn's knee. She smiled back.

Lynn squirmed throughout chaotic Act Three. The Mother and Father wheeled out a towering tree, like a palm, or maybe it was a huge sunflower. Yellow lights ringed each floppy petal. They cuddled beneath the tree's margarine glow. A row of missiles lined the lit back stage. Then Sy Terlinger, as Fury, dressed head to toe in burlap swaths, made his entrance under a strobe light, wielding a whining chainsaw. An oily, acrid smell drifted. Baby Johnny directed Fury, pointing toward the tree. Terlinger ran about the stage, swinging the whizzing saw over the audience—Lynn squeezed Lance's arm tightly—before pruning all the petals of the tree. Mother and Father cowered behind a boulder. Terlinger let out a terrifying cannibal scream before cutting the trunk itself, a metallic ring echoing. Diamond sparks flew and the tree crashed to the stage, Fury hustling out of its way.

The play closed with Father turning his back on Baby Johnny, crossing his arms and shedding a gloom across the stage. The missiles rumbled and blasted off. LaCoss kneeled as Liz Williams cradled his head. He sobbed as she stroked his upturned face. Lance sensed LaCoss's tears were real, and that was impressive.

Backstage, he and Lynn congratulated LaCoss. Sitting, LaCoss seemed frazzled and exhausted, peering from his blackened eyes. "I screwed up my lines during the monologue." He hung his head.

"I couldn't tell that. You did great, man," Lance said. He shook LaCoss's neck at the shoulder until LaCoss lifted his head. "That last scene killed. People in the audience were in awe."

"You covered perfectly. I didn't notice a thing," Lynn said, smiling, using the neutral tone she always reserved for LaCoss.

"I hope you guys are right. I gave it all I had."

Around a corner, Wallace Dennis yelled at Terlinger. Terlinger stared down the director with a smirk, unfazed by him. The trunk cut had been Terlinger's ad-lib. They would have to do expensive repairs. Terlinger had risked electrocution. "You're out! You're fired!" Wallace Dennis yelled. Lance and Lynn rolled their eyes. He had his arm around her hip and she was being very touchy-feely since they'd gotten out of their seats, hanging on him now. LaCoss invited them to the cast party that night.

"We're there!" Lance said, making his hands into fists.

LaCoss smiled. "It's really good to see you guys together again. It's a happy sight. You two belong together."

The night air was brisk, scented with decay and traces of charcoal. Lance pulled up the collar on his jacket. He could see his breath. They took a different route to get back to her place, via the length of The Lawn, holding hands.

"Did you like it?"

She raised her eyebrows. "Yes and no. I'm not sure it's gone beyond the experimental phase." Then, after a few crunching steps over leaves, "It was like a form of programming."

"It was heavily metaphorical, though I found it entertaining." He felt energized by the avant-garde expressionism. He wanted to wander the streets of Munich in a dark raincoat and fedora and mutter about the bleakness of life.

"Couldn't they have had normal dialogue? Poor Ian."

"He did a good job under the circumstances." Lance tried to read her passive face in the concentrated dark of the tall pines near the Chemistry building.

"He was awful."

"Hey. Come on." Lance raised his hands.

"I'm sorry. But he was spastic half the time."

Her brattiness was an irritation. This critique from someone who never missed a dreck-filled episode of *thirtysomething*. They walked under a lamplight, shedding their anonymity.

"Maybe we shouldn't go to the cast party if that's the way you feel," Lance said.

"I don't think we should go for other reasons."

"Such as?"

"So we can just spend the evening alone. And if we go to the cast party you'll drink too much."

"That can be regulated, you know."

"Oh, hon. We need to talk about moderation. You are a junior now."

A spike of discomfort, of indignation, rose at mention of the word junior.

"I don't want to talk about grades," he said.

"I wasn't talking about grades. But you know you're avoiding your responsibilities. That's why you're thinking about grades. Are you trying to throw your future away? Are you scared? Is that it?" The fact she was right in every way, that she so easily destroyed the delusional way he preferred to see things, made it all the more stinging.

He let go of her hand, shoving his hand in a flap pocket that provided little warmth. They had stopped and she was lingering before him, turning in a slow circle, like she wanted an answer. He took a step off the walkway, a chain pulling tight against his shin. She was looking at him in a penetrating and self-righteous way.

"Who was that girl you were staring at in the lobby?"

"What girl?" A hardness entered his voice.

"You must know her. She was looking at you like she knew you."

An almost Orwellian sensitivity. That she was capable of such ultra-sensitive observations amazed him. "There were a lot of people. I can't control who looks at me." The integrity of this statement gave him heart, but he chafed at the unfairness of this questioning. He wanted to kick her, hard, to knock her over.

"She lives off-campus somewhere. She's one of those girls you've been chatting with."

"Are you the Chief Inspector?"

She turned and they continued walking into the night. He was incredulous, heartbroken she was pulling this. It was violence. She was completely rotten inside. Everything seemed fragile. Terrible things would happen if he breathed too hard. A madness pulled at his jaw.

At the steps of the History building she sat, her knees pulled together. He sat beside her. He was on some kind of probation, he realized, thinking of her rejection the other night. He considered confronting her about this. She stared out at nothing in particular, acting like she was alone. The marble was uncomfortably cold on his rear end. His veins constricted. He was surprised to hear himself shouting, "Why are you doing this? You're ruining the night! You're ruining everything!"

"I couldn't have cared less when I mentioned that girl. But you've been so defensive I really wonder."

This is what I get, he thought. Laughter echoed from the opposite side of The Lawn. He felt completely panicked, stumped about what to say. A silence twisted between them. The next sound I'll hear is her apologizing, he thought.

"I should probably go," she said softly. She stood and smoothed her skirt. She set off across the grass, her hands dug deep into her coat. He expected her to turn around, to say something else. He fought an intense desire to chase her and scream in her conceited little ear how stupid, how completely stupid she'd been to ruin things. He cracked his knuckles, his ears getting colder.

What did you do when the woman of your dreams was walking away?

What could you do?

Maybe there were limits.

Maybe he should run after her.

Maybe some things were inevitable or impossible.

Even with the bulky coat she cut a familiar silhouette. In a glow of soft yellow light between two dark buildings, her form gently diminished, moving away steadily, shrinking. Then she was lost in shadow and dark.

Cold crept under his jacket, prickling at his ribs like

carpenter nails. He sat a full hour, until his face had numbed and the air made his lungs ache.

Then he got up to leave.

His father called from the airport. Using a flat, dark tone, he said, "I'm in town. I need to see you." A late lunch (Lance couldn't think his way out of it) was arranged at an upscale bistro near Langford. Lance waited in the empty place, his thoughts misfiring. He'd been unable to think straight since Lynn walked away, and now irrational thoughts plagued him: a phalanx of white Imperial Stormtroopers would clack in before his father; Al Pacino and a coterie of Cuban thugs, circa *Scarface*, were about to kill him. His father filled the front door briefly, then approached the table in a beautiful dark overcoat and pinstripe suit, an odd light in his eyes, his lips tight: he was going to close a deal. It gave Lance chills. He patted Lance on the back, then took off the overcoat, explaining in a rambling preamble that the Senate had just made an important change in a procurement law, saving his clients billions; for weeks his father had been directing the work of a select team of high-priced lawyers, flying to Arizona and London, and cornering two key senators on a yacht in the Potomac. I've got no chance, Lance thought. His father was superior on all fronts, with no indication this would change. He cycled between the gravity of Gregory Peck and the edge of Clint Eastwood.

His father settled into the opposing seat. "It's good to see you," he said directly, in a way that possibly touched on the ducked phone calls.

"And you."

His father collected menus from a waitress, giving her a suave smile of gratitude for bringing waters. He carefully studied the yard sale jacket Lance had forgotten he was wearing. A green blot from a Sy Terlinger paint bomb, Lance noticed, marred the sleeve. His father smirked and said, "Nice jacket."

"Thanks." Lance was surprised by the compliment, before realizing his father, at Lance's age, might have worn a similar jacket. An association that diminished it.

His father flexed his elbow and said, "Played tennis this weekend. My tendons are still barking." He played in a competitive league, winning more often than not with steely resolve, hustle and a precision topspin serve that was unstoppable when accurate. "I lost badly. Unfortunately, my backhand is nothing like yours."

"My backhand isn't that great."

"Oh, but it is," his father said, tipping his head forward for emphasis.

"It's average," Lance said, resisting the longstanding hoopla his father made about his tennis game, yet also welcoming it. His father had personally taught Lance, offering a steady banter of rowdy encouragement and corrective critique from across court. The day Lance beat his father the first time—a rare time—his father bought him his first beer.

"I disagree. Yours is a natural. I wish I could graft your elbow onto mine," his father said, flexing his elbow rapidly in a comical way. Lance had to smile, relax and lean back. He considered his backhand could be rather fierce, it had zing. His father was easily the greatest guy in the world.

"Order whatever you like," his father said. "I've got the check."

"That's good. These days I got no spending money." Lance's smile withered as his lighthearted plea was met with a stone-faced stare. Suckered by his father's charm, he'd blundered into a weak position. This was the actual start of their lunch, he realized—the agenda. Now he knew his father's leverage point.

They ordered food. His father stared at the table with a deeply pained expression, his bottom lip pulled high. He weaved his hands before him, as if trying to crush an object between them, and raised his voice. "We're going to have a serious conversation. Right now. This one is as serious as they come," his father said, without concern at being overheard. He had known a bistro near a college would be empty. Essentially, he'd bought the whole room.

"Fine. Let's talk," Lance said, feeling exactly the opposite.

"Now you're willing to talk."

"Absolutely." Lance planted his elbows firmly on the table.

"You have a problem returning phone calls. Never did I think speaking to my youngest son would be so difficult."

Lance winced. "There are things going on in my life—"

"Not that you tell me about them on the phone."

"I've had…if you're interested, I've had a difficult time recently."

"I'm all ears." His father did the head shake, a tremoring while keeping his eyes locked—a warning he was building angry momentum.

Lance sipped his water, wanting no part of explaining his difficulties. "I'm having problems with Lynn, my girlfriend. Basically…my heart's been ripped out."

"I'm sorry to hear that." His father nodded in a bothered way, as if heartbreak were a tiresome tangent that had been introduced. "Dating can have its challenges."

"It's not just dating. Lynn is…she's so far beyond just dating. She's…I mean, she is just the most amazing girl…" Trying to express this to his father was unbearable. All the Lynn-oriented physical manifestations began: the churning stomach, the weepy eyes, the desire to punch something hard. He shut them all down.

His father tensed his wide face, as if he'd eaten something unpleasant. Also, he flashed incomprehension. Lance realized his father didn't buy this flowery bit about overpowering true love; he had never experienced it and didn't care to. "This sounds like a problem that is a proximate cause of your biggest problem. There are priorities. Such as, your studies. How are they improving? How are your business school applications going?"

Lance lowered his eyes and adjusted the positions of his knife and fork. "I'm doing the best I can under the circumstances."

Shoulders squared, his father stared until Lance's eyes rose to meet his. He tossed his reading glasses on the table and pressed his fist toward Lance. "Once again I'm getting nothing. Nothing." A growl entered his father's voice: once reserved only for arborists who tried to cut a tree on his father's property, for loud drunks who disturbed his dining. Lance stared in disbelief. For the first time, he experienced his father as other people did, as an imposing stranger. "Your mother and I have had to make calls, to scramble around like spies to get the real story. You haven't been honest with me. You haven't been honest with yourself. You're not trying. I can't figure out what the hell is wrong with you—"

"There's nothing wrong with me." Lance glared back. Under the table, his middle finger extended. The hateful finger trembled like a ballistic missile about to blast off and destroy his father.

"You're cheating yourself. There is no reason. You're damned smart. Always have been. Are you on drugs?"

"I'm not on drugs, for God's sake. This is bullshit!" The obscenity—had one ever been directed toward his father before?—hung in the air precariously.

His father sighed. "Do you not care where you end up in this world? Do you not care what happens?" His neck strained, his voice trailing to a high note. His shoulders—Lance had never seen them do it before—slumped. Forced to slump, as only the greatest disappointment of his life could force them. A disappointment verging on permanence. Lance's stomach felt like it had been cut in half with a sword.

"I'm not trying to push you to do anything," his father said, lowering his voice in a conciliatory way. He shook his head sadly. "I'm just trying to explain the way things are. Maybe you don't want to accept this. Your actions have consequences. You're throwing opportunities out the window. Follow-through is everything. People who don't follow through learn very painful lessons." He crossed his arms meditatively and rested his eyes, as if alone. Suddenly, Lance seemed in danger of ending up a loud drunk, and homeless, of having every family member turn their backs, of being growled at by cruel passersby until an anonymous death occurred. Hard, terrible truths existed and could no more be avoided than talking to your father. But no! It surged inside him: he could still become the person he had so fervently wished to be, growing up under the steady eyes of his father. He craved that high GPA and yearned for a way to pull it off, until this collided with frustration at that stupid system.

"Hold on a second," Lance mounted a counterattack. "You forget about my internship with Patterson French. You're totally overlooking my achievements." In fact, Patterson French had just dissolved, principals such as Jack Dalrymple joining Arthur Anderson and getting a $3 million guaranteed bonus out of the reorganization. His one career prospect now a footnote. Also, according to an administration letter, he was flirting with academic probation, words his father would have thrown out had he known.

His father smiled. A smile so crafty, it disproved this overlooking by itself. "I'm not discounting achievements. You've given effort. I'm just wondering where it has gone."

Lance picked at his club sandwich, forcing a tomato and a slice of turkey into his mouth. His father pushed forward an empty crock of onion soup and wiped his mouth. His eyes flitted surreptitiously over his napkin to Lance. Lance recognized this look. His father had always glanced this way after Lance saw Dr. Henry Shatzer—a distant judging, fraught with worry. This without ever speaking of the appointments, as if to his father, they had never occurred. Lance stared back over his sandwich, anger raising hairs on his neck.

"Before we go on, I need assurances," his father said. "Without them, we will not go on here at this university. What I'm paying for—" he gestured vaguely in Lance's direction— "you can easily do without my paying tens of thousands of dollars."

Lance slapped his napkin on the table, said "Excuse me," and stood abruptly. It was unclear where he was going. For a moment the front door beckoned. Two waitresses glanced over. He walked slowly to the men's room. He locked the door of a stall and sat on a toilet. He pulled his Walkman out of his pocket and lost himself in "Béla Lugosi's Dead," the rambling middle with its screeching pyrotechnics. Eyes closed, he wished he were Mel Gibson in *The Road Warrior*, tearing across hot Australian wasteland in the last of the V-8 interceptors, with no one to rely on but himself, and his trusty mutt, every utensil and weapon he needed hanging from his leather gear. He crammed the headphones into his pocket, appalled by his wasteful escapism. Outside the toilet stall, he kicked the door hard, banging it inside the stall. The banging galvanized a plan. He smoothed the lapels of his Secret Agent jacket, picked at the green paint blot but decided not to remove it. He buttoned the top button.

He walked back to the table. His father put away a business report into his accordion briefcase, and removed reading glasses, having utilized this intermission constructively. He stared mutely, in recognition that it was still Lance's turn.

"I can always try harder," Lance said in his calmest, sunniest voice. Suddenly, he was channeling the unflappable Gerald Grafton. "I want to try harder. Have I done things perfectly? No. But hey, what is college about anyway? I'm learning to live my life." The truth of these statements was unclear; his full focus was on negotiating a desired result.

His father nodded, seeming eager to agree. "I don't expect perfection. I just want honest effort. I've always had high hopes for you, Lance." A pleading smile seemed to sneak up on his father, despite his efforts to suppress it. His father's forehead wrinkled, his face seeming grayer, older.

"I have high hopes myself, you know," Lance said. It was the truth, almost too truthful to state. "Look, I want to do better—"

"All right." He produced an envelope, containing a blue check, and slid it across. Lance put it into his own jacket, feeling like a fraud. His father finally leaned back in his chair. His eyes solemn, he told a story from his college years. His own father had sent him a spending- money check. He used part of the check in a poker game, losing the money. Trying to win that money back, he lost the rest of it. Lance stopped eating, hooked by the story (his father, the gambler! and losing money!). His grandfather, chiefly experienced from behind his mother's legs, had been a loud man of brutal opinion who somehow inspired great devotion. "As you can imagine, I was quite distraught. Somehow, I don't know how, my father knew this had happened. At first when he asked about it, I denied it. Then I came clean. When my father died, it was something I kept remembering—I gave him the true answer. If I hadn't, things with him would have been ruined." His chin lowered, he dabbed his lips with his napkin. A moist sheen came to his eyes. "Relationships are fragile things. More delicate than you realize. But I've always thought our relationship was good." He reached over and touched Lance's hand.

What kind of creep gave his father the finger under a table? A father who had come to help his son and give him some advice.

His father studied his watch, his chest filling with air. "I'm glad we did this. I think we understand each other. Do we?"

Lance studied his father, noting how quickly he'd gotten back to business.

"I think we do."

In the bathroom again, Lance vomited up scraps of food.

For distraction, Lance buried himself in reading. A newspaper theater critic, Irwin Claypool, had reviewed *The Complete Nuclear Family*. He called the play "a unique, though uneven experience." He said, "One wished for a conclusion so that Baby Johnny could be released from the hell of Ian LaCoss's hammy creation. The amateurish character was unable to handle any portion of reality, but was able to hijack attention, at times ruining the production…"

Lance gasped, cutting his reading short. He looked up at LaCoss, whose attention was focused on a small television. A pipe-smoking Dutch anthropologist with an overbite was giving an engrossing account of seeing a mammal with the locomotion of a big cat crossing an English moor. *In Search Of…*, as narrated by Leonard Nimoy. LaCoss's mouth cracked open as eerie music floated around Nimoy's authoritative scrutiny of the show's thesis.

Lance held up the article and said, "This is fascinating reading," which sounded unkind, but it was going around.

LaCoss pointed at the TV and said, "That flake, I wouldn't believe if he said the sun rose every morning."

"Big cats roaming around England? Sounds implausible."

"Oh, they are. I just think that dude is wacked. Plus he looks like my dad." LaCoss frowned and shook his head so vigorously his neck cracked. LaCoss's father was famously oblivious to everything LaCoss did. No amount of motocross trophies or vitamin sales or roles in school plays could stir him from his couch and the prison of his defeated thoughts. He was unsure where LaCoss attended college. And so LaCoss was winging everything. Lance wondered whose father was more problematic.

Lance guessed LaCoss was in similarly painful denial of reality.

"Did I tell you about the very worst movie I have ever seen in my life?" LaCoss asked.

Lance put a hand over his face and moaned like a derailment victim. He'd heard what a rotten flick *Mannequin* was three times already; it was about a sculptor who falls in love with his department store mannequin when it comes to life.

"It was unbelievable. Virtually every portion of *Mannequin*, the script, the acting, the soundtrack, was complete and utter waste. It was painful."

"What did you expect? It's a romantic comedy."

"And that Andrew McCarthy!" LaCoss shook his fists, complaining about McCarthy's elevated whine, that passive-aggressive, sensitive-guy-in-a-blazer nasal sneer talk. Had McCarthy practiced this? Was he still coming out of puberty? The same drippy guy in every movie. LaCoss could do McCarthy perfectly—the slight stoop and expression of deeply wounded pride. The thriving career of Andrew McCarthy had long bedeviled LaCoss, from his sensitive journalist character in *St. Elmo's Fire* ("Kevin"), to the rich kid who befriends poor girl Molly Ringwald in *Pretty in Pink* ("Blane"), to his starring role in *Mannequin* ("Jonathan"). LaCoss paced about the room, kicking bits of clothing and seething.

Lance also found Andrew McCarthy an irritant, but suspected LaCoss craved these emotive teen hunk parts, and felt threatened. Late that afternoon, LaCoss got a phone call from Sy Terlinger.

"We're meeting Terlinger at The Antler," LaCoss said joyously. If Andrew McCarthy occupied the lowest rung of LaCoss's respect, Terlinger was on the highest.

"I'm beat. Not me. Why does he want to go there?" The Antler was a dump, a dive bar, far enough away and degenerate enough that Langford students rarely went.

"You are going. Stop thinking about your former woman. That's over. It's time to smell the coffee and read the writing. The Antler is exactly what you need."

Lance crossed his arms tight, threatened by the "over" comment. His thoughts of Lynn came in waves; he was fine, then it felt like an important internal organ was being stomped.

"It's too far to walk."

"You've got wheels."

"My clutch is out."

LaCoss looked out his attic window, pulling it up. Norton Skinner was walking down the sidewalk and LaCoss yelled to him. Then moments later he stood in the room, wearing a bulky down jacket. Lance hadn't seen much of Skinner that year. He had had a life-changing revelation, a Jimmy Swaggart moment, and he'd quit drinking and stocked the trunk of his convertible with religious pamphlets. He handed them out in front of the Student Center with a spacey smile.

"We're going to The Antler. Want to go there with us?" LaCoss asked.

"Hell, yes I want to go."

"I thought you'd given up booze."

"Man, I'm pretty tired of these misconceptions. People think because I'm a believer I never have any fun. That's all crap." Skinner smiled, showing all his teeth and nodding like he was ready to have fun right then.

Skinner's TR7 was now hospital-white. Lance took shotgun in Mary Ann. LaCoss sat in a cramped area behind the seats. A Langford Police cruiser pulled up behind them, and tailed them through several turns. Lance glanced back at the two blank-faced officers. One talked on the radio. As young men in a sports car they were suspect, and considered likely to destroy, break, undermine or molest something. They were no better than dysfunctional beasts. They were either not to be taken seriously or to be punished for every infraction and shown zero tolerance. That cruiser faded off, then another one pulled behind, escorting them off-campus. Skinner drove using only the first two gears. There was a problem getting into or past third, Skinner explained in a shout above the redlining engine. The car was sensitive to taps on the gas at these inflated RPMs, pitching the car back and forth.

"You're destroying your car!" Lance yelled.

"It's fine. It always sounds like that."

The to and fro sensation intensified Lance's carsickness. He'd eaten nothing that day. He sniffed the odor of fried oil coming from under the dash. Lance shut his eyes, praying the movement would end. He flashed back to seeing Lynn at the gymnasium. He'd stared for several shattering seconds from a remote point while she led a Power Aerobics class in a knee-pumping maneuver. He left through the south entrance to avoid her.

They pulled into the gravel lot of The Antler: a squat cement building. A red neon Bud sign peeked from a window crossed with bars. Terlinger wasn't there. Inside, it stank of cigars and unemployment. Old guys in polyester caps sat on wooden stools. Lance wanted to leave. They chose a booth. They ordered two draft beers, one Coca-Cola. Lance worked at his beer with lugubrious sips, his throat feeling full. This wasn't recreation; it was punishment.

"It's a classic good time we're having here," LaCoss said, frowning, staring across the table at Lance and Skinner. He leaned toward Lance accusingly. "I know who's still on your mind. And I'm very disappointed."

Lance's hands sprung before his face, helping him clutch at his point. "Listen! This is Lynn Van Oster. She is the kind of woman who…you could kick yourself, you could really regret losing."

"I find the conditioning here astonishing. I warned you. Now you're paying the price. She's one girl. Do I have to tell you the analogy of the fish and the ocean?"

LaCoss had forgotten the exact cliché. Lance laughed, leaving behind a hysterical sadness no amount of lame-brained, tactless advice from fathers or best friends could prevent. He placed his forehead on the table. Something collapsed inside him with the force of a body hitting pavement from eight stories up. He had found a small, delicate thing with gilded edges, a fairytale treasure. The best thing he had ever had. He'd found it within, at a depth he had never thought existed. It was gone. He wanted to cry. He pressed his glass into his mouth, gagging himself to prevent this.

"I know," Skinner said in a bored voice. "That stuff can hurt like hell."

LaCoss put up his hands in mock surrender. "Am I being a ham? Perhaps an amateurish ham. Would you say…hammy?"

"Know what? You guys aren't having any more fun than I am," Skinner toasted them with his remaining sip of cola.

"Yes we are," LaCoss said, pressing his teeth together demonically.

"Nope. I can tell you aren't." Skinner's eyes brightened, his face coated with a saintly bliss. His consistent level of happiness had always been a mystery. Were some people naturally happier? Skinner was lower-middle-class, yet had no designs to improve. He was an English lit major, a poetry fan, with no expressed ambition beyond how he intended to spend the day. Maybe some lack explained the happiness. Or maybe he was more evolved. Either way, Lance wanted to smack the bliss off Skinner's face.

"Where is Terlinger?" Lance asked.

"He's coming. Be patient."

"I was just hamming it up," Lance said. "I'm no Andrew McCarthy, though."

LaCoss shook a slow fist at Lance.

Sy Terlinger pulled up in a rumbling, rusted primer gray Mustang Fastback, wearing knee-high fringed moccasins. He made a phone call behind the bar, yelled something about Van Halen tickets and then rumbled off. LaCoss's face drooped in a defeated way. They got up to leave.

Skinner's car, Mary Ann, screamed down the road with the urgency of an escape, jerking and bucking in second gear. LaCoss, somewhere above Lance's head, yelled to startled pedestrians about ham sandwiches, about honey-baked hams.

Lance leaned against his door, nauseous, beyond exhausted. He wanted to punch Skinner for yanking the car around, and to tell LaCoss to shut up, but instead, carsick, he hung his head over the door, his body convulsing in spasms. Wind ripped spittle from his lips. The window poked into his neck. LaCoss's booming voice cut through the air, like a Sam Donaldson question bellowed above the chopper blades of Marine One as Reagan crossed the East Lawn: "Fuck you Irwin Claypool, you worthless idiot! You and everyone you know! You're not going to stop me or my career. No waaaay! When it's all over I'm gonna write it on my tombstone, in giant letters: I...FUCKING...WON!"

Lying in bed, Lance stared upward, vaguely hoping the ceiling might collapse and crush him and end his misery. He turned onto his side, his eyes picking up a naked square on the wall of stripped paint, where tape had once affixed a picture of Lynn.

Then his eyes shut and nothing he could see reminded him of her.

CHAPTER FOURTEEN

MAYBE YOU SHOULD

How Lance and LaCoss had missed the first run of *Blue Velvet*—the latest from David Lynch, their favorite filmmaker—was a mystery. Lance blamed a certain girl, whose name he wasn't speaking, who had left one phone message after she walked away in the night (that was how little she cared!). Luckily, a local art cinema was showing *Blue Velvet* at midnight. Two girls were visiting LaCoss from California. Raylene, the strawberry blonde, was more possessive of LaCoss. Joan had a pixie face and squeaky voice. In greeting she offered a friendly hug to Lance, who moved back, resisting her, fearing trickery from her gender.

Lance proudly wore his yard sale jacket, the Secret Agent jacket. At first people said it was ugly, but more and more he detected an unspoken respect, as though he had recognized the jacket's overlooked qualities, and through his own personal brashness, a certain Lancesque bravado, he was now pulling off this look. He'd achieved the impossible—a fashion statement. Sure enough, the fall J. Crew catalog had a similar jacket, worn by a guy romping at a fake clambake barefoot people were forever attending within its pages. Before leaving for the movie, they went downstairs and knocked on Charles Boyd's door to invite him. Only the faint chatter of a Japanese language instruction record answered.

As they sat in pre-movie gloom, Joan admired Lance's jacket, feeling the sleeve, but she could not have his jacket, no way, not even if she paid fifty bucks. He discreetly pulled his arm away. In the opening scene, slow-motion firemen waved as an old-fashioned fire truck floated through an idyllic neighborhood. Bobby Vinton's honeyed vocals dripped in the background.

LaCoss leaned over Joan, saying to Lance, "My mind is already blown."

A chilly sensation spread across Lance's chest. He connected with every subtlety, in awe, as though thunderous truths were being revealed. That Dennis Hopper could act. Lance identified with the main character, Jeffrey Beaumont, who found a human ear in a field, which led to a hometown mystery and a hidden, dangerous world. It was quite thrilling, the way movies could make ordinary things, even terrible things, seem fantastic and wonderful. Maybe your own experiences could be similarly transformed. It was good to see weirdness and suffering and confusion resolve and add up to something. He sensed there was higher logic brewing in his seat, in this theater, on this night. Their aisle exploded with wild laughter at the dry jokes and hip absurdities Lynch had peppered throughout the narrative. At other times they stared reverently. During the credits, the girls stirred, stretching their backs. Lance didn't want to talk for several days, though he felt refreshed and oddly centered. When the lights came up, he moved to the edge of his seat and looked at LaCoss.

LaCoss, still slumped in his seat, said, "I have witnessed cinematic perfection. I am worthless. I am nothing. I have no talent whatsoever."

The group filed out. In the lobby, Lance wandered across carpet flaked with popcorn, his friends lagging behind. A group of girls in dark coats lingered near the glass doors, several stepping outside. He stared dreamily at a coming attractions poster, feeling unreal, like he was inhabiting a movie, in a slow transitional point before the hero was challenged again. A girl in a black pea coat with intricately embroidered dark hosiery turned around. It was Veronica Boyer. She took a half-step toward Lance. "So…what did you think?"

"I think…I don't know what I think." He smiled unevenly,

like he had no brain.

Her face was level with his chest, black hair pulled back and bound with bobby pins. The frill of a dark vintage dress caressed her neck. Her green eyes accentuated the sharp delicacy of her nose and lips. She always dressed like an off-duty chanteuse, which amused him. She gazed past his loopy grin to LaCoss, Joan and Raylene, loitering near the concession area. "I see your deceitful friend is up to his usual tricks."

Lance could think of nothing to counter this. He shrugged.

"Care to get a bite?" she asked lazily. "I've got my car."

Unsure of the words falling off his tongue, he automatically said, "That would be great," then worried about this social obligation and his ability to be normal. He had spent the previous day shut in his room, eating stale crackers and contemplating a strategy of avoiding females the rest of his life. He considered canceling, but her invitation seemed human and innocent. Lance signaled he was taking off with Veronica. LaCoss flashed a wry smile.

He opened the door for Veronica and they both bristled in the cold. Veronica walked fast, her slender neck sallow in the poor light. She put a key into the driver's side door of her canary yellow two-seater Karmann-Ghia, that strangest variety of Volkswagen. Stickers covered the rear bumper and trunk; obscure bands with ominous names: Killing Joke, Corrosion of Conformity, Misfits. Inside, she scooped up a shoebox and a red bra from his seat. A rubber tarantula hung from the rearview mirror. The car smelled of fast food and patchouli. She reached over him to pop the glove compartment and retrieve cigarettes, her unleashed hair brushing his arm. A trace of fermented grandmother perfume remained after she pulled back.

"I hope you're not asthmatic," she said, an unlit Kool Milds menthol between her teeth.

"Smoke away. It's your vehicle." A gnarled tube of toothpaste was down by his foot. "There's a Waffle House just around the corner."

"How very charming. I had another place in mind." Her voice had a permanent understatement with an ostentatious edge.

The car drove with a clatter Veronica made no apology for. He noticed her ghostly pink chalk lipstick, and fixated on it. At first it seemed corpse-like; an old programmed part of himself was weirded out. But the eroticism of her glowing lips and an appreciation of this bold don't-give-a-shit statement won him over. She drove the two-seater with an ease, but a fierce control as well. Her slender hand shifted, then fixed a lock of hair. She clipped in a barrette, checking her hair in the mirror while noting a transit bus on the left. Despite these conflicting purposes, Lance decided against a late deployment of his seatbelt. She drove with an invincibility and competence other female drivers did not display. She percolated with high-strung brunette energy, a lost cousin of Joan Jett and Ally Sheedy, with some Vivien Leigh thrown in. The engine heated the floorboards and a musky sex-like smell rose off the carpets, filling his nostrils. Lance glanced to pick up changes in her facial lines. The radio ached with the strange songs of college stations, the underground exotica she favored. She sang in a melodic soprano to a Siouxsie and the Banshees song, lyrics Lance never could have deciphered on his own. He suddenly felt oddly happy. These things were supposed to happen in life—he recognized he'd been waiting for this—a joyride with an art-loving bohemian ingénue with great calves.

She parked at a diner hangout. Local hipsters had latched onto the brick walls and the peasant skirt waitresses. At their table, she turned her back to him and shed her coat. He caught it at the last moment.

"That was my second time. I think I finally understand the movie. Follow me." She touched his wrist lightly. "In the first scene Kyle MacLachlan's father has a heart attack while watering the lawn. The camera pans down to the lawn, to blades of grass, then bugs and beetles underneath. It's the darkness under everything. MacLachlan's dark side comes out when he meets Dennis Hopper and Isabella Rossellini."

"Very clever." Lance's brain burned with satisfaction at this insight. "And then…MacLachlan gives in to evil. He ends up using Rossellini sexually the same way Hopper does."

"You're right," she said, nodding with interest.

His order of scrambled eggs arrived. She picked at a cottage cheese salad, using her fork while still holding her knife, European-style.

"Hold on." Lance put down his fork. "Think about all the fours. Laura Dern honked four times outside Rossellini's apartment. And MacLachlan held up four fingers for Double Ed at the hardware store."

She studied him closely, not blinking. He couldn't tell if she found this observation brilliant or moronic. He cautioned himself against caring. But here came an unexpected thought, as if from another brain: what would a bed romp with this vixen be like? Her corneas enlarged and seemed to quiver, as though she'd intercepted the thought. She admonished him with a scolding flick of her eyelashes. A blush swept up his neck and reddened his face. He stared into his plate, telling himself complication with Veronica, at this time, would be the worst of bad ideas.

When the waitress delivered the check, Lance slid his hand over and plucked a flake of lettuce off Veronica's plate. She turned quickly, her eyes chiding him. She didn't miss anything. Beneath the curtain-like bangs of dark hair and the makeup she was quite elegant, even beautiful.

Lance reached for the check and said, "I'll get it. My treat."

"Absolutely not. I have money." She pulled the bill out of reach.

"I'll take it. Really."

Her nostrils flared, as if her entire honor were at stake. "I'd like to pay for mine, please."

They split it. Back in the Karmann-Ghia, the ignition

sputtered without starting the engine. "Dammit, Edgar," she said. The car seemed like an Edgar. Once they were going Lance asked her where she was from. Raising her voice above Edgar's clamor, she spoke in clipped sentences like she was reciting a prayer. She'd been born in Mexico. Her parents were Methodist missionaries. As a toddler they lived in an adobe pueblo without electricity. Her parents divorced and she and Mom moved to California. Mom ditched the faith, started selling Mary Kay, her new faith, and made a whopping bundle, then remarried and they moved to backwoods New Hampshire with her new dad, Randy, the trouble magnet. He was on the run from federal crimes, so they lived in Vermont backcountry, enduring terrible winters, like Laura Ingalls Wilder. She read stolen library books in tree forts until Mom ditched Randy. Mom sold more Mary Kay in Bangor, made a second whopping bundle, and drove around in a pink Cadillac. Veronica graduated from high school, the valedictorian, then hung out with troubled punk teens on the Lower East Side of Manhattan. Her father was in South America saving souls. Every Christmas, he sent her a poem.

Advanced, thought Lance. One of those advanced hybrid personalities.

They were taking streets along the fringes of the North Downs, in an old expensive neighborhood. "I live in an awesome place," she said. "I'll show you." She turned a corner and parked in the driveway of a rambling corner lot dotted with huge seasoned maples. A two-story Tudor mansion rose into the trees. Lance bent forward to peer up at the big house. "Don't tell me this thing is a rental."

"I live up there. The whole top floor to myself. A very old, wonderful lady lives on the first floor. It's her house. I pay almost nothing because I check on her."

"Is she weird about noise?"

"Deaf as a stone. You can come up for a while but do not, I repeat, do not get any ideas. Is this completely clear?" Her eyes were stern beads.

"There's not a thought in my head." He flashed the Scout's Honor hand signal.

For several moments she seemed to judge his sincerity. She got out of the car. "Boys and their heads," she muttered. On the dark porch she flicked around her key rings. Inside, Veronica hung her coat on a stand, then paused at a bubble mirror to study herself. The place had a funereal quality: white lace covering tables and dried flower arrangements. A staleness hung in the air, but it was mild.

"Is she awake?" Lance whispered.

"No chance," Veronica said in her normal voice.

Lance followed behind as Veronica clopped up the carpeted stairs, her black dress setting a fine silhouette, snug to her hips. She stopped on the second floor, pointing one foot before the other and unfolding her arms grandly, like a showcase model. "This is my fabulous abode!" she said. She popped off her heels, lowering her height significantly. It was easy to tell what was hers and what was the old woman's. A Cure concert poster hung next to a mahogany armoire, a lemon yellow bean bag sat next to a Queen Anne chair, framed pictures of Eisenhower and Morrissey graced the hall bathroom.

A sitting room, which connected to a small kitchen and her bedroom (not included on the tour), seemed her chief haunt. A prominent poster—a flopping halibut next to a Schwinn—showcased the Gloria Steinem quote: A woman needs a man like a fish needs a bicycle. A collection of wax skulls and miniature skeletons on a bookshelf. Lance noticed a row of books with French titles. The French language, which attracted waves of beret-clutching brunettes, generations of them, from every tedious corner of the America, *je ne sais quoi* and *savoir-faire* trickling from their pointy superior tongues. Veronica was capable of thinking French thoughts. Impressive. Was she smarter than him? Quite possibly. Another shelf was crowded with Russian writers: Dostoevsky, Tolstoy,

Solzhenitsyn. Also Betty Friedan, Steinem, and *Sex Tips for Girls*. She explained she had read the novels during the fierce Vermont winters, thinking of herself as a Russian.

A crude painting was propped against a futon sofa—a nude girl with a ponytail on a stool, her knees turned away from the artist, feet propped on the rungs. A naked nymph, her rump perched on the seat. Lance hesitated to say anything, in case Veronica had painted it. Then he realized she was the girl. She looked over her shoulder toward the artist with classical innocent surprise, but the way she lowered her bottom lip put her into the Lolita category, creating an air of ruination, of porn.

"Who's the lucky artist?" Lance asked, downplaying his interest.

"Just an art student. I had to sit in that position for two weeks." It captured the elegance of her neck and shoulders, the proud face worthy of a Renaissance seraph. Once you got under that vintage clothing she was hot. One of those girls who had never exerted herself and never would, but who looked incredible exactly the way God had hatched her.

Lance cautioned himself against leering too long. She sat on a wicker plantation chair, curling her feet under her. Lance sat on the futon couch.

"Do you feel like the artist guys are checking you out?"

"I do it for art. There is a long history of artists paying tribute to the female form." She arched her back with nobility, running her hand slowly along her torso. "A sculptor did try to feel me up once."

"It must have been weird to take off your clothes the first time."

"Nothing has to be hard the first time." She lowered her chin and voice. "It's just the human body. So what if some art student gets an erection looking at me? I'd offer you a beer or something," she said, "but I don't have alcohol or drugs on hand."

"That's OK—"

"Except for very powerful drugs."

"Wow…what kind are we talking?"

"I did heroin for two years."

"Oh, my God." His hands jumped from his lap.

"Wrong." She opened her mouth, agitated, and shook a finger at him. "Do I seem like a junkie? Come on, Mr. Lance. And what is it like to have a phallic first name?"

"I never thought of it that way."

She laughed to herself, then dropped her head onto her shoulder in a sleepy way.

"What do you know about me?" he asked, feigning shyness.

She pulled a hair out of the corner of her mouth. "I know you have good taste in entertainment. And your girlfriend is Lynn Van Oster."

Lance tensed, like a scab had been ripped off his arm. He wrapped his arms protectively around his stomach. "Past tense. You're a few weeks behind."

"Lynn was in one of my classes last year. She's…an interesting girl." Veronica narrowed her eyes competitively, seeming to remember a conversation or incident that had crawled under her skin. A mocking edge entered her voice when she asked, "Was it true love?"

"I don't know what it was." Fatigue washed through him. He distrusted Veronica briefly, reminded of the cruel snarkiness Lynn had lashed him with. He wondered if Lynn and Veronica had ever gotten past the blonde versus brunette tensions to talk and develop a relationship. This possibility both creeped him out and excited him.

"Aww, poor baby. I apologize for bringing that up." She straightened her body, allowing her wrists to hang over the armrests. Her eyes closed and she yawned.

He sensed he was moments away from eviction. It was 2:30 a.m. He grabbed a Key West postcard from the table, waving it to get her attention. He told her about an epic summer car journey his family had taken there. Her eyes brightened. He moved easily into new subjects, amazed by his knowledge and eloquence, his ability to hold her focus. He lowered his voice on certain points—a technique of his father's, but without his father's condescension. He rambled about extemporaneous theories, that the second Miles Davis Quintet had been the Dark Prince's apex, producing real genius, i.e. the complex modal structures. He veered into other topics (she conversant in them all): the movie career of Pia Zadora; whether Nixon's foreign policy accomplishments offset his Watergate disgrace; Sting's solo career. Sting led to Madonna and Veronica's disclosure that she very much admired The Material Girl. She gathered her hair ends into a bunch, twisting them into a rope. "Women can't avoid their sexuality when it comes to liberation. Sex has to be part of it."

"Madonna has made herself into a sex object. You're saying all women should?"

"Yes and no. Women are sexual objects to men. They always have been. It's biology. It's a matter of controlling sexual identity without it being defined for us."

"It's a matter of controlling her bank account."

"Madonna is a strong, sexual woman who doesn't run away from herself."

Lance wondered if she was talking about sex as a test. Or maybe it was his misinterpretation. He was annoyed by his inability to read her. She crossed her arms, her face prim. She'd given no hints she wanted companionship. In fact, the opposite. He wasn't angling to attack her either—beyond his conversational magnetism, which he couldn't control. He'd been a gentleman, except when she'd leaned forward and he'd taken a healthy peek down her dress into the supportive shadows of her décolletage, spying the heave of her sketch-worthy breasts.

Veronica yawned fiercely, then explained she had to get up early. She closed her eyes in bothered fashion. "It's going to be a day of toil. A nursery is delivering plants. I promised Mrs. Perdue, my landlady, I would help plant them. It's going to involve digging in dirt."

"I could help you dig." He looked off, but prayed she would say yes.

After a moment she said, "How chivalrous. Actually, I could use help."

"I could meet you here tomorrow."

"The truck will be here at 8:00. You might as well stay."

They moved the coffee table and folded out the futon into a bed. She brought out some sheets and a blanket. He took off his yard sale jacket and untied his shoes. She held up the jacket. "Oh, this sport coat. Love the style. It's very cool." Her eyes twinkled at him with admiration, seeming to grant him the same status. He bowed, gladly accepting this designation from a cutting-edge woman.

Veronica pointed imperiously to her bedroom. "I will be sleeping in there. You will be here. Is that clear?"

"You got a revolver in there?" He made a funny face, breaking the tension.

"It's a .38 with some rust, but it shoots straight." It was unquestionably true. She turned to her bedroom, her stocking feet swishing on the floor. Her door shut and a lock clicked with authority.

He turned out a lamp, the hardwood chilling his bare feet. He stood gazing out a front window. His eyes adjusted to a dull street light. He'd understood nothing would happen between them; he didn't really want that either. After a near-drowning, you stayed away from the ocean awhile. Just being there, standing in the strange house was satisfying.

He had a vivid Kurosawa-like dream about alpinists stranded on a rocky ledge during a blizzard. Japanese alpinists, himself included. We have to jump! Lance pleaded with his unmoving companions. Jump! Snowflakes had gathered on their numb, hypothermic faces. Waking from the dream, he crawled over to her door and listened to a creak from her bedframe, a shifting of covers. In early morning, light poured from a window and cold air gnawed at an exposed shoulder. He pulled up the blanket to his neck. He felt content with unfamiliar surroundings, far from familiar problems and safe from looming decisions. Foreign sheets always cheered him, reminding him of vacation, escape, and being around strangers who didn't know the first thing about you.

The racket started outside. Doors slammed. The hard staccato of boots banging and scraping in a metal truck bed. Then one piercing, warbling voice. Lance wrapped the blanket around his shoulders and shuffled to the window. From a truck on the front lawn, two men dropped seedlings wrapped in burlap. A hunched figure in a tan raincoat leaned on an aluminum cane. Veronica appeared at his side, sans makeup yet chipper, in a blue terrycloth robe and matching furry slippers. "She gets up at six a.m. every morning. She's a terror. We better get out there."

Lance pulled on his clammy socks and jeans. He borrowed a maroon Harvard sweatshirt. She emerged from her room wearing tan riding pants, green wellie galoshes, a heather wool sweater and a scarf, like the daughter of a country earl on *Masterpiece Theatre*.

The air outside was moist, drops falling from branches. Too cold for just the sweatshirt. Veronica, her voice climbing several decibels, introduced him to Mrs. Perdue. The old woman, leaning like she expected a weight to fall on her from above, pivoted to face Lance; she raised her watery eyes. She regarded him with interest. "Hello there!" She put her non- cane hand forward and he held it, scaly and light, as if it had no weight or force.

"He's going to help plant the new bushes," Veronica said happily, sidling up to Lance and putting her arm through his, like they were entering a prom.

"I didn't see you arrive this morning," Mrs. Perdue said in

her powerful, throaty voice. More perplexed than accusing.

"You must have missed me." Lance looked to Veronica, who smiled, offering no help.

The workers unloaded the shrubs, mostly squat bushes with waxy leaves, pyracanthas; and they waved and drove off. Lance had thought they would help dig. The three of them walked alongside the house, Mrs. Perdue picking her way slowly along wooden stakes with red ribbons. She pointed at one that leaned. Veronica scooted over to it to make it upright. The old woman stepped closer to face Lance and said in a more restrained voice, though still quite loud, "Veronica is a nice girl, but she wears these old clothes." A tension set into her face, of disappointment and sorrow. "And black makeup!"

Lance nodded in sympathy, in this moment of intimacy, as though he harbored similar misgivings about Veronica's fashion choices. Mrs. Perdue then held a hand up, recanting a bit. "She is really very, very nice." Over the old woman's shoulder, Lance could see Veronica holding back laughter, doing a strange dance of waving her hands and shaking her shoulders. She snorted, then stuck her tongue out at Lance, hoping to break him up. Maybe it wasn't so good, he thought, that Mrs. Perdue's family put so much faith in Veronica.

The sky darkened and a light drizzle began. Veronica thought it best Mrs. Perdue,–whose face looked more ashen, should go inside. Veronica turned her around and they walked toward a backyard door. Lance held the screen open as she and Veronica climbed the stairs into a large kitchen. Antiquated appliances lined the counters. A tiny city of green prescription bottles filled a tray alongside a black rotary phone. Veronica helped the old woman out of her raincoat, then disappeared into another room.

"Where are the shovels?" Lance asked Mrs. Perdue.

She stood in the middle of the kitchen, in suspended animation. She stared at Lance, motionless, like she was in shock. Had she heard? In the stillness of the kitchen—her element, her smells—Lance tensed. Most of his life he had somewhat feared women of her age, the church-aisle dainties, the grocery-store creepers. Her mottled skin was almost translucent. Her hand tremored. He shuddered, thinking one day his youth would be gone.

Veronica walked into the kitchen and Lance recoiled, shaking himself out of a stupor not unlike that of Mrs. Perdue.

Random smacks of rain fell on Lance and Veronica as they dug. The trees swirled from winds that hinted at a more serious drenching. Veronica was a surprisingly good shoveler. She'd plant her spade and jump on it with her full weight, which wasn't much, but enough to sink in her implement and turn up ground. She made grunting noises; there was something sexy about her abandon and determination. Damp hair fell into her face. He liked her. He'd been wrong about her. She was the kind of girl who, if marooned, would construct a jungle shelter, then gleefully slice open pig bellies.

Once they had four holes of sufficient depth, Lance dropped a pyracantha into each hole. He undid the ties and pulled the burlap from under the roots. They shoveled dirt around the trunks and packed it down. Veronica wiped some grime off her wrists and shook hair out of her face. Her sweater sagged from moisture. "It's official. I'm now disgusting."

Lance made a clicking sound and winked at her. "You look fabulous as ever."

"You're a damn liar."

"Watch your mouth, young lady."

Only the dogwoods were left to plant. Veronica went inside to check on Mrs. Perdue.

A blister was on the verge of surfacing on his thumb. He paused to catch his breath, an even mist settling over him. He finished digging the second hole as Veronica came down the back steps into the yard. She smoked a cigarette near the steps, then walked over.

"You're doing great," she said. "All we need to do is drop

those babies in."

Lance leaned on his shovel, flicking moisture off his hair.

"I can finish. You don't have to get yourself wet again."

"Are you sure? I'm excused?" She reached out and touched his elbow, gazing up at him with sarcasm.

"Yes, you are." Lance bowed in a mocking way, feeling loopy from the exertion.

"In that case I'm going to take a shower." Veronica turned and took two steps away.

Lance exhaled heavily. He easily could have said nothing, but as a suave joke that slipped out, he said, "Maybe I should join you."

Still walking, she half-turned her face, exposing her rosy cheek, the tip of her nose and a line of dewy eyelashes, and said, "Maybe you should."

Then he saw the back of her head, and her steps in the grass trailing away. Maybe you should. It echoed in his mind as she reached the steps, opened the back door without looking back, and was gone. A slow-motion sequence he was powerless to affect. It had been impossible to make out her complete expression, though he sensed, from her eye mostly, scrutiny of her entire face would have revealed a sly, cutting look, a look that was an entire conversation. How had she said it? Maybe you should. The same voice she'd used during the conversation, with a slight emphasis on should. No, she'd pulled back a little, saying it more softly, more shrewdly, which made it a joke. That was her, a joker. She liked laughing about things, laughing at people and being mysterious. She liked to shock. But she also liked directness.

The not knowing was pure agony.

He grabbed the base of the dogwood, lifted it and crab-walked over to the hole, dropping it in with a thud. He replayed the image of Veronica's face and her exact tone. Her head had been tilted back a few degrees, consistent with teasing. She'd been totally frigid last night, emphatic about it. She was a fish without need of a bicycle. Had she added some shake and bake to her walk? Her lips had been pursed. She had touched his elbow.

He couldn't budge the knot on the burlap. He dug his fingers inside the string and tried ripping it open. The tree shuddered with each furious yank, his heart thumping wildly. She had those amazing calves. He yanked out the burlap and shoveled dirt around the hole. He thudded his feet with an even rhythm—a war dance to pack it down. She was a nude art model, a wild child. Water speckled his upturned face, falling on his eyes and teeth. He heaved the other dogwood into the remaining hole. More stamping.

She wouldn't tease about such an invitation; and he most definitely would join her.

He tossed the shovel onto wet grass, to rust. He ran to the front door, which creaked and shook. He heard nothing inside, save the imperceptible whoosh of plumbing delivering water upstairs. He locked the door, his heart clocking at a steady rate, and flew up the stairs two at a time. Maybe you should. On the second floor he paused again, his blood thicker in his chest. Maybe—she'd only said maybe, not please do, or will you. She was a kidder. A teaser. She had been kidding, that was all. If he hadn't made the joke first, she would have said nothing. It was a huge mistake. He crossed the hardwood floor of her living room, hearing the steady flick of water against a plastic curtain. How many people had been bloodied by her rusty revolver? He stepped gingerly into her bedroom, as if the floorboards might collapse. Candles and makeup littered a vanity. A black and white photograph of a barn hung over her four-poster bed. He stood staring into the bathroom. A white clawfoot tub was inside, an eggshell curtain pulled around its perimeter. Wisps of steam crawled over the threshold into the bedroom. He barely knew this girl.

He stood still, still enough to disappear. Let me have what I want.

He stripped off the drenched sweatshirt. Standing barefoot on the cold tile, he unzipped his jeans and peeled them down to his ankles. Water splattered against the tub as she moved inside. It would either be the most courageous or the most humiliating, disastrous thing ever. He tossed his lucky bandanna-print boxers aside, feeling oddly exhilarated. He imagined burglars and murderers experienced something similar—a blend of not really being there and not being supposed to be there. He reached for the curtain, then put his hand down. He didn't want to frighten her.

He cleared his throat, then said, "Is there any hot water left?"

The curtain near the showerhead sprung back, her drenched head poking out, dark hair dripping. She looked him up and down. She disappeared into the shower. After several moments she said with nonchalance, "There's plenty. It's fabulous."

He stepped in. She was impossibly small compared to him, a touching sight. He put his hands at her slippery hips and they kissed, a menthol flavor circulating. On her tiptoes, she strained to reach him under the warm stream. His mind shut off, overwhelmed by his senses. They ended up on the bathroom floor, her slender back against a fuzzy blue rug. Tiles pressed against his knees, the cold of the floor contrasting with the heat of moving inside her. Each of them, gulping air, drove for every possible iota of pleasure, her feet propped against his legs, then braced to either side. He struggled to stay centered, his elbows and knees slipping. So overwrought with passion, he barely recognized himself, or the surreal sight of her underneath him.

Lying on the floor next to her, he felt relaxed, but mildly disorientated. He tried to sort out what had happened, what would happen next. They showered, then wrapped towels around their dewy bodies. She pulled out a tube of cherry ChapStick and put a hand to his face. He jerked back from the approaching lip balm.

"Your bottom lip is dry, darling. You're about to flake. Trust me."

He held still while she dabbed with oily strokes. She put ChapStick on her lips, strained upward and kissed him. She smiled in a secretive way. A feeling of warmth toward her came over him, of thankfulness and affection. There would be no uncomfortable silences or power shifts. She stared into the mirror, her eyes solemn and purposeful. She combed out her hair, flicked it straight over her head and arranged it with her hands. She gave him a white cotton robe from a Marriott. She put on a flame-red velour robe with a feathery collar. They spent the rest of the day sitting or lying on the floor, as if some extra-gravitational force kept them off furniture. In her living room, they stretched out on the polished pine, each propped up by an elbow. They intertwined like the yin yang symbol.

"Were you expecting that from me?" Lance asked.

"To be honest, no. But I was vaguely hoping. Then I couldn't resist."

He felt disappointed she'd doubted him. "Why did you not expect me to join you?"

She studied him, running her tongue over her teeth. She stared off, silent awhile. "I wasn't sure you were the type. At first, I didn't think you were."

"What type?"

"You know—a type of person. A certain adventurousness, a sensual openness."

"But I did turn out to be that type of person."

"Maybe you were that type of person all along, but you never knew it. You can thank me for that." This sounded better, though he still wasn't totally happy with it. Her free hand and wrist were perched on the curvature of her hip. He was mesmerized by her periwinkle fingernails tapping on her thigh, as if their rhythm was an important clue about her.

"When I was coming up the stairs, I kept thinking—"

She covered his mouth with her cupped hand and shook her head slowly. She whispered, "You think too much."

At dusk the rain became harder, making a hushing sound on the roof. A chill rose from the floorboards. Veronica padded down the stairs to crank up the thermostat. She came back with a jumbled stack of photographs. Lance plucked one off the top. She tried to snatch it back, too late. Veronica as a puffy-faced middle schooler, in an ultra-preppie getup: hair band, forest green monogram sweater. She grabbed it back. She kept shuffling pictures to the bottom of the stack.

"You're holding out on me," Lance said, craving her full story, wanting her to share all the photos.

"I'm showing you only what I want you to see," she said, uncharacteristically modest.

He studied an upside-down picture in her lap. Veronica's bangs were down to her eyes, heavy mascara: a Chrissie Hynde phase. In another she had scary razor slices on the side of her head a la Cyndi Lauper, but rougher, with black lipstick.

"Now." She held a picture to her chest. "This is why I got these out. I had a huge, huge crush on this guy. You remind me of him, in fact you look exactly like him."

In the picture, a guy sat in an American sedan in a parking lot. All the windows down. He wore a sleeveless white t-shirt with a red Japanese character, and was scowling. A shadow inside the car obscured his upper face. "His name was Jasper Ross. I was so in love with him I thought I would die!" She threw her head back and groaned like she had been stabbed. "He was three grades ahead of me. The first guy in school to hear of New Wave. He wore pointed purple shoes. He dyed his hair silver, wore an ear clip, a checkerboard jacket and a brown leather tie that was one inch wide. So cool. He would drive around the school parking lot at like 4 mph during class hours, blasting songs by The Cars on this expensive sound system. He had a canary yellow Buick Le Mans with a sunroof he had cut out himself.

"I was in seventh grade, waiting for a ride home after classes, standing there, paranoid about getting my period or a pop quiz or something stupid, and Jasper Ross drove up blasting this music. The song was 'Let's Go'—The Cars' song. The car echoed with that buzzing keyboard sound, these whirring spaceship sounds and that fat, futuristic guitar. It changed my life. I heard these sounds, that pop beat. And the lyrics! It was like a narration of my life. I was the girl being sung about. No, don't laugh. This was totally real to me. I didn't even own a radio. I wanted to be a librarian. He was creeping along and he slowed down when he saw me, so I heard the music extra clear, like I had never heard sounds before, like my ears hadn't worked until this moment. It was so loud his door panels were vibrating. He was playing the keyboard parts on his dashboard. Just as he crept past he tossed an old sneaker at me. It upset me, but I was flattered he noticed me."

There was something about the guy's nose and chin Lance found familiar, only that; but he loved the idea of this doppelganger spirit, a rebel who had earned Veronica's lasting devotion. "Did you date him?"

"Not really. Jasper sort of tolerated me." A rare, fleeting vulnerability flashed in her eyes—he questioned if he'd actually seen it. "He did take me to a Depeche Mode concert in Hartford. That was before anyone had heard of them. I begged him again and again to make love to me, to be the one I lost my virginity to. He kept saying I was too young, that he could go to jail."

"And what about this guy reminds you of me?"

"He was sweet and defiant. He wasn't very liked at school. This was small-town New Hampshire and he was very un-New England. The rustic kids gave him a hard time. They slashed his tires. Somebody took ipecac from a chem lab and put it in his sandwich. He got really sick. He struggled with self-esteem and embodied this freakishness I felt but didn't show. During his senior year he moved away. It was weird, he stopped wearing the clothes and listening to his music just before that. It upset me because I thought he'd done it for the wrong reasons." Lance wished he hadn't asked. Being in the League of Rebels was great, but he disliked talk of faulty self-esteem. There was a fine line between principled defiance or cool independence and being the kid who fell on the wrong side of the fence.

The upstairs windows had fogged over, the air turned sharp and hot from the ancient metal radiators. Lance loosened his robe belt to ventilate himself. His forehead felt tropically moist. "It's so hot," he said. "Mrs. Perdue is going to keel over down there."

"The hotter the better for her. She's like a reptile."

Veronica loosened her robe and slid a hand over her chest. "It feels kinda good. Like we're in the desert." She let her robe fall off her shoulders. She pulled her slender arms out of the sleeves and leaned back on the floor. She calmly stared at him, as if planning.

It occurred Veronica might be a nymphomaniac, that she had done it with him for reasons beyond his overpowering charm. Was she a bad girl who slung herself around searching for connection with her lost father, her sex life a series of infatuations beginning with her New Wave man? Lance had always shied away from bad girls: the roller rink sluts who did it on dirty mattresses in the woods, the hallway girls with their vulgar stares, tight skirts and submerged hatred. They didn't care who knew, or so it seemed.

But Veronica was too smart for that, too cultured. She wasn't the kind. Something else was going on with her.

Veronica swung her legs around, putting her feet on either side of Lance's ribs. She inched her hips forward. Her sheer, pale legs vibrated. Lance matched her benign silence, her curiosity, as his stamina gathered. A wicked desire rose into his throat—an animal surge. They kissed. He lifted up her hips and they went at it like spiders, like naked Twister players, as if they had never stopped before. He imagined a fresco in a crumbling palace, a Hindu nobleman doing it this way with a courtesan. An unwelcome tap at his shoulder reminded him of the recklessness of these trysts. He wasn't using birth control. Unclear if she was either. Would a venereal disease be part of his future? That list of seven or eight of them, with their embarrassing, hard-to-spell names, some incurable. He dropped this thought, all thoughts, slamming a door in their dour faces, happy to be done with them. He closed his eyes, relishing she had also deemed him worthy of rolling the dice.

They ordered Chinese food and spent the evening naked, sitting and lounging around. They listened to music and nibbled at pot stickers. Predictably, her collection was heavy on gloomy British rockers: Love and Rockets, Echo & the Bunnymen, New Order and the Cocteau Twins. She had a curiously complete selection of Human League. A Ted Nugent record hid in the stack. She put on one of the middle Cure albums, the one with rambling songs he didn't really care for, and they played backgammon. Veronica, with an impassive expression, used a scorched earth policy of taking his pieces captive at every chance, stacking them like round candies in the penalty box. He retaliated by taking her exposed pieces. She rolled doubles several times and whipped her pieces around the board, laughing at him. She glanced at him mischievously as she considered picking off a stone of his.

"Just make your move!" Lance said. He despised losing at games. He would have been beating her if he could get any decent rolls.

She hummed a bluesy tune and jiggled her breasts, considering the fate of the piece. The sportsmanship of a wicked medieval queen, yet it only made her more captivating. She generated constant excitement. He retaliated by holding her pieces hostage; they gave up in stalemate. She stood up, oval red spots on her butt, and changed the music. She crouched by the record player, setting the needle down delicately, then stood and smoked a cigarette. She took a long draw, her elbow propped on a wrist, like Jack Benny, as the music came on.

"These are the Pixies," she said, "and for my money they're the best rock 'n' roll band in America right now."

They were tricky little songs carved with a savage guitar attack. A rotund lead singer screamed non sequiturs in a hysterical falsetto. A girl was on bass and also sang. The album was called *Surfer Rosa*. After a few songs he understood what she saw in them, this band's obvious genius. He was destined to never be the first to know about these things, and that hurt, but knowing second beat not knowing at all.

She danced nonstop to most of the album, mimicking the lyrics in a sultry lip-sync. She used a straight back and elongated neck and bounced on the balls of her feet, making quick delicate movements with her hands, moving them like a Balinese dancer. A startlingly original dance. That was Veronica—you had to watch closely to see what she did next. From his perspective on the floor, she shook her butt slowly near his shoulder, doing this go- go stripper thing that was very sexy. He was moved to get up and dance with her, feeling self-consciously naked for a moment, then greatly enjoying the innovation of swinging freely and the lack of restriction. He could have shown hippies at Woodstock a few things. He showed himself a few things. They got a wicked groove going.

He poured a glass of ice water. She lit candles around the room and turned off the lights.

"Is it time to sacrifice the chickens?" Lance asked.

"Ha-ha. Maybe I'll sacrifice you."

"I'm ready with my *Blue Velvet* theory," he said.

"Let's hear it."

"The villain, Dennis Hopper, is the alter ego of Kyle MacLachlan's character. Hopper even says to MacLachlan at one point, 'You're just like me.' All the other characters are pulled between those two. Hopper corrupts Isabella Rossellini, then she corrupts MacLachlan. But he resists evil and he prevails in the end."

"But does he really prevail?"

"Of course he prevails. Dennis Hopper's character dies in the end."

She shook her head, not at all convinced. "At the end of the movie MacLachlan's character has changed, and has he changed for the better? Is he the same sweet innocent boy? No."

Sitting with their knees touching, they debated into the evening. Around midnight she turned down the thermostat. Both of them yawned. Without saying a word they climbed into her bed, flipping her comforter over them. Feeling dewy and sentimental, his arms fit easily around her.

He dreamt of the Japanese alpinists again. His companions on the snowbound ledge were blue, motionless, like rocks, as Lance circled above with outstretched arms, riding powerful currents of air. In the dream, he couldn't figure out if he had sprouted wings of salvation, or had died and was leaving the mortal world.

Soft rays of morning slid around the window blinds. On his stomach, he moved his head from a drool spot on his pillow. He noted a sudden pressure on his lower back. For some reason, Veronica had straddled him. He considered asking about this, but decided it wouldn't make any difference. Her thumbs dug into the base of his neck, then worked down his back. Morning shiatsu. Oh, the pleasures of those fingertips! Muscles along his spine protested, then loosened into submission. He moaned as she worked out a kink. She rolled him over. She worked the same magic on his pectorals and his facial muscles. During intercourse, confusing and intense realizations swept through him: he was impossibly tired, and they were breaking all known records of frequency, and it was all quite insane, practically *Last Tango in Paris*; and was this really him, was this really happening, and it seemed he'd known her all his life, but who was she really, and how had he ended up with a girl who read Dostoevsky and wore black makeup? It became exhaustive, hovering forever near completion, his nerve endings flaring and berserk. He felt himself struggling, beat, consumed with wonder about how he had ended up in this house, in this bed, on this morning, with this girl, and wonder about the raw conjugal act, and just when it seemed a conclusion was impossible to reach, he got one.

They recuperated in separate heaps. With a wrist propped over her eyes, her legs lay akimbo. In a soft, breathy voice, she said, "Unbelievable. That was the best ever."

He pretended he hadn't heard, but he most certainly had.

He said in a woozy voice, "Why did you decide to do all that this morning?" He was thinking aloud, not expecting an answer.

"Why not?" Veronica described her theory of lovemaking. Of life itself. Nature was the key. What were humans but a part of nature? Hair grew from our bodies and we ate vegetation and the flesh of rival creatures. We were born into the world sticky and yelping we sought the warmth of sunshine: the same as the Alaskan brown bear or the porcupine. She gained these insights from watching *Mutual of Omaha's Wild Kingdom* (as well as a crush on Marlin Perkin's proactive sidekick, Jim Fowler, safari jacket unbuttoned to his sternum, sleeves rolled tightly over his tanned arms). In her ninth year she became an avid watcher of the show. She delighted in the capture, safe transportation and release of animals, of the protection of rare species from human plundering, ensuring their survival for years to come. She marveled at the surreal beauty of a giraffe, the comical American prairie dog. While documenting these animals in the wild, Marlin Perkin's narration always came around to springtime and the search for mates. Cougars scanned valleys from a rocky crag, sniffing the air. Bighorn sheep cracked their skulls together in preparatory combat. And then, male and female would emerge from separate parts of the wilderness and circle each other, perhaps nuzzling. Then the male would rise onto its hind legs, or the bull sea lion's massive girth would ripple as it rose over the female and then…footage of pups squealing in a den, or a fawn trying out spindly legs.

This frustrated her, this censorship of the mating act. All the other action—the gory dismemberment of prey, the galloping chases—was captured so artfully. If the soaring of the condor or the stride of the leopard was so beautiful, and Marlin was always pointing out the grandeur of these creatures—we must learn to respect and value them—then why not examine their linkage to produce young? No one wants to see disgusting animals rutting on television, Veronica's mother explained. Human beings are too much like animals as it is.

But why this aversion to the natural order? Animals weren't ashamed of their mating. Within the shiny pages of *National Geographic* she found cultures more willing to embrace their own reproductive selves: Kalahari tribeswomen with oblong breasts like flat sacks; Amazonian pygmies, their bare bodies caked with mud; New Guinea headhunters with horns grandly affixed to their penises. They shared communal wives, performed public circumcisions; babies suckling at nipples were an everyday sight. They seemed happy enough. On a return trip, her missionary father pointed to these pictures as evidence these crude people needed spiritual guidance.

Little Veronica wasn't so sure. She realized she wasn't alone in her thinking the day she climbed her backyard jungle gym. Standing precariously above the rope swing, she looked over the high fence of their neighbor, Mr. Urmson, the aging bachelor. Mr. Urmson lay on a chaise lounge in brilliant sunshine, wearing only aviator sunglasses and flip-flops. His entire body was a rich, glistening chestnut color. He had sagging male breasts, a hairy belly and a slumbering purple and red wee-wee in a scraggly black nest.

"Did it freak you out to see his thing?" Lance asked.

"No. He reminded me of a Bolivian tribesman."

The next day, using a ladder propped at the side of her house, Veronica climbed onto her roof. She stripped off her clothes and sat her baby-soft behind onto the sandpapery shingles, rested her head back and spread her arms and legs. She wanted the nut-brown skin of a Nicaraguan Miskito Indian, or a deep-chocolate Ivory Coast shade. She wanted to be a native. The scorching sun prickled at her porcelain skin like tiny needles and she dreamed of a swarthy warrior lover, his hands bloody from wrestling and spearing a giant anaconda, making his way through the jungle to their smoky hut to make love to her. She got the most horrific sunburn of her life. She spent a night in the hospital and for weeks she peeled painfully, like an artichoke. Her mother put her on probation for two months and confiscated every *National Geographic* she had.

Lance imagined Veronica's bedroom to be a cave, or a den, and the comforter he pulled over them to be a rough bear skin. She in a cozy ball, he wrapped his arms and torso protectively around her; in comparison his shoulders seemed massive, indomitable.

When they finally rolled out of bed, Lance was ravenously hungry. He ate, in rapid succession, three full bowls of cereal drenched in milk. Leaving the house seemed out of the question. What they were up to could not be interrupted. This thing with Veronica was so advanced, so modern. They were celestial comets pulled into the same spectacular orbit. He found her exhilarating, irresistible, and together their energy was crazy, maybe not love but something equally intense—perhaps better than love—the energy of people who committed crimes together, who packed up cars in the night to drive to distant cities. He wanted to be exhilarated by her a long time.

"You know," he said with a full mouth, "I don't even know your major."

"Speaking of, we're missing classes today."

"What day is it?"

"Monday." It was hard to believe, like their whole time

together (three days? four?) had been one drab continuous November day. "I'm a double major," she said proudly. "Anthropology and art history."

"Are you completely insane? That's a huge workload."

"It's not so bad. I could graduate early if I wanted. I'm on track to be summa cum laude."

"Won-derful. Thanks for making me feel like a big turd." Just as he had suspected. Veronica was more competent, more connected than her wardrobe suggested. He spooned the remaining sodden bits, expecting and dreading her asking about his major, his plans. He prepared to offer his usual litany, his stated purposes, his memorized justifications. His eyes dove under the lip of his bowl. She kept looking at him, as if she might have said something aloud had she been alone. She studied him intensely, in a raw way, her mouth slightly curved: with mild amusement, or perhaps puzzlement, or charm at his naiveté, or as he wanted to see it, with affection.

"Don't you want to hear about my major?" he asked.

"Only if you want to talk about it," she said quietly. She genuinely seemed not to care.

"Aren't you curious about my big plans? My plans for huge success?"

"Exceedingly." She flattened her hands, fingertips together and placed her chin atop them. She smiled innocently, as if imitating a young schoolgirl.

"Plans so glorious I'm not sure what they are at this point." These things seemed funny in the old house. So distant they were absurd. Like he had begun some counter life beyond the reach of established rules. He liked this idea. They were making their own rules.

"What does your soul say? What touches your soul?" she asked.

His soul? It seemed an obscure tangent; for a moment he was stumped. He told her the first time he'd heard "Tainted Love" on the radio, it had deeply touched him. And reading *The*

Stranger, and seeing *Apocalypse Now* on the big screen, and his moment with that Jackson Pollock painting were also very intense. He thought of making love to Lynn Van Oster the first time, without mentioning this to Veronica. How did these things translate into money? They seemed not to. In this context they were ridiculous, nonserious things. He frowned.

"Don't sweat it. You're young. Every time I think I've figured it out, I learn I haven't. You don't have to automatically sacrifice yourself to corporate paternalism." Veronica opened her eyes wide for emphasis. "Ultimately, you can do whatever you want."

His shoulders loosened. Amazing. Just what he needed to hear. For the first time, it seemed more than a throwaway homily. Under her roof it seemed possible. Everything seemed possible. An immense happiness spread within him. Of course, this was an easier stance for her. She had her shit together. She had this brave integrity, this originality. Every flick of her eyelashes, every nuanced vowel that slid from her pink lips was a work of art, and possible only with her. She was the coolest person he had ever met. He wanted to inhabit her skin.

They dragged her futon into another room and plopped it onto the floor. They recovered by splaying their limbs across the futon. Motionless, they stared upward. The room had bookshelves packed with crusty volumes and moss-green wallpaper. Veronica told of the apartment—no bigger than this room—she'd lived in on the Lower East Side of Manhattan. After high school she'd spent a year punting in Gotham (God, she was so advanced!). She arrived wearing a man's dress shirt and tie, like Patti Smith, with a notebook of poems under her arm. She knew a guy in this band, these performance artists who played acid metal badly. Veronica slept in the closet of their apartment. The band did a lot of inhalants and hung off the fire escape hallucinating. After a few months she got out of there. "That was the last guy I have so-called dated. These pathetic girls thought they were dating a guy in the band, but to these guys it was just which girl he chose to screw and for how long. Dating is outdated."

"You're so right," he said. "It's this shallow social posturing. Gee Sally Sue, I thought you were dating Jim Bob. It's like a means of inflicting pain. There are all these expectations, but no one can measure up."

Her voice became louder, more strident. "It's a dinosaur, an abusive institution. There's this pressure to announce feelings, to profess bullshit to please the other person. And it has possessive connotations, that women are willing to become chattel for some prospect of marriage."

Lance propped himself up on an elbow and looked down into her face. "And at Langford you can't tie your shoe without ten people interrogating you about who you're dating."

She laughed in her approving way. She swept her head toward his supporting arm, her dark hair covering his hand. Her body softened, her knees pulling up in a trusting, self-satisfied way. She nuzzled her smooth cheek against his forearm. Feeling enormous affection, he traced a finger from her shoulder to the dip of her waist.

"So what happens when we see each other on campus?" His eyes blazed with an abrupt surge of mischief.

"Let's pretend we don't know each other. We'll fake everyone out. We'll tell no one."

Exactly what he'd been thinking, like he'd willed her to say it. "But in private, we are lovers." He lowered his head, hovering for a moment before kissing her.

"Yes. We'll be secret lovers," she said from a dreamy place.

It was so brilliant, so advanced he couldn't stand it. He rubbed his lips against her soft ear and whispered, "Hey, secret lover."

When he woke up, gray light was growing outside. He pushed

aside the comforter and rolled onto his feet. Only Veronica's face was exposed to air. He shuffled over to the moist window. He folded his arms and gazed over the brown yard, its heavy coat of dew. What was Lynn doing this morning? He didn't care. Beyond branches of the dreary trees the world churned on. Fortunes were being made. Election rallies were being held. Admissions offices at business schools took in the daily bushel of mail.

A car door slammed. A solitary old blue sedan was parked on the street. A guy with a shaved head stepped up to the sidewalk and stood looking toward the house. Veronica wrapped bedding around her shoulders, then it slid across the floor behind her like a royal cape. "I'm going into the shower," she said in a sleepy, absent-minded way. "Join me if you like."

Lance stood dumbly, blinking, and watched her go. Outside, the shaved-head guy made his way across the lawn. Tight black jeans snug against wiry legs, the jeans tucked into combat boots with yellow laces. A black nylon flight jacket puffed out his upper body. Chains swung from his belt. He walked with a surly bounce, his mouth clamped tightly shut. He disappeared from view. Lance waited for a door chime from this delivery guy, or paper guy, or whoever. The shower whooshed in Veronica's bathroom, curtain rings rattled. The house shivered as the front door opened downstairs, then heavily closed. Muffled thumps came up the stairs. It occurred to Lance, in a moment of ringing and decisive clarity, he needed a plan since a skinhead boyfriend of Veronica's was making his way up the stairs. He rushed back to the futon and pulled on his jeans. He fumbled with the button fly, shuffling back toward the hall. Heavy footsteps and the creak of floorboards. The skinhead stood looking into the living room from the hall, his back to Lance.

"Could I help you?" Lance asked warily.

The guy spun on his heels, surprised, and inspected Lance with dull eyes. He was an inch taller than Lance, but that was from the boots. Thick wrists and hands, scratchy stubble on his battering-ram head. The odors of armpit and cigarettes trailed him. In a suspicious tone he said, "I came here to see Veronica." The corners of his mouth curled up in an uneven way, like he was trying unsuccessfully to smile or had been overcome by a wave of dementia. He stood immediately before Lance, staring aggressively. His face was creased by thick eyebrows. Dark shiny eyes with wide pupils like black camera lenses. This fellow had spent the evening snorting speed and drinking with his shorn buddies, raising their scratchy voices to some fascist racket band. Lance straightened his spine and stared back, observing a Reaganesque peace through strength approach. He'd learned at an early age that the appearance of weakness fed the malevolence of bullies, but machismo indicated doubt about one's abilities and invited challengers as well. The best course was the assumption nobody had reason to bother you.

"I'm Lance, by the way."

"I'm Splitter, by the way."

"Spitter?" Lance deliberately misunderstood, unable to resist mild antagonism.

"Splitter."

"Like a split-finger fastball?"

"Maybe."

Splitter rubbed his hand; the letters P.I.S.S. were tattooed across his knuckles. He turned his head suddenly, seeming to hear the shower. Splitter studied the twisted sheets on the floor mattress and the discarded male sweatshirt on the floor. "Are you the new lover boy? Lover boy Lance." This was a bad development. The idea of Splitter being the old lover boy turned Lance's stomach. What did she see in this creep? Surely, he hadn't been her lover.

"I suppose so," Lance said. A stupid answer. He became fearful. These guys supposedly enjoyed fighting. It was a fun hobby. He imagined himself in a patrol car, cuffed, his face horribly bloodied, minus some teeth. But he reminded himself that Splitter was ultimately a knucklehead with a goofy middle school picture, whose mom had given him loads of crap, who'd been stomped by older kids behind the mall too many times to mention, and whose life had been generally traumatic and dysfunctional enough that he had adopted a fascist uniform.

"That must be Veronica in the shower." Splitter turned and took a step into the next room, his boot scraping the floor. Paradise was about to be ruined. Lance took a deep breath.

"She's not here."

"Who's in the shower?"

"Her friend Julia, who's visiting."

"Julia?"

A mocking edge lined Lance's voice. "You never met her before?"

"Mind if I check?"

"Julia probably won't appreciate that."

Splitter stepped back toward Lance, his eyes zigzagging around Lance's face, as if considering where to plant his fist. A sour breath blew into Lance's face. Lance puffed out his chest, then blew a hot breath into Splitter's face. Splitter's nostrils made a tiny whistling sound. Lance readied himself to strike back when the moment came, to pound this asshole and win. He imagined Veronica wiping his bloody, yet victorious face, impressed with his devotion.

Splitter turned and ambled toward the stairs, like he was browsing in a museum. "Tell Veronica I stopped by," he said.

Lance stood at the banister, gloating. "See you around, dude."

Splitter stopped halfway down and pointed a grimy index finger. He opened his mouth, revealing stunted teeth. From the inscrutable expression on his face, he could have been about to announce that anybody who stole his girl would pay, or that he'd be back with his best buds to take care of business. Instead he said, "I went to high school with a guy who looked exactly like you."

The triumph over Splitter produced a satisfying contact high, as well as a new sense of power and ability to manipulate danger. That wasn't so hard. Now he was staring down skinheads, running them off. Terrorizing them! Danger could be fun.

Veronica toweled off. It didn't register with her that anything had happened.

"You never mentioned skinhead boy," Lance said. He couldn't hide his jealousy.

"What's there to mention about Splitter?" Her eyes lowered. She seemed to be weighing a past set of circumstances, and adding Splitter's latest visit to that chain.

"Like maybe, who he is and that he might barge in here." His voice got higher with irritation. What had she seen in Splitter anyway? He felt devalued. He wanted her to say that it was over, and she would have nothing to do with Splitter.

"He's just a guy I know. Relax, lover." Her eyebrows tensed, indicating the topic displeased her.

"But what—"

"Relax!" She whipped her wet hair over her head.

He realized jealousy wasn't very advanced or modern. It was incompatible with Veronica and the secret lover thing, so he dropped it. He resolved to do better.

She wanted to go to a club in downtown Atlanta that evening. One she frequented. Her pink skin wrapped with the towel, she put her hands on Lance's chest. "Now. If you are going to accompany me to Club Rio, then you must tell me the truth. Going with me, you must go all the way. I have a reputation to uphold. It's a scene. No party poopers allowed."

"Fine. I'll wear whatever."

"But will you go all the way, darling?" She pouted, her wide green eyes searching him.

"All the way, baby!"

She smiled radiantly and it melted him, made him rejoice.

"Good. Thing two. You can tell no one at Langford about

this place. If they all started showing up there I would just die."

"You have my word."

Lance showered and stepped out into her bedroom. She paced in front of her huge closet. It took up an entire wall, clogged, bulging and spilling over with hung leather and velvet and suede and chenille and silk. Piles of other clothes dotted the floor and space underneath the hangers, shoes wedged in the mounds like digging utensils stuck in a sand castle.

"First we'll outfit you," she said, rooting through dresser drawers packed with socks, scarves, complex underwear and accessories. She found a black t-shirt and a pair of black jeans with sliver studs that lined the seams. They were somewhat big, but she cinched them with a metal link belt. Then from a box she produced vintage Cuban heeled boots with side zippers. So many male clothes, he thought. Where did they come from? Amazingly, the boots fit. He tried on a motorcycle leather jacket which he liked, but she said didn't work; then a black silk coat with plum-edged lapels she was very pleased with. Next, she worked on Lance's hair. After spraying even rows of mousse on his wet scalp she experimented—he unable to monitor what she was doing—until she settled on a high plateau ducktail, reminiscent of Jerry Lee Lewis or Jack Lord. She cemented it in place with a hair dryer, the sides plastered to his head in a uniform sheet. He patted the stiff upper reaches cautiously.

She assembled her outfit, picking out black patent leather boots that flared at her knees, a dark suede skirt and a painful-looking lace corset contraption that bound her waist and squashed her breasts together to form a horizontal shelf. A black leather jacket and velvet gloves to her elbows completed the outfit. She sat at a vanity and created an Asian vampiress look with her eyes and lips. She made 1920s-type wet squiggles with her bangs and volumized the rest of her hair, waving the hair dryer and commanding no fewer than four different combs and brushes. Reviewing her work, she tapped her ass and made a sizzle sound. With a catcall whistle, he concurred.

They stood before her full-length mirror. For a moment, Lance felt he was meeting new people, two fascinating strangers. And it was satisfying to be a stranger. More things became possible. Other things could be discarded. He remarked that they looked like Bulgarian agents infiltrating a London mod clique. She laughed. He was feeling ultra-hip. So hip and cool that lesser hipsters would stare in envy, dumbstruck and dislocated, shamed by their outdated conceptions, and be forced to modify their idea of what was cool. It seemed conceivable, even likely, that photogs who worked for oversized European fashion magazines, seeking young remarkable specimens, so brash, so very now, might snap photos as they crossed a street.

"Let's hit the road, baby!" he shouted.

"Not just yet." She came toward him with a mascara wand.

He put up his hands and said, "Whoa."

"It'll bring out your gorgeous eyes. You'll be surprised how many guys tonight have it."

"Ahh…"

"You gave me your word, darling. You promised."

Lance fidgeted. Then, as a man of his word, he let her stroke his eyelashes with the tar wand. She didn't put that much on. It really did bring out his eyes. Using the timer on her Instamatic, they photographed themselves in an haute couture pose.

Outside, they held hands and walked across the damp lawn in darkness. It seemed a new world, a world with fresher air. At her car, Lance stared at the mute reflection of himself in the window, invigorated—for this night, people like him would look at him like he wasn't one of them.

She insisted on driving Edgar. The car was temperamental with strangers, and it stalled at the first stoplight; Veronica talked to Edgar sternly and the little Volkswagen seemed to improve. It was a long drive. He lit a cigarette for her, taking a hot puff, then passing it over. She placed her gloved hand on his leg, rubbing toward his inner thigh when she wasn't shifting.

The dressing up and going out, he could see, was an extended flirtation, a kind of elaborate foreplay. They flashed teeth at each other, the taste of great sex already floating in the car. Feeling liberated and outside of himself, he told her he'd written a screenplay (not mentioning LaCoss's association with the project), and explained the entire plot of *The Man Who Would Be the King*.

"…So in Las Vegas, Wyatt becomes a regular for an oldies review. He's the Elvis impersonator who goes on after the Fab Four but before the Sinatra impersonator, who is a prominent coke dealer. Wyatt gets a raging cocaine habit and his act suffers, his life falls apart. Meanwhile his arch rival impersonator, The Big E, becomes a headliner on the strip. Wyatt gets into enormous debt with the Sinatra guy, who gets real-life mob guys to try to kill Wyatt. Wyatt flees Vegas, fearing for his life."

"And what happens at the end?"

"I can't tell you that or it would ruin it." In truth, he wasn't sure how it was going to end. Or if the thing could be ended. Lance had made up the part about the cocaine dealer recently and had yet to write that in.

"I don't understand why," Veronica said, "even if he does believe he's the reincarnated stillborn twin of Elvis, he feels the need to be an Elvis impersonator."

"That's the whole movie. Maybe it's the belief that if he hadn't been born dead, he would have actually been Elvis. Or it's a sibling rivalry thing maybe."

"Impressive. I had no idea you were a writer." A glow of fresh discovery, of titillation graced her face. He allowed the idea to wash over him, enjoying it, even considering it might be true. But it was a lie. He was no writer and *The Man* was a colossal piece of garbage. It was a movie he himself wouldn't see. It was going nowhere. But this was mere detail.

"Writing is a turn-on," Veronica said.

"Apparently."

They took a ramp off the expressway and into the bowels of downtown. A place of towering futuristic hotels, next to old hotels with faded facades and pay parking lots. No people on the sidewalks, like microbes had killed them off. At a stoplight, brief paranoia rippled through Lance, that the murky figure with a bottle across the street was going to run over and jiggle the door handles. His mother was forever cautioning him to be extra careful downtown, worried about her innocent boy. He dismissed that as overreaction. Urban felt mysterious and good. She seemed to know her way around. She pulled Edgar into a metered spot before a narrow storefront with a neon sign: Marco's Tattoo.

"I don't know about getting inked," Lance said, crossing his arms.

"You're getting a piercing." She tugged on his earlobe. "That will complete your ensemble." She stepped out of the car. He gazed down the street a moment in contemplation, then got out. He had promised. A pierced ear wasn't such a big deal. It was kinda hip. Starter posts had been appearing on male lobes around Langford. Kyle MacLachlan had a micro hoop in *Blue Velvet*.

Inside Marco's a thin woman with cat-eye glasses and a pageboy haircut sat behind a glass counter. A money-green Nosferatu tattoo on her forearm. Lance stood on threadbare carpet and looked at tattoo designs. Intermittent buzzing came from behind a curtain.

"God, I love that corset," the woman said to Veronica.

"Thanks. Got it at Salvation Army. He's getting an ear pierced."

Lance sat at the end of the counter on a stool. The woman loaded a brass stud into a gun-like device. He opened his eyes wide, pretending to be terrified. Veronica winked at him. Two buzz-cut military guys were checking her out, whispering things.

"Be gentle with me."

He heard a click and felt a pinch in his right ear. He paid the woman eight bucks. She told him to disinfect it every day for a month with alcohol to prevent infection. He twisted the intriguing metal in his earlobe as they drove to Club Rio.

"See the trouble you've gotten me into," he said, but he felt happy.

"You are looking extra hot, lover." She squeezed his thigh.

They got back on Peachtree Street and took a right on International. Club Rio was at a bend in the street, figures loitering around the entrance. They parked in a lot across the street. Booming, thrashing sounds drifted from the doors of the club. Veronica batted her eyes at the sturdy door guy, who lifted his hand to wave them in without asking them to show ID. Inside, Veronica chatted excitedly with the cashier woman. Ominous music came down a marble stairway, a disembodied roaring and gnashing mixed with driving percussive sounds. She pulled him inward, to an atrium-like bar with theatrical blue lighting. Veronica waved at the bartender, who reached for her hand and kissed it. She introduced him as Sydney. In red leather pants, a red t-shirt and wrist spikes, he waved apathetically at Lance. Two inanimate figures—at second glance, two live people—sat in ornate chairs to the left of the bar. One had exploding bushy Robert Smith hair, black makeup and a gray shapeless smock. The other, with ultra-frizzed white hair, wore a yellowing wedding dress. They were disturbing.

Veronica sat on a barstool and Sydney leaned over the bar. They talked secretively. She held the bartender's hands tightly and they laughed about something. Then she opened and closed her purse underneath the lip of the bar and put her hand on Lance's arm. Walking out of the room, Veronica said, "We're in luck tonight."

Lance asked what this meant but loud music garbled his voice. She pointed up a metal stair to a second level. People noticed her, looking over their drinks. The metal stairs dinged underneath their feet. A long mirrored wall bordered a dance floor, a few tables and a small bar across from it. She barged into a group of girls next to the bar in dresses and torn fishnet stockings, giving hugs and shrieking, the group convulsing and chatting around her. She introduced Lance to them: Heidi, Linda and a pudgy girl named Delia. They all had pasty, corpse-like complexions and seemed to be reserving their judgment of Lance. Heidi was weirdly thin, with a gloomy cigarette-girl aspect. Linda, the bleach blonde, wore a long velvet dress and red Doc Martens.

"How do you know Ronnie?" Linda asked Lance. Lance realized then he'd heard the cashier women say Ronnie instead of Veronica also.

"We bumped into each other at school."

Heidi complained about her workday to the group, her soul-crushing job developing pictures for wedding photographers. Veronica had been whispering something to Linda and pudgy Delia. She pulled Lance aside and pushed something small and solid into Lance's palm.

"We're all X-ing out tonight. Sydney set us up." She stuck her tongue between her teeth, curling the tip. Her eyes glowed with mischief.

"X?"

"As in Ecstasy. No big deal, it's a kick."

Lance wanted to inspect the pill in his palm, though Veronica held his hand in both of hers. What was the stuff LaCoss had taken?

"Geez. I don't know…" Lance smiled in a fake way, suddenly very tense.

Her face moved up toward his, the inviting shelf of her bosom looming closer. She had the most gorgeous eyebrows.

"Secret lover," she said, "you promised me you'd go all the way." She gazed at him, her lips parting slightly—a look of supreme feminine poise. He wanted to keep that sweet vibe going between them. He wanted to see that carnal look on her face forever, and above all he didn't want to think too much, the way old Lance would have, and ruin everything. She put her hands on either side of his jaw, pulling him down for a kiss, a succulent kiss with her tongue dabbing at his teeth. With a nervous twitter, he took a breath, then popped the beige octagonal tablet into his mouth and washed it down with beer. He tried not to think about it, about a supernova exploding inside his head, about Brian Wilson confining himself to his room for a year. Veronica was already moving to the music. He did think about the way Veronica's hips shifted appealingly under her miniskirt.

Veronica and her friends shifted to the dance floor as an extended-version New Order song twitched in an infinite cycle. A swirling overhead light strafed them with colors. Lance joined them, fronting with Veronica, but being fluid, and having dalliances with the others. He threw out his usual *American Bandstand* routines. Veronica was a formidable partner, a whimsical and unpredictable mover, shifting herself toward others and lashing them with stomach rolls. He tried to keep up with her. By the time a high-energy Shriekback song came on he had found the groove, adopting a proper level of absorption and incorporating some clever shoulder twists. A wild, inventive chemistry flowed between Lance and Veronica. The club was filling up, the throng around the dance floor growing. A sticky heat built up under his jacket, a coppery taste in his mouth.

He wondered about the pill, if it was already happening. He hoped so since he felt loose and energized. He weaved his fingers into Veronica's fingers and he leaned down to her, almost touching noses. The DJ changed the music to a more industrial sound, a thrashing beat punctuated by crashing pows, his heart rate escalating with these sonic punches.

A spike of energy bolted through him, along with nausea that inched up his esophagus. He sensed a berserk quality entering his movements. The music seized him, made him an instrument of it, a puppet. She put her arms around his neck. He struggled free, a horror reflected on his face that she didn't notice. He was aware of bodies heaving and shifting around him, too close to him, the cloying odors of essence oils and perspiration. He faced the wall mirror, searching for himself among the frantic bodies. He located Veronica. Her friends had melted away. Arms at his side, he stood still for several moments and found a similar, solitary guy dressed in black head to toe with odd hair and dark, stricken eyes and a panicked face. He studied this frozen person, wondered about this person. This poor guy was clearly out of his league and in trouble. In another moment, he recognized that guy as himself. People around him gyrated with their wet mouths, flashes of teeth, the struggle of their arms. An enormous dark bubble rose from his chest and stole his breath.

Veronica asked, "You OK?" He pointed away from the dance floor, mouthed something he doubted made sense and walked off. He needed to be in a confined space—the bathroom. Was he hallucinating? Did he have a desire to jump off a building? He rushed past bodies at the periphery of the dance floor, these gray people like ghosts or ghouls. Then a familiar face, peculiar in this setting. Gennifer, Lynn's roommate, stood there. Her eyes swept across the crowd, settling on Lance, who made eye contact with her. She seemed puzzled. He cracked a frantic smile; his pierced ear pulsed with a single heartbeat.

In the men's room—had he gone into the right place?—he let cold water pour over his hands; the faucet grime sickened him. He took concentrated breaths. It was dank and steamy in there, weirdly crowded. Too many legs sticking out the bottom of stalls. A woman came out of one stall. A guy with shocked black hair teased it with a comb. Trickles of anxiety fluttered through him like rain on a car's hood. Was music being piped in overhead? He dabbed his face with water, his sleeves becoming soaked. The corner urinal was free. I can't pee this stuff away fast enough, he thought. Something banged against the partition and startled him. People were unwrapping things, whispering. Wait! somebody shouted. The scrape of heels on tile.

Once he stepped outside Veronica said to him, "Whatever Sydney gave me is shit. I don't know what it is. Heidi thinks it's great. She's insane." Veronica was perspiring heavily, but otherwise seemed no different.

"Let's go. I'm having a bad experience."

"Me too. Let me find my friends to tell them I'm leaving."

She moved off into the crowd and he found a marble bench at the edge of the second level. Sitting in an uncrowded place helped, though there was no escape from the raging music. People coming up the marble stairs ignored him. A woman with a leashed ferret on her shoulder went by. As hip and cool as he'd felt an hour ago, the vulnerability and conspicuousness of sitting alone on a bench, like a shunned middle schooler, now descended upon him. His Jack Lord hair drooped comically. His clothes were soggy. His mascara was smudged. Veronica tugged on his sleeve. "I can't find them. Let's just go."

Outside, a grim stillness had settled upon the city, the sky ink black and impenetrable above the streetlights. Veronica's heels clicked as they ran across the street. His ears were ringing. At the lot, Lance went around to the passenger side of Edgar. There was a fresh peppering of glass on the ground, the window of a Thunderbird smashed. Jagged glass teeth sat in the doorframe.

"We're lucky that wasn't us," Lance said, shutting his door.

"Thank God they didn't get my tape deck." Veronica put a hand on her chest.

"Are you good to drive?"

"It's totally worn off."

Lance wasn't as sure about himself.

She tried the engine three times before it turned over. They sputtered down a one-way street, looking for signs to get to the expressway. Following a succession of signs, they took a bridge over a highway, then block after rough block went by without another sign. They drove along in silence. A harsh yellow light burned at the dirt corner of a public housing project. The monotonous brick two-stories were raw and stripped. They passed a weedy lot with abandoned car hulks. Two men in a rusty parked car turned their heads as the car lights passed them. We're totally lost, he thought. He prayed for another sign.

"We missed it. Let's turn around," Lance said.

"Shit! There should be another sign."

"I don't think so."

At an abandoned gas station, she pulled into the parking lot, her turnaround arc blocked by a stack of bricks. She put the car in reverse and it stalled.

"Damn you, Edgar!" The reluctant car wheezed without starting. After about ten tries she said, "We'll have to wait twenty minutes for it to cool down."

"This ain't a good spot to wait."

She clicked off the headlights and pulled off her gloves. She sighed. The boarded-up gas station was in a twilight between streetlamps. Lance looked around. He was sweating. A chain-link fence was topped with razor wire. A scruffy field with a worn dirt trail was littered with bottles. He cracked his window open. A hysterical male voice shouted or laughed somewhere, echoing in the night. He couldn't believe it. It was everything bad he had been warned about his entire life. A car with a boom boom didda boom stereo slid down the street.

They breathed quietly in the little yellow car.

"What a night." She lit a cigarette, then bent the rear mirror down to examine her makeup. Her mouth and eyes, heavy with cosmetics, looked fiendish. Her calmness irritated him, infuriated him.

"Try it again!"

"No. We need to wait." She held up her hands.

Lance reached over and tried the key and the car started.

The drive back was interminable. Cold air whipped through his cracked window. The night's traumas had left him fragile, something flapping loose inside him. Lance almost asked her about Splitter, and what the deal was there. Had Veronica screwed him too? He wondered about the deal between himself and Veronica. He needed to know, badly, but the topic was forbidden.

They got back to the house at 1 a.m. The last of his energy waned as he stripped off his borrowed clothes. Lying naked in her bed, a falling sensation took him quickly toward sleep. He thought he felt something nipping at his feet, but dismissed it as leftover delirium from his chemical adventure. Never, ever again, he swore. More nips around his calves, a bite above his knee. Startled and suddenly frantic, he threw aside the comforter. She was down there in a crouch, giggling.

"What the hell is that about?" It came out hard and accusatory, like something his father would say when angered.

She raised her eyebrows high, then hopped out of bed and went to the bathroom.

He woke up fearing he'd forgotten something extremely important. A deadline had passed just days ago. An application deadline? A term paper? The phone bill—did he pay it last month? And exams, they were coming. They were always coming.

He felt next to him but Veronica wasn't there. It bothered him because he wanted a sympathetic ear. Squeaky shower noises came from the bathroom. It felt like the inside of his skull had been scraped with a rock. He rubbed his eyes and moved his shoulder to the edge of the bed. He stretched. Turning over on his stomach, his arm trailed to the hardwood floor. His fingers ticked against a box under the bed, behind the dust ruffle. He pulled out a Kinko's box, sliding it along the floor. A thick stack of copies inside. He picked up one, expecting to read her resume.

THE LANGFORD AMAZON SOCIETY SAYS:
THINK ABOUT IT

All the press can think to say about singer Sinead O'Connor is that she is bald. Where is the similar dissection of the hair choices of Michael Jackson or Michael Hutchence? Do they use coloring? Is it real? Why so long? Are they trying to look like women? These questions are never asked.

But have a women shave her head—an option men enjoy—and an explanation is demanded. The premise is that long hair, supposedly preferred by men, is the proper choice for women. To decide against long locks must be an act of insanity or hysteria. The obsession with Sinead's hair exposes the oppressive heterodoxy that women exist only for the pleasure of men and that their exterior qualities must conform to male conceptions of beauty. Must the media reinforce this notion through its obsession with one performer's scalp? Sinead's real beauty comes from within. Ask about that, Mr. Reporter.

GET A CLUE, AMERICA

Veronica walked into the bedroom in a white bathrobe, rubbing her hair with a towel.

"You didn't tell me you were one of the Amazons," he said. A grin gathered on his face.

She flicked her hair to one side, then fixed on Lance holding the paper. She snapped it away from him and pushed the box back under the bed with her foot. She pointed a finger in his face. "None of your business." Her jaw stuck out.

Lance reached out for her finger and she walked away.

"I would have told you about something like this," he said.

"That's not the issue. It's a violation of my privacy. Who do you think you are?" She tightened the tie of her robe, her face going red.

"It was under your bed. I'm not going to blab that you're one of them."

"You don't know anything about that, or about me."

"Why else would you have two hundred copies of their handout?"

"You know nothing about me!" She slammed a plastic comb on the floor, bouncing it, and Lance sat up. She retreated to the bathroom. "Maybe you're making too many assumptions and maybe you've been here too long."

The horrible seriousness of this scene depressed him. He had wanted to tell her about the stack of business school applications gathering dust on his floor and the heavy feeling in his heart and to get some advice, but after a night of drugging they'd become Sid and Nancy. Lance followed her, naked, his feet clomping on the floor. "You act like I'm a stranger. We've been sleeping together, remember that? How about some trust? I'm not going to tell anyone."

In front of the sink mirror, her eyes shifted to his reflection behind her. She put her teeth together, her nose and cheeks seeming sharper: the same withering gaze she'd used to fend off strangers the night before. Her voice became cold. "I don't want to say nasty things to you."

"I see—so you're about to!" It came out as a bark. His neck muscles were taut, like bridge span wires. He put his hands on his hips.

She looked into the mirror innocently, at herself, and he regretted chasing and barking at her. He plotted a salvage operation, the kind of turnaround John Wayne engineered in every war movie, setting things straight with his gal after a tiff. That would never work on Veronica, he realized. He couldn't stand there forever naked, so he held his arms out in a contrite way, moving toward her for a conciliatory hug. "Hey, look…" She backed away toward the toilet while staring him down. He'd thought this primal appeal might work, on the very tile surface where they'd begun their relationship, hoping it would reignite good feelings. Instead, she glared at him like a cornered deer about to buck, a woman about to scream and call the police. He hovered a moment, then retreated into the bedroom.

It was the end, and nothing he could do would change this. The full arc of their time together now was clear. It was under museum glass. It had taken place years ago. It would all go back. She'd treat him like every other jerk. He felt sentimental about every possible dumb thing: eating Chinese food, her dancing to the Pixies, Edgar's breakdown, burrowing her face against his forearm, their vow to be secret lovers. They had had such promise.

He searched for his original clothes, his yard sale Secret Agent jacket. She strolled over to the doorway and glanced out, as if trying to hide her concern. She disappeared, then came back. "You're certainly in a hurry to leave."

Now she was pinning it on him? After inventing this means to evict him! He pushed aside a stack of clothes, looking for his jeans. So many hordes of men had gone through here, they'd shed their clothes like exoskeletons. Some chink of his own armor would likely be left behind also. He picked up a white sock that appeared male, trying to identify it.

"This is so typical," she fumed. "Such stupid patriarchal bullshit. I'm really disappointed in you."

"This is what you want! It wouldn't be progressive enough for the modern woman to admit affection for an evil male."

"Now you've done it! You asshole!"

Having found his jeans and jacket, he fumbled with his shoes. "I'll show myself out."

She came after him in her bathrobe. "I will show you out." Her voice cracked a little.

At the top of the stairs, he waved without looking at her.

Leaning over the stairs, she said, "Go run back to your precious Lynn Van Oster. That's who you're still in love with."

He stopped and glared at her. "How could you possibly know that?"

"I knew when I first mentioned her and I know it now."

"What is it with you people? You think you know

everything. You don't. Only I know what I want." On this high note, this affirmation, he continued down the stairs and out. The door clanged behind him. A cold gust nipped at his fingers. He fumbled in his pockets to confirm his wallet and keys were there. He made his way quickly to the sidewalk under a blustery sky. Wet leaves clung to the walk. His heart seemed about to fall out of his chest.

He had never walked before in this neighborhood. The edge of campus was around somewhere. It felt good to move, to be anonymous in the world, though he sensed all the old rules still applied. His hand wandered up to his ear. Lance fingered the brass stud with amazement. A piece of metal now punctured his earlobe. I'm a rebel, he thought sarcastically. A real outlaw.

Two weeks later, he would pull the post out, painfully easing it from red swollen skin which held it tight. A yellow bulb of puss would ooze out the hole.

CHAPTER FIFTEEN

BLOWING IT

L ance's head was full of mush, his tongue heavy with confusion. How to explain the full impact of Veronica? Had their time together been wonderful or awful? LaCoss nodded slowly, hesitantly, as Lance offered anecdotes, details, snippets of conversation, jumbling the chronology and feeling like an achy person after twelve hours on a Greyhound. Each time Lance mounted a grievance against her, it evaporated.

"I can't believe you stayed so long in some old woman's creepy house," LaCoss said, shuddering.

"The end was so wrong. Get the hell outta here, basically. But Veronica—Man, she is so deep, so wise. She's got the sensual capacity of an ocean."

A long, biting laugh came out of LaCoss. "What's wrong with you? She shakes her vampire dress in your face and you think it's a marriage made in fairytale land. You know, there's something familiar about this scenario." He inspected a blackened carburetor. He was reassembling a Vespa scooter engine which lay in greasy stinking heaps on his floor.

"That's not helpful!" Lance yelled, suddenly appreciative of the female ability to listen and sympathize, rather than ignore and ridicule when soft spots were conveniently exposed. Lance realized an unexpected truth. As brutal and unfair as the end had been, he still cared deeply for Veronica Boyer. He missed her already. Explaining these emotional implications to LaCoss was problematic; he only got so much.

"Let's review," LaCoss said. "It was an intense several days, then you flamed out. So where's the problem, chief?" His disavowals of attachment always seemed forced.

"I feel bruised. There are emotions involved here. Ever heard about them, ever experienced one?"

"Speaking of hearing things…" LaCoss paused to scratch his knuckles, as if considering holding back. He raised his eyebrows. "Here's something you should probably know…I heard from Gira Singh that Carson Wombley, Jr. has been calling your old flame, Lynn."

"You…what!" His heart leapt into his throat, and something tightened in his lower abdomen, like his pancreas had been stepped on. "That can't be true. No way."

"According to Gira, Wombley was asking her out. That was almost a week ago. I don't know if they've gone out yet. Probably."

Lance's chin fell to his chest. His vision blurred. "How could she do that to me? How could she?" Even more disturbing and infuriating than Carson Wombley, Jr.'s pursuit—that lame pompous wanker, going after his Lynn—was Lynn's apparent receptivity to this. It was some twisted, elaborate revenge of hers. She was obviously planning to flaunt this, likely tongue-kissing that bastard in front of Lance, tumbling out of his room in the morning holding her socks. She knew the nuclear hurt she'd cause; she was doing it anyway.

"You guys did break up," LaCoss said sheepishly. "Not that I'm on his side. But those are the breaks of the game."

Facing an extreme personal crisis, Lance did what he always did. He went back to his room and shut the door. It was time to be alone and tend to the gaping wound growing between his ribs. The alone strategy insured no one else could reflect on and magnify the crisis, which helped, though thoughts of Lynn and Carson Wombley, Jr. could potentially torture him indefinitely if he didn't get control of himself.

He retrieved the picture of Lynn fallen between the bed and wall. She was laughing with her mouth slightly open, teeth exposed, showing off her spectacular neckline. It all came back. He rewound the full cassette tape on his answering machine.

Knowing this sentimental immersion was a bad idea, he left it running once he heard Lynn's voice: *Hey, there, it's me again!* He listened to their entire beep-laden messaging history. *Whoops, you're not there, but I sure wish you were.* The warmth of her voice. There was an immediacy, a body language he sensed. Hearing her fed the illusion she was still a phone call away. *Don't worry about that exam, you're going to do so well.* Her voice was assured, though with a softness that was incredibly sexy: (laughing) *maybe you won't find that funny, but I do.* This glow from her, even recorded, cheered him up. He had once been worthy of her love. He put his head in his hands, pressing, his desperation reaching a crescendo. Her nicknames still tickled him: *Hello Mr. L.* There had been Lanny Lance, and his favorite, Hey La-La. As problems developed between them her voice faded. I really wish you would call me. How could he have abandoned her to the cruelty of the world, to the predatory morons who stalked her? He hated himself.

He had betrayed her.

His breath became choppy. He felt a tear on its way, humiliating even when alone, because he was still there to witness this lack of control. He braced against it, against a sudden, terrifying and overwhelming force—a fifty-foot tsunami which crashed and destroyed his crumbling barriers. He crumpled over to his knees, then his forehead hit the floor. Wet lines trailed down his cheeks as never before. The hot tears flowed and flowed, straining his eyes. He cried and made anguished sounds into the carpet. Above him there appeared a panel of fathers, coaches, male authority figures, senior vice presidents and older brothers shaking their heads in disgust. In his vulnerable state, he was defenseless from their glare, as they stood shoulder to shoulder, silent, perfecting deep disapproval of this emotional outburst, not to mention his enthusiastic fornicating with a questionable girl, his sissy dress-up games, his recreational drug use and his reckless neglect of his high-priced education. And was that an earring? They scowled, arms crossed, considering their wasted efforts. What a poor boy, tsk tsk. What a sad, dwindling future. We were wrong about him.

Lance lashed out with an arm to dispel them. He could not. The crying went on.

Veronica had been right about his still being in love. Only something as powerful as actual love could do this to him. His love for Lynn was so obvious it assumed physical form and sat beside him. He was pacing wall to wall in his room, wiping his face, then he was out in the hall with a demented expression and a metallic taste in his mouth, that big vein near his hairline taut with pressure, his eyes casting around for Carson Wombley, Jr.

At the door to Wombley's second-floor room, Lance took in a huge breath. At his shoulder, LaCoss whispered *fight fight fight*. Lance banged on the door and it swung open. Wombley's air conditioner buzzed along. One of those people who complained unless arctic air blew into his face in every house, car and restaurant. A framed picture from the '87 *Sports Illustrated* swimsuit issue was near a lamp: Elle Macpherson's sequined bosom and impossibly long legs glowing in Caribbean sunshine.

Lance pushed at the edge of a king-size waterbed with a bamboo headboard. It gurgled and waves rolled the covers up and down. He imagined Lynn climbing onto this very surface and the surprised sound she'd make when it undulated. His mouth became hot and stuffy. An eight-by-ten of Wombley's car, his cherry red BMW 540i, was taped near the bed. Another picture showed his family gathered before their custom ski chalet in Steamboat Springs.

Next to the pictures was Wombley's prized possession: an autographed San Francisco 49ers' #9 jersey from Joe Montana, under glass. Every time someone asked about it, he increased its value. Right now it was worth six hundred dollars. Wombley had no association with San Francisco other than their consistent domination of the NFL. Every Sunday Wombley, wearing an identical jersey, was on his feet in front of the TV clapping for Montana. Did you see that pass? he asked after every touchdown; or during a drive, OK, now we're getting somewhere, Joe. During the week he was full of clichés gleaned from ex-jock TV commentators. Joe had the winning knack, the nose for victory, he could maximize opportunities. Wombley emphasized these inane concepts that had the official stamp, like the non-quit factor (which Montana had in abundance). He glowed from association with the best quarterback in the history of the game.

An embarrassment at ever being friends with this shallow idiot, this Jack Dalrymple in training, now nagged Lance. A checklist taped to the wall over the desk listed every business school he'd sent applications to, date mailed, deadlines, decision dates and responses. He had gotten into Stanford, UNC and Wharton and was still waiting for Princeton, among others. Lance put his fingernails on the checklist but restrained himself from clawing it off the wall.

With an X-Acto knife, Lance scratched this message on the display glass over the Joe Montana jersey: STAY AWAY FROM LYNN.

They went up to Lance's room to clear their heads and wait.

Hearing a clamor of footsteps on the stairs, Lance stepped out into the hall. LaCoss, who had more experience with fights, had said earlier: You can take him. But Lance had no intention of fighting. He remembered successfully defusing Splitter, the skinhead. A crowd behind him, an enraged Wombley marched toward Lance, his jaw set and hair slicked back. In an expensive outfit of wool plaid sport coat and gabardine trousers. He seemed taller than usual and wagged an accusatory finger, shouting all the way. "That shit is not appreciated, Rally. Where do you get off vandalizing my property? That's unbelievable! I'm going to tell you that…"

Lance's blood became warm at the sight of his competitor: the ass-kisser, the resume- cheater, the rich bastard. His adrenaline spiked. Wombley kept charging, shouting, his mouth in attack mode and working very fast, like he had gotten terrible service at a restaurant. Each bombastic word struck Lance's ears unpleasantly as Wombley marched up, trying to knock over Lance with his mouth. Lance shouted back, halting his progress. "I don't appreciate you trying to steal Lynn!"

"What? That's bull…" Wombley continued with his cannon mouth, as if getting his way were a simple matter of volume. A sharp point of hatred grew within Lance, his face getting red. Wombley moved closer, flashing his teeth and waving a pointed finger near Lance's nose as he blathered with his peppermint and cola breath.

Had Lance thought about it beforehand, it never would have happened. But the gatekeeper thoughts, the Rally moderation, were missing and in an instant hatred and frustration poured forth and his fist, his right fist, lashed out like a rogue missile, with what boxing commentators would have called a right cross. He stepped into it with a solid shoulder turn and launched the lightning-quick fist into the hard cavern between Wombley's nose and eye socket, catching him unaware and in midsentence. The impact made a peculiar series of sounds, a squashed, cracking noise and a thud. Wombley's skull kicked back as a single piercing bolt of pain traveled up Lance's arm. He cocked his left fist, anticipating return punches. The crowd gasped. Wombley staggered backward, as if unsure of himself in darkness. Then he dropped to his knees, collapsing like an empty bread bag: a satisfying thing for an adversary to do.

Wombley shrieked in a high-pitched voice: "Oh! Oh, Jesus! My contact! You probably ruined my eyesight!" He leaned one shoulder against the wall and whimpered, a palm pressed over his eye. A trickle of blood ran from his nose.

A deep throb began in Lance's hand, his first two knuckles aching. He was torn between the remnants of anger and a growing pity. He waited for a return charge, but it never came. Wombley's non-quit factor was much smaller than Joe

Montana's.

Wombley looked up, his good eye blinking. "All I said was that I thought Lynn was hot. I never called her. Jesus!"

Lance didn't believe it. He considered punching Wombley again, harder. Just for humiliation's sake. But he remembered the pain of the first punch. Wide-eyed, he looked around at LaCoss and the others, awed by his own violence. He felt claustrophobic. There had been no glory in the first fight of his adult life. The pain in his hand sharpened. His heart pounded in one knuckle. Who knew a face would be hard as concrete? People were holding Wombley's eye open, looking for his contact. Can you see out of it? everyone was asking. LaCoss patted Lance on the shoulder and said something congratulatory. Lance considered that Wombley might be telling the truth about Lynn. He resolved to find out.

In the car Lance thought intensely of Lynn, imagining an introspective, vulnerable version of her. Wind from the darkness blew throughout his car. A tear—it was habit- forming—spilled from his eye. His left hand on the steering wheel, he winced when he shifted with his right. His palm on the stick shift, he tried not to use his fingers. He expected flashing blue lights to fill the car from a pursuing patrol car, chasing him to lock him up for his unprovoked assault.

Well, let them come!

It seemed perfectly logical, even urgent, he should confront the woman he had just fought over, on whose behalf he had assaulted another guy. He sensed—his mind careening unpredictably, somersaulting, an aquarium full of hyper fish—this combat would make her understand the depth of his feelings for her.

She might take him back.

He parked in front of her apartment building, which he hadn't seen in weeks. He put his chin on the steering wheel to see up to the second floor. His stomach twisted. He wondered if his scattered thoughts would cloud things, if he would come across as insane. As if on cue, her car settled into a parking spot several cars away. Her proximity cheered him, allowed him a screaming hope he might influence her in the old way—she might smile or even hug him. He opened his door and shuffled to the sidewalk, holding his damaged hand up by his armpit. She detected his presence immediately and glanced over. Her car door was open, shielding her. The most beautiful girl to ever grace a dim parking lot. She casually reached inside the car for a plastic bag, then shut her door. Her facial features drew tight as she stepped on the sidewalk.

He tried to fit his hand in his pocket, then crossed his arms. "Is it true?" he asked, projecting his voice. An adversarial tone, which was all wrong. Everything was wrong and doomed. Everything was happening around him, like he was in a zoo cage, powerless and staring out.

"Hello, Lance. Is what true?" Her voice was chilly, controlled, like a phone operator.

"About you and Carson Wombley, Jr.?"

She had come a few steps toward him and now she turned up the walkway toward the stairs. She raised a cheek, squinting. "Which one is that?" She bristled. None of it was true, he realized. She strode confidently without turning her head toward him. Again, she was walking away from him. She was destroying him in the cruelest way possible: pretending she barely knew him.

"You don't have to give me the silent treatment," Lance said.

"The first thing you say to me in weeks is to accuse me of something—I don't know what." Her feet dinged on the metal stairs.

He rubbed his forehead with his good hand, then held both hands up. "Just stop for one second." It was useless to try to go up the stairs to touch her, to get near her. An impenetrable circumference had descended around her. He struggled to process things correctly. Couldn't she understand the turmoil within him? "I...I got into this fight...I think I broke my hand, maybe..." He held up the throbbing Quasimodo hand, the pain becoming horrible.

She gave him the hardest, most arctic of stares and said in a dull voice, "Maybe Veronica Boyer could help. Maybe she could kiss it for you."

She knew everything. They all knew everything. Lynn's feet plinked up the stairs. At the door, she rattled her keys. It was the most dreadful of cinematic clichés, but as he cleared his throat to shout, only it would do: "I still love you!"

The door smacked shut behind her.

Inside his car, he studied his swollen, misshapen hand. Shading blue, it was transforming into a lump, a rock.

Sunk into an armchair, Lance held up an album cover. He clamped one side with his left hand and braced it against the white plaster cast that encased his right hand. He studied the artwork carefully, a photograph, allowing himself into the picture. The music washed over him, pops and whispers coming from Ian LaCoss's turntable. He mouthed each sad, stirring lyric silently as he heard it. Was there any music more attuned to the pangs of youthful male misery than The Replacements' *Let It Be*? Lance couldn't think of any. Even the album's coopted title, borrowed from the hallowed and untouchable Beatles, had a feeling of hopeless resignation and being second best.

The album cover: a black and white photo of four guys sitting on a slanted shingle roof. An older house in Minneapolis. They all wear Converse Chuck Davis All-Star canvas sneakers, the ancient high-top design. Dark jeans and heavy, working-class shirts. Their hair is grown out and longish, but unteased. They are bleary and scattered, probably hungover from a gig. The bass player rubs his eye and Paul Westerberg, the songwriter and leader, is turned away, saying something to the others. A moment typical of many, Lance wanted to believe, when they climbed out on the roof to escape their parents' lives, or let off steam after a fight with Dad, or were on break after hours of battering their guitars in the basement. They didn't know what would happen to them, Lance sensed. But who did? They had thumbed their noses at MTV (unwisely), releasing a video with a single shot of a throbbing speaker playing their song. Their roadies made more money than they did. Blame their audience, insecure teen males, who taped their latest release from a friend of a friend, denying the band even these meager royalties. Girls were scared off by the belligerent thrashy vibe and Westerberg's gravel-throated vocals. The lead guitarist leans forward with a curious, goofy expression, his face puckered. This guy seems to have problems, and later he drops out. Lance felt worried about him. Why leave the band just as they were finding some recognition? They didn't have much, but they were a band, a unit, and they had songs that broke your heart, so they were OK.

Two athletic trophies sit on a window sash above the drummer; tributes to forgotten glory, to boys playing in slow motion. One trophy so squat it's barely there. The other is a frozen metal torso. They are picking up dust, waiting for the day they go in the yard sale. If anybody wants them. There had been great joy when they were handed out. Lance recalled past soccer seasons: the tense concentration on assigned tasks, the guilt of a blown play, the constant threat of demotion from the starting squad. The coach would shout, demanding more intensity, demanding a precision that was never quite possible to achieve. So Lance had run madly and collided with other boys, pushing through physical pain, never stopping until the whistle blew. And with the trophy the team's competence had been proven. They had defeated an opponent, and the coach was finally satisfied. Then, over the years, the trophy shrank and became obscure, and you saw hundreds like them at trophy shops where anybody could buy one.

Lance first discovered The Replacements shortly after the

Prom Incident, and the beautiful though masochistic pleasures of *Let It Be* were the perfect companion to the confused weeks thereafter. It was a difficult and gray place to visit, but when you're there why not take a good look around? Recovering from double heartbreak, it seemed a logical choice now.

At the end of side two, the ultra-poignant last chords of "Answering Machine" faded into a wide silent place. Lance rubbed the top of his scalp with his plastered hand, careful not to clock himself. LaCoss stood up to tend the turntable. Lance said, "I can't take any more. Not one more song or I'll have to sharpen razors. Put on some classical music or jazz, anything else."

LaCoss flipped the Replacements record and settled it back onto the turntable, then lowered the needle for another listen. This was a surprising thing, but then again, lately LaCoss had taken some knocks himself. He slumped in his opposing chair, his fingers tightly entwined before his nose. Dusty craters had opened underneath his normally rested eyes. His hair was pulled back against his head and tied with a green rubber band. Waxy rebellious strands hung around his ears. Patchy, reddish hair was thickening on his face and neck. He'd had no enthusiasm for ridicule of the latest Arnold Schwarzenegger movie and he'd listened patiently to Jerry Falwell on television without yelling obscenities.

It started with his demotion from the cast of *The Complete Nuclear Family*. Fired. I was fired, LaCoss told people who asked. Wallace Dennis took it badly that his production had been ambushed by the theater press. Sniping from cast members, that LaCoss was hogging attention and stepping on their lines, didn't help either. He missed a Thursday rehearsal (who rehearses at the end of a run?) then got a one-minute explanation from Wallace Dennis a half-hour before the Friday show that a lighting guy would be doing Baby Johnny in the last two performances. That night's programs had LaCoss's name whited out. Neutral observers thought LaCoss's performances had not improved since the opening. After watching *The Pope of Greenwich Village* six times in a week, LaCoss had started doing Mickey Rourke doing Baby Johnny, which meant hanging his head, shifting his mouth around as if working on a cough drop and speaking too softly. Nobody could hear in back. Sy Terlinger walked out in protest of LaCoss's dismissal so Wallace Dennis himself donned the burlap and filled the role of Fury.

Fresh from this humiliation, LaCoss got a letter from Lucinda Falcon, his model girlfriend and main girl in California. He pulled her personalized salmon-colored stationary out of his mail slot and sniffed for perfume traces. The kind of happy mail you touted and waved around the Langford Post Office at students who only had phone bills and university announcements. Looking around to see if anyone had noticed his good fortune, he slit it open. He thought of his last letter to her. The one with a poem he'd written. (Actually, he'd ripped it off from Keats, substituting antiquated verses with some imagery of a Pacific sunset.) He had also begged her to visit in the spring; he anticipated her answer as to when.

He scanned her letter for a specific date.

There, a yard from his open P.O. box, he became painfully aware of his naked presence, an existential aloneness he had never fully grasped when studying Jean-Paul Sartre. A terrible vulnerability, a slow-burning panic, crowded him as he stood on a floor littered with junk mail. He shook his head, his eyes flitting over the words. He folded the letter and jammed it in his pocket, lest someone start reading over his shoulder, or ask Hey Ian, what's in the letter? or guess its contents from his expression of sick disorientation. He passed a throng of students entering from a courtyard—they clogged the door a long moment—and made a quick escape.

At a safe distance from the P.O. he pulled the letter back out. It read the same way. Our relationship has meant everything to me—past tense! He shuffled over to an unoccupied stone bench and sat. You are truly a wonderful guy who has taught me so much. Like birds in flight, neither of us is ready to settle or marry…have been seeing another guy…a producer who is working on a major project with Paramount…honesty is everything. I hope we can fly again. A pigeon waddled out from behind a trash can and picked up a speck of popcorn.

Paranoia surged within LaCoss that people were staring. He was lost as to the meaning of this letter. It seemed an error. When it came to ending things, ending relationships, he had always been the first. It was his choice. He was Ian LaCoss. If he didn't take action they would keep hanging on with stubborn hope, many times taking his calls years afterwards. He stood and tested his legs, then was walking again, moving briskly, putting his mind elsewhere; but he couldn't leave the thought behind, couldn't shake it, couldn't squelch it.

He'd been dumped.

On Parson Street he slowed down, students with backpacks passing him as they hurried by. LaCoss couldn't get past a feeling of terrible change, a sense that the earth now had two moons, or that objects might fall sideways. Maybe his assumptions about himself had been incorrect. Omens, karmic energies, cosmic dust pelting the planet? He'd have to consult his mom to interpret the letter. On the sidewalk, the face of Greta Hargrove, the tiny blonde, flashed by. Going in the opposite direction, her face there and gone before he could react. She'd given him a peculiar crafty look, a knowing look. They'd had a thing that had lasted ten days last semester. He dug his hands into his pockets. He was just walking, his legs aimless robot legs.

So Lucinda had cut him loose. OK. Fine.

He turned down Langford Way, headed toward The Lawn. He paused at the pedestrian light with two other students as a refrigerated truck rumbled past. A neon lime-green poster with black letters caught his eye. It was stapled to a light pole. He could see another one stapled to a pole across the street. He'd seen that color green in other spots that day. The poster said:

THE LANGFORD AMAZON SOCIETY
PRESENTS
THE TOP FIVE PREDATORY LANGFORD MALES

Interviews with numerous Langford women have confirmed that these males are disrespectful, misogynistic, phallic-obsessed, conquest-mentality, atavistic males. We hesitate to call them men. Langford women are hereafter warned about them and are advised to AVOID THEM. Knowledge is power.

* Phillip Duffey
* Ian LaCoss
* Patrick "Joe" Handlon
* David Issacs
* Serge Kristofferson

GET A CLUE AMERICA

His first thought: It would never be the same at college. Every time he walked into a classroom or a bar, they would see one of THE FIVE. It would be on the mind of every girl.

His next thought: Was he only number two? Had Phillip Duffey pushed him out of the top spot, or did the list consider them all equals? He reached to rip it down, but walked across the street instead. No use. It would just become part of the story: LaCoss was so mad he was ripping them down! He entered the concrete courtyard between the research labs and the old Bursar's Office, his long hair slack at either side of his head, allowing only a narrow portal for his nose and mouth. Normally he pushed it back with his thumb and middle finger, shaking to clear his face. Now he receded into anonymity. Two girls sat on a concrete wall eating lunch. One girl leaned toward the other, whispering behind her sandwich. The wall retained a square clump of lawn and a statue of Fritz Szabo Langford—LaCoss's favorite Langford, the wild-ass brother who was always pissing everyone off. The neon green flyer was pinned to Fritz Szabo's back. He sighed deeply, and quickened his pace. THE FIVE, like he was a criminal! Like he had only taken, when in fact he had given his time, his affection, his spirit. This was not insignificant. Once again, they wanted to shackle his spirit.

He felt like a kid again, the kid who lived in a trailer and a teepee, who wore the same patched pants every day, who wrote his sentences backwards and might have been retarded. No better than trash behind a fence. But he'd sprung out of puberty with high cheekbones and a rare, startling face, and the girls had started addressing him with dignity, then started following him around.

At the old Math building there was a rowdy lunch scene. LaCoss ducked his head, the laughs and giggles buzzing his ears like attacking blue jays, the word atavistic repeated. He'd have to look that word up. The humiliation was just beginning. It would take days to peak. His neck grew warm. He remembered Lucinda's letter. That was worse, even more depressing. Droves of people were now passing him on the east path of The Lawn.

He could see the Langford Owl mascot ahead, hamming it up with passing students. In yellow stockings, floppy feet and an oversized Owl head with googly eyes, it shook its tail feathers at an amused girl. As LaCoss was about to pass, the Owl waddled over. It bent at the waist and with a yellow gloved hand, shook a solitary, accusatory finger at LaCoss. Onlookers laughed, realizing the subtext. Then the mascot whipped a black medicine ball at LaCoss which collided painfully with LaCoss's arm and midsection. More laughter, louder.

The Owl, waving its hands, egged on LaCoss to return the throw. LaCoss picked up the medicine ball and tossed it at the Owl, who popped it back like it was a volleyball. Walking away, the ball thumped LaCoss on the shoulder and knocked him off stride. The Owl put its hands to its head in mock concern and churned its knees. LaCoss smiled broadly, picked up the medicine ball and socked it into the midsection of the Owl, who doubled over in pretend agony. Using the wooly costume as cover, LaCoss socked the mascot with a short, vicious body punch. The Owl winced with a groan that could only have been real.

"How do you like that, you bastard?" LaCoss muttered, the Owl hanging onto him for balance. It crumpled to its stockinged knees.

The Owl tipped up its costume, and under the dark head LaCoss could make out the perspiration-dotted brow and crossed eyes of Norton Skinner. Who would have guessed? "It's just me, dammit," Skinner said, wheezing.

"I'm really sorry. I'm having a bad day."

LaCoss walked on, the Langford Owl lying on its back in a pile of leaves. After he vented this anger, cockiness reentered LaCoss's stride. The flyer hadn't been the first act of vengeance he'd endured. There had been the girls in high school who had tried to put sugar in his gas tank; so many times he bought a locking cap. That insane redhead girl had stolen his wallet. The bare threats were too numerous to mention.

He halted and his mouth fell open as he recalled the latest: Celie Banks and Mindy Turnbull had somehow teamed up. Mindy came over to LaCoss's table in Compton Hall—he was waiting for Liz Williams at the time—and told him that they knew he had a serious girlfriend who was a model in Los Angeles named Lucinda and that they were going to write a letter to her, detailing LaCoss's infidelities and telling her what a jerk he was. LaCoss furrowed his eyebrows and gave Mindy a wounded look, a contrite look, to indicate that his feelings for her were deeper than she realized (and they were; he still thought Mindy was terrific). This approach defused girls like her (it had worked on Mindy before). Mindy stormed off, but LaCoss suspected it was just talk. If they ever wrote a letter it would be hard to track Lucinda down. She changed apartments often.

Obviously, they had done so and gotten the address right. It explained Lucinda's letter, which stunk of hurt feelings and payback. The crap about birds in flight was code, designed to be as insulting and patronizing as possible. This was a crucial realization. Lucinda hadn't really broken up with him. She was just hurt by the accusations. Things could be fixed!

So LaCoss picked up the phone. His usual phone confidence was tempered by the insistent and unsettling feeling he really needed to fix things, this need unfamiliar in an inner-preservation way, a need so strong he feared he might beg. He had to preserve his vision of himself and Lucinda, which, he had to admit, he had come to rely on. Despite his dad's three divorces and the ruin and depression and deep scars which followed each, and despite his dad's warnings to his son, LaCoss had allowed himself during intoxicating moments to dream about Lucinda and allowed love's sweet tentacles to creep in. He'd envisioned their rise together as young stars, as a Hollywood power couple. They'd jack each other's careers to high heaven with their romance, maybe doing a romantic comedy together. But it wouldn't just be a romance: they were going to marry, she bearing his children. It would be an acting empire, like the Barrymores.

So he did prep work about explaining the letter from the jilted girls. He prepared to offer a complete confession. He would change. Then he dialed. There was confusion on the L.A. end of the line from a roommate. Finally her voice came on, "Hello?" The confused interval had thrown him—him, Ian LaCoss!—and he felt off guard, so he chattered about getting her letter. His palms were moist. His mouth went dry. He hinted at any letters she might have received lately—

"Listen, babe," she cut him off. "I know my letter was kinda shitty, but it was a start. I do want to talk to you. The last thing I want is to hurt you…"

He wanted recriminations from her, hurt, some outpouring of grief with the poison letter crinkling in the background. He was supposed to be calming her, apologizing for his mistakes. He knew from her reaction: she'd never gotten the poison letter (he later confirmed it had never been written).

"Are you listening?" she asked. "I'm going to a party in a few minutes. It's at this beautiful house in Malibu and it's for a major project I just signed onto. It's important. Hello?…" He was reading between the lines and watching his vision of their relationship fade, evaporating into the telephone ether along with his suddenly porous self-esteem. His mouth hung ajar. "…Call me in a day or so. You sound hurt. Sorry. I don't have time."

Click.

Lance and LaCoss sat staring listlessly at the walls. The music touched their ears, but without pleasure. It rang on and on in the endless fashion of Muzak in a doctor's office. They made attempts to express themselves, but for a long while relied on Paul Westerberg's vocals as the lone voice of their angst, and sat mired in silence and confusion. The kind of bitter silence common to losers of the most painfully uncool variety.

Lance wondered aloud, "Do we have any control?"

LaCoss's t-shirt, hands and chin were blackened with Vespa grease. "You mean with women? That would be a resounding no."

"I mean control over anything, over the future." Lance's voice trailed off into doubt as he said, "That we could have things our way…"

LaCoss's face knotted up in disbelief. This idea seemed to upset him. He pinched his eyes together and made a long groan. "Don't go there! That's a useless question." Staring at a fixed point, his eyes glazed as he appeared to go there. He sadly scanned the engine parts on his floor he'd failed to fit correctly together in his attempt to fix his Vespa.

"But don't you wonder? Don't you look at what's happened so far and think: when are they going to go my way, or will they ever? Or is the world another kind of way?"

LaCoss slumped, as if a large object had struck the top of his head, and for a long while this unwanted notion seemed to confound him. Maybe things weren't as easy as they seemed. Maybe listening to your favorite song, all the noise and power and craziness and dreams you felt in your chest were only that, and it didn't translate into anything you had, or could do, or that would come. The world wasn't simple, happy, predictable Bryan Adams but was hard-luck, kicked-in-the-ass Springsteen, and the tough times not just in rust belt Jersey but in your own backyard. The world wasn't quirky dialogue and get-what-you-want-in-the-end John Hughes, it was David Lynch. LaCoss ran his fingers anxiously over a gear, then threw it, denting the drywall. "Those Langford Amazons!" he yelled. "Who are they anyway? Are they like the secret society of Nazi women?"

Rhetorical questions, but Lance was tempted to divulge the identity of one particular Amazon. He toyed with the idea, though he knew he couldn't. He had promised Veronica and his sense of loyalty to her was strong and getting stronger. He was sentimental about her second-floor paradise and his banishment from it, about their days of passionate abandon, part of him wishing he'd run into her, part of him still hurting. Over the space of two weeks two women had lured and crushed him, had vandalized his inner fine filament. Strangely, each still made him rejoice in a small way. That was beyond pathetic. Pathetic, thy name was Lance. And such opposites. Lynn had wanted superhuman assurance of his love, wanted it constantly, and Veronica would have been offended by its very mention. Where was the logic? What could be learned from this? He had made zero progress. He'd learned nothing. His ability to understand their hearts was deteriorating, a negative vacuum, an expanding universe of doubt. How horribly naive to think he could achieve otherwise.

Lance worried he had a dangerous vulnerability to the fairer sex, a weakness, and this might not change. He might forever be stuck in the playground sandbox, wide-eyed and immobile, staring stupidly at them. He wasn't alone though. LaCoss's decline had proven a live beating heart existed under the guy's t-shirt, not that he was admitting it.

"What about Veronica? Are you still seeing her?" LaCoss asked. It was odd after the Amazon mention, but Lance was sure it was just coincidence.

Lance shook his head. The thought of Veronica in her bathrobe deeply depressed him. "That breakup was worse than the one with Lynn."

"You only were with her five days. Get real."

"Oh, I'm real. Don't underestimate the intensity of those days."

"I wonder if that all happened to you because Veronica was trying to get back at me. Maybe it was an elaborate revenge plot."

"You're a paranoid one. And you're giving yourself too much credit."

LaCoss's tone grew deeper: "You're underestimating their viciousness." His eyes became fixed, two frozen marbles, which added credibility to his statement.

Veronica's gleeful destruction of their relationship did bother Lance. She had kicked him out like a homeless person, taunting and renouncing him. He was angered that Lynn had turned on him so coldly the other night, his damaged hand dangling before her and crying out for compassion—a medical emergency. Each was sure to be broadcasting Lance's secret flaws and weaknesses into radiating rings of gossip. Veronica did have a sworn curse on LaCoss; and she bore enough of a grudge to put him in the top five. The ugly truth was that lots of girls like Veronica might do something like that. They possessed ample treachery for such a scheme, Lance thought, his anger and pain feeding this feverish theory. Their self-centeredness had to be considered. They prized above all else *how I feel, what I need*, their worldview rotating smoothly around themselves and their favorite mirrors.

"Oh, man. Here's the final kick in the crotch," LaCoss said. "Look who I found in the latest issue of *Rolling Stone*." He handed Lance the issue and quoted a page number. Lance expected to find Lucinda snarling in tight jeans or with a look of surprised dazzle in a hair spray advertisement, and to hate her, to hate all of them, especially the one who had trashed his friend.

It was a soap ad. Lever 2000. It took Lance's breath away. His hatred softened and passed, draining off easily. In soft light and mild shadow, Lucinda hugged her bare upper torso, her arms crossed before her breasts. Her hair bundled on top of her head, she stared off to the right of the camera, her stark face tilted toward a hand at her shoulder. Her full lips were closed, though relaxed. That look! That snapshot of their souls. A soft look, infinitely sweet, but resolute. A look as honest and unadorned as the scrubbed skin at the gentle swell of her womb. The look hinted they weren't going to believe much they heard. After all, they had to deal with men. The look was their armor and their salvation, their stare-down of the world.

On second thought, he had learned some things, some facts: often they were brutally dissatisfied with themselves, and their competition with one another was fierce. But other things he had less learned than absorbed, witnessed, achieved an intuitive understanding of, like how to open himself and glom onto her vibe, and in this space achieve a mirroring which tapped into her luminescent glow, which, if you were lucky, might shed some rays into your gloomy recesses and stoke your own sorry light, and make everything less about being a guy and a girl and more about sharing as two human beings. Who could give up on that?

"Wow. She is really something. Or, she was…" Lance handed back the magazine, open to the advertisement.

"Tell me about it." LaCoss placed it on his desk like a blind person, his eyes focused above and away from the picture. But he couldn't resist one peek. Little blood vessels popped out at the corners of LaCoss's eyes, making them pink and watery. Moisture pooled, his lacrimal ducts suddenly pumping. He sniffled; his body quivered. Lance was ready to be embarrassed, and amazed, to witness the breakdown of the mighty Ian LaCoss, the punk rocker. LaCoss did take two unsteady breaths, then whipped out fingernail clippers and did some digging at his cuticles with the attached nail file. Clipping skin and drawing blood seemed to steady him. He looked at the time and snapped his fingers. He switched on the television to catch, five minutes in, *Viva Las Vegas*.

Lance's mood improved as he lost himself in the movie, and so did LaCoss's. It costarred Ann-Margret. God, the vivaciousness of that woman! Even on LaCoss's fuzz- afflicted black and white portable with the tinfoil ears. She wouldn't have been any hotter in life-size 3-D. Her quick brain popping out zingers to slay Elvis, with her cha-cha pillow talk voice, and those crazy beatnik go-go dances she threw herself into, like voltage injected into her body. Those high steady cannons occupied a wondrous category of their own. Presley lost every scene to her. No one could deny such a woman, that goddess in Capri pants.

LaCoss clicked off the little television as the credits rolled. Then a light entered his eyes, a supernova of the corneas, and he smiled, putting his hands behind his head. His body seemed to relax, to ripple and absorb some notion. He started talking excitedly. Afterward, Lance couldn't decide if it was a split-second decision, or something LaCoss had been considering awhile.

"I figure I'll start looking for parts in two weeks," LaCoss said. "That will give me time to get back to the land of sunshine. I've taken my last exam."

"Huh?"

"I'm outta here. My Langford days are over."

"You haven't graduated yet. You've only got two more semesters."

LaCoss teetered on the edge of his seat, ecstatic. "Don't you see? Can't you see what it all adds up to? The stars have aligned, my friend." He clapped his hands. As much as could be followed within the Unified LaCossian Thought System, his reasoning was: Just as the band Devo had described, he himself had been devolving in the last year. The disasters both personal and professional illustrated this. The basic alignments were out of kilter, not because he had made mistakes at Langford, but because he was at Langford in the first place. He had been trying to bodysurf feet first.

Lance shook his head. "So, you're going to be a dropout?"

LaCoss beamed. "Yes. I'll be a dropout. All the most successful people are dropouts. And I'll be one of them!"

Lance covered his face with his hands, then pressed on his eyelids. Now his friends were deserting him. It was all too much. He sensed his own liability; perhaps he had triggered this decision, this horrifying waste of education. He considered arguing more forcefully, but in a blink this fancy had become a fait accompli. Such was the high wire act of LaCoss's decision making.

"My life can't wait any longer. I'm like a phoenix from the ashes, like Sugar Ray Leonard up off the canvas, like Mr. Smith going to Washington."

"That makes no sense."

"They don't want me here. But it's like the cosmic forces of destiny intervening in what was a flawed system anyway. Don't you see that?"

All Lance could see was his best friend sitting in a chair with a crazed expression. LaCoss saw himself as being pushed out because of his infamy, as being unfairly tarred and ostracized. In fact, before leaving, LaCoss would enjoy a surge of sympathy from Langford girls, as well as new interest in the official bad boy. They clawed one another, trying to be the one to mend his wayward heart.

Lance feared for LaCoss's future, for the volatile mix of his hysterical ambitions, his middling talent and his quixotic belief system. He was certain that for the rest of his life, he would get phone calls with tales of financial mishaps, strange diseases, forced career changes and peculiar personal crusades. But then again, who knew? LaCoss was always so sure of himself.

LaCoss stood, his fists stabbing the air. "The worm has turned!"

He started shaving his scraggly face with his electric razor, pacing around the room and talking about the nineties. The nineties were coming and you had to be ready because it would be a decade like no other. "It's going to be our decade!" LaCoss said, crouching behind Lance and shouting in his ear. The nineties! All the dumb fashion, the unfairness, the flashiness and misguided energy of the eighties would be gone and a whole new thing would be forged. Totally new and improved. An enlightened decade! Lance could find no enthusiasm for the new decade.

LaCoss studied his clean face in a mirror, rubbing his cheeks. "Wow! Yes! Oh, man!" He rooted under his bed and found an electric hair cutter. He shaved above both ears and around the back of his head. Clumps fell to the floor, leaving wide swaths of stubble on the sides and a mane flowing on top. Studying himself in the mirror, his eyes widened then narrowed. He stared fiercely, as though his face were about to reveal an important clue, some impetus for further genius. He snapped his fingers. Riding a wave of inspiration, he shaved off his eyebrows. One, then the other.

IV.

CHAPTER SIXTEEN

THE APARTMENT
Fall 1989

At the beginning of his senior year, Lance rented a cheap apartment. After another summer in Oswald Dorm, another school year in noisy, chaotic Oswald was unthinkable. Also, the previous year, Charles Boyd had been banned from Langford residence halls. After his month of seclusion, he had emerged from his room to be discovered on Oswald's front lawn, standing on a milk crate and wearing an American flag as a cape. Rumors were flying: Boyd had a raging crack habit; he had had a psychotic break; he had written a blockbuster political manifesto akin to *The Communist Manifesto*, or *Mein Kampf*. His hair weirdly flat, he loomed over the yard like a scavenger bird. He flung off sunglasses and then shouted to the crowd of onlookers that a presidential election was coming up and their democratic system was born out of acts of protest and violence, and so in the spirit of freedom and encouraging democratic rejuvenation…he flicked a lighter at the lower hem of the flag and flames licked at his legs. Boyd then ran, cackling strangely, pulling the flag behind him like a tragic kite, filling the air with smoke and a scent of burning toys. Pursued by patriotic students and Langford Safety and Security officers, he was tackled near the street, the flag pulled away. Lying in the grass, he wrapped his arms around himself and closed his eyes. Then the strangest thing of all, which Lance would never be able to get out of his mind: a grand smile of dreamy self-satisfaction graced Boyd's upturned face. The smile of vacationers, of lottery winners. As though his plan had worked to perfection.

The idea of an apartment was appealing to both Boyd and Lance. They could cook meals; they would have private bedrooms, a bathroom, a living area, direct mail delivery. The way real people lived. Lance imagined they would throw legendary wild parties, have student and non-student acquaintances, watch cable TV, stretch out by the pool, and get killer tans. Females would drop by at all hours. In short, the apartment would be a dynamic social cell. This was his conception. His ideal.

But they only had so much money.

A week before fall tuition was due, Lance got a letter from his parents with that year's tuition plus one thousand bucks to live on. The Last One! was written across the seal in his father's jagged hand. One of his father's hysterical jokes that held significant truth. His father had pledged they would support their son through college, which Lance now realized, holding the envelope, meant until the moment of graduation and not a second longer. Further arrangements could be made once he got into business school. Lance had led them to believe this would happen, while dodging particulars and once again maintaining a misleading secretiveness regarding the true nature of his GPA (a shamefully low, dangerously low number he wanted to bury deep in the earth). He gathered from his increasingly terse, uncomfortable phone conversations with them—his limbs jerking involuntarily during these calls, his hands sweating—that they fully expected this to occur.

But if and until, a thousand bucks was it. So he was determined to hoard this final cash until he figured out how to get more. Surviving on what money you had while trying to get more was the essential game, he realized. The game was on. In this light, his managing to slap together and mail applications to several mid- and lower-tier business schools last spring, though he had been recklessly ambivalent at the time, now took on new wisdom and urgency. It was a utilitarian long-term move to succeed in the game, and a short-term means of getting more parental cash.

He now hoped and prayed a school would accept him. He felt alone and wanted a tangible outcome from his rapidly ending college years. He wanted a lifeline to hang onto.

Charles Boyd had more budget flexibility—he paid no tuition as a Langford Scholar and got a stipend for expenses, a sort of academic welfare—yet he was cheaper than Lance. He hadn't spent any repair money on his lime-green Ford LTD. Not ever. Every nonessential system of the car was broken.

They saw a banner for the special deal at Widger Arms, the $450 two-bedroom "courtyard apartment" deal. It was far enough from campus, on a forlorn corridor of fast food joints and auto body shops, that it couldn't be considered near campus. Their building was a three-story box of faded bricks connected to a grassy area, a courtyard formed by the patio sides of two other matching buildings. It wasn't until they moved in that Lance noticed a metallic, dusty smell which never dissipated, or the kitchen linoleum curled at the edges, or that looking down the metal front stairs to the mold-stained slab at the door of 10A and its subterranean twin 10B was like looking into a dungeon, or more charitably, a basement apartment.

On Lance's first night in 10A, he turned out the lights and lay on his floor-bound mattress. Headlights from a parked car leaked through the blinds with surprising intensity. A shudder vibrated through the building as a door slammed overhead. Thuds and creaking sounds crisscrossed the ceiling. Then a chorus of bedsprings, like angry predators around a carcass. Sleepless, he found himself tracking this person's movements by the creaks. He imagined killing this person. The grocery-store butcher lived overhead. He wore the tall white hat and seemed strung out.

On another night, he was awakened by quick pops, what sounded like firecrackers. It was a shooting at building two, a drug deal gone wrong. The laundry room was on the same level of their apartment. Lance lost his best pair of Levi's from the first load. Almost supernatural thievery—he had only left his stuff alone for five minutes.

Lance ate cereal while leaning against the dining room wall. He walked into Charles Boyd's room and said, "We need to get some furniture."

Boyd, his attention focused on a hardback of *The Ugly American*, said emphatically, "I'm not going to spend any money on that." He sat on the floor in a half-lotus position next to a pillar of books against his bedroom wall. His unruly dark mop of hair sprung in all directions and obscured his ears. It seemed as natural for him to be on the floor as for Adlai Stevenson, his cat, who slumbered near him in a nest of shredded tissues. Boyd's spot on the carpet was outlined by a peppering of cracker crumbs, which would remain there for some time. The only decorative accent to Charles Boyd's barren quarters was his modest corner shrine to Bob Dylan.

Lance realized then it was probably a mistake to have a roommate who was cheaper than you. Luckily, piles of abandoned furniture were often stacked next to the Widger Arms entrance. Other renters were being evicted at a regular pace. One afternoon they found a couch, a huge sectional rattan thing that formed a U-shape. The cushions were a colonial plaid of earthen hues and smelled of pet urine and sweaty human legs, but only if you pressed your nose to the fabric. It became the living room centerpiece. They cooked out of two pots. They used a crate as a coffee table. Lance suggested they buy a microwave.

Boyd shrugged. "I'll be in D.C. this time next year, or overseas, so why should I spend money on that?"

"But what if you don't make it all the way through the process?"

"What if I do?"

Charles Boyd's unshakable faith that he would win an appointment to the Foreign Service was an annoying, demoralizing thing. Even more so after he explained the system he had to conquer. First, as administered by the Educational Testing Service, there was the Foreign Service examination—a standardized Confucian exam like the SAT, the GMAT, the LSAT, etc. (Lance had sat for the GMAT before applying to business schools, and memory of it triggered nausea and flashback hypertension). Like alerted cult members, tens of thousands of young people across the continent congregated at locations on the same day and same hour. You and fifty other people gathered at 8:00 am outside the doors of an auditorium, your test center, clutching #2 pencils, eye drops, No-Doz tablets, cough drops, breath mints, lucky trinkets and positive I.D., wondering if fate was with you at that rocky hour, if two or three more correct answers might change your life, thinking the guy in line before you seemed a long shot, but the girl behind looked scary smart. You glanced at them with belligerence—they were trying to take your spot. You settled in for the six-hour ordeal. You received a pale green answer sheet filled with circles you would darken to form mysterious patterns, like the cycles of coughs and sniffles echoing around you. You began! Each breath taken and sentence read had a time consequence. A compression crowded your ears. Your mind chatter contrasted with the odd, enforced silence of the room. Then during one question, that simple though sublime, impossible-to-answer brain-freeze question, whose contemplation stretched far beyond the time allotted, you reached into an abyss of knowledge—a breaking point—and relied instead on instinct and superstition, feeling rotten for it.

In three months you got the results in a rip-away carbon letter, smudgy hard-to-make-out numbers which were invariably disappointing, as Lance's results had been.

Only ten or fifteen percent of the Foreign Service takers passed and were given an invitation to the next stage, the ominous Oral Assessment. Of the three thousand people who were orally assessed, smaller and smaller groups appeared before Interview Panels, withstood Background Investigation and cruelest cut of all, the Inquisition-like Final Review, after which only a handful were hired as new officers. As Lance considered these impediments, Charles Boyd stared blankly, even yawning and becoming distracted as he was questioned on details. He pointed his finger down into his opposite palm. "They should just give me my appointment now."

Where did you buy confidence like this?

An austerity within the apartment bugged Lance. It seemed a transient place where he didn't belong, didn't want to belong. He couldn't sleep. He had no appetite. This incomplete feeling was helped one night when they reclined on the giant couch, each with their feet up, heads sunk into the cushions, and drank Bacardi and cola and watched TV late into the night. The wall they shared with 10B shook with a cranking roar. The lone wall picture, a scene of dogs playing poker, fell to the floor. Then the didididi of an electric guitar doing a speed metal riff. It was Rodney, their amateur musician neighbor. He and a woman named Alice were holed up next door, having shouting matches. They had matching black nylon Megadeth concert jackets and similar shoulder-length dirty blonde hair. Outside their door, wet paper bags spilled open with empty liquor bottles. I am not them, Lance told himself. I will not end up like them.

More didididi. It became impossible to hear the TV, or themselves, so Lance and Charles Boyd yelled Shut up! at the top of their lungs. Lance really enjoyed the yelling, their voices melding with the heavy chugging riff. He was moved to do a stamping Neanderthal dance while pounding his fists on the wall and yelling Shut up! Shut up! The dance was self-affirming and strangely cathartic. Silence; then the guitar started again. Lance bounced a basketball against the adjoining wall several times and it went away for good. Charles Boyd yawned and put down his drink. "I got that test tomorrow."

"What test?"

"The big one. The Foreign Service exam."

"You're up at this hour—drinking! Are you insane?"

"I'm going to sleep like a baby. You've got to stay loose. That's crucial."

"My God, why haven't you been studying! What's wrong with you?" Lance shouted. He was pacing and pressing his fingers into his forehead. It wasn't even his exam.

"I've been studying all my life. It's like life itself. There's no way to study for that." Boyd rubbed his eyes and staggered off to his room, his socks flopping around his toes.

He saw few people he recognized on campus, the thick layer of underclassmen pushing him out. They were still deluded enough about the world to enjoy themselves. How strange that from a distance a shock of blonde hair remained destabilizing, making his heart tremor. On campus, an apartness lingered around Lance like invisible twine. He had driven from Widger Arms and before the day was out he would be back. People sometimes assumed he had already graduated. Always they asked the same question: What are you doing after graduation? It became a nuisance, a feared question. He anticipated it and gritted his teeth a second before it happened. He had sent out business school applications—an accomplishment of sorts, a display of initiative—and was waiting on them, so he told people this fact. I'll see what happens, Lance would say, or, I don't know if I'm ready to go just yet, as if he might have the luxury of turning a school down. Though with some people, a professor he liked, or the French circulation woman at The Ivan, he might huff and admit he just didn't know.

His chief routine was getting the daily mail at the apartment kiosk. It was exhilarating to find important mail, though nerve-wracking and crushing also, like watching the Super Bowl after betting everything on it. He would unlock their aluminum box, extract the clutter and flip through credit card offers—Congratulations Recent Graduate!—searching for an official envelope from a business school.

The rejections came in even installments. Just as he had forgotten about the last one, or conned himself into believing he never had wanted to go to U. of Wherever, but could stand to attend the remaining places, another thin letter with curt language arrived. He got a rejection from a prominent school, then a week later another letter from them. A change of heart? An apology and an offer to attend? He had sensed the wrongness of the first letter. It was the same rejection, dated a week later. As the rejections came he grew to resent the time he'd wasted typing applications, the hell of taking the GMAT, the $45 application fees, the humiliation of brainstorming to put something in the Awards and Honors category, and the misery of writing sugarcoated essays about his most memorable character-building lesson; and to resent the pinhead admissions people who had pushed him aside. He'd known his chances weren't good, but he had tried anyway; hoping a decision maker might overlook his anemic falling-into-academic-probation-and-below GPA, his unimpressive GMAT score, and might recognize some well of potential in his application, a semi-desperate though honorable quality, and find him a spot.

He held the letter from the last remaining school. With shallow breath, he ripped open a jagged end. He scanned the first lines. Every time he was tricked into thinking it might be good...we regret to inform you...He took a deep breath and looked about the mail kiosk, seeing nothing before his eyes, an absence, a finality, the end of a long family line of distinguished postgraduate degrees. His hand dropped to his side, the letter crackling against cement. A breeze tumbled it into the street, where it lodged in a puddle. He now clung to nothing. He had tried, but his mistakes, derelictions and failures had been many. He had fucked up, which meant, he was...The moment stretched into a time warp, and though he rejected the moment and earnestly wished it were not happening, it persisted. A hot stuffiness crowded his ears. It was vivid, probably the most real moment of his life. He both experienced the moment and monitored his reactions to it, to see if being a fuckup was as bad as he had always dreaded (it was), or if earthquakes would shake the planet, or if he would blink out of existence.

In the same batch of mail was a proud-looking letter to Charles Boyd. A bulky letter from the United States Department of State with raised gold lettering.

Lance numbly extended the letter to his roomie. Sitting on a pillow, Charles Boyd took off headphones and slit it open. His eyebrows jammed together in concentration as he read. He sighed and smacked his hand against the letter.

"I knew it. They must have graded against me on those two questions."

"Did you pass?" Lance grabbed the letter, semi-hoping Charles Boyd would need commiseration.

"Of course I passed. I missed two questions in the geopolitical section. I was worried about them. They could be construed different ways, depending on which specialist you asked." His other scores were perfect. Lance shook Charles Boyd's hand and slapped him on the back. He stuffed his wet rejection letter deep into his pocket, along with his feelings, electing not to tell Boyd. Though Boyd knew the poor direction of the process and had stopped asking.

"Two questions missed?" Lance laughed loudly. "Who gives a crap about them?"

"They might hold those questions against me. I should write some kind of addendum to my application explaining my reasoning."

"Probably nobody gets a perfect score."

"It's happened before."

Lance's face turned red. He kept rereading the State Department letter, shaking his head and clearing his throat. "This letter is so great. I'm really, really proud of you. Really, I am proud." He felt like vomiting.

"Are you OK? What happened today?"

"Nothing. Nothing at all." Lance backed into a wall, then

wandered into the kitchen.

In early fall, the sun still blistered the sky. He spent lots of time at the Widger Arms pool, reading South American writers, sweating and hoping the forces of sky and water might lift his depression. In the radiant pool light, he tried to imagine himself on the Caribbean coast of Colombia, at a beach shanty like some Gabriel Garcia Marquez character. But this prospect seemed unreal, like someone else's life. The pool was oblong, corralled by a high chain-link fence. Sun worshipers often stubbed their toes on the inch- high blue tile shelf near the water's edge, sending them into hopping frenzies of pain. He pulled his lounge chair away from the others to avoid conversation. He wanted to be left alone to the penitence of the scalding sun. His stomach grumbled; he refused to feed it.

He slumped into the rubber straps of his chair, his eyes shielded by mirrored sunglasses. He picked up a magazine full of doomsaying articles that hinted the economy was going south, the great American postwar boom being choked off by Japanese and German competitors who were exploding the trade deficit with their cheaper, superior goods.

The consensus from last year's grad crop of Langfordites was that there weren't any jobs. None. Corporations were nervous. The boomers were hanging tight to the positions they had scratched out and the meager openings for college nobodies were so fiercely contested as to be unobtainable. The very top graduates were doing fine, naturally, the summa and magna cum laude scholarship whiz kids. This applauded ten percent hogged the campus interviews and were being recruited by Fortune 500 concerns. They weren't being denied. They never had been, or would be. Older former whiz kids were gathering in the new crop, seeing their own proud selves in the crisp resumes. But everybody else was relying on pulled strings, or they were hopeful and working for nothing in internships, like amorphous semi-slave relationships, or they had surrendered to the service economy with other bottom feeders; or had wandered off, jobless and dazed, unaccounted for, which seemed more and more a likely fate for Lance.

A man with a saddle-leather tan often hung around the pool. Graying hair grew on the sides of his head, long enough to tie into a ponytail. He wore photosensitive glasses which outside darkened to a rust brown. He placed a small portable typewriter before him on the straps of his lounge chair. Lance would drive past the pool and see the guy sitting there, alone, staring off toward the trees or mumbling things. In violation of posted rules #3 and #5, he usually had a glass tumbler of scotch he slurped, then placed with a clink on the cement. He wore short red plaid trunks, faded and frayed, a relic from another time. He sprayed liquid from a plastic bottle over his chest and legs which smelled like coconuts and kerosene.

On a sunny day Lance read Marquez's *Chronicle of a Death Foretold*. Light wrinkles pulsed calmly along the bottom of the turquoise pool. The tan guy clipped past in flip-flops, ice cubes clacking in his glass. He paused at the foot of Lance's chair, pointing at the book, and said, "That's a helluva good read. Marquez is solid. Too bad he fell for that minimalist crap that polluted the water in the '70s."

He walked on, shaking his head. Later, Lance learned the guy's name was Hetrick Curtain. He was with the journalism program at Langford.

One Friday night, Margaret Zanger walked through the door of the apartment with Charles Boyd and never seemed to leave. Lance had been lying on the couch, sleepy but awake. He had watched TV awhile, then turned it off and stared at the ceiling. A blank suspension occupied his mind. The plaster's uneven topography of silhouette, dimples and smudges was like a strange map, a puzzling universe. He studied it, as if it hid some design that might provide important guidance to his life. Hours went by, yet the plaster yielded no clues. He sang lyrics from a recent song, that annoying radio song by the guy with the strange hat. Then he realized, sadly, the song was three years old. The front door opened and Charles Boyd and Margaret stepped inside. Boyd had gone to the annual Langford Scholars Banquet without a date, but had returned home with this strange girl and a roguish glint in his eyes.

Lance's horizontal form in shadow, he studied the slender dark-haired girl, who looked young, prim, with detailed makeup. In a black cocktail dress and dark coat, she walked in behind Charles Boyd, holding his hand with both of hers. Boyd, his tie disheveled and a shirt tail hanging over his belt, glanced across the living room. Her hazel eyes stayed fixed on Boyd, with a look of muted expectation, of secret joy. When Boyd looked back at her she became demure. She pulled off a crushed velvet hat and tossed around dark fluffy hair. She had a bland kind of prettiness. Her personality helped her features. Her legs were inviting in dark hose.

Lance stirred, putting a hand behind his head. Margaret was startled and clung to Charles Boyd.

"Who are you, the creeper?" Charles Boyd asked.

"It's impossible to creep when lying on a couch," Lance said.

"I totally didn't see him there," Margaret Zanger said, breathless.

Charles Boyd introduced Margaret and Lance waved, without bothering to get up. She composed herself, squinting to see Lance and checking out the apartment.

Margaret said, enunciating precisely, "Well, it was officially announced tonight. Guess who won the Stella Pitts Langford award for this year?" She rubbed the shoulder of Charles Boyd's jacket, beaming at him. At graduation the winner received a $2,000 cash award and a yearlong scholarship to the Sorbonne in Paris (Boyd would decline the scholarship part).

"That is terrific, my friend," Lance said, clapping his hands slowly.

Charles Boyd gave a modest bow. His face glowed impishly, both acknowledging the prestige of the award and dismissing it as ultimately a minor thing considering the magnitude of his self-opinion.

"It's a lot more than just terrific. I mean, it's a big honor," Margaret said. She had gone to the banquet with another Scholar and met Boyd when she complimented him on his award.

Lance went to his room and read awhile. Then, before going to sleep, he went to the kitchen to get water. Margaret and Charles Boyd were in there kissing, slurping and pawing each other in front of the stove while coffee brewed. Lance pretended he didn't see them. Though he was lonely and depressed, he pretended he had no desire to suck face with a lovely young thing. She stayed that night in Charles Boyd's room, leaving in the morning before Lance got up. She and Charles Boyd stayed up all night and talked and played chess and read tarot cards and messed around.

"She's got a three-week rule," Charles Boyd explained the next day, frustrated and weary. Hickeys dotted his neck. He ran his hand through his shaggy-dog hair and groaned loudly.

"You seem to manage pretty well by yourself. You'll survive."

An exuberant sparkle in his eye, Charles Boyd reported things he'd learned, each detail a wonderful omen to him. She was a sophomore, though a year younger than most in her class. Her New England family had lots of money via a string of dairies. She was a third cousin to John Belushi. She'd spent a year living in Austria. She was a fanatical tennis player and had been the #2 ranked under-eighteen female in Connecticut.

Charles Boyd's overall mood improved hugely. He had met a woman worthy of dating, who tolerated him, even revered him, and the days quickly went by. He took her to movies three nights in a row. He volunteered alongside her at a homeless shelter. Margaret hinted a waiver might be issued after two and a half weeks. At long last Boyd's personal drought was going to end, coal black rainclouds hovering over fields. On the night, Charles Boyd took her to La Salle's, a restaurant he complained about bitterly to Lance after learning the cost of the average entree. Twenty freaking dollars! Charles Boyd had theater plans, but he and Margaret came back to the apartment after La Salle's and scooted into his room. After brushing his teeth, Lance came out of the bathroom and paused near Boyd's door, hearing one faint moan (hers). He admitted to himself, grudgingly, Margaret Zanger was probably a tigress in the sack.

The next morning Lance walked into the kitchen in boxers, extracting lint from his bellybutton. Margaret was bouncing a teabag in a mug. Either she had already applied today's makeup or yesterday's had lasted really well. She was by the sink, her legs and feet bare, wearing one of Charles Boyd's t-shirts. She opened the refrigerator and shoved a carton of cold orange juice into Lance's belly.

"This is probably yours. It's gone bad."

Lance opened the top and sniffed it. She took it out of his hands and dropped it into the trash. "I tasted it. Very sour."

Lance brushed his fly to make sure it was closed. Margaret leaned against the counter and crossed her arms. She had olive eyes, dark eyebrows and an amused stare so bold it made Lance nervous about the next thing she was going to say. "Charlie says you're going to business school. Which school are you planning to attend?"

Lance blinked a few times. "Uh, well, I'm still hearing from them. So, I don't know."

"What are your primary choices?" She turned to get some tap water. She had these incredibly toned legs. "Hello? Did you hear me?"

"Well, you know. It's very early, it depends…" He flopped his hand in a circular way.

"I can tell I'm asking too many questions." She stepped toward him, then looked around him impatiently. He stepped out of her way so she could get to the refrigerator. Charles Boyd walked in wearing pajama bottoms and rubbing his eyes. He kissed Margaret on the lips. She threw her arms around his neck and her t-shirt pulled up, revealing beige underwear.

Boyd had totally lucked out; Margaret was smart, fun, sassy. Sexually, she was more advanced, experimental even, intimidating, but he was happily catching up. Fashion-wise, she combined designer clothing with revival hippie touches: odd scarves, tie- dyed shirts, jean skirts. She thought she was more beautiful and popular than she actually was.

A week before Charles Boyd was to fly to Washington for his foreign service Oral Assessment, Margaret took him to a salon, Le Hair Académie. Had he ever had a style before? He usually snipped it himself with scissors when it got too long, leaving a rough outline for his face. He came back with his hair cut weirdly short, parted smartly on the left and slicked back, like a member of the Rat Pack. Like Dean Martin. It was shocking to see Boyd's hair tightly organized, to see a clear expanse of forehead, and his ears—he had handsome ears! He looked professional and worthy of diplomatic responsibility. He also had an armful of shampoos, conditioners and wet gels he'd bought at the salon, and a commitment to using them.

Margaret helped him select a charcoal gray wool suit from an outlet store, black Balmoral oxford cap-toe shoes and a selection of three silk ties. She got him to use a Speed Stick deodorant on a regular basis, even trimming his mass of underarm hair to a more respectful hedge. He listened patiently to her entire discography of Joni Mitchell. Boyd was on record as despising Joni Mitchell, but he pretended it was all new to him. Margaret explained her dreamy interpretations of the music while he sat with a rapturous expression, though maybe love had colored his taste and opened him up to the folk singer. Margaret rented *Three Men and a Baby*, which Charles Boyd claimed wasn't too bad a movie, really. They watched Tex Avery cartoons together on Saturday mornings, giggling and falling over each other like kids on a Halloween sugar high.

Charles Boyd insisted upon driving himself to the airport before his Oral Assessment in Washington, D.C., a daylong process involving hypothetical questions from a panel and group negotiation exercises. Lance wished him luck in the parking lot, Charles Boyd looking suave in his full suit and tie regalia and his new, precise hair. Margaret adjusted the handkerchief in Boyd's breast pocket and teared up. She hung inside the window of his car and hugged him. Black exhaust kicked up from his car as he waved, flashing the Casio calculator watch Margaret had given him as a good luck present.

"I just know Charlie is going to do so well," Margaret said. Only his mother dared call him Charlie. Lance had been sure Boyd would put a stop to it when she started doing that, but he hadn't. "So much is riding on it for Charlie, for both of us really."

Lance realized the depth of her feelings and was tempted to suggest perhaps she was taking things a bit too fast. He suspected Boyd had no intention of letting some girl tag along on the early foreign adventures of his career. But maybe there was more between them.

"He'll do fine," Lance said. "They would be fools not to hire him."

Margaret looked at Lance for a long moment, as if noticing something about him for the first time. "What exactly will you be doing next year?"

"I'm still in the process of figuring that out."

"What do you think you'll do?"

"I'm considering all my options."

"Which ones are you favoring?"

"It's a very long story."

"Tell me."

"Back off, Margaret."

Margaret gazed at him knowingly, her thin lips pressed shut. Her face softened into a sympathetic expression, implying Lance was a deluded person, a sad directionless person who had neglected to do vital planning. At that moment he hated Margaret Zanger and all her smugness about the world. It had become this way with females. Lance looked at them, unsure what to say, and they looked back in quiet judgment. He was experiencing a catastrophic loss of mojo, a wipeout which made small talk painful and intimacy impossible. He shoved his hands into his pockets, walked into the apartment, went into his room and shut the door.

CHAPTER SEVENTEEN

THE PARTY

I n late October they hosted their first party. Lance was adamant they give a really good one, a memorable one. At least one of his visions of apartment life had to be realized. Charles Boyd was ambivalent. Margaret was enthusiastic. The theme was her idea: an Art Party. Each guest would get a big sheet of paper to produce a work using the media of their choice. The winner would be given a grand prize.

The original plan was to buy many cases of cheap beer, but Margaret and Charles Boyd found a *Mr. Boston Deluxe Official Bartender's Guide* and became crazed about mixing arcane concoctions like White Elephants and Irish Rickeys, as though Manhattan socialites who could distinguish a Pink Pussycat from a Cadiz would be in attendance. Lance also got swept up in the novelty of serving sophisticated libations. They went overboard stocking their cart in the package store, gathering scotch, peppermint schnapps, triple sec, vodka, grain alcohol and Banana Snowshake mix. It added up to $297. Lance groaned. Charles Boyd started putting back half of it. Margaret, who would bartend, insisted she needed it all and chipped in with a hundred bucks.

Lance and Charles Boyd carried in boxes of booze, then jumbo sketch tablets, watercolor sets, Magic Markers, colored pencils and deluxe boxes of crayons, while Margaret planted two tiki torches in the grass just beyond the patio. She set up two card tables with a picnic cloth to serve as a bar. Then she changed into her bartender outfit, a Playboy Bunny costume. She wore it every Halloween. The fishnet stockings and cottontail were flattering, but the cups were too big and they caved toward her chest like clam shells.

In his room Lance donned his own party outfit, one of two matching burgundy velvet smoking jackets he and Charles Boyd had bought from a secondhand store. It smelled like hay and was a bit small, his wrists showing from the sleeves, but it had a debonair effect nonetheless. Charles Boyd walked in wearing tuxedo pants and his own smoker, which complemented his new slicked Kingston Trio hair. A cigarette hung leisurely from his mouth.

"Are you ready for this tonight?" Charles Boyd asked, gleeful, rubbing his hands together. Now the whole thing was his wonderful idea.

"I am ready for anything, baby." Lance smoothed the lapels of his jacket.

In a casual, yet secretive voice Charles Boyd asked, "Did we invite Sandra Stoppard?"

"Yes we did," Lance lowered his voice. "Is Margaret not enough for you these days, champ?" Suddenly Boyd had delusions he was Warren Beatty.

Charles Boyd grinned and play-punched Lance in the arm.

Lance attached a JUDGE tag to his lapel, after struggling mightily with the safety pin. He handed the matching tag to Charles Boyd, who frowned and tossed it into the garbage. "I'm not wearing that. It looks ridiculous."

"Lance, Lance. Come here, quickly," Margaret called, waving her arms and standing at the makeshift bar. "Drink this! Drink this!" Lance took a plastic cup with dark liquid. He drank the awful stuff, a firewater explosion singeing his throat. "Oh, no. Not that one," she said. "I wanted you to drink this. Sorry." She handed him another cup. This one had green, candy-smelling fluid. It tasted like toothpaste. Lance smacked his lips and felt popping sensations across his scalp. "OK, now try this and tell me if it's better," she said, handing him another cup.

"What are you trying to do to me?"

"I'm perfecting my Peppermint Rickey."

Lance swallowed another cup and tried to discern the ingredients. "The first one was better."

"Nope. I put in too much crème de menthe in the first one."

Lance shrugged in surrender. She sipped something frothy which left a mustache above her lip. "Mmm. Very yummy." She knocked over a steel shaker, popped a strawberry into her mouth and said something to herself. Her bunny ears shifted and became crooked.

Twilight was fading into evening. He opened the sliding door and stepped out to the patio. He sensed a vague though pleasant intoxication. He lit the tiki torches, the burning citronella oil mixing with the pleasant autumn smell of the wet ground. The air felt bracing and good. He gazed at the austere patios of another building. It was quiet and he felt tranquil in a remote way. He resolved to put anxiety regarding his future aside and enjoy the evening. In his jacket pocket he found a yellowed strip of paper, a fortune that read: You are the master of every situation. He said aloud, "Yes I am."

He turned around to go inside and the apartment was packed with a throng of girls. They swirled around the bar as Margaret handed them cups. Inside, Charles Boyd said sourly to Lance, "It seems Margaret invited every cheesy sorority sister she has."

These girls were ripping out sheets of paper and laughing and spilling their drinks on the floor. Lance met several, but forgot their names as soon as they said them. They all looked alike in a Banana Republic leather jacket meets pastel Lycra skirt kinda way, each with long frizzy hair, cowboy boots and the same vocal pitch. One of them put a tape into the stereo, banal rock music that was no longer popular, turning the song up to a shattering volume. Charles Boyd moved from the far edge of the room, waving his arms. He ejected the tape and tossed it on the ground. Lance got a beer in the kitchen. He surveyed the partygoers. He nibbled on a chicken wing; a needle of spice stuck in his throat, watering his eyes. The nuclear hot sauce—whose decision had this been?—burned his lips and he swigged beer, splashing it over his lips with his tongue. He rubbed his mouth with his hand, then was blinded by the flash of an Instamatic camera.

Lance waited for golden suns dangling in front of his eyes to subside, to find Norton Skinner holding the camera, in a tan corduroy jacket and brown knit tie.

"You'll never guess what I'm gonna to be doing." Skinner puffed out his chest and put his hands on his hips.

"You'll be performing the Russian dynamite trick later on."

"No, man." Skinner dug into the pocket of his khakis and pulled out a ring box. A tiny diamond on a single gold band. "My sweetie is going to be in town next week. Anna. I'm going for broke, man."

"What about that other girl, the other one you were engaged to?"

"That was all wrong. This one is the one for life. As soon as she says yes, we're doing the ceremony." A semicircle of girls now surrounded Skinner, drawn to the shimmering contents of the ring box. He recounted to them his relational history with what's her name and how he'd worked as a roadie for Anthrax on their summer tour to afford the rock, how after an extensive prayer vigil he'd determined it was time.

Shut out by the box onlookers, Lance said, "We need to talk about this," before moving on.

A fresh swell of people crowded the apartment, covering every surface of the giant couch. Retro Brit rock buzzed through the stereo speakers. People had taped sheets to the wall and were using crayons and watercolors. Artists shouted things Lance couldn't make out; he gave the thumbs up to their crappy scribbling and yelled encouragement. Margaret was pouring straight liquor into cups, holding pouring spouts over people's mouths. Her hands fumbling, she babbled in a high pitched staccato. Lance's bedroom door was open. The activity in there worried him briefly, but the party needed space to expand and these people were all friends, or at least he kinda knew these people and they had come to the party so it was like they were friends. He finished another beer and shook someone's hand, saying something that escaped from his mouth before he knew what he was saying. A weird, chaotic elation ran through him. He wobbled like a jellyfish. The room convulsed with flashes of white paper, brilliant Magic Marker designs, running watercolors, plastic cups draining caramel liquid into mouths, hugs, a kitchen group using a length of tube and a funnel to inject beer directly into their stomachs—regular drinking took too long. A tangle of dancers gyrated and circulated within a small contained area, a cute girl being lifted in the air in a quasi-Heimlich maneuver. A guy and a girl sat on top of Charles Boyd on the couch and tickled him.

Lance pointed at a circle of people on the floor working around the crate coffee table and then tapped his name tag. He shouted, "I'm the Judge, you people! Ho ha-ha!" and one guy looked up at Lance strangely. Someone tugged at the back of Lance's jacket. He turned to find a guy with stringy blonde hair in a black satin concert jacket. A beer was tucked into his jacket pocket, full drink in hand. Rodney, the doomed rocker from next door, who said, "Did you hear about the shooting?"

"Huh?"

"The shooting two nights ago. A guy was shot dead at building five." A terrible acne pockmarked Rodney's face.

"You don't say," Lance said with disinterest.

Lance recognized Rodney's partner in fashion, Alice, over by the bar, negotiating for some straight up Wild Turkey.

"I saw him afterward. Blood was runnin' all over the pavement."

Alice came to Rodney's side. "Didn't you hear it? It was a drug shootout." She was slurring and her tone was boastful.

"I guess I missed it," Lance said. He was tempted to evict these two.

"Lance! Lance!" Margaret was screaming his name. She

had been yelling for a while. Hetrick Curtain, the tan pool guy, was standing next to the bar holding a drink. The tiki torches and the stereo were attracting Widger Arms people like moths. Curtain wore an untucked red batik shirt, black tennis shorts and sandals which seemed made out of tire treads. Beads of moisture dotted his scalp. Curtain introduced himself, shaking Lance's hand with a fleshy palm, holding his hand sideways. "Margaret, let me say this Delmonico is the absolute tops." He made a barking sound. He stooped a bit, looking at Lance out of the corner of his eye. "She tells me you have written a screenplay. Tell me about the project. Do you have backing yet?"

Margaret gave Lance a hopeful, encouraging look.

"I cowrote it with a friend of mine. I think it's pretty awful."

Curtain faced Lance. Bifocal strips on the lenses of his glasses contorted his dark eyes. "Do not, I repeat, do not let this coauthor sell it behind your back."

"I don't think—"

"Give me a synopsis. Hold on. The first rule is to trust no one. Who the heck am I anyway?" Curtain explained he taught at the journalism school. He'd worked for the *Miami Herald* for years, he said, rolling his eyes like there was something indecent or infuriating about this institution. He had several screenplays in development with his people in the movie business. Screenplays jumped around like foster children, he explained, and then, in the right hands—whammo! payday! Lance hooted and touched drinks with Hetrick Curtain, like he was waiting for a similar mythical payday.

"I write the serious stuff too," Curtain said. "More serious than you could imagine. Enough to zoom right over the heads of English-lit types." He wrote commercial novels as well. He had penned a catalog of action books that he had yet to publish. One was *A Genius for Torture*, about a sadistic KGB master spy who defected to the West and worked under the direction of the Joint Chiefs of Staff. Another was *Killer Trident*, about a deadly bacteria spawn that induced psychopathic behavior and infected the crew of a Trident nuclear submarine. Lance tried to keep up, these plots hurtling through his head. He was thankful when Curtain turned back toward the bar for another Delmonico.

The letter! Lance remembered Ian LaCoss's letter, and patted his jacket to locate it. LaCoss had sent two letters, one Lance had already read and one sealed with the instruction: "To be read aloud to the guests of the first party in your apartment." LaCoss, bless him, understood the importance of this milestone.

In the first letter, LaCoss described working as a roofer in L.A. alongside Mexican coworkers, climbing aluminum ladders to the vaunted roofs of the Hollywood Hills. He sounded ecstatic to be a working man, or, as he described it, "an honest laborer making an honest wage." He'd shaved his head clean. He'd given away most of his possessions. "I realized, did I need all this stuff?" Shirtless all day, tearing tiles from roofs, he drank artesian water and was cleansing himself with each shower of sweat, erasing the fallacies of the ivory tower. And celibacy—the mental clarity cultivated was amazing! The exhausting work and exposure to sun and air had connected him to a "primal serenity," as he put it. "You'll never guess whose roof I just finished," he wrote. "Gina Lollobrigida! All day I look over the roofs and pools of the moguls and stars, into the city and beyond. Above them all! I'll share their view in few years, if I don't get skin cancer first. Ha!"

Finding a milk crate, Lance stepped on top of it. He motioned for the stereo to be turned down. "Could I have everyone's attention, please? Hello!" Lance smiled, holding the second letter in the air. He waved his arms. He waited for heads to turn to him, then opened the letter and skimmed LaCoss's handwriting. Voices still came from the bedrooms, but Lance started anyway. "I have here a letter from Ian LaCoss in California, who we all know. I'll read it."

Dear Langford Friends,

I am well in the entertainment capital of the world. With the tuition money I've saved I've purchased a Lincoln Continental. Not! OK, serious stuff. My three years were great and I miss you guys. The other morning I realized something. It was my first thought upon waking. The thought was waiting for me, like someone had planted it in my brain. The thought was this: Not one person actually knows anything. I include myself in this. Let me explain.

We are surrounded by modern complication. Our cars, our satellite communication, our databases, widespread use of aerosols. We have theories and categories up the wazoo. People sit in offices all day. But what does all this actually add up to? Nothing. Think you've figured it all out? You're deluded. We haven't changed in the last thousand years. In the shower, water feels a certain way against your skin. When you're in love, it's the best. Hearing a great song can be better than sex. Take off your shirt and the sun warms your skin, burning it after too long.

So take all your theories and throw them out the window. Is this a bad thing? If you accept it, it's good. So don't forget it, you naked hairy know-nothing people, or your lives will be unhappy.

Your loyal friend,
Ian

"That's it," Lance said. A second of quiet followed, a beat. Lance looked out at the faces, absorbing the letter himself. The message was odd, though sincere, in a LaCossian way. Open laughter broke out near the door. Several faces near him twisted with sarcasm and silent indignation. Two girls hissed; one tried to quiet the other when Lance looked at them. Low-grade conversations restarted, like nothing had happened.

Lance stepped off the milk crate, pissed off, wondering if

he had done justice to the letter. You'd think at his own party people could have at least said nothing. Margaret was absent from the bar and blitzed people jostled against the card tables, mixing their own. He felt like a sheriff as people asked about the contest. The art contest had given people license to rearrange the place and mark up the walls. Near the bathroom, the wall was being painted with acrylic paints—they'd brought their own supplies! Life-size likenesses of himself and Charles Boyd wearing tuxedos, these wretched and cartoonish likenesses. An off-center mandala of Magic Marker colors was on the wall next to a closet. An elaborate psychedelic mural of a Viking babe was going up in Charles Boyd's bedroom. Lance was speechless, a sick wooziness consuming him. A rumor had circulated that the object of the party was to decorate the walls. How embarrassing, how stupid. The people they had invited had been nitwits enough to believe this. He wanted the vandals to leave.

Two girls stopped Lance by the couch. Their round faces bobbed toward him. "That's really great you're going to work for the State Department," one said. The other one said, "My brother-in-law wants to do that also."

"It's my roommate. He's the State Department guy."

"Oops. What are you doing next year then?"

He couldn't think fast enough to deflect the question. "I don't know."

"You are a senior, aren't you?"

"Yes. I am." Langford girls could be so linear, so careerist and demanding with their expectations. Always with expectations. The two girls waited politely, but their eyes betrayed them. A senior without plans was a waster of money, a rudderless and vacillating personality. A loser.

Lance found Charles Boyd talking in the kitchen, gesturing with his hands over his head, likely recounting his latest triumph—his high marks from the Foreign Service interview panel, leaving only the Final Review between him and his ultimate goal. He would be high on the rank order list and get his area preference. Frederick Rich, in a black turtleneck, and Chip Grassley, in a khaki army shirt, both part of the Langford radical fringe, stood as acolytes, admiring Boyd's train of thought. Lance opened the last beer from the sink, taking blithe, absentminded sips—no point to it really, other than continuing the slog to his gray destination. Frederick Rich took a deep tug on a fresh joint. He held it toward Charles Boyd, who extended his hand to accept.

"What are you doing?" Lance asked with exasperation.

"What does it look like?"

"You've got drug screening coming up!" Also, the Background Investigation process was underway at that very moment, determining Boyd's character and suitability for a security clearance.

"Who are you, his mom?" Grassley said.

"Who are you, an asshole?" Lance stared down Grassley, feeling dangerous and ragged. Grassley blinked back, acting wounded.

Charles Boyd finally took the joint and reached into his pocket for a relight. Lance slapped the twisty out of his roommate's hand, this swipe focusing his anger: Boyd was so contemptuous, so maddeningly confident about his future, he did things like turning his nose up at academic honors, and insulting party guests, and trying to burn the American flag in a public spectacle after a long episode of drug abuse and psychologically erratic behavior. And he would get away with it all! His talented brain would cover him every time. The world was presenting him with a platter of delicacies while he sneered and gave it the finger.

Charles Boyd glared back, his eyes flaring with rage. He erupted, taking a clumsy swing which grazed Lance's shoulder. Lance, with gritted teeth, grabbed his roommate by the lapels and drove him backward, clunking him hard against the wall, ready to pummel him. Charles Boyd thrashed and snarled. With blood swelling in his cheeks, he hissed, "The rejections you've gotten aren't my fault. They're your fault!" He snaked a hand onto Lance's neck, a claw hold. Lance slammed Boyd's shoulders and head against the wall, harder, as breathing became difficult. Guests rushed toward the kitchen to see the guys in matching burgundy smoking jackets fighting. Hetrick Curtain picked the joint up off the carpet and pocketed it. Lance and Charles Boyd, their faces turning bright red, quickly became exhausted. They each let go. Margaret rushed into the kitchen as redness drained from their faces. They stood, breathing hard. Charles Boyd smiled, like it had all been playacting. He brushed his lapels. Lance mugged like he was about to attack again and laughed, though he still wanted to punch Boyd.

"What about the art contest?" several guests asked, waving colored bits of paper. "When will the judging take place?"

"We were just conferring about that," Lance said with crazed effusiveness. "The judging will be right now!"

"I'll be the judge of that," Charles Boyd cracked, still doing his jolly person impression. The bleary-eyed people standing around holding cups didn't seem to be buying it.

Lance looked around at swatches of art. "What looks good to you?" he quietly asked Margaret, hoping for some help. She shrugged. Charles Boyd, officiating like an insane mayor, made a big show of examining the wall murals. Lance held up a charcoal landscape. "The winner! Right here! Someone named Tracy has won! Congratulations!" As echoes of disappointment and mild protest sounded, no one came forward. Tracy had left hours ago, someone reported. The winner has to be present! they were all shouting at Lance, from every side. Has to be present! they yelled, these people wired from beer, liquor, high-energy dancing, the tension of artistic creation, Tabasco sauce, and other stuff they'd discreetly inhaled or swallowed.

Charles Boyd slunk away from the crowd which had locked around Lance, his eyes wide. Lance tore through the entries again, choosing a watercolor of the Langford Bell Tower he recognized that a plump girl, one of the louder shouters, had been clutching. "New winner!"

"What do I get? What's the grand prize?" the girl wanted to know.

Lance drew a breath. His eyes searched over the heads of the mob to find Charles Boyd leaning against the wall. They exchanged looks of sudden recognition and shock: they had neglected to buy a grand prize.

"The grand prize," Lance lowered his voice, "will be awarded in a few days." The crowd surged a step, their hard voices biting from every side and growing into a cacophony. Angry red faces bobbed all around.

"Here it is! Here's your prize." Charles Boyd held the VCR over his head—technically Lance's, though it was old and unreliable—a wire trailing down to his head and the electric cord swinging by his arm. This offer of tribute turned the angry heads. Boyd's presentation of the VCR to the girl and her inspection of it seemed to placate the remaining partygoers. People checked their watches and headed for the door. The stereo was turned down.

Lance shut the bathroom door and had a long pee, gratefully alone. He tried not to look at or smell the vomit in the shower. A persistent despair clouded his mind. He considered the party. It had seemed wonderful for a few boisterous minutes. This had been false; it had been terrible, awful. Nothing uplifting or unique about the party. The usual low-rent degeneracy Langfordites favored, the standard drinking, gossiping, lusting and vomiting, all done on Lance's limited tab. Part of him—a weak and delusional part—had held out hope Lynn Van Oster would show up, without an invitation. That she would want to see his place and her wholesome face would appear, exuding humanitarian concern and a longing for him. Or maybe Veronica Boyer's face would suddenly stand out, the pale temptress stalking the edges of the crowd until she sidled up to him and said something coy and snappy. Another part of him was relieved neither had discovered him in his muddled state of decline.

Opening the bathroom door, a smoky, cloying odor greeted him. Smoke filled the hallway. A moody, nameless rock song played. Then, a vision so warped it seemed like fantasy: Rodney, the doomed rocker, had shed his concert jacket and now stood bare-chested, in obscenely tight jeans, on the coffee table crate. He was spinning a lit tiki torch, majorette-style, like a fiery wheel of death, the flame licking the ceiling and leaving a black streak on each pass. Doing a sassy lip-sync of the vocals, each flick at the ceiling was syncopated with the beat.

Hetrick Curtain and Margaret were near Rodney, cringing and holding their hands up defensively. Charles Boyd got there before Lance could, grabbing the torch from Rodney's hands. Rodney held on and the crate beneath him tilted, then shifted and cracked, shooting his legs to the side. He landed in a horizontal position, flattening wreckage beneath him. Outside, Charles Boyd extinguished the torch in damp earth. Alice gathered Rodney from the floor and propped him up. A red crack opened on his forehead and blood dripped onto the carpet. As she dragged him out the door, Alice promised there would be a lawsuit. She had a thirty-dollar bottle of Absolut tucked under her free arm.

In a post-party daze, Lance picked up cigarette butts. The carpet was nicked with acrylic colors and marshes of spilled liquid. Sticky cups and bottles lined the floorboards. A back cushion from the couch was unaccounted for. Traces of cigarette and armpit odor lingered in Lance's bedroom in a ghostly vortex. His loose change jar (containing forty quarters and numerous smaller coins) and his beloved Bauhaus bootleg tape were missing.

Charles Boyd and Margaret were locked in a venomous argument in the kitchen. Loud enough to interest cops. Margaret held onto the refrigerator handle, her knees bent, her neck veins tweaked, as she slapped bunny ears against her leg and chewed out Boyd for flirting with Sandra Stoppard by showing her his coins of the world collection. Charles Boyd, hands braced on his hips, leaned into Margaret's face, yelling, as if testing his lung capacity with the force of each word, "I SHOW EVERYONE MY LAME WORLD COINS!" Unnerved, Lance put a finger in each ear and backed off from the kitchen, making slow circles. They reached a crescendo, their voices overlapping like argument opera, and Margaret burst into tears and hustled out the front door in her bunny costume. Charles Boyd called her a total bitch. Then, suddenly apologetic, he ran after her.

All this would have been fine if Lance could think for just one moment. He lay on the couch, placing his head down gently. What he wanted, more than anything he had wanted in a long time, was to think clearly, to concentrate and figure out what to do with his life. He feared if he didn't do so right then, and unless something changed, he would be stuck in his dingy apartment forever and would die there, an old man, broken and bitter. He would be penniless, riddled with tumors and hideous lesions, the subject of horrified whispers by his college classmates. He was in no shape for this kind of concentration, however. A watery sensation nagged him, blurring the edges of his vision. His mouth was dry. A pinching and throbbing against his forehead plagued him, like hammer blows with every heartbeat. His thoughts spun off in a disconnected fashion, like a tiny wobbling gyroscope behind his eyes. He prayed for a return to clarity.

He noticed radio station music playing on the stereo. The sound froze him. It invaded his ears, his being, in a way never before experienced. The unyielding pulse of sounds and voices filled him with dread. The song's lyrics were pointless. On a Saturday night…yeah, baby…gonna be all right…The cheesy melody and generic guitar solo were physically jarring. A wall of audio garbage. But this band was hugely popular and had appeared on recent magazine covers. Their albums flooded the nation. Teen girls wept at the sight of them. Their haircuts and fashion touches were being widely mimicked. They were ubiquitous and considered highly cool. He was in the wrong, in a minority. He was a roundly rejected guy with a paltry GPA, with no girlfriend, in a crappy apartment, wearing a thirty- year-old smoking jacket which was too small and reeked of mothballs, which meant he was …uncool? Or maybe the crowd had it wrong. He sensed they did. Maybe their collective clamoring had destroyed what once was cool. Too many people in a room sucked out all the oxygen, but one person in a room, well, nobody wanted that either. That was lonely. The more he analyzed it, the murkier it became. To consider it was to disintegrate it. Maybe those who truly possessed cool never talked of it or even considered it, like Zen.

This relation to others, the mob factor which had once made the designation attractive, now made it unattractive. Maybe it had all been a colossal waste of effort. But what of the cool things he loved—the music, the movies, the dance moves? All the things that had lifted him up and made him feel special. It saddened him to abandon them. That didn't seem necessary.

It was hard enough to just be himself. He was whatever the hell he was.

He clicked a button and to his relief, the noise went away. He closed his eyes and exhaled. Now he could think. He sensed something circling his mind, a crucial bit of intuition. He rolled to his feet and stood, unsteady at first. This minor bit of momentum gave him hope. He gazed around inside his bedroom, suddenly wired, restless. He noticed paper. Piles of paper on his desk, beside his desk, in boxes. He rifled through the stacks, curious about all these sheets. There were syllabuses, suggested reading lists, course catalogs, clinical study extracts, old issues of the *Langford Owl*, illegible loose-leaf notes from freshman year, wire-bound notebooks with hieroglyphic diagrams, a rough draft of his Crimean War term paper, announcements, academic guidelines, handouts, Xeroxes, carbon copies...The excrement of his educational experience. It tired him just to look at them. The papers seemed to be clogging him, obscuring his way, as if each sheet still demanded attention and was leeching his energy.

He gathered up an armload of papers. He left the front door open and climbed the metal steps to the world above, to a parking lot in shadow. He heard wind shaking and dislodging leaves from the tops of trees. Cold air prickled his arms. He walked toward the corner of building nine, to the Dumpster. The muscles of his arms and shoulders strained. He flung the armload over his head into the metal Dumpster in an exhilarating heave—haaaho!—papers whistling and banging against the hollow bottom.

Gathering up the next load in his arms, a slim hardback slid out from between stacks of Xeroxes and hit the floor. Theodore Ivan Langford peered up indignantly from the cover of *From Ignobility to Glory*. The thought of bespectacled Theodore Ivan upended among Dumpster rot saddened Lance for a moment. Then he set it on top of his stack. He'd toss that kook's vanity scribblings and be done with them too. He took a running approach, twisting and slinging his armload into the air. The load gonged against the inside of the receptacle. Unburdened, Lance spread his arms gloriously and tilted his head back. He gathered up the final stack. With tired arms and a sore back he made the last trek. Before he reached the Dumpster, the load shifted and a mass of paper bound with rubber bands hit the pavement. He tossed his armload and stooped for what he'd dropped.

In a slash of light from an insomniac's window in building nine, he made out words on the top sheet in the bundle: *The Man Who Would Be the King*, the screenplay he had coauthored. The heft of this bundle cried out to be flung, to be liberated and forgotten. He flicked the manuscript's edge with his thumb. He ran his finger over the title and recalled all the work he'd put into it. He walked back with the screenplay in his hands. The title page reminded him of its unexpected arrival in the mail in the summer of 1987, during the pinnacle of the Lynn Van Oster era and his salad days at Patterson French. That magic time. That summer when each day had the promise of a bright future, when the smooth tendrils of love were a phone call away. Or maybe that was revisionist crap.

He sat on the floor and spread out pages, an appreciation of the crazy veerings and tangents of the screenplay surging within him. He felt a responsibility for the protagonist, Wyatt Burris, the fated Elvis impersonator. It occurred to Lance—with shocking clarity, with obviousness—that he and LaCoss had gotten it wrong. They had missed poor Wyatt Burris altogether. It was all wrong that Wyatt Burris wanted to replace his famous twin. It was a delusion. The only proper ending was the guy realizing this and moving on with some kind of real life, with his own life. He wasn't cut out to be a performer. That was why he and LaCoss could never end the thing properly.

He whooped, celebrating this bolt of inspiration. Energized, he started arranging scenes and imagining how to cut and fill holes in the narrative. He made notes on the back of a page. After an hour he flicked on his Macintosh and started typing. He rewrote old scenes, new scenes scrolling through his head with remarkable vividness. His fingers were in constant motion. Alcohol leached from his pores, his brain working with razor clarity. His stomach cried for food; he ignored it. Had he ever worked more steadily, more wholeheartedly at anything? That morning, around 8:00 a.m., Charles Boyd and Margaret walked in, hungover. They peered through the open door as Lance slurped coffee and banged away at his keyboard. He waved over his shoulder.

By that afternoon a profound confidence in his creation overtook him. That evening Lance fell to his floor-bound mattress with his party clothes still on and slept solidly, satisfied the new *Man* was worthy. He pictured scenes flashing twenty feet high on a big screen. *The Man* was now imbued with magic. It seemed like an answer to his future, reason for a crusade. Oh, sweet passion!

Late the next day he awoke. He decided he would show Hetrick Curtain his creation. He'd need some guidance in order to sell it. At the leasing office, they frowned and shook their heads at mention of Curtain's name, though they gave his apartment number.

Curtain opened the door wearing a black kimono with red stitching. Without glasses, his eyes were goofy and sensitive. A half-mane of peppered hair hung to his shoulders.

"I'd like your opinion of my screenplay," Lance said, holding up a red floppy disk.

Curtain looked at the disk carefully, like it was a rare artifact. Then he invited Lance in. Lance had expected a typewriter set up at an altar, or diagrams of Russian subs on the wall, or to find the guy smoking opium. Instead, the walls were bare except for a primitive object that looked like a tomahawk. A flat, little Asian-type couch against one wall and a matching side table. The place smelled of spices, like an Indian restaurant. A portable typewriter was on a kitchenette table out on his porch. Lance sat on the couch and Curtain brought out a red plastic chair to sit on. He rubbed his photosensitive glasses with a cloth. "That was one hell of a wing ding the other evening." Curtain whistled appreciatively.

"Thanks. It seemed to go fairly well." It had been a fine party, Lance thought, perhaps underrated.

Curtain squeezed sinus spray into each nostril, then opened a box of foreign-looking skinny brown cigarettes, putting one between his lips. He paused, closing his eyes, as if remembering the whereabouts of his lighter. There were problems with several of Curtain's toenails. They were yellowed and opaque.

"So you know people in Hollywood?" Lance asked, feeling a sudden skepticism.

"I know people all over." Curtain took a deep breath,

becoming thoughtful and distant. He laughed suddenly. "Not that it's done me a damn bit of good. I sense you've just completed a powerful rewrite." Curtain nodded toward the disk.

"I have. I just revamped the whole thing." Lance felt a great pride. He leaned forward and rubbed his hands together.

Curtain pointed with two fingers, holding his lit cigarette. "Good, man. Sometimes you've got to rip the guts out. That takes courage." He pulled out some drawers of the side table and then gave Lance a faded hardback book. *Screenplay Mechanics and Aesthetics*. They chatted about movies, about books and Langford. Curtain spoke of his Southeast Asian travels, about meeting Fidel Castro in the sixties. It was captivating stuff, Lance envious of these worldly stories. He thought: Here we are, two writers hanging out. Lance had thought Curtain was about to go teach a class, or about to eat lunch or about to do something. But he was in no rush. He seemed glad for company. A phone call pulled Curtain into the kitchen. He spoke in low, inaudible tones.

Curtain promised to look at the screenplay within a day or so. He let Lance keep the *Screenplay Mechanics* book. They shook hands briskly.

In the following days Lance reflected on the coincidences of nearly throwing the original *The Man Who Would Be the King* away, of Hetrick Curtain showing up at the party. He became convinced fate had called. *The Man* would be his horse and he would ride it to glory. Lance smiled grandly, the assurance that comes with grand purpose making him generous. Charles Boyd kept asking him, "What is so funny?" Margaret wanted to know if he had met a girl. He told them about his rewrite, about how destiny had called and the screenplay was finally ready. "I'm going all the way with it," Lance said, smacking his hands together. "All the way, baby!"

After four days Lance could stand it no more. He went over

to Hetrick Curtain's apartment in building three to get Curtain's opinion. Two black men were taking furniture out the front door. They shuffled past Lance with a battered desk. Inside, Lance looked around at blank walls.

"What's going on? Where's Hetrick Curtain?" Lance asked.

"Your friend has been evicted. If you see him, tell him he owes four months' rent. He didn't leave much behind. Mostly coat hangers."

The leasing office people didn't know where Curtain had gone. He had moved out in the night and never turned in his keys. Since losing his job at Langford two years ago he'd been a problem tenant. The FBI had phoned the leasing people to ask questions about Curtain six months ago. Walking back to his apartment, the whole business seemed puzzling to Lance, though not unsolvable. The guy had promised to get back to Lance. Curtain seemed decent enough, even if he was broke. It was disappointing, though not necessarily disastrous.

At the apartment Charles Boyd was watching television, transfixed. There was a great commotion of people on the screen and excited narration from a reporter. Lance sat on the opposite side of the great couch.

"You're not going to believe this one," Lance said. He explained the whole thing, using a light, ironic tone. Boyd's eyes shifted between Lance and the set.

"Oh, Jesus! That's the worst thing I've ever heard," Charles Boyd said, holding his forehead as if he'd been told a close friend had died. "At least you've got other copies of the thing."

Lance's mouth went dry. His eyes glazed. "Uh-oh. I didn't make any copies."

Boyd's jaw dropped. "Then you're screwed. That guy is probably on a plane to California right now. How could you possibly trust that dude?"

The question illustrated Lance's colossal ineptitude so precisely he couldn't answer. There was no answer. The screenplay was forever gone (he'd thrown away the marked-up hard copy he'd worked from). He hadn't even grasped the full nature of the tragedy on his own. He had been stupid enough to give the sole copy of his screen gem to a fast-talking stranger. A burning sensation burrowed at the bottom of his windpipe. He gazed off to the ceiling and its familiar landscape and fought waves of nausea and dizziness. He knew he had done dumb things in the past, had used poor judgment and had poorly executed things; but this particular reversal of something he had poured his soul into seemed so cruel and out of proportion to his ineptitude, it had the makings of a curse or divine disfavor. His spine seemed fused. Couch fabric scratched the skin at his elbows and neck, but he was unable to move. He felt deranged. His mind was wiped blank, part of him fearing that if he did think, the thought he would never recover would be so persistent and crushing it would become true, and his life, his shot at any happiness or competence in any career, would be ruined. So he tried not to think.

For some unknown reason, he stood. Or he found himself standing. His arms stretched over his head, his fists pulling and elongating his body, his torso stiff. This stretching felt good, then it felt awful. He seemed to lift, as if another force were pulling him by the wrists. He sensed an instability, a precariousness as he wavered, tottered, and became short of breath, the nicks in his superstructure widening, becoming gaping—the thousand cracks in his support pillars, from the ubiquitous numbers and the million deadlines, from his failures and misdirected efforts, and from the girls, the smiling girls with their impossible expectations, the indecipherable girls with their tiny chisels and hammers, hungry for soft tissue, and their constant invasive mindreading. He winced, his muscles taut, so taut they seemed hardened, until at last they gave. His arms fell to his sides like toppled columns. His knees weakened, but held.

In the vacuum of his clean-scoured mind, his eyes darted around for relief. Some diversion or reason for hope. He noticed people screaming on the television, shouting, crying and celebrating. Bundled people in a cold climate waved flags and hugged each other and danced. They whacked picks and sledgehammers against a graffiti-strewn wall.

"What's going on here?" Lance asked.

"The Berlin Wall is coming down. The Cold War is over. And we won." Charles Boyd crossed his arms. He smirked with the satisfaction of someone who had expected this all along. Which he had.

It was shocking, this crumbling of the Soviet empire. It was less likely that warheads would be falling on them. Reason to breathe easier. Somewhere high above him, a vast peaceful space opened in the sky. He was happy for the East Germans, born on the wrong side of the line. They were free, which he had always wished for them. This mere fact of freedom, just the raw promise of liberty, was driving them to hysteria. It was refreshing.

"Maybe you could track that guy down," Charles Boyd suggested.

"Huh?"

"Curtain, the guy who stole your screenplay. Maybe you could track him down."

Lance latched onto the idea, considering it seriously. So seriously his mind attacked the idea from all angles until what remained was a raging absurdity. Tracking Hetrick Curtain, the fugitive, the raving lunatic, through cheap hotels, on the lookout for his bald pate and the smell of curry. It was ridiculous, a B-movie plot. Lance laughed—a raw, possessed laugh that made his insides ache. The laugh continued, gathering force until his voice drowned out the television. A nervous electricity tweaked his arms and legs. So much of his struggle became absurd.

Charles Boyd half-smiled, seeming disturbed and baffled. "How is that so funny? If he ever did make it into a movie, you could always sue him."

This was more ridiculous, the idea Hetrick Curtain would succeed at anything. And still more absurd, this Perry Mason court battle. "I'll hire the best legal guns!" Lance shouted. "I'll unleash a torrent of litigation! A torrent! There will be hell to pay!" His possessed laughter filled the spaces between his words. By the time his laughing, hopping and panting had ceased, he stood before the television. Charles Boyd tried to look around him, irritated, waving for him to move.

Lance looked at him quizzically. Then for maximum disruption, he switched the set off.

CHAPTER EIGHTEEN

A NEW AND POWERFUL DRUG

L ance opened his eyes and stared up at a new day. Then he rolled off his floor-bound mattress. A jujitsu reverse roll that flung his feet and knees above and over his shoulder. He had the correct dexterity for this maneuver on this morning and landed solidly on his feet. He pulled on a pair of boxers—his lucky hooked game fish boxers—and opened the door to his bedroom.

He gazed across the living room to the sliding doors and the courtyard beyond. Silvery, fresh sunlight bathed the grass. He took in this unexpected beauty. On this day he sensed within himself a delicate and satisfying strain of mischief. An autonomous inner chunk that glowed solid and strong. Also, a molecular awareness of himself, as if he were a single atom, which, upon leaving his bedroom, would careen and collide however he wished with all the other atoms of the world so as to affect them and leave them scattered. He enjoyed this thought.

A rich coffee scent was in the air. He inhaled, noting the sensation inside his nostrils. He walked to the kitchen and found Margaret, with her back to him. She poured water in the coffeemaker. The hem of her Langford Coed Naked Lacrosse t-shirt rose as she lifted her arm, revealing beige underwear with a faint, metallic shimmer. She measured a precise amount of grounds and made a hmm sound. He observed her for thirty seconds.

She gasped and turned around, putting a hand to her chest. "I didn't know you were there." Surprised in a cheerful way.

"Sorry. I didn't mean to startle you." He stepped toward the sink, amused at his entrance.

She shook her head in a sorrowful way. "Oh, Lance. You poor thing. I heard about your screenplay. That is so awful. I would be so destroyed if something like that happened to me." Her words smelled of sympathy intended to make your own life seem better.

"Oh, come now." His tone was meant to comfort her. Lance stood a foot from Margaret, staring directly into her eyes. "The screenplay thing is a pure hobby. Probably a lucrative hobby, but I've got too much going for me professionally to take that seriously now. I've got some real decisions to consider career-wise."

"Such as?" She licked jelly off her fingers. Then she put her hands behind her on each side of the counter. Her full attention created a temptation.

He gestured as he talked, his hands filling the space between himself and Margaret. His hands mirrored each other, his fingers insistent and precise, hypnotic. "I interned with this huge outfit the summer before last, Patterson French International. Big-time consultants. Professionals to the professional. They were bought out by an even bigger concern, but the beautiful thing is that I've got mentors and people I've worked with all over now. A network. So the question is where I throw my hat." Lance sighed, these prospects weighing heavily on him.

"Networking. That is so crucial these days."

"And once you've got a network in place, it's like you've multiplied yourself by a factor of that many people."

"Sure. Consulting is so hot right now. That sounds like a great plan."

Lance nodded. It was all new to him. From Margaret's glowing gaze he gathered it was rather brilliant bullshit. There was a mild plausibility to the consultant thing, he supposed, because of the money, the sharp suits, the clever phone banter. Somebody might put in a good word for him. He might crawl under the door somewhere, like a bug. He might. But the stress involved, and being marooned in an office. And the bastards who yelled. Upon consideration it was unlikely, a remnant of past insanity. It no longer translated.

"I had no idea. I've never heard you talk about these things." Margaret stood on one foot, balancing. She held her hand before her mouth, smoothing her lip, as if she was trying to hide for a moment. She cleared her throat and narrowed her eyes. He reached around her, apologizing, to get a bottle of Vitamin C. Then he popped a thousand-milligram pill into his mouth. He stood at attention, offering his profile as he washed the horse pill down with water. He'd started a regimen of fifty pushups before bed and his shoulders were responding nicely.

They stood silent in a drowsy morning way, occupying the same kitchen space. Eyes level and unfocused, they gazed past each other. He noticed goose bumps on her bare arm. He considered Margaret's likes and dislikes, her talents, her weaknesses and blind spots. He liked her spirit, always had. Suddenly, he was intensely, madly curious about her. It was Thursday and Charles Boyd was out for teaching-assistant duties.

He stared at her until she pulled his eyes up to him.

"So," he said. "Tell me about the world of Margaret."

She straightened her neck, and picked up her coffee mug. She reached toward him with her free hand. "I am so frustrated with a professor. This stupid old man, Harnecker, in Sociology. He's really mad at my class and he's going to flunk all of us."

Lance nodded, thinking it was the most miniscule problem she would ever have. He lost track of himself, entirely focused on monitoring her reactions: her breathing, eyelashes, the quick changes of her hazel irises. He took her in, his curiosity overpowering. He wondered about the chemistry he'd sensed when he'd observed her, unguarded, that first night she walked through the door, about the mystery that always existed between people.

He listened to her talk about her life. They had always had a decent rapport, though today they were reaching more depth. She admitted her mother was a heavy drinker. Lance shared concern about this. Margaret made a joke about the guy who lived upstairs—the butcher, the mouth-breather. Lance, leaning against the counter, slid along and bumped her arm in a chummy way as he enjoyed her joke. Lance impersonated the butcher coming down the stairs and she laughed, bending forward and leaning against his elbow. He held her hand to help her balance. He was razzed by a startling bolt of energy, a spike of emotions. He decided to trust the moment.

He put his free hand on the small part of her waist, then pressed his lips to hers. He amazed himself. He was either observing a stand-in, or he had gotten way ahead of things. She absorbed the kiss, but with her hands up, defensive. Her eyes were frozen with awe, stunned by the corruption and illegality of the kiss. Her face was serious, as if, thoughts racing, she was being confronted by the direst of decisions. Then it softened, her lips sealing together into a playful look.

"Oh, my God. I can't believe it. Maybe I can," she said, gushing.

"I can't believe it either." He smiled. What was his intention now? Was it merely to rub noses with Margaret? In one sense, his curiosity was satisfied. Though as he gazed into her eyes, as her fingers traced a slow path along his arm, as they breathed each other's air, he found himself in another moment, a tender moment. He lacked preparation for this moment. But this newness and freedom was quite delicious. Their embrace had an inevitability to it, a call from fate, like it was a beginning in which Charles Boyd might become a footnote over time. The feeling was both unreal and too real.

"Oh, boy," Lance said, as they stepped back at the same time.

"What just happened?" she asked, taking a deep breath.

"You tell me." He was surprised he enjoyed this melodrama as much as he did. Lance felt mild guilt. Charles Boyd was a good friend, a valued friend, who probably loved Margaret. Then the guilt was gone. "Maybe we should just forget that happened," he said without conviction.

Leaning against the counter, she studied Lance playfully. "Some things are hard to forget," she said. Lance smiled at her. From her return smile, he could tell she had no intention of forgetting their kiss.

Protesters marched up Ivan Drive past the Bursar's Office behind a banner that said: WOMEN'S STUDIES NOW! They turned heads on a crisp and otherwise sleepy November day. The thirty ragtag people, mostly pasty-faced women, their clothing primarily black, made a slow procession up the street doing a chant Lance couldn't quite make out. Something about gender equality now. He paused on the sidewalk as they made their way up Ivan. A breeze smelling of leafy rot kicked up. Wearing a green British commando sweater, Lance dug his hands into his jeans pockets to warm them. Others stopped to watch the commotion. The protesters shuffled along, a few carrying difficult-to-read signs.

He remembered this group had been collecting petition signatures for several weeks to expand women's studies classes and make it a full department. The march was to deliver the petition to the Head Dean. He would have thought no more of them had he not spotted Veronica Boyer walking with this pack.

He focused on her, his pulse quickening. In a black leather jacket with a short, turned- up collar and a long dark wool skirt, she looked sleek, elegant. Her dark hair was a shade more auburn and seemed longer. It was pulled away from her face, her features sharp and beautiful in the chilled air. Her eyes bright. Something about being wrapped up in this cause, her stridency, made her vibrant as well. He strained to see as walkers shifted around her. Once the stragglers of the march—one of them a sign-carrier—had gone past, Lance stepped out into the street. Veronica's dark hair spilled over her collar and she wore boots with spiked heels. Her shape was so distinctive and familiar, even among this throng.

Standing in the middle of the street, Lance smiled. He got a charge out of seeing Veronica marching, her lips moving. He thought he could hear her voice. He imagined her role in organizing the march, what she had said to other marchers. Then there were things he knew about her the marchers would probably never guess. He watched the walkers move away a few more moments, then hurried to catch up with them. He overtook the stragglers and hustled up into the bulk of the female crusaders, then adjusted to their pace. The marchers either didn't notice or were indifferent to their new comrade. He caught his breath. The brisk walking felt good. A new chant started that he pretended he knew. Lance made his way up to Veronica and hovered behind her. Her legs rustled against her skirt. He tapped her back and said "Hey!" with an overly surprised tone. She smiled at him and answered with a coy hello, though her eyebrows reflected puzzlement.

"Imagine meeting you here today," he said, facing forward and swinging his arms.

"Imagine that."

Going up the hill toward the main Administration building, the group labored. The banner-carriers spread further apart to keep the long banner off the ground.

"Am I not welcome?" he asked, not being serious.

"All are welcome if they support our cause," she said dryly.

He flashed an enthusiastic thumbs up. "I'm a longtime equality supporter," he said, catching himself before tacking the word babe to this sentence.

The novelty of being next to Veronica Boyer in a feminist protest march was a thrill. Since their commune last year he'd only seen her once around campus, at a distance, and another time driving her car, Edgar. He didn't think she had seen him. A chant went up: Hey hey, ho ho, women's studies is the way to go! Lance started a hand clap as he chanted, trying to whip up the fervor. The group sounded bolder, tighter as they neared their destination. A few campus cops were posted at the entrance to Administration. The chant became punctuated with fists thrust in the air. Lance and Veronica, in unison, pumped their left fists forward. He remembered the propaganda under Veronica's bed, the Langford Amazon Society thing. He guessed he was walking with them right then, which made him an Amazon sympathizer, sort of an auxiliary Amazon. An Amazon for a day!

As the marching and fist-thrusting reached a rhythm, Lance put his arm around Veronica's shoulder in a spirit of protester solidarity. They strode several steps this way—Veronica not seeming to mind—then Lance bent to her ear, his nose tangling in her almond- scented hair, and said softly: "Hey, secret lover."

She stared toward the campus cops without blinking. He took his arm away and was rocked by another wild electrical spike of emotions: terror, excitement and perverse joy, this glorious sensation. He waited for her reaction. He thought he might have ruined things, that she might be horribly annoyed. She looked up at him with amusement, a trace of a smile, but also cautioning him to cool it. The group filed into the Administration building and took elevators to the fourth floor. A woman with a red beret presented the petition to the Dean's secretary and a *Langford Owl* photographer snapped a picture. Outside again, the protesters scattered.

"So, Mr. Lance," Veronica said, with her usual urbane composure. "On what day did you sign our petition?"

"Saturday? I'm pretty sure it was Saturday."

"Uh-huh." She knocked him in the chest with a play punch. He faked being in pain.

"Are you still living in the same digs?" he asked.

"Yes. I don't know for how long. Mrs. Perdue has been in and out of the hospital lately." She wet her lips with her tongue.

"I'm sorry to hear that."

She moved hair away from her face with a gloved hand, her defiant nose pointing into the air. The sublime joy of witnessing this gesture overwhelmed him. He felt he understood her in a way she didn't realize he did. His eyes fixed on her. He wanted to kiss her, wanted to melt in her little hands like a Popsicle. Their long separation seemed a natural thing. Beginnings, endings, middles…they were advanced enough to not be confined by these concepts.

"Her family has told me this is my last lease," Veronica continued. "I'll be in New York next year anyway."

"The state or the city?"

"Which do you think?" Her act broke down and a restrained smile came through. Her light green eyes seemed to study his face. They had so little time left, he thought. He could make the transition to a big city with a resourceful woman like her. She looked off and kept talking. "I have an offer from a commercial design firm. A boutique firm a friend of mine started a few years ago."

"You and those friends of yours."

"Are you mocking me?"

"Of course not. I'm one of those friends of yours. Though I have a different title." He leaned closer to her, glaring to get a reaction.

With crossed arms, she stared a moment at the tips of her boots. Her hair, the lack of jewelry, her approach—they were all different. She was already moving into the next phase. She'd be cutting-edge. She gazed at him with a lowered chin and withdrew into herself, like she was put out, but clearly she wasn't. In fact, the opposite.

"What about you? What about your future, young man?"

Spinning records with Veronica flashed through his mind. "What I'm thinking is possibly becoming an A&R rep for a record company," he said. "It seems like every time I turn around there's this hot new band I stumble across, so what better than to be paid for finding them?" His face lit up, his explanation growing more energetic until the idea peaked, slowed by the reality he'd never found a hot spot or hot band on his own, and a record company was more likely to give him a free promotional EP than a job. But why ruin a bright notion with bothersome facts?

Veronica listened with a consuming interest, rocking her hips slowly. She deemed him worthy. A month ago it would not have gone this way, but today he had the touch. She was concentrating to hold back, to keep a steady demeanor, but behind her eyes he sensed an oozing satisfaction, a blessing. He had crashed her event, behaved in a mocking fashion, flirted inappropriately and been presumptuous, and she loved it.

She peeked at her watch. "Oh, shit. I was supposed to be in class ten minutes ago." She straightened and took in a graceful breath which acted as a pause. She considered saying something.

"Say it to me," he said.

She furrowed her brow, not understanding.

"Say the words I want to hear," he said. "Repeat after me…secret…"

"Oh, please."

"…Lover."

She rolled her eyes, then held Lance's hand with both her hands. "Call me."

"I will."

He winked at her and was on his way.

Lance strolled through the lobby of the Student Union, intent on collecting his mail in the post office. Alerted by an extra sense, he paused, listening to the echo of chairs scraping the floor and the murmur of voices bouncing off hard surfaces. His eye was drawn to an aggregation of girls near the student programming window.

Lynn Van Oster was among these girls, leaning against a

wall in faded jeans, her legs propped at an angle under her. Lance's favorite jeans. The stonewashed ones that fit her just so. Her face was bright and relaxed, absorbing the comments of girls around her. The sparkle of her blonde hair created a light around her face: a beacon that singled her out. She waved goodbye to these friends and blurted something, confirming future plans. Her cheery mask drooped as they walked on. She pushed off from the wall. She combed a hand through her hair ends, then glanced at her hand, distracted, becoming lost in herself. She was smarting over a tragic documentary about the mistreatment of Native Americans, or lamenting the one kitten from her friend's litter who hadn't survived, or there had been a tiff with her mother. It was bringing her down. Her insecurities were right at the surface, pulling her toward self-loathing.

He knew this to be true of her, and knew that no one else would see it.

He moved toward her, sucked into her path. Her books were spread on a lunch table. As she was about to sit, she flared her nostrils and stared at him in a flat, forceful way—the way she usually did. A circle-the-wagons look, a stiff arm. But the idea of talking with her became an imperative, something he had to accomplish. Before he died and left the world, he had to receive the Lynn Van Oster shine one more time.

She reviewed a page in a notebook, head down, as he approached the neutral ground of her table. An excited burst went through him as he pulled out the opposite chair, an electrical twitch, which was strangely manic though assuring. A mad confidence. He had been experiencing this more often lately. It was like adjusting to a new and powerful drug. He tried to slow himself; he wanted things to proceed in the right order, to perceive everything. He sat and placed his hands palms down on the table. Clutching a pen in her fist, she looked up at him suddenly.

"How are you?" Lance asked.

"I'm doing well. And you?" It came out stiffly. Her bottom

lip was rumpled.

Lance smiled. He couldn't help himself. "I guess I'm doing all right."

Her eyes were uncertain, but not unfriendly. The tender expanse of skin from her chin down to her clavicles was soothing. Her hands knotted in her lap and she pulled her shoulders closer, like she was trying to shrink. He was close enough to pick up her scent—the sweet flowery essence from her hair which permeated her clothes. He enjoyed a lengthy inhale.

She squinted at his elbow, becoming disturbed. He glanced there and found a sizable scab: cracked and rust-colored, a real nasty. He'd tripped playing soccer.

"That looks terrible," she said in an offhand way. "You might want to use a Band-Aid." Her reserves of maternal compassion still existed.

He took his elbow off the table. She unwrapped a cough drop and popped it into her mouth. An old fantasy surfaced, that he and Lynn were much older, married, and on vacation. Away from their grown children. While sitting around a tropical resort pool, Lance had a heart attack or some sudden dire medical condition. In tears but still resourceful, perhaps speaking a foreign language, Lynn directed the local medical people to save his life.

"I thought about you the other day," Lance said. "I heard a U2 song on the radio." Not true. He made this up.

"Which one?"

"Bono hits that really high note. The video where they walk around…"

She thought seriously, staring off with a hand propped under her neck. He felt guilty about this. He loved her and always would. The best things about her remained. She wouldn't last long once she got out of college. He hoped she would marry someone decent, but feared she probably wouldn't.

"It's not important," Lance said. "How are your roomies?"

"Gwen went through a freak-out period. Her parents are broke. Gennifer is moving back to South Carolina and wants to get married."

"I can see that."

It was good to sit across from her, to dispel the rumors his mind had started about what she was up to that semester. He noticed a silver bracelet on her wrist. That was new. A single charm on the bracelet. An elephant? A rhino? A troll?

He sensed her guard slipping.

Looking over his shoulder, Lynn's face brightened suddenly and she lifted her eyebrows, mouthing a silent greeting. Lance turned to see who this social gleam was directed at, finding a stream of students behind him. It was probably one of the guys Lance had never been able to kill off, who would circle Lynn until she settled on one of them, then keep circling.

"You seem well," Lance said. "It's good to see you. I've missed talking to you." A big risk. It opened a door she might slam, a potential avenue of hurt if she said nothing or stuck out her tongue.

Her mouth opened to reveal the tips of her lower teeth and she tilted her head, signaling she felt vulnerable too. "It's nice to talk with you." She dropped her gaze. Her feelings toward him remained, but for the sake of self-preservation she would never admit it. Lynn cracked down on the candy with her molars. "How have your business school admissions gone?"

"Thankfully, they all turned me down." He hadn't looked at it this way before, but there was a certain relief. In fact, it was a blessing, a reprieve from the governor. "I mean, what the hell was I thinking? I hate economics!" How obviously flawed was this idea? He became consumed with an odd, aggressive laugh.

Lynn looked worried. He was venturing dangerously outside her value system.

"Here's a totally better idea than the business school thing. Remember the screenplay I wrote with Ian LaCoss? I'm going to try and sell it in L.A. Now, probably nobody wants it, but you never know, and I figure things will happen along the way. I'll find something else. And I'll be in L.A. Every major trend in America starts right there…" He was tempted to stretch things more, to really blow smoke and make it outrageous. But he couldn't do this to Lynn. And she'd know better. He tried to stick to some semblance of truth (lacking possession of the screenplay was one obvious deviation). The entertainment industry was a natural fit. Plus, the idea wasn't completely misguided—he'd gotten critical encouragement for *The Man*. He took Hetrick Curtain stealing the disk as a vote of confidence.

This latest idea he had introduced days before on the phone. It had been an awkward, strained length of time since speaking to his father and mother. He figured, why not? He had expected a rich cocktail of emotions, was hoping for them to make things really interesting, but listening to the insistent trilling at the other end, he was surprised by his own calm. A calm that needed shattering. His father answered in his serious voice. Lance announced he would not be attending grad school, now or at any time in the future. An artery in his chest flared like a pressurized hose. He smacked the couch with his hand. He said he was sick of school, sick to death, and could stomach it no more—realizing there was great truth there. He went on, measuring his words, waiting for his father, expecting him to interject. Air pushed angrily through the thick lattice of hairs guarding his father's nostrils. Lance kept talking. He was an army pouring through a forward position, tanks gunning through a gap in the lines. Where was the reply? His father was not talking, not instructing, not screaming, not arguing. Then Lance got it—his father was listening. A caution born of respect. So Lance went into his L.A. plan. He sensed anger at mention of a screenplay and Hollywood, a line crossed. He paused and experienced a silence, a gulf within the phone universe as his father managed a confounded breathing. The astonishing gulf widened. The first time he had ever found his father at a loss for words. Each listened to the white noise of the phone ether, to the hush, as though great forces of reordering might be faintly detected. The line crackled; it fizzed and popped and then another hush, as if a galaxy billions of miles away had contracted, smashed itself, then blinked out, in an explosion noted as a blip in the wires.

It was difficult to recall the minor exchanges at the end. That cosmic crackle rang in Lance's ear and muted what remained, and gave the room a bluish hue. Though he recalled his father saying in a perfectly even voice, "Very well," then clicking off, and Lance had imagined—a chill inching down his spine, then down his legs—his father rising from the conference table of a dead deal, checking his watch outside the room and anticipating a connecting flight through LaGuardia.

With Lynn glancing at him, Lance troubled his eyebrows, recalling how he had stared at the cradled phone for twenty minutes anticipating, once his parents had regrouped, the return call. He considered telling them his L.A. plan was speculative. But after an hour, then a day, then three days, it had not come. Might it never come? A confusing sadness swirled, as if he were continually entering rooms without knowing why. He knew calling them again would put them on different terms; he wasn't sure what they were. He was still making them up. He ached to tell Lynn, but she seemed unreceptive to anything which could not be explained in thirty seconds.

Lynn stared at him, unmoving, a little spark of what seemed affection rising in her eyes. "Could I say something to you?"

"Yes." Giving her permission worried him.

She became weirdly serious. "I realized something while listening to you. It is something I think I was grasping at when we were dating, but never quite realized. How to say this? It's…that you're nuts." Her teeth together, she strained her neck. "I mean that in a good way, though not totally in a positive way." She opened her mouth, trying to find a way out. "Not that there is something wrong with it. Or that it detracts from your better qualities."

Lance put the tips of his fingers together before his nose. She might be right. It seemed a damning comment at first, being nuts; then it had a certain charm to it, hinting at initiative and imagination. There were worse things.

"You're going to have to explain this theory further. I sense emotional scars rising." He half-closed his eyes and shook his head slowly.

Lynn's eyes shifted away from him, focusing on a distant person.

"Maybe we could discuss this another time," he said.

"Maybe. Right now, I don't know." She did the pained look.

He leaned over the table, his chin dipping close to the surface. He put his face against the wood. Glancing up at her, he twisted his eyebrows, puffed his cheeks and gnashed his teeth like a Neanderthal. She seemed puzzled, disturbed.

Then she laughed, her cheeks glowing. It was what he wanted.

That evening, banging from the front door echoed around the apartment. Through the keyhole, Lance made out a bald figure, fidgety, standing in the stairwell gloom. He opened the door. Hetrick Curtain stood in an all-weather parka. He reached into a pocket and gave Lance a red disk, which Lance confirmed, via the handwriting on the label, to be *the* disk.

"Sorry for the delay in getting back to you." Curtain looked over his shoulder. "I relocated recently. Do not ask."

Stunned, Lance invited Curtain inside. Curtain refused. He cleared his throat, pointed at the disk and spoke in a loud voice. "Now. Let me say of this story, it is not without flaws. Most are structural. However, I think it has something. I believed the story of Wyatt Burris and I think others may as well."

"Do you think a producer might buy it?"

One edge of Curtain's mouth drew up. "A producer might buy anything." He fumbled in his pockets and took out a book of matches and a pen. He scribbled something on the match cover. "Call this gentleman if you are ever in L.A. He knows everybody. Tell him I told you to call. Don't listen if he says rotten things about me. Most of them will be false."

Lance wasn't sure he wanted the disk. He'd written it off. His mind struggled to adjust to its return. He was tempted to hand it back, to tell Curtain he was beyond it, or that Curtain was welcome to take his best shot and they'd split the proceeds. Curtain hustled up the stairs. Lance closed the door.

He stared at the disk. He opened the matchbook and inspected the scribbled phone number. It had only six numbers.

It was under random and unforeseeable circumstances that Lance ended up in the passenger seat of Norton Skinner's convertible. They sped down a major highway. Skinner worked his way past larger vehicles, using all of the lanes. Frigid air whipped over Lance's head and pounded his ears. Skinner had painted the car an outrageous, sparkling gold and they zipped through traffic like an oversized trophy car. In honor of his coming marriage—was it now a family car?—Skinner had painted, replaced the old seats with leather red and black Recaro sport seats, installed an expensive in-dash compact disc player, added a custom aerofoil and bought new Pirelli tires. He'd plowed all his savings into the mutant Frankencar. All refurbished, with the exception of the original engine block.

Just minutes earlier, Lance had stepped out of the History building. Lance climbed into Mary Ann, expecting a lift over to the gym. While Skinner drove he described the arrival of his girlfriend that day, the woman he was going to marry. A girl so perfect, so luminous and wonderful, mere talk of her choked him up. She'd won beauty contests; she volunteered with deaf kids, and wanted to be a television anchor. Then they were on the road to the airport to pick her up. No time to waste. They were late. Lance wasn't sure where she was going to sit, but he was dying to meet this girl. Skinner reached for the stereo knob. Lance expected a heavy metal barrage of power chords. But instead it was Italian opera. An interlude of strings gently surrounded them.

"Why don't you let me drive?" Lance asked. He remembered driving the peppy TR7 once long ago, and wanted to test the new version.

Skinner shook his head. "How about…you can drive on the way back?"

"Deal."

Skinner downshifted to pass a tractor trailer, then slid left into the fast lane. The engine whined and brayed. Lance thought he heard another sound from the engine, a sound within a sound, like a rock in a can. He wanted to ask about the noise but decided not to. Skinner's reddish hair was plastered back in a monolithic ball. He pushed the little car up into the high eighties, jerking the wheel and flashing his brights in frustration behind a slow Mercedes. He veered near the shoulder. The new Italian tires spit gravel bullets.

On another day, Lance might have been worried about accidents and possible death. But anyone with the grand and detailed plans for bliss Norton Skinner described surely was immune from mishap. Skinner was going to marry the woman of his dreams, then enlist in the United States Marines, attending sniper school and serving five years—longer if wartime required it. Then he was going to enter a seminary. He was putting country before God, though both figured prominently.

Traffic became thicker. Skyscraper icons loomed before them. A blazing drip of sun hung low to their left, its rays blinding, warm on their faces. These lowered rays were fierce, making the car shine like the center of a lighthouse lens. Skinner's face was perfectly content, as if always at the center of brilliance. Without Lance asking, Skinner had started talking about his future plans. Then he looked over at Lance. "What about you? What are you going to do?"

Lance thought a moment, but said nothing. He was enjoying the momentum and the expressions of other drivers who stared at the car. A purposefulness and rightness settled into this detour. It was an obscure meaning, though getting clearer. He didn't feel like stretching to come up with an answer to the question. He wasn't going to push himself on such a beautiful day. Each thing he had said recently had felt semi-genuine. He felt no remorse that each had been different. In retrospect, they were lies. His only regret was that they had not been bigger, more outlandish lies. Today the answer seemed more complex, but unnecessary. He was speeding toward exactly where he was going.

Lance nodded happily at his friend, both of them bouncing their heads out of the sheer joy of hellbent transportation. Skinner talked in a singsong, his voice raised to counter the engine noise and the gale blowing over their heads. "...So then, once she finally says that she's going to marry me—"

"Hold on. I thought you had already asked her and showed her the ring."

"I did. She said she needed some time to think."

They zinged past a Greyhound bus, its fumes in their nostrils.

"How long has she been thinking?"

"Two weeks."

This was a really bad sign, and Lance was tempted to say so. Though maybe she had a difficult time making up her mind or was waiting for a divine signal. In any event, Lance didn't want to cause upset before they got to the airport.

Skinner's face became tense. He gripped and regripped the wheel. He looked at Lance with hesitation. "Do you think her waiting could mean...?"

"I don't know what it means. But you deserve a straight answer about what she's thinking."

Lance became certain: it would turn out badly for Skinner at the hands of this girl. He had always considered Skinner to be well-adjusted because of his social nature. But he was naive, Lance realized, with a lot of painful lessons coming his way; or maybe no lessons, just misunderstanding and pain. Maybe nobody was immune. Lance considered himself; ultimately, he was weak and pliant with the fairer sex. He loved them all. They would shine on him and nourish him, then carve their initials into his organs like scalpel-wielding surgeons and sew him up again. It would be glorious.

In the fast lane, the car suddenly lurched, as if spooked. A gunshot sound rang out, an engine part shooting through the hood. Smoke gushed out the jagged hole. Skinner braked, steering into the left emergency lane, a tiny shoulder between a concrete divider and cars rushing past. A terrible stew of odors, of smoke, burning oil and stressed metal flooded the car. They crawled to a stop as varooming cars whipped past. Tendrils of flame poked from the hole in the hood. Lance opened his door, paranoid that traffic would rip it off its hinges. When they were both out of the car, Skinner fumbled with keys at the trunk latch. He tore through the trunk, upending things.

"Extinguisher?" Lance yelled.

In lieu of producing an extinguisher, Skinner cursed savagely. Flames leapt between the dash and the windshield, smoke growing riotous from the hood. Skinner moaned and shook his hands, his eyes panicked, as flames licked at his new seats. Lance pulled Skinner away from the car. As if Mary Ann had been dipped in rocket fuel, the flames raced each other to form a bonfire. They cringed, anticipating an explosion. It was shocking to stand at an interstate median, buffeted by the steel herd whizzing by. Lance sensed his human frailty; he was puny, soft, and easily destroyed. Multiple lanes of traffic slowed as rubberneckers stared.

Oh, boy. He's about to cry, Lance realized. Skinner leaned a hand against the divider, his mouth open. While flames consumed the car, he bent at the waist, shaken, as though all his plans were in question. Lance put his hand on Skinner's shoulder to steady him, and felt himself drawn into a similarly deep hole of anguish. It was terrible, awful, the worst thing imaginable. Lance felt fatigued, like the car had been burning for hours.

Then his mind disconnected and jumped wildly ahead, looking back on these events, at the terrific story it would make—the chance ride, the girlfriend, the dramatic immolation of Mary Ann. His heart leapt; he was briefly overjoyed, as if telling the story to a receptive audience. He wanted to laugh and do a victorious tribal dance, wanted to celebrate this future perspective. But this was out of place; Skinner's hands were trembling, his distant eyes casting about with uncertainty.

Nonetheless, it became imperative that Lance remember each detail: the smell, the dense smoke column; the noise from stereos leaking out car windows, from a helicopter, from brakes squealing, from sirens, from rubber hissing as it melted, from the whoosh of cars. These noises built into a collective hum, like a soundtrack. Wind tossed his hair. His nostrils flared and his eyes grew big and riotous. He took in the arctic blue sky with its cathedral-like opening and the strange rolled clouds at its fringes. The edges of his mouth crept upward, lifting. It was all quite overpowering, quite amazing, as if his senses had gone awry or he was already embellishing details of the story.

ABOUT THE AUTHOR

Robb Skidmore writes upmarket fiction. He lives in southern California with his wife. To receive news of his latest release please sign up for his mailing list at robbskidmore.com.

Made in the USA
Lexington, KY
20 April 2014